ONCE IN A LIFETIME

Once in a Lifetime

DELUXE
EDITION
WITH BONUS
MATERIALS

HARPER BLISS

CONTENTS

PREFACE

February 2021

Dear Reader,

Who doesn't love a second chance at love? All the characters in this 'deluxe edition' of *Once in a Lifetime* took their shot when the opportunity presented itself again. It's up to you to find out if they succeeded.

Leigh and Jodie's journey in *Once in a Lifetime* started in a short story I wrote a very long time ago called *As Years Go By*. I was so smitten with the passion between them that, at my wife's urging, I decided to give them a full-length novel to tell their love story in much greater detail.

Even though I've written more than thirty novels by now, some of you still consider *Once in a Lifetime* your favorite. And I get it. Leigh and Jodie simply belong together and their bond (amongst other things) is so strong that it transcends all the obstacles they face.

I don't write second-chance romance that often, despite having a soft spot for it. I'm usually too busy writing age-gap romance (my first love) but, as I write this introduction to this deluxe edition, I'm actually working on a second-chance age-gap romance (called *At Your Most Beautiful*) and the second chance element is absolutely crucial to the book. This made me think of other second-chance stories I'd written and gave me the idea to collect them. What better way than to include them as bonus material alongside my ultimate second-chance novel, *Once in a Lifetime*?

In this edition you will find the very first second-chance story I ever wrote, *I Still Remember*. It's full of nostalgia and also features a massage that may leave you a touch (or a lot) hot under the collar.

No Greater Love Than Mine is a story I wrote more recently featuring two fifty-something ladies between whom there isn't a lot of love lost any longer, until they unexpectedly cross each other's path again (and sparks start flying.)

One of the things I love most about second-chance romance is all the emotions it evokes and *No Greater Love Than Mine* might only be novella-length, but I guarantee you a novel-length dose of emotion.

The final bonus story, *Lovely Rita*, I originally wrote for an erotica anthology and for that reason it's more second-chance hotness than second-chance romance, but with a bit of a twist. Do go forth and find out what I mean by that.

Enjoy all the goodness that makes second-chance romance so great: nostalgia, emotion and, of course, scorching hot scenes when the love is, at last, rekindled!

Thank you,

Harper Bliss

ONCE IN A LIFETIME

CHAPTER ONE

J odie has always looked too damn glam to be a social worker. Look at her. She's only just gotten out of the shower, and already she seems to have this sheen to her. A sheen I used to find irresistible—all glossy and inviting and yes-I-will-let-you-do-that-to-me—but now it shrouds her in a distance I can't seem to bridge anymore. As if she's made her decision already.

On top of that, she knew I didn't want to come here. Not to Gerald's place, with all its man things, and a few of Troy's toys always lingering, no matter how many times the cleaner comes before we arrive for the weekend—I guess even people who get paid to tidy get tired of the never-ending task of stowing a child's toys.

Jodie has her arms wrapped around her body, clothed in the light-blue silk robe she always wears after taking a shower. She looks out over the beach, as if answers are there, in the sand that has been brushed clean overnight by the ocean. Answers to how to resolve this always-returning argument between us, the one that's been wearing us down for months.

"Hey," she says, finally, turning away from the window. "Did you manage to get some sleep?"

I wonder how I must look to her now. And how would Gerald feel about his ex-wife's partner sleeping on his Chesterfield sofa in nothing but a t-shirt and panties?

"Some." In the beginning, when Jodie and I had just gotten together, it was a thrill to come to her ex's lavish Hamptons beach house for a dirty weekend. But now, six years down the line, when she suggested coming here as a sort of last resort it felt more like she was trying to tell me something. The way she also does sometimes without words. Her face all brooding and unreadable, although I don't need to see her eyes anymore to know that it's over.

I could have slept in Gerald's room—or Troy's—but deciding to sleep on the sofa last night felt like a defiant stand. Now, in the cold hard light of day, it feels like a decision made by someone foolish enough to put stubbornness before a good night's sleep. At thirty-three, I'm not old by a long stretch, but, all the same, my bones prefer a soft bed.

It's only Saturday morning, and already we're in the middle of this fraught stand-off. How will we get through the next twenty-four hours without biting each other's heads off?

"Coffee?" Jodie asks. Her expression is not unfriendly but her face is not exactly folded into a peace-making one either. And I can't help myself. I suspect she's naked underneath that robe, and I still feel it—I still want her—but too many ugly words have passed between us and neither one of us knows how to take them back.

"Sure." I sit up straighter. Stare at the coffee table. I have to hand it to Gerald; he has excellent taste in furniture. If we got along better, I'd ask him where he got this table, as a way of making small talk and being civil and all that, but Gerald and I have been wrapped in a silent, mutually agreed upon mild hostility since we first met, and I never had the inclination to do anything about it. I'm not in a relationship with Gerald, so why bother?

"Can't you try a bit harder?" Jodie used to ask me in the beginning. "If not for me then at least for Troy's sake?" I can still see her shake her head at me. "You can be so ruthless sometimes."

"My mother is called Ruth," I would tell her. "And as long as she's alive, I will never be Ruth-less." The first few times I used that line Jodie actually giggled and dropped the subject.

I get up and sit at the breakfast bar, looking out over the ocean, which is savage this time of year, the waves loud and brash—the way I like it.

"The waves are like you," Jodie once said, "they never know when to stop. They just keep on going and going. The tide may retreat twice a day, but it always—always—comes back with full force."

"That analogy does not add up at all, Jodes," I'd said. "You're just babbling." And I had grabbed her, pushed her down on Gerald's sofa, and shown her what it was like to just keep on going while she looked out over those waves.

"What would you like to do today?" I ask. Her hand trembles a bit as she pours me a mug of coffee and she spills a few drops on the counter. Neither one of us cares.

Disappear, her face seems to say. It's so pale, it seems all pigment has drained from her body. Jodie's always pale, what with her Irish blood and skin, but I can tell this... phase we're going through has worn her out. If only it were just a *phase*. "Go for a walk, I guess." She actually shrugs when she says that, as if it doesn't matter anymore what we do. "Maybe have lunch at Gino's."

I shake my head before sipping. The coffee is strong, the way we both like it.

"What?" Jodie stopped bothering to keep the irritation out of her voice months ago.

"What are we even doing here?" I know she'll blame me again for actually saying something, but I can't stand this anymore. All the love I had for her, everything we've built between us over the years, is not enough anymore to bear this.

"You know why we're here."

I look up from my coffee. Try to find something inviting in her eyes. I come up empty. "It feels to me like we're here for one thing only." I pause, ignoring the nervous contractions in my stomach.

Something I learned to do in my first year in court. It's harder to do when a relationship is at stake. "To break up."

Jodie's eyes narrow. "If *you* want to leave *me*. You're free to go."

I purse my lips together and nod in mock understanding, my chin going up and down in the most passive-aggressive way I can muster. "Sure. Because if this ends, of course I'll be the one leaving *you* and you will have nothing to do with that."

Jodie just sits there shaking her head. "I can't change you, Leigh," she says after a while. "I want what I want, and you want what you want." Her voice breaks a little. We've said these things to each other before—in different versions, with alternative words—a million times, as if they need to be said a certain number of times before a decision can actually be made. If we're waiting for the pain that comes with them to go away, we'll have to wait until that ocean outside freezes over.

"Let's get out of here." I don't want to stay in this house with her. I don't want to spend my weekend drowning in this tension and not finding my way to the surface. My lungs are full of spite and anger and resentment already. Maybe it's better for her if she can hate me. After all, I'm the bad one here. I'm the woman who has the audacity to go through life without any apparent desire for motherhood. "Or better yet. I'll go." *I'll pack up my things and be out of our apartment by the time you get home tomorrow evening*, I want to add, but I can't say the words. "It's time," I say instead.

That she doesn't burst into immediate, passionate protest is like a knife in my gut, but it's not as if this was ever going to be pain-free.

"I think it is, as well. This is killing us one day at a time." We don't look at each other. In my case, for fear of seeing something in her face, her demeanor, or anything else, that I could latch onto. And I'm tired of fighting. Of coming up with arguments that won't win her over, because some things are just how they are, and no reasoning stands up to them.

But can this really be how it ends? The pair of us drinking coffee in Gerald's house? After all the shouting has been done, and the harshest words have been spoken, can it just be this calm conclusion that we draw?

"Okay. I'll go." I don't get up though. How can I? How can I walk away from Jodie Whitehouse? The woman who has given me everything. Why can't I be a bit more accommodating? After all, I don't mind Troy being around. It's not as if I detest children. It's not as if Jodie expects me to become a full-time mother. But it feels as if I have to give up a crucial piece of myself to stay with her and honor her wishes. Her fierce desire to have another child clashes so ferociously with my own wishes and it's laying bare a fundamental difference between us—one that can't be overcome by a thousand conversations, or the best sex we ever had in our lives.

"Leigh." Her leg touches mine for a split second, but is gone before I even get the chance to register her touch properly. "I—" But Jodie has run out of words, too. We knew months ago that words wouldn't save us.

"It's fine." This time, I do get up. Gerald's place has floor heating, so I don't even get punished with cold tiles under my feet. On the surface, it may look like I'm walking away scot-free, all limbs intact, no skin broken. Beneath my ribs, though, my heart breaks because I know what I'm walking away from. I know all too well, yet, I can't stay. Because staying would only mean more of this, more of this chipping away at what we once had, at each other's confidence and essence. It has to stop sometime. It stops today. At 11.34 a.m. on Saturday, the twenty-second of April 2003. The day Leigh Sterling and Jodie Whitehouse cease being a couple.

And we were a good one. We had it, that unidentifiable chemistry, that boundless passion, the knowledge that we saw each other for who we were and that, just maybe, this might be forever. But it wasn't enough. And the mere fact that even a love like this, a love like ours, is not enough, scars my soul here and now. I head to Gerald's guest room—the room Jodie and I have always used—where I left my bag last night, just to pretend that there might be a possibility of us sleeping in it together.

I don't bother showering; just throw the few items that made it out of my bag back in, slip into a pair of jeans, a washed-out gray hoodie, and my trainers. I glance at the bed Jodie slept in. The sheets are twisted and the pillows scattered, indicating she had a rough night. Nights before break-ups usually are. It was a quick drive to get here last night, because no one goes to The Hamptons when the weather is gray and heavy like this, and the icy silence in the car was only broken by muffled radio voices and nostalgic songs from the oldies channel. I guess our break-up was already a done deal and coming here just a formality. As if we couldn't break up in our home, as though the many memories we made there would stop us. The sight of our bedroom door, some paint peeled off the upper right corner. The picture of us above the fireplace, of Jodie and me in Hawaii, when, perhaps for the last time, we looked immeasurably happy. I'd just left the D.A.'s office for Schmidt & Burke and we'd splashed out. Maybe I should never have left the District Attorney's office. Perhaps me crossing over to *the other side* was what kick-started this entire process.

But I know I'm only fooling myself. I know very well what has brought me here, bag in hand, ready to leave this weekend place where we never really belonged anyway. It's me, and the immutability of what I feel inside, of not being able to meet Jodie halfway in this—not even a quarter of the way really. I know what I'm walking away from, however, and it hurts so much I find it hard to put one foot in front of the other, to leave this room in which we haven't slept together for a very long time. We came here to talk, to smooth things out, or, at least, that's what we told ourselves. It's not as if we could say, "Hey, let's go to The Hamptons and finally get this break-up over with, shall we?"

But then I somehow find it in myself to start walking. I descend the stairs for the last time—because why would I ever come here again? Jodie is in her robe, her hands clasped around that coffee mug that should be empty by now. What do we do? How do we say our final goodbye? I can't just walk away. Not after six years with her. There needs to be a gesture of closure.

"This is it, then," Jodie says, fingers wound tightly around the mug. Outside, the wind howls, and I feel its echo in my heart. My heart wants to scream. I want to cry. But I need to hold it together, need to make it to the car in one piece.

"Will you be okay getting back?"

But Jodie is a public transport girl, and she can train her way out of anywhere. She nods. Why am I prolonging this agony? Her hair is almost dry now. I always envied how she can wear it long and never has to do anything to make it look fabulous. "It just dries into perfection," she used to say when she was feeling sassy.

Will she walk toward me? Or, because I'm the one who's doing *the leaving*, should I make a detour? I'm by the door already, but only because the stairs end there. Again, I'm frozen in my spot. Am I doing the right thing? I recognize this last question as panic. Last-minute nerves. Fear. What am I going to do without her? Without our apartment to go home to? Where am I going to stay? And what will she tell Troy when he gets back from Gerald's on Monday evening?

"Bye," Jodie says, her voice a dagger in my heart.

"Yeah." The way we're doing this stands in such stark contrast to how we were as a couple that, perhaps, it's fitting. Perhaps this is the only way.

I reach for the handle and open the door.

CHAPTER TWO

I watch the door for a long time after Leigh has let it close behind her. As if she might come back. Change her mind. Undo everything. As if, on the way to the car, on those few steps between the front door and the driveway, something magical has happened, and an idea that will save us has sparked in her brain. But we—Jodie and Leigh—are not to be saved. So, I just stand there, looking at a shut door. It's a beautiful one. Large in a classy, designer way, and shiny in… ah, hell, I don't know which tint of brown. All I know is that Gerald's money bought it and that Leigh never wanted to walk through it.

I'm still clasping my hands around this mug. I can't let go because it's the mug I drank from when we shared the last coffee of our life together. Everything I do now has this ring of finality to it. Or, if you look at it differently, of new beginnings. The start of my life without her.

Fuck, I love her. And I've let her go. Does she know how much I love her? How much she has changed me? Six years is hardly a lifetime, but it sure as hell feels that way now. And what am I going to do with myself, right now? I chose to come here to The Hamptons so I feel like I should stay.

I wait a few seconds longer but the door remains shut. I heard her car leave the driveway minutes ago. My wishful thinking is based on pure fantasy. And what if she did walk through the door again? I still couldn't take her back. The first thing that changes in this tableau vivant of *Broken-hearted Woman in The Hamptons* I imagine myself in, is the mug slipping from my fingers. As if all strength is draining from me and even an empty cup is too much to hold. It falls to the floor, but it doesn't break. It's empty, so there won't be any stains to wipe away either. My legs give out next. I crash to my knees—shattering the way the wretched coffee mug wouldn't—and I know I will have bruises, but what does it matter? Leigh is gone. Then the tears come in waves, like the ocean outside.

We didn't even hug. I can't even remember the last time we touched. Have I really become so cold that I let her leave without even the briefest of touches? Tears rain down on the floor, next to the unbroken mug. I try to wipe them with my robe, but silk is not very absorbent. Fuck, I scream on the inside. What have I done to us? Because Leigh might be the one who walked out, but I'm the one who made her do it.

Still, it's not as simple as that. I spread myself out on the floor in a dramatic fashion, arms wide, head to the side, as if I've fallen and can never get back up without the help of someone else. Without her.

I first saw her in court. I could tell she considered herself a bit of a hot-shot, even though her only task that afternoon was to sit there and observe. She'd only just joined the D.A.'s office, but I could already tell she was the kind of person who wouldn't keep on fighting the state's battles for the rest of her life. Even in a cheap pants suit, she had some glitz about her. Her hair was longer then, with sideways swept bangs that covered her eyes when she didn't brush them aside. She pushed her hair away from her face a lot that day.

After the court hearing, her colleague, Dan Mazlowski, quickly introduced us, but they both had other places to be. Leigh shook my hand with determination, like a woman who knew the importance of a strong handshake—like a woman working in a man's world. If I registered on her radar at all that day, she didn't let on. It would take five more weeks until we met next.

I saw her exiting the courthouse, coming down the steps with sure strides, as I made my way inside. She just nodded. I've always remembered that she wore pinstripes, and I considered that an odd choice. I only allowed myself a brief frivolous thought of another woman that day. I was still getting used to being a divorced woman, living in a small apartment on the Upper East Side, sharing custody of a child. My mind was overflowing with babysitter schedules and how to make my modest city paycheck last until the next payday. And there was Alexander to consider, the boy on whose behalf I was testifying that day.

The main reason for my divorce from Gerald was crystal clear to me, but I simply hadn't had the time to pursue anything. Nevertheless, despite our very brief introduction a few weeks earlier, and this quick, courteous nod on the steps, something did register with me. I didn't realize at the time, but looking back, I had to acknowledge that somewhere deep inside, I already knew I wanted to see her again.

The next time I saw her was at my office. There was that handshake again and I noticed for the first time how broad her hands were, as if slightly out of proportion with the rest of her. Her fingers were long, like her, but also wide, and so strong.

"I'm here for the Cindy Latimer case," she said, her brown eyes resting on me. "Good to see you again, Mrs. Dunn."

"Oh, it's Whitehouse. I guess my name change hasn't made it through all the channels yet."

She tipped her head a fraction to the right. "I guess not," she said, and only then let go of my hand.

"Please, call me Jodie." She was wearing pinstripes again. I escorted her to my cubicle, where we huddled so closely over a case file I could smell her perfume. I recognized it as DKNY, one of my personal favorites.

"I guess I'll see you in court then, Jodie," she said, a broad smile on her face. I felt it then. I didn't have much experience at picking women who were into women out of a crowd, but somehow, with Leigh Sterling, I knew. Built-in gaydar, perhaps. If only it had worked when I looked in the mirror before I married Gerald.

"I look forward to it." I extended my hand and suddenly I couldn't wait for her to take it in hers again. As she did, her smile transformed into a crooked grin.

"Poor word choice, perhaps," she offered. "Considering what happened to the girl on whose behalf you'll be testifying."

I was so taken aback, I didn't immediately know what to say. I still stood there, slightly entranced by this woman who opened up rather a few possibilities in my mind, that I could only mumble, "Sorry. Didn't mean to be unprofessional about it."

She gave my hand one last squeeze. "Day after tomorrow, then?"

"See you there." I watched her walk off.

"Earth to Jodie," Muriel in the cubicle next to me whispered. "Come back to us, please. The New York City Administration for Children's Services needs you. The children need you."

"Shut up," I hissed, feeling caught out.

"You're smitten." Muriel couldn't let it go.

I sat back down, hoping that disappearing from her sight would put a stop to her teasing.

"You don't giggle like that when Dan comes to see you, Jodie. And you especially don't stutter like that."

I wheeled my chair back so as to get a good look at her. "I wasn't stuttering."

"Hm-mm." Muriel rolled her eyes at me. "Sure, girl. Believe what you want. I'm just an innocent bystander, that's all."

"What do you think of her?"

"Of *her*?" She pursed her lips together. "Hot piece of ass, for sure. As for what I think of you, *Mizz* Whitehouse… I think you want a slice of that."

I shook my head. "Please, Muriel. Must you be so crass?" I said it in the voice I used to impersonate our supervisor.

"I must." Muriel stretched her legs and rested her feet on an overflowing trashcan. "I *must* also discuss this further with you over drinks after work."

"I can't tonight. I have Troy."

"Then you and Troy must come to dinner and we shall discuss this further while Francine helps him with his homework."

"He's five, Muriel. He doesn't have homework yet."

"Then she'll build a fort with him. Whatever. God knows the woman is broody and she loves that child. Do it for her." She tapped her thumbs together. "And you'd better know who to call to babysit when you and the sexy ADA go on a date."

The ringing of Muriel's phone interrupted our conversation. Before she picked up, she pointed her forefinger at me, as if to say that what she'd just proposed was non-negotiable.

Our first date happened weeks later. After the Cindy Latimer case, Leigh rushed to another appointment and we barely had a chance to say goodbye. A similar case put us back in court together, only this time Leigh didn't win and instead of being placed in a state facility for his protection, Joey Williams, the child in question, was sent back to his family.

"Drink?" was all she said.

It was October, and the city was cold and wet. I'd stepped in a puddle on the way over to court and one of my shoes was soaked. Troy was at his dad's and when I looked into Leigh's eyes to say "Yes, please" I already felt a little bit better about the unfairness of the system and its repercussions on Joey.

My instinct and Muriel both turned out to be correct. Not even fifteen minutes into our date, Leigh said, "Just so you know, Jodie, I'm into women and I like you."

"That's very forward." My heart was thumping beneath my thick woolen sweater.

"I mean," she continued, "I could be all coy about it. Throw out some feelers. Probe gently into your personal life, but after the afternoon we've had, I don't really have the energy for games like that."

I nodded pensively, as if mulling over what she'd just said, while really I'd been dreaming about a moment like this—in various degrees of hotness—for weeks. From the get-go, she was someone whose presence in my life, no matter how small and infrequent, I couldn't shake. It sat there, at the back of my mind, coming to the fore out of the blue, and often late at night when I couldn't sleep.

"Additionally," Leigh hadn't finished yet, "I get a rather distinct sort of vibe off you. I wouldn't be saying all of this if I didn't." She ended with a wide smile. One that shot straight through my flesh, to body parts untouched for years.

"Well." I looked into my glass of cheap wine. Despite its acid taste, it was nearly finished. "I guess I'd better buy another round then."

"I'd much rather do something else with you than sit here and get drunk," Leigh said.

"Like what?" I asked, already mesmerized by the twinkle in her eyes.

Her response came in the shape of another smile. She bit her bottom lip, and I wished my teeth were doing that to her.

I pull myself from the floor, avoid the view of the ocean, and go straight upstairs. I pull some clothes out of my overnight bag, and as I turn, I catch a glimpse of myself in the mirror. As expected, my eyes are red-rimmed, my skin blotched, my cheeks puffy. I can't help but wonder if I'm looking at a woman who has done the right thing. Because if it was right to let her go, then why does it hurt so much?

Why this urge to undo? To go back? To sacrifice, now that it's too late?

But I'm a mother. First and foremost, I am Troy Dunn's mother, and I want another child. It was one of the first things I told Leigh six years ago. Nothing is more important to me than my child. And I will have another. Was she not listening when I said that? Because I said it often, and in a clear voice. Of course, I waited. I needed to know where things were going with her first. Needed Troy and her to get acquainted. Needed to build our life together first.

Judging from the woman looking back at me in the mirror, I've gone and destroyed that life together. Yet, despite the blistering pain, somewhere beneath my ribcage, a sense of relief builds. I'm free now. No more fights. No more energy wasted on trying to convince her that this may actually be something she wants as well. No more talking to deaf ears. I know what I want. I can see it so clearly. Troy and I in Central Park pushing a pram. The look on his face when I first bring his brother or sister home. The wonder in his eyes. The first time he realizes he's someone's big brother now.

Over the past year, those thoughts have become my fantasies much more than anything I wanted Leigh to do to me.

I push a finger into the pillowy flesh of my tear-stained cheek. These signs of heartbreak will fade away over time, as will the most acute pain. I'll pull myself together. Go for a walk on the beach alone. Return to the city tomorrow. Go to work the day after and pick Troy up from his dad's in the evening. I will hug him, and explain to him why Leigh couldn't stay with us, and then I will hug him some more—for both our benefit. And our life will go on without her, until it's not just me and Troy anymore, and we welcome a newborn baby into our home.

I nod resolutely at the woman in the mirror. Her eyes brighten a tad. Then I catch a glimpse of the bed behind me, the bed Leigh didn't even sleep in, and it hits me again that she's gone. For good.

CHAPTER THREE

When I arrived at our apartment on Saturday after the drive back from The Hamptons, I was in such a state, I'm surprised I managed to throw some spare panties in a suitcase. Ours was not an easily uproot-able life. I moved into Jodie's apartment on York Avenue not long after we got together. My place was bigger, but hers was rent-controlled and located only a few blocks from Gerald's townhouse on East 78th Street. The plan was to find a place together after I'd been with Schmidt & Burke for a while, but that never happened.

So, now, I feel like it's Jodie's bell I'm ringing. I can hardly still call it *ours*, not even in my head. She buzzes me up. She knows I'm coming to collect my things. I already know that I won't be able to move everything I want this time either. She'll just have to live with my stuff for a while longer, until I figure out a more permanent place to stay.

I don't knock immediately when I reach the front door of 3B, but the door opens anyway.

"Hey," Jodie says and gestures for me to come inside. It's strange to have her do that while the key to this apartment still sits snugly in my pocket.

My heart sinks when I see the two suitcases and the couple of boxes she has piled up in a corner. She wants me out so badly she packed up my things.

"You've been busy." I head over to the boxes.

"Look, I know you wanted to see Troy, but he's staying over at Jake's after his soccer game."

"How is he?"

Jodie stops in her tracks and looks at me as if I have absolutely no right to inquire about the well-being of her son, a child I shared a home with for almost six years. "What do you want me to say, Leigh? That he misses you? That you leaving has him crying himself to sleep at night? Because, yes, that's what he does. You know he adores you and it hurts."

I bite back the tears. "I wish you'd stop saying that I'm leaving you." I lean against the boxes, looking for some sort of support. "Because, to me, it feels much more as if you're not giving me an option to stay."

Jodie holds up her hands. "Let's not do this again." Almost instantly, her arms go limp again, drooping by her side. She's not looking very glam today, despite the glossiness of that skirt she's wearing. "I can't."

"I want to say goodbye, Jodie. I want to see him."

"Of course. I'll set something up. I promise. Today, I just couldn't —" Jodie wrings her hands together.

"I understand." It's not as if I have any claims to make on her child.

"Where are you staying?" She struts to the couch and sits, not looking me in the eyes.

"At a colleague's." When I arrived back in the city on Saturday afternoon, I decided to call Sonja on a whim. Most likely because I was in dire need of some admiration.

"Not Sonja?" Jodie asks, the inflection in her tone indicating that she already knows the answer. And that I've just reached a whole new level of despicableness.

I just shrug. It's easy for her. She still has a home.

"I can't take all of this now." I point at the boxes and think of the rickety pull-out couch in Sonja's broom cupboard which doubles as a spare room. "I just came to get some essentials."

"You seem to have gotten by without them for the past week." In a way, it satisfies me that she's getting worked up because I'm staying at Sonja's. Perhaps it wasn't the most dignified choice, seeing as Sonja blatantly hit on me one time Jodie joined us for after-work drinks, but what's the point of caring about that now?

"Can we please get through this in a civilized manner, Jodes?" I sigh. "It's hard enough as it is." My mind flashes back to that night when Jodie met Sonja. Jodie sat there pouting like a wronged teenager, sulking with a martini glass in her hand, her back to me and the rest of my colleagues. After I'd let her stew for half an hour, I took her home and showed her how much room there was for another woman in my life. "No one takes it like you, Jodie," I'd said to her while ripping her panties off her. "And you know it."

She nods and rests her head on her upturned palm, fingers cradling her jaw. "This place is not exactly spacious either. Just... don't wait too long."

I try to find her eyes, but she doesn't let me. I suppose asking if we could, at some point, still be friends, is out of the question. "I won't." I turn to the suitcases. "Are my suits in here?"

"They're still in the closet. I wanted to leave them hanging up." And it's this mundane, homely piece of information that kills me the most. Because Jodie can't help but care about things like that, just as she can't leave any dishes in the sink before she goes to bed. Having my stuff linger here must be terrible for her, not just on a personal level, but it must seriously mess with her OCD.

"I'll just take those and the suitcases. I'll come back for the boxes as soon as I can." I can't begin to imagine what opening these boxes will do to me, knowing that she packed them.

"Okay." Suddenly, she stands. "Please, come here." Her voice has grown small.

I don't question it, just go to her.

"Just… one last hug. To say goodbye properly." Jodie's a few inches shorter than I and when she looks up at me like this, her eyes pleading and her lips trembling, I actually want to question my desire not to have children—again.

I wrap my arms around her. Her head presses against the flesh above my breast, as it has done countless times, and at first the embrace we stand in is strangely soothing, until wetness spreads where my blouse is open, and Jodie is sobbing, her tears hot against my skin.

"Hey." I curl my fingers around her neck, also a tried and tested gesture between us, and pull her up so I can look at her. I know this sucks, I want to say, but what the hell kind of difference will it make now? I wipe away some of her tears with the back of my hand, but it's pointless, because a gazillion more of them moisten my hand and her cheek, as if something has broken behind her eyes, something that, right now, looks like it can never be fixed again. So, instead of talking, I slant my head toward her, and I kiss her. Her lips taste salty and they are slippery, but she easily allows me access to her mouth. My tongue slides in and I try not to think of the circumstances. I try not to wonder about the uselessness of break-up sex. I'm not even sure I can do it. I'm not sure this can go further than this sloppy, wet kiss, which could be considered as part of that goodbye hug she asked for.

Or perhaps she was asking for more.

Jodie's lips are frantic on mine. She bites and sucks as if there's no tomorrow. I can't blame her, of course, because for us, there is none. There's only now. One last moment. One last opportunity to be Jodie and Leigh. One last chance to change our minds, perhaps? But no, I think we both know that ship has sailed. This is just a way of saying goodbye, as opposed to the hurried manner in which I fled the house in The Hamptons.

Jodie's tugging at my shirt buttons already. Her mouth has descended to my neck. Her hands are on my belly, crawling upward, and her fingers slip under the underwire of my bra. I have no more time to question if I really want to do this. Jodie has decided for me. For once, I let her. We can have this. Even if it's just an instant during which we don't have to face the consequences of who we have become. Two people wanting vastly different things from life.

So I hoist Jodie's top up, and we unglue for a second, and I still can't find her eyes. She can fuck me, but she can't look at me. Somehow, I understand. Understanding each other was never an issue. We're both very good at laying out arguments, displaying logic, and making each other see why we want certain things. If only life's issues could be resolved by understanding each other.

Because I understand what Jodie needs now. She needs to forget. She needs a moment to hold onto, something between us to look back on other than all this pain we've caused each other. And right now, in the state we're in, this can only be physical.

Jodie doesn't wait for me to undo her bra. She rips it roughly off and throws it on the sofa behind her. She barely gives me the opportunity to take in her breasts one last time. Those tiny nipples of hers, that can grow hard just by being gazed upon. They're so pink and perfect, but there's no time to dwell. Jodie practically grabs me by the neck and shoves them in my mouth. She's not usually one to be so forceful, but that, too, I get. She wants to leave an impression, make a memory. And, perhaps, she also wants to make sure that, grief-stricken as I am, I don't end up in Sonja's bed.

Her mouth is by my ear and at first she just sighs and moans, but then she says, "Fuck me, Leigh." And if she wanted the hinges to come off, her wish has been granted. I move away from her breasts and let her nipple fall from between my lips.

"Look at me," I say, my voice demanding. "Look at me, Jodes."

Her eyes are still filled with tears and her cheeks are smeared with mascara.

"Take off your skirt." I hadn't noticed before, but it's the one we bought together a few months ago, during a weekend which we both firmly believed was to bring us closer together again. Because the human brain can trick you into believing anything if you really want it to. Is that why she wore it? It doesn't matter now. It's coming off, slipping into a puddle of dark-green fabric on the hardwood floor.

She's taken off her underwear as well and she stands before me naked. Quite the parting gift, I think, without a hint of cynicism.

I strip quickly and methodically before pulling her toward me because, as always, this is going to be my show. The one where I call the shots.

Together, we sink to the floor. Only part of it is carpeted, but it'll do. Jodie stretches out beneath me, her legs already spread. But some of the earlier frenzy has escaped us and the atmosphere is now morphing into a more solemn one, like a moment that needs to be cherished. If we rush this, we're lost forever. We will have spent our last moments on a quick orgasm built on heartbreak. I think we both know it can't be like that. Making a memory like that now would hurt too much, and everything is already so unbearably painful.

I lean over and kiss her. Slowly. Savoring her, although all I taste are salty tears. Our breasts press together in this final embrace, our nipples meeting in that way that can be so exciting. The way only being with another woman can feel. Softness on softness. Every-where we touch, pillowy curves and smooth skin. It's what Jodie said to me after our first night together. "I can't believe how soft it is," she'd said, and it had made me laugh, although it was true, but she was just so damn cute when she said it, as if it was the biggest revela-tion of her life. Maybe it was.

While I kiss her I let a hand roam down her belly. I wonder how many fingers would be appropriate for a goodbye fuck. I can't give her less than three, but all five seems too much for the occasion. Too intimate.

"Fuck me," Jodie says again, her hands in my hair. And then I do. I let three fingers slither through a wetness that baffles me. Then again, it always has, and it's almost cruel that even now, during our very last moment together, it still does.

And it still turns me on as much as it did the first time I let my fingers wander between her legs. And this time, she gazes back, she stares up at me, and I know what that look means, because I know Jodie better than anyone does, and, especially in these circumstances, I know her better than I've known anyone in my life. She wants more. That's what the non-blinking is about. The open mouth with no words coming out. Because I can't give her anything else anymore—and, more particularly, the very thing she wants most in life, more than me—I give it to her.

I push three fingers inside of her, but quickly follow up with a fourth. To be inside of her after such a long time, because the past six months we spent most of our private time either in fraught arguments or in cold, distant silence, makes me well up. I can't help it. The sob starts in the pit of my stomach, engaging my entire body. Because I'm fucking Jodie. I can feel my clit throb between my own legs, and this might be the most painful fuck I've ever been a part of. There's pain, and more pain, but also the look of longing in Jodie's eyes. Those beautiful green eyes, which were probably the first thing I noticed about her that time, so long ago when we were introduced at the courthouse. Green eyes are so rare, so of course they captured my attention. And I liked what I saw. I still do. Even though a mist of tears clouds them and our faces are so close my own tears add to the wetness of Jodie's face, and I can't see them right now. And then I realize that what we're doing right now is just as messy as what we've become. We're lovers who will turn into exes, perhaps even strangers.

I'm inside a woman who will disappear from my life. A woman I've loved for six years. A woman who opened herself up to me in ways we both deemed unimaginable when we first met.

"Oh Leigh," Jodie moans, in that way of hers, and this is a million times more painful than when I walked out of the door at the house in The Hamptons. But maybe we need this pain. Because how else could we possibly mark the end of our affair than with regret in our hearts and tears in our eyes?

Then she comes for me for the very last time, and I can feel her climax shudder through me, like a parting gift. And then, it's over. Then we're just two naked people on our—her—apartment floor, trying to wrap their heads around what just happened, and quickly realizing that nothing has changed. I still need to drag my suitcases down the stairs and leave.

CHAPTER FOUR

My alarm clock is one that Leigh bought. She'd broken the one I'd had for years after slapping it with all her might one too many times. She was never much of a morning person. And now I'm stuck with it. It sits there, during the night when I can't sleep, its red digits mocking me. I should have put it in one of her boxes. I still can. She left them. I'll never know if that's because she still wanted to leave a piece of herself in our apartment, or if she genuinely didn't know what to do with them. And if she thinks it's easier for me because the lease on this apartment is in my name, she can think again. Even with most of her things packed up, her presence is everywhere.

Not for the first time, I wonder if this agony is worth it. But I can also hear Leigh's words in my head: "We're fundamentally different people, Jodie," she said, in the aftermath of one of our fights, after we'd calmed down enough to use a normal tone of voice again. "Perhaps, if our differences were about something less important than the desire to procreate, we could maneuver around them, but this… it's too big for negotiations and compromise. The last thing I want is to make you unhappy. If I stay, that's what will happen."

When she first said it, I still believed I could change her mind. That my love was powerful enough to accomplish that. That was my mistake. Perhaps I should have run at the first sign of our incompatibility.

"Do you want children?" I asked over a breakfast of mimosas and croissants. We sat half-dressed on Leigh's sofa after one of our early dates and a wild, wild night that had left me so dazed and satisfied, her reply didn't even matter at that point. I was just thinking of Troy, the way I always did after waking up.

Leigh put her mug on the coffee table and reached for her champagne flute. "Can't say that I do."

I was so smitten her words barely registered, even though, somewhere in the back of my mind, a red flag was being raised nonetheless. But this was our third date, so not exactly the time to plan how many kids you see yourself having. But there was no hesitation in her voice when she said it, only determination.

"Is that a deal breaker?" she asked.

"Well, you know I have a son." Troy was at Muriel and Francine's, most likely being spoilt rotten.

Leigh smiled the sort of smile that could make the more susceptible kind of judge melt on their bench. "Whom I would love to meet." She locked her big brown eyes on mine. She'd slipped into the silk blouse she'd worn the night before, but hadn't buttoned it properly, and it had slid off one shoulder. Those shoulders. I could look at them for days. "But I don't want any of my own."

It was more than enough to placate me at the time. "Maybe we can pick him up together later?"

Leigh nodded thoughtfully. "As long as later means I get to do this now." She disposed of her glass and reached for my legs, pulled me toward her and flattened me on the sofa. The first year of our relationship, we didn't spend a lot of time talking. She fucked me again then, and not even in the way that would change me forever.

. . .

The first time Leigh really took my breath away, we'd stayed in at my place during a weekend that Troy was at Gerald's.

"Why go out?" Leigh had asked when she'd arrived. "When there's plenty to do in the comfort of your home?"

I was sure my eyes had started glittering with anticipation, but I only saw Leigh's eyes when she said it, and something I couldn't place shone in them. A darkness I hadn't yet encountered. It ignited a yearning in my belly I'd never felt before.

She barged her way in, shut the door behind her, and with subtle but clearly noticeable force, shoved me against it. She looked into my eyes, waiting for some sort of approval, but I was already too aroused to give her that. The stupid grin on my face was probably enough for a woman like Leigh to understand that she was on the right track.

Slowly, she trailed her fingers along my arms, only to snap them around my wrists hard, denting skin. She hoisted my arms above my head and pinned my wrists to the door with those strong fingers of hers. All the while, her lips sported a grueling, sneering sort of smile that left me wet like a river. It was as if what I had seen in her the first time we met, what I had seen flash in her eyes, that unquantifiable spark that had passed between us that I had mistaken for gaydar, was actually something else entirely. A sort of recognition, perhaps, an unexpected encounter of kindred souls.

She didn't say anything, just looked at me, giving the impression that a few glances were enough to read the entirety of my being, my desires, what—bone-deep—I really longed for. That sneer told me that she had it all figured out, and the wordlessness of it was the biggest turn-on of all.

One hand grabbed my wrists in a tight grasp while the other unbuttoned my jeans. No kisses, and certainly no displays of tenderness, were exchanged before she slipped her fingers all the way into my panties and caught my already swollen clit between two digits, pressing hard.

My breath caught in my throat, my knees giving a little.

Then, she broke eye-contact and brought her lips to my ear. "Here's what's going to happen, Jodie," she said, her voice all command. "I'm going to fuck you against this door and you're going to come for me. Don't make me wait for it, or else..." She released my clit, and the walls of my cunt clenched around nothing. Not for long, however, because one of her fingers was already sneaking closer.

Leigh dug her hand deeper into my pants, her wrist rubbing against my clit as she sought entrance to my cunt. She jammed her fingers inside in a rugged manner while her teeth sank into my earlobe. The fingernails of her other hand dug into my palms as— there's really no other way to describe it—she took possession of me. And I knew, there and then, that nothing else would ever do for me again. This was it. Nothing I, or even we, had ever done together had impacted me so profoundly. Because it wasn't pain I felt. It was something beyond pain, something beyond physical awareness, like a life-long thirst in my soul being quenched.

All my senses stood to attention as Leigh fucked me. This was not making love, as Leigh would later point out. This was fucking, and the fire in her glance when she said it left no room for contesting. Her DKNY scent filled my nose, and her teeth kept biting, rhythmically, and her fingers kept delving, and I was spread so wide, and filled to the brim, that I had no idea how many fingers she was using, but what turned me on the most was the immobilization of my hands, the sense of surrender that came with her controlling me in that way. What she'd asked of me earlier, came easily, although I was quite curious about the 'or else' she had threatened me with.

She must have known I was about to come and brought her face back across from mine to glare at me. She pushed harder with both hands, pinning my wrists painfully to the door, probably leaving bruises, while down below, she seemed to take hold of me, of everything of me, my pussy the entrance to the core of my being. She was in charge of everything.

My brain went blank as the climax momentarily paralyzed my limbs. Leigh pushed her body against mine to keep me upright, otherwise I would surely have crashed to my knees, weeping, as if this was my first time coming at her hands.

When I came back to my senses, her lips were on my neck, and both her hands in my hair. I remembered how I'd said to her the first time we had sex that I was blown away by the softness of it. Maybe that had inspired her to try something else because there was nothing soft about what she'd just done to me.

"This is just the beginning," she whispered, her lips on my cheek. "Just an introduction, Jodie." And only then did she kiss me.

I toss and turn in the faint red light of the alarm clock. I'm not wondering where and when I'll ever find a woman like Leigh again. I know I won't. I don't want to, either. I had the passionate, all-effacing love affair. Now it's time for something else. A visit to my ob-gyn, for starters. I'm thirty-six. If I'm lucky, I have more years for this, but now feels like the right time. If I can't have both Leigh in my life and another child, I'll choose another child. For the longest time, I held on to the belief that I would never have to choose, that life would arrange it so it would never have to come to that. But here I am. Alone in bed. Leigh's side unoccupied from now on. Because I can't possibly imagine another woman taking her place in my bed. Not because we only just broke up, but simply because I can't envision another woman doing what she did to me.

—————

At the first light of dawn, I can't bear to be in the apartment on my own anymore. I take a shower and go for a walk. My plan is to keep walking until the hour is decent enough for me to pick up Troy from his friend's house. I need desperately to spend every minute of this day with my son. Life always goes on when you have children. When you have someone to take care of.

"Up at the crack of dawn." I hear a voice behind me. I don't need to turn around to know that it's George from 4A. "Are you sleeping like us old codgers now?"

I wait for him to catch up with me. He's probably gone around the block a few times already. It's what he does to pass the empty hours of his life. His words, not mine.

"Just going to fetch Troy." It's not a lie and I don't feel like getting into the real reason behind my early Sunday morning walk.

"Missus having a lie-in?" He cocks his head like he's asking about a secret between us. As if Leigh hasn't lived in the same building as him for the past five years, carried his groceries up the stairs, and even watched baseball games with him on his tiny, old TV. As if she only moved in yesterday, and it is still news-worthy that I am shacking up with another woman.

"She left," I blurt out. "She's gone. It's over." It comes out in a rush of short words, like something that really needs to be said. As though saying it to George equals announcing it to the world.

"Oh, dear." George leans on his walking stick a bit more, like he's the one who needs the most support. "I sure am sorry to hear that."

Not as sorry as I am, I think. But sorry is not the right word. A car swooshes past us, obviously over the speed limit, and this would normally snag George's attention, but he doesn't even bat an eyelid.

"Are you okay?" he asks, and this old man asking about my emotional well-being shakes me again.

"Not really. But I will be." I catch a sly tear that has escaped with my thumb.

"Anything you need. I mean it." He stomps his cane, as if his voice alone is not enough to make the point. "If you need some quiet time when you have the little fella, let me know. I'll look after him. He loves my model plane collection. Can play with it for hours."

"Thanks," I say, and it suddenly hits me that, although Gerald and

I share equal custody of Troy, and I've never really been a single mother, that's kind of what it feels like now. Me and my child against the lonely world Leigh left us in. Gerald and I had only been divorced a few months when I met Leigh. When she came swooping in and, so quickly, became a massive part of our lives. "I may take you up on that."

"Any time," George says. He tips his forehead with his fingertips. "I'll leave you to your business now."

I watch him wander off and it feels like all I've done of late is watch people walk away from me.

CHAPTER FIVE

Six months after Jodie and I broke up I jump at the chance of trading New York for San Francisco. Everything in New York reminds me of her, especially in October. We met in October and I can't seem to separate the month from all the first times we shared during it.

I don't care that I've only just settled into my new mid-town apartment. That I only found the strength two weeks ago to unpack the last of the boxes that, in the end, remained in a corner of Jodie's apartment for months. When the offer from my firm comes to join the new office on the west coast, I don't hesitate. I grab the opportunity to leave with both hands.

Because I need to start over. I crave new surroundings. A clean slate. Soon the ice skating rink will be up in front of Rockefeller and I won't be able to walk past it without memories of Troy's and Jodie's gleeful smiles at my attempts to venture onto the ice with them. How Troy put his tiny, gloved hand in mine and said, "Come on, Leigh. I'll teach you." And how even a genuine, beautiful gesture like that wasn't able to sway me. For I fell in love with Jodie's son too. My heart is not made of stone and ambition alone. I loved Troy, but as soon as Jodie started talking about another child, something in my brain failed to compute.

By the time the New Year rolls along, I'll be on the other coast. Maybe Jodie will be pregnant by then. Who knows? We have gathered mutual friends and acquaintances over the years, of course, but, as if they've all secretly agreed on the best strategy, they never mention my ex when we meet up, not intentionally anyway.

Granted, it was awkward when I ran into Muriel and Francine at the Chelsea Market a few weeks ago. Sonja had looped her arm through mine and I guess someone not in the know could have mistaken us for lovers, which we were, sort of, but it was all very lackluster on my side, a fact which Sonja didn't seem to care much about. All I could think when Muriel and Francine appeared in my line of vision was, *please don't let them see me* and *please don't let them draw the obvious conclusion and tell Jodie.* Then I was ashamed that I even had the audacity to think of Sonja that way. Sonja who had only been good to me, who'd given me a place to stay, and a shoulder to cry on. It remains unclear who actually took advantage of whom. I guess we're both guilty.

But they're not blind and Muriel has an inclination to latch on to other people's drama, so she swept us up and the four of us ended up in one of those trendy places in the Meat Packing District.

Muriel, one of Jodie's closest friends and someone she sees at work every day, apparently couldn't help but look at me disapprovingly, as if to say, "You've moved on quick enough." But she didn't know that I hadn't moved on at all. That leaving Jodie was far and away the hardest thing I'd done in my life, and that I doubted the validity of my decision every single day. Especially, too, during those long dark nights, when Sonja lay purring beside me, and I would drift off into slumber only to wake up again and again to find that the person next to me was not the one I wanted it to be.

"Please excuse me," I said. "I'm going to find the washroom."

"I'll go with you," Muriel cooed, right on cue.

As soon as we reached the bathroom, fitted out in nothing but ostentatious black marble, I cornered her. "It's not what you think."

"No matter what I think," she said, squaring her shoulders. "But let me tell you this." She brought her hands to her sides matron-like. "Jodie is in pieces and it's a good thing she has Troy because he's the only one getting her through this. So, if you're in any mind to reconsider, please do."

I knew she was forward, but I had never realized quite how much until then. "It's complicated," was all I could say.

"Hm-mm." Muriel shook her head dramatically. "Not in my eyes, it's not. She loves you and you love her. What's the problem?"

"Really?" I narrowed my eyes, gearing up for a fight. It had been a while since I'd had a good one in court. Maybe in her naiveté Muriel was trying to help, but she wasn't doing a very good job of it, and I could do without the lecture. "That's the line you're spinning me? How long did it take you to come up with that?" Muriel was at least two heads shorter than me and I used my height to my advantage by towering over her. "You're her best friend. You should know better."

"Listen, Miss Fancy Lawyer who has it all figured out." She didn't back down an inch. "Have you perhaps considered—you know, with that academic brain of yours—that what was valid six months ago may have changed? A break-up changes people. Shifts their perspective. Makes them see things differently and rethink their goals."

"Wh—what are you saying?" Suddenly, my heart was thumping wildly. "Has Jodie said anything?"

"It's really not for me to put words in her mouth, just… get in touch." With that, she turned on her heel and headed toward a stall.

"Muriel," I called after her. "Please don't tell her about Sonja. It's really nothing. We're colleagues and I've been staying with her, that's all."

"Oh, I know all about Sonja." She pushed open the door of the stall and disappeared.

I steadied myself against the wash basin, peering at my reflection in the mirror. Outwardly, our break-up had definitely changed me.

My cheekbones were as sharp as in my teens, my eyes sunken deep into my face from lack of decent sleep, my skin grayish from too much booze. Looking back at me was a wreck of a woman. And then there were Muriel's words. Should I get in touch? Did Muriel mean that Jodie's wish to add another member to her family of two had waned?

I contemplated calling her every day after that washroom conversation with Muriel, but a week later the offer for San Francisco came in. It was not that I didn't love Jodie enough to check in with her and the status of her wishes—it was that I loved her too much. And I couldn't do it again. Couldn't give in to what might turn out to be false hope. My heart hadn't yet mended from when it was torn out of my chest after our first break-up. What if we ended up on her living room floor again, and I had to walk away all over again?

Muriel might be her best friend, but yet that didn't mean she knew Jodie better than I did. I knew the dark cavities of Jodie's psyche. I knew what she craved and what she could and couldn't say. I could read her, and, even though a part of me wished it hadn't, the past year *had* happened. That year in which we'd danced around the subject, playfully at first, until there was no more room for play, nor joy, because I couldn't picture myself walking, living, and waking up next to a heavily pregnant woman, not even if that woman was Jodie Whitehouse. A woman with a teenage son, a newborn on the way—both equally important to her—and me, trailing behind.

It wasn't only the absence of maternal instinct, nor the focus I put on my career—although they were the main reasons—that drove us apart in the end. For me, Jodie always came first. She had done from that evening in the bar around the corner from the courthouse in 1996. I even passed up on a faster track to my career goal to spend time with Troy when the babysitter bailed or something else came up, because I always enjoyed my time with him—even when it didn't fit my schedule. But I had to draw the line somewhere because if I didn't, where would that leave me in Jodie's life?

I witnessed first-hand, and on more than one occasion, how motherhood so fundamentally changed the lives of women whose ambition equalled mine during law school—former peers who, because of time constraints and shifted focus, are no longer a part of my life. It was as if they'd had a personality transplant. As if a switch in their brain had been flicked as soon as they gave birth, and all their previous, often loudly vocalized goals and dreams took an immediate and permanent backseat to their new role as a mother. A sudden transformation my logical brain can fully grasp, even though it was never something I wanted for myself. Not even with Jodie.

So here I am, on the first of many flights from New York to San Francisco. My boss, Steve, told me I'd most likely be flying over there every other week, until I move permanently by the end of the year. Perhaps it could be seen as another cowardly move on my part —as running away—but I know that only distance can heal that hole in my heart. Bumping into Muriel made that perfectly clear. Because what if I had run into Jodie? Or Troy? What would that have done to my heart? New York City is a huge city, but it's not big enough for my pain.

Sonja knew she had to let me go when I told her. At first, I was afraid she'd convince someone at the firm to let her relocate as well, but as it turns out she's not that besotted with me, after all. And New York is threaded through the fabric of her being too much. She can't leave it, not even for me. Not that I want her to.

The first night I allowed her to slip into my makeshift bed in her spare room, all I did was throw my arms around her and cry on her shoulder, cry until I believed I was empty, until the next night, the tears came again. That's what Sonja did for me. She let me cry, my tears gathering on her skin, wrinkling it, until I ran out. Until I was dry. Then we had sex a few times, but to me, it felt like encountering a trickle of water in the desert when all I was used to with Jodie were shattering, uncompromising waves of the wildest ocean.

When the plane touches down, I inhale deeply. I'm ready for my new life. The arm of the passenger next to me bumps into mine as she finally relaxes. Clearly, this woman is no fan of flying, just like Jodie, who always held on to me for dear life when we flew somewhere. I'd try to distract her by whispering silly things in her ear, making her laugh, or playing one of our favorite games.

Our last trip together was to Hawaii. We had an early morning flight back to New York and had gone on a massive bender the night before. I usually don't break a sweat while flying, but lots of turbulence and a martini hangover made even me shaky. Jodie, the sweetest person I've ever known in my life, took my hand in hers on that flight, brought her mouth to my ear, and whispered, "Tell me what you're thinking right now." The memory of that moment sparks another. Of the very first time I asked her that question.

"Tell me what you're thinking right now," I asked. We'd gone for a quick dinner at a restaurant around the corner from her apartment after dropping off Troy at Gerald's. I was cradling a glass of wine in my hands and Jodie kept staring at it.

"Don't think about it. Just say it," I urged. "Just blurt out whatever's going through your mind."

"Those hands of yours." Her voice had dropped into a lower register I could barely hear over the restaurant murmurs around us. "I wonder what else they can do."

I know she didn't mean spanking. We'd successfully graduated to that not long after I had pushed her against her apartment door on our seventh date. This was our tenth. I knew what she meant. "I'll show you." I swallowed a lump in my throat and called the waiter for the check. I couldn't get out of there fast enough. On our way to York Avenue, her shorter legs could barely keep up with me. But a fire in my belly had been stoked. I had considered it before, of course, as a natural progression of the sexual dynamic that was unfolding between us, and it was on the schedule, so to speak, but I definitely hadn't had any plans toward it on that particular night. In my mind, it was still much too soon. In the beginning of our relationship, reading Jodie, gauging her desires, was still very much a careful balancing act, even though I made it out as anything but.

"I want it all," Jodie said, as soon as we fell through the door of her apartment, and she pulled me close.

"You've got it." I injected a shot of bravado into my voice I didn't really feel. The prospect was exciting—almost unbearably so—but when someone asks that of you, it always comes with a burden of responsibility. Also, by then, Jodie was not just *someone* to me. The fire that crackled between us every time we met left me with more than growing desires and that ever-present wish to push boundaries. I was in love with her. We stood at the beginning of our journey together—a long and rewarding one, I hoped—and I didn't want to screw that up by making a false move.

Our kiss grew frantic in no time, our teeth breaking skin, until I pulled away and stared at her, until the silence around us became too loud. "Take off all your clothes," I commanded.

She did as she was told. It was a Saturday so she was dressed casually in jeans and a sweater. The way she stepped out of them indicated that she'd been waiting for this moment much longer than I could have suspected. The enthusiasm in her demeanor soon exterminated my nerves, because that was the thing with me and Jodie. We fed off each other's energy all the time. It was all cause and consequence. Sometimes it felt like a perfectly choreographed ballet of movements, intentions, and desires. It was the way it always clicked for us in the bedroom, the way we erased each other's doubts and got to the essence so effortlessly.

"On the bed." I stripped off my own clothes and followed her to the bedroom. There could be no disparity in the state of undress between us for this. We had to meet on a level playing field. The beauty of our give-and-take was always the equality in it. I never made her do things, I merely unearthed them from her psyche and then we did them together.

"Spread your legs," I said.

I moved onto the bed and sat between her legs, looking at what lay in front of me, mesmerized by the sight. I doubled-down in front of her and licked her wet pussy lips until she almost came. I could easily tell by the rapidly increasing twitches in her legs, which she pressed against my ears when I went down on her—unless I told her not to.

Then I stopped and pushed myself up so that I could see her eyes. She didn't say anything, but I felt electricity zing in the air between us. She let her knees fall open, spreading herself wide for me again, her breath coming in labored gusts. Clearly, she was on the edge of climax, and I was right there with her. Only, this time, we would go about it a bit differently.

I only looked away from her briefly to bring my hand in position, and my eyes were back on hers when I let the first three fingers slip in. By then, three fingers was our standard. Nothing less, nothing more.

"Oh christ," Jodie murmured after the first stroke, her head falling back a bit, but not breaking eye-contact. I could still see it in her eyes. She was begging for more.

Adding the fourth finger was a mere matter of transition. She took it easily, as if she was used to it. Her pelvis gyrated, her pussy swallowed, enveloping my fingers in exquisite warmth.

"Yeah," she started saying then. "Oh yeah." Her hands had curled into fists, clenching the sheets between tight fingers.

I eased back and inched my thumb closer to the tips of my other fingers and spread her wider. I didn't go deep at first, let her get used to the changed shape of my hand, caused by only the slightest of alteration on my part, but making a world of difference for her.

"I want it all." She repeated what she'd said before, but now her voice was drenched in lust, and low with animalistic want.

Slowly, slowly, I let my knuckles touch the rim of her pussy, seeking entrance. It was the most I'd asked of her. I had to avert my gaze from her face and examine what my hand was doing. I watched as my knuckles slid over the entrance, and then all the way inside.

Jodie lay completely still, the movements of her pelvis having ground to a complete halt. It was all me now. I kept my hand immobile for a few seconds and reveled in this moment of complete surrender. I felt it burn throughout my flesh, underneath my skin, like the biggest, most immersive present anyone had ever given me. It was.

Then I started fucking her, the knuckle of my thumb sliding in as well, and to have someone spread so wide for you feels more like a spiritual experience than anything else. My clit swelled between my legs and I could feel moisture gather on my inner thighs, that's how wet I was.

I scanned Jodie's face. Her eyes were shut, her features a mask of concentration and utter bliss. And it had all started with a simple question: *Tell me what you're thinking right now.* Then her lips parted, but no sound came from her mouth. All the while, I shifted my hand inside of her with minute movements. This wasn't about motion so much as it was about being inside of her to such an extent it made both of our hearts explode.

Even though my task at hand wasn't strenuous, beads of sweat pearled on my forehead. This was a meeting of the emotional and the physical, and it was taking all I had.

"Oh Leigh," she said then, breaking the silence around us, and how she said my name chased a chill of pleasure up my spine. "Oh… Oh… Oooh."

Her entire body contracted around my fist. Jodie threw her head into the pillows and her fists uncurled, then curled back up again. That was the first time I witnessed someone totally surrender, to the moment, the action, the intimacy, and the feelings that blossomed between us. A new bar was set.

Ever so gently, I slid my hand out of her. I looked at it incredulously for an instant, as if I could hardly believe what it had just done, but then Jodie called for me, and I clearly remember the single salty line that a tear tracked down my cheek as I folded over her to kiss her.

CHAPTER SIX

From the moment my ob-gyn confirms I'm pregnant with a girl, I know I want to call her Rosie. Not Rose, or Rosamund, or Rosalyn, but just Rosie. Rosie Whitehouse. My dream come true.

My friends, Ginny and Susan, who had put me in touch with their fertility specialist and accompanied me on my first appointment, had warned me about the path of hope and disappointment artificial insemination would take me on. They'd had to try—and pay for—four inseminations before Ginny had gotten pregnant and successfully carried the baby to term. But, as if the universe knew I was more than ready—and that I had already sacrificed greatly—my very first insemination took, despite the odds being small. Dr. Barkin confirmed my pregnancy, monitored me closely, behaved moderately optimistic but always with an edge of caution to her words and demeanor, until I was in the second trimester and she gave me the go-ahead to start telling people.

Gerald is not necessarily the first person I want to impart the news to, but I'm so elated, so completely over the moon and buzzing with excitement, that I just blurt it out when I go to fetch Troy.

I see my beautiful boy who's growing up so fast and I'm so overwhelmed by love and hormones and joy, that I crouch down next to him, pull him to me, and say, "Guess what, handsome? You're going to be someone's big brother in six months' time." Gerald stands behind him and almost shrieks.

"For real?" he asks. "Oh, Jodie." From where I'm kneeling, his voice sounds teary. Gerald is a tall, broad, dark-haired man. Our marriage suffered from many more issues than my growing attraction to women and, to his credit, he never felt the need to blame it all on me. Always a cordial, well-mannered guy, he was the one to make sure we made it through the divorce as something akin to friends, for our son's sake.

"Yep." I stand and face him, my hand on Troy's shoulders because I can't let go of him.

"That's such great news." I can tell from his smile that he's genuinely happy for me.

Troy shows his excitement by leaning against me. He barely asks after Leigh these days. He's too preoccupied with starting High School and balancing on the edge of puberty.

And it is great news. And Gerald is Troy's dad and still a good friend. We've successfully co-parented our son for almost seven years now, so why not tell him first? For a fraction of a second, it takes me back to when I found out I was pregnant with Troy. I was only twenty-five. Barely out of college. We'd only been married a few months. This pregnancy couldn't be more different from my first. The biggest difference will be that there will be no one to rub my feet after a rough day at work, when carrying a baby may weigh on me, and have me sink into the sofa with pure exhaustion. If something were to go wrong, or I need emergency help, I'll need to actually think about who to call first, as opposed to having the automatic reaction of calling a husband or partner.

"Anything you need, Jodie. This guy and I will be there for you. Right, buddy?" He holds up his hand for Troy to high-five. Troy slaps his palm against it, and I do feel a twinge of guilt for robbing my baby of having a father. But he or she will have a big brother. And me. And Gerald in the background. And Muriel and Francine. And Ginny and Susan. And even George on the floor above me. And my parents in Connecticut. We will not be alone.

"Thanks." I nod at Gerald, then turn to Troy. "Ready to go, Troy-toy?"

"Don't call me that, Mom. I'm too old for that sh—" He realizes his error and doesn't pronounce the last word. It's true what they say. Once they're in school they grow up so fast. It doesn't matter that Gerald pays for Hunter College, they learn the same ugly words everywhere.

Most times, I don't even pick him up from Gerald's anymore. He just walks the few blocks that separate his father's home from mine. He'll be going off to college before I know it.

"Let's go," Troy says and reaches for his bag. He's not too old to let his dad kiss him on the cheek and give him a big hug. Thank goodness.

"See you next week," Gerald calls after us.

Troy is silent on the way home, but I can tell a million questions are flitting through his mind. I explained the process to him as best I could, going into details where it was appropriate but leaving out the information that no young teenage boy needs to know about his mother.

"So we'll never know who the dad is?" he asks again when we've almost reached our building. "Not even my sister or brother will know?"

"I chose an anonymous donor." I remember going through the details of the men who had donated their sperm. The donor files only consisted of a list of characteristics like height and hair color, medical history, and level of education. At first, instinctively, I sought out tall, blond lawyers until I realized I didn't need that sort of reminder for the rest of my life. "We only know a few things about him." Troy already knows this, but perhaps learning the news while at his dad's has triggered some new emotions in him that need to be processed.

"Mm." He just shrugs and reaches for the key in his pocket. I take him by the shoulders and make him face me.

"Any questions you have. Ask them, please. Okay?"

"Yeah." He pushes his hair away from his forehead awkwardly. "What are we going to call... him or her?"

The fact that he says 'we' makes my heart sing. "Any ideas?" I ask, although I already have plenty of my own. He opens the door and we walk up the stairs in silence, while he ponders.

"How about Rufus for a boy?" he asks.

Personally, I was thinking more along the lines of Jack or Tommy, but I don't want to dash his hopes. "Maybe." He's already half-way to his room. "Why don't you make a list? Give it to me in a few days?"

He nods pensively. Pushes his hair away again, then shoots me that grin. "I'm very happy for you... for us, Mom." And my heart is in my throat.

"Thank you, baby." I lean against a hallway cabinet with my hip. "Are you up for all the extra chores that come with being the child of a pregnant woman?" I shoot him a smirk.

"I've got homework." He takes a few hesitant steps toward his room.

"And you'll have to learn how to change diapers. You'll make the perfect husband for someone some day, baby," I joke.

I never meant for the age difference between my two children to be so big, but what with Leigh coming along and diverting me from the path I had laid out for myself for such a long time, this is how it's going to be. Troy will be even more of a teenager by the time this baby joins us. I've worked with enough moody, irresponsible, hormonally imbalanced teenagers to know exactly what they can be like—and that it's foolish to hold most of their mistakes against them, unless they break the law. It will be an interesting combination. And Troy is not just any teenager. He's my son.

"Come on, Mom." I can see a flush rise up his neck. It's the Irish in him. "Lay off."

"Go do your homework. But stay off the internet." I smile as he exits my field of vision, and then, as it does so many times, my eye wanders to the one picture I kept of her. The only one on display. It's only hanging on that wall because Troy insisted. Because every time I took it down he would stare at the empty spot with a trembling lip. Now, I can barely remember the last time I saw him cast a glance at it.

It's a snap of Leigh and Troy and a giant Lego castle. That's what they did most together. Build things. I never had much patience to sit on the floor with Troy and help him, but Leigh loved it. She could spend hours studying the instructions, laying out the pieces, and making Troy feel like he'd been the one who'd put it all together, with just a tiny bit of help from her.

He beams with pride in the picture, and Leigh's smile is so wide, so genuine, you would never have pegged her for a woman with no desire whatsoever to become a mother. I know she loved him. But she left, anyway. Now I have another on the way. I put my hand on my belly. I'm not really showing yet, but just putting my hand there makes it more real. And then that sneaky feeling, that if she were here, that if she'd stayed and could put her hand on my belly, she would have felt it, too.

———

Six months later Rosie is born, and my life becomes a whirlwind of not enough sleep, breastfeeding, never-ending noise, folding baby clothes, and never having enough energy to start a new day, but always doing so anyway, and enjoying every minute of it.

A few months after bringing Rosie home, I find myself standing in front of the picture of Leigh and Troy, Rosie in my arms, introducing her to Leigh.

"This pretty woman next to your brother," I say, "is Leigh Sterling." And I'm not overwhelmed anymore by a sense of loss, or missing out on another life, because I know that I've become what was in my cards all along: a mother, again.

"She was a bit crazy, this woman," I say to Rosie. "She didn't want an adorable, cute, awesome baby like you, Rosie. Can you believe that?" And I can smile now because the hurt has been replaced by so many other emotions. "She must have been crazy for not wanting that, huh?" I inhale my daughter's scent while staring at Leigh. I pondered sending her a birth announcement card, but it felt like rubbing it in too much. Like exclaiming, *look how happy I am without you*, and that didn't feel right. Because I could never in my right mind claim that Leigh leaving had made me even remotely happy.

Thus, I haven't seen Leigh since she came to pick up the last of her boxes, months overdue. Last I heard she moved to San Francisco. I bet she's a hot-shot lawyer there. I bet she gets all the girls. I bet our lives are now so completely different we couldn't even be friends if we tried.

CHAPTER SEVEN

Another weekend, another woman, I think, as I let Karen into my apartment. It's my third rental place in San Francisco. After I first arrived, I lived in the financial district to be close to work, but it was too dead and lonely after dark. Then I moved south of Castro, but that brought too much temptation for one more martini after I'd had three already. Too close to Cherries to not pop in and see who would give me the time of day.

Now, I'm on Lexington Street in the Mission District and I've sworn it will be my last rental before I buy a house. If I keep working the way I do, the road to making partner is wide open. My very own house will be the reward for the life I chose when I left New York.

I don't tell all this to Karen. Karen is not here for a chat. We both know what she's here for. She may as well be called Lynn, like the woman I brought here last week, or Fran, like the one from a few weeks back.

"You're playing the field, huh," Sonja said when she came to visit a month ago. "Good for you." Only, it didn't feel good. It doesn't feel good now, either. Yet, I can't seem to stop myself. What felt good at the time Sonja said it, though, was seeing *her*, someone from what I now consider 'my old life'. San Francisco has given me everything I thought I wanted, and my life is not an unhappy one—from what I hear from tipsy colleagues and acquaintances in bars it might even be an enviable one—but let's just say it doesn't feel exactly how I had expected it to.

Take this woman who is sitting on my sofa while I fix us another drink. She's petite, with slicked-back dark hair, and her eyes sparkle when she looks at me, as if she knows what she's in for—maybe I've built a reputation for myself in more than one field? Even this sort of formulaic foreplay doesn't satisfy me anymore. And it used to be such a thrill. Sitting at the bar at Cherries. Occupying my favorite spot in the corner, the one with the best view. A shot of whiskey at hand. Scoping out the place. Sometimes, I don't even have to try. They just walk up to me, as Karen did earlier. Because I knew what I was there for, I didn't fend off her barely concealed advances. And every time I meet someone, there's this twinge of hope, like a feebly flickering flame that gets a fresh rush of oxygen, that this time it might be different. That I won't know if I don't try. And then I try. And run out of oxygen after one night.

Maybe it will be different with Karen. I have to believe that, which is why I repeat this cycle of hello-goodbye over and over again. This is San Francisco. The number of happy lesbian couples must be higher here than anywhere else in the country—except, perhaps, for Portland. I see them everywhere. Doing groceries together at Whole Foods. Strolling through Dolores Park hand in hand. Every time I go to the movies, one of my favorite means of escape, a *Happy Lesbian Couple* is seated in the row in front of me. As if destiny is trying to tell me something. I haven't figured out if it's that I could be part of a couple like that as well, or that I was a fool to destroy the one I was part of in New York.

"Cheers," I say, as I hand Karen her martini.

"What a lovely place you've got." The wrong remark. After moving three times in the course of two years, my decorating touch has become lazy instead of sharp. I just don't bother with hanging up picture frames or having the right color of curtains made anymore. Why would I if I know I'm just passing through?

"Thanks," I say, anyway. I can hardly dismiss her because she's trying to make polite conversation. There's also something about her that draws me to her more than to others who have sat on that couch. Maybe it's the tint of her irises. They have green flecks in them. A rarity I've always found highly attractive.

We've already covered the what-do-you-do and where-are-you-from bits of our biography at the bar. The preliminary work has been done. All I need to do is swoop in—because God forbid someone swoops in on me. The closest I can get to allowing someone to make the first move is having them walk up to me while I'm nursing a drink, my demeanor an open invitation. After that, it needs to come from me. I determine the pace. Decide where we go— always my place. And with me on top.

"Have you lived here long?" It's this small talk I can't stand.

"Long enough," I say, and move in. I take her glass and deposit it on my designer coffee table. I take her now free hand in mine and examine it, giving the impression I can read her palm. Run my thumb over a line. Press a little. Her lips part already. Then I drop her hand and bring mine to her jaw, cup it briefly, before rubbing my thumb along her lips, demanding entrance. Perhaps it would have been politer to kiss her first, but I need to gauge the sort of woman I'm dealing with. This is how. If she protests too much it's probably not going to work out.

Karen sucks my thumb between her lips with the kind of gusto that never fails to turn me on. This night may not be a total loss, after all. There's promise in the way she twirls her tongue around my thumb, and in the way her green-speckled eyes find mine. Okay then.

I grin at her as I remove my thumb from between her lips. The main issue with a string of one-night stands is that the first time can touch the edges of what I really want to do, but it can never go any further. The irony of what my love life has consisted of these past few years is not lost on me. Always searching, never finding. At first, I was just looking for the next Jodie, until it dawned on me that that was hardly fair on anyone.

Karen lets her head fall back, exposing her neck to me. Is she not the kissing kind? We'll see about that.

"Get up," I say and lead by example. "Come here."

Before she stands, she peers at me from under her lashes for a few seconds, as if she wants me to make her. Then she rises, and I pull her toward me, hoist her top over her head in the same movement. No bra. Just a pair of leather pants and the sort of high-heels I only wear in court when I have something impossible to prove. I do like what I see. I feel it twitch in my muscles, and between my legs.

I walk us toward the nearest wall and push her against it. I curl my fingers around her wrists and bring them above her head. Her breasts jut out and the desire to take her nipple into my mouth overwhelms me. But I resist. Instead, I unbutton her trousers and lower her zipper.

"Keep your hands above your head," I murmur before taking a step back and taking in the view. She looks so vulnerable and defiant at the same time. Her skin is pale against the black of the leather, her lips smudged red. This is a test for me as well. I wish it didn't have to be. I wish I could just enjoy these few hours we have together. Give her what she wants while tending to my own needs. A perfect transaction of fulfilling emotional and physical needs. But sex is rarely so uncomplicated.

Then I give in. Take a step toward her and kiss her fully on the mouth, my tongue meeting hers in a soft crash of desire and lust and trying to make up for too much accumulated disappointment. But maybe I *am* ready. The thought shocks me at first. But why wouldn't I be? I've relocated. My career's on track. I know Karen doesn't have any children. The first thing I will have to ask her about in the morning is where she sees herself in five years.

I pinch her nipple hard and she barely even shudders. Her lack of obvious response turns me on. I pinch harder and she writhes a tiny bit against me and it reminds me that all I really want is someone who can take it the way Jodie did. To meet my match in this game of give-and-receive.

When we break from the kiss, my fingers still on her nipple, she stares into my eyes and flits her tongue over her lips. "Harder," she says, and it's as if someone has flicked a switch in my brain.

———

The following morning, the light wakes me, pouring in through the flimsy curtains that came with the apartment. Before I open my eyes fully, I align my memories of the night before. The bar. The walk over here. A woman named Karen who got to me. Three hours of sleep at most because I couldn't get enough of her, and she kept asking for more, harder, wider. Already, my lips are breaking into a smile. I open my eyes to slits. Karen is so tiny, she's barely a presence in my bed. She's moved to the edge, her body curled into a ball, her head next to the pillow.

I crawl toward her, spoon her small frame with my tall one. We fit snugly together. That's a start.

"Morning," I whisper in her ear. I revel in the absence of regret.

She turns on her back, my arm sliding onto her bare chest. My bedroom smells of sex, of good times had. "Hey." She smiles up at me. Her lipstick is smudged all the way around her mouth and her mascara has left black marks on her cheeks.

There's no awkwardness, no anticipation for a hurried walk of shame out of my apartment.

"Coffee?" I ask. If we drank too much alcohol last night, we sweated it out in bed after. I feel no signs of a hangover, only an already returning pulse between my legs. My eyes wander to the scarf with which I tied her wrists to the bed and I feel all fuzzy inside.

"Sure." Her voice is a bit hoarse. "But something else first." She pulls me toward her and kisses me. It's deep from the beginning and

I get lost in it so much I don't realize she's pushed herself up and is now half on top of me. She kisses my cheek next, then my chin, and moves down with more incremental pit stops, and by the time she's reached my belly button, I spread my legs easily for her. I want her there. And when she licks me, I don't think of anyone else. My mind just goes blank while my body surrenders. And I know it's the beginning of something.

CHAPTER EIGHT

"You need to get laid, girl," Muriel says. "How long has it been?"

She says the exact same thing to me every Friday after work. This time, I try to humor her with a truthful reply, but the truth is that I can't even remember. "I honestly don't know." The last time I had sex was with Leigh, that I do remember. First I was grieving. Then I had Rosie. It's Rosie's first birthday next week. So, I guess I could actually count the months—years—since that time Leigh came to pick up some of her stuff, but the prospect is too depressing.

"All jokes aside." Muriel's face goes all serious. "You need affection, honey." To prove her point she puts her hand on my arm.

I stare at it as though she's making a move on me. "Oh, hell no." She doesn't remove her hand, however, just squeezes a bit harder. "Francine won't be having any of that." She cocks her head. "Besides, it would only put our excellent working relationship in peril."

I swat away Muriel's hand. "I've got you. I've got my children. I've got my job. My friends. I don't need anything more."

"Keep telling yourself that until you believe it, sweet pea." Muriel drinks from her mai tai.

"Maybe you're right." I don't usually concur so easily. "But I come with a lot of baggage."

"Everyone does at our age." Muriel shrugs. "Does this mean I can finally set you up with Amy?"

Amy Bernard. I've heard so much about the woman from Muriel I feel as if I already know her, although we've never met. I even googled her, just out of curiosity.

"We'll babysit. You'll have nothing to worry about."

"Nothing to worry about? How about selling myself to another woman with my stretch marks and scars and two children?"

"Amy has children." Another fact I already knew. It's supposed to reassure me, but it doesn't. I can't stop thinking about all the possible complications. But I also know I need to start somewhere. A woman hand-picked by my best friend can't be that bad a starting point.

"Fine. Set it up."

Muriel takes a deep breath, as if she's just been bequeathed with the most important task of her life. "I won't let you down, Jodie. I promise."

———

Much to Muriel's delight, Amy and I click. I've *gotten laid* several times, and it has certainly taken an edge off, but when I say 'harder' to Amy she can't interpret it in the same way that Leigh used to. Instead, she narrows her eyes and looks at me with a tad too much disbelief displayed on her face. She tries, I know that, just as I know that it's not really a matter of trying.

But I'm not the same woman that I was with Leigh. My relation-ship with Amy is based on entirely different pillars than supreme and, at times, shocking satisfaction in the bedroom. Amy has two teenagers who are around Troy's age. Two boys. When we're all together I sometimes look at Rosie's crib in fright, what with so much unbridled youth running around the house. Troy is fiercely protective of Rosie, and sometimes it feels a bit like an us-versus-them situation, but then I'm reminded of the solace and comfort I've found with Amy, and more than anything, the deep understanding of each other's lives that we share.

I don't question Amy when she cancels a date because one of the boys is unwell. I don't wake her up for a bout of uninterrupted sex on the rare Sunday morning when we can both sleep in and have either her house or my apartment to ourselves. I don't have to ask her what her week will look like because my week looks about the same.

"I knew you needed more than to get laid, Jodie," Muriel tends to say. "That was just my hook, you see?"

It's only over brunch to celebrate our one-year anniversary, when the conversation turns to moving in together, that I experience the first major doubts. Being with Amy is the complete opposite of being with Leigh. Amy and I never had the urgency of desire I had with Leigh, but the sexual component of our affair has gone from taking a back-seat to a tired, almost reluctant show we put on every few weeks just because it's part of the relationship deal. We've never sizzled in the bedroom, but a spark now and then would be welcome.

Amy has a big house in Park Slope—an inheritance from her late father's side of the family. One that would fit me, Troy, and Rosie easily, but just the notion of leaving my apartment and my neighborhood makes me queasy—not a pleasant sensation when having brunch.

"Think about it, Jodie." Amy has a million freckles on her face and a huge mane of red curly hair. "Rosie could have her own room." Rosie's room at the moment is a glorified broom closet, and the fact of the matter is that on my salary I can't afford to leave my rent-controlled apartment. As far as persuasive arguments go, Amy has come out with the big one from the start.

"I'll think about it."

"Don't sound so enthusiastic." Amy's eyes dim. Sweet, sweet Amy.

"It's only been a year, though." What if it doesn't work out, I add in my head, and I will have lost my apartment.

"Yes, but what a year it has been." Amy reminds me of the reason why we're drinking champagne today. She raises her glass. "I love you, Jodie."

Amy didn't have any issues with the fact that her boys are practically grown and I brought an infant into the mix. The way she is with Rosie, treating her like one of her own, warms me to my very core. In front of me sits a woman with the same desires as mine. The sort of woman I wanted all along. Someone to share my life with— the kind of life I always dreamed of. So what's stopping me? I drink from my glass, which I still hold in toast position.

"Okay." I nod, more to convince myself than her. "Let's do it." In the back of my brain, I can't help but conjure up possible scenarios to keep my apartment. As though a little part of me already knows this relationship—shacked up or not—can never last.

Amy beams me a smile. She is gorgeous. I should have taken Muriel up on her offer to matchmake much earlier. Even Gerald likes her. Most of the time, Troy loves that he's gotten two step-brothers out of this. Sometimes, though, he just wants to be alone. He grew up an only child for the longest time. "Let's have another." She points at the near-empty bottle in the ice bucket. "Make this a proper celebration."

We planned this day like it would be a wild one. Luxurious brunching followed by luxurious fucking. The boys have been carted off to their dads and Rosie is with Muriel. But I know exactly how this will end. Stomachs too bloated from too much food and booze. Libidos remaining dormant because, in my case, what's the point, really? I'm not sure how Amy feels about our lack of fireworks in the bedroom. Maybe I should ask her. She's sufficiently tipsy to give me a straight answer.

"Are you sure?" I lean over the table. "We could also get out of here semi-sober and, you know, go home."

"*Our* home." She quirks up her eyebrows suggestively and extends her arm over the table. "I'm so happy."

"Me too, babe." I grab her hand. "So, what do you say?"

She glares at me for a minute with glazed-over eyes. Amy is no fool, of course. Not even with a good amount of alcohol in her blood. But, suddenly, I feel we need to have this conversation now. If we don't, there will always be something more important keeping us from having it. This is *our* day alone.

"I say that you look like a woman who has something on her mind." Amy's voice sounds skittish.

I look at our intertwined fingers instead of at her face. My cheeks grow hot already. Leigh and I never had to have these sorts of discussions. It was all so effortless and easy. Then again, Leigh proved allergic to my wish for another child, so what is more important to me? Amy, who wants to lead the life that I want? Or someone like Leigh, who thrills me in the bedroom but can't stick around for the hard stuff? The stuff life is actually made up of. Ideally, I'd find a combination of both in one person, but that's proven to be impossible—as though the two lifestyles are mutually exclusive. Except for me, I think.

What I really want to say is, "I want us to go home and fuck," but I can't use that line on Amy. It's not who we are.

"Sweetie?" Amy urges. I've probably been silent for too long. "Are you okay?" Sometimes, without her being able to help it—and I know this because this happens to me as well—she uses her baby-addressing voice with me. It makes me feel like the most unsexy creature that ever walked the earth.

"I'm fine." I straighten my spine and wave her off. "It's nothing." My liquid courage evaporates. What am I doing anyway? I should thank my stars for having Amy in my life. Or, as Muriel puts it, shower my best friend with eternal displays of gratitude. Normally, I would discuss the lack of bedroom action with Muriel, but she introduced me to Amy, and it seems ungrateful. The fact is I don't have anyone to talk to about this. Perhaps if Leigh had stayed in

New York and we'd found some way to become friends. Perhaps we could have discussed this sort of thing. Or would it have led us somewhere dangerous? Either way, there's no point in contemplating this. Leigh Sterling is long gone, and probably rocking another woman's world on the other coast.

Then Amy surprises me. "Come on. We're getting out of here." She signals the waiter for the check. Has she been reading my mind?

"Tell me what you couldn't say at the restaurant," she asks when we're in the cab. The Brooklyn Bridge looms in the distance. I don't even particularly like Brooklyn with all its hipsters and gentrification, I think for the umpteenth time.

I pull her toward me until her ear is close enough to my mouth. "I want us to fuck," I whisper. I put my hand on her upper thigh and dig my fingers in hard. The thing about making demands like this is that it doesn't really suit me. It makes me sound like someone I'm decidedly not.

"Then that's what we'll do," Amy replies, but there's a sort of resignation in her voice I find hard to bear. Like it's a chore that needs to be ticked off a list. "Let's just behave for a little while longer for the cabbie's sake." She glances at the front seat nervously and puts her hand on mine, detaching my fingertips from her jeans.

The rest of the ride passes in a tense silence. While Amy searches her purse for her keys I look over the facade of the house, all three floors of it. There's a basement playroom for the boys, and a woman comes in twice a week to clean it. Rosie could have a well-lit space of her own with room for all her toys, and a desk when she gets older, and real privacy. Maybe I have to do this for my children.

So, I remain silent when we go inside, dump our overcoats and bags in a specially designed closet, and fall onto the sofa, both of us lazy and heavy-limbed. Amy flicks on the TV and there's an episode of *Law & Order: SVU* on and we both love that show, so we watch it and the day passes quietly. Almost politely.

When we go to bed, I'm painfully aware that we have the house to ourselves, like a ticking clock reminding me that it's now or never. Come tomorrow, Rosie will be back, and the boys will arrive in the evening, and our attention will be divided among them, with only a fraction left to spend on ourselves and each other. Then Monday will roll around, and along with it the frenzy of a working week, during which we usually fall into bed completely exhausted at ten.

I'm more put off by my own ambivalence than anything else. I'm fully aware that our lack of a sex life is as much down to me as it is to her. Perhaps even more. Sometimes, when I want to instigate lovemaking, I stop myself because I know I won't get out of it what I really want—hands tied to the bed and five fingers inside. What aggravates me most is that, before Leigh, this more gentle love-making would have been more than plenty. Happiness would have been a given. If only Leigh hadn't looked into my soul and given me what I truly wanted.

"Good night, babe," I say to Amy. I kiss her on the cheek and there's a brief moment during which the chaste kisses we exchange may turn into a full-blown French kissing session, but the moment passes, as do so many, and a few seconds later the lights are off and we've both turned on our side.

CHAPTER NINE

"Tell me about your ex," Karen says. We've gone for a walk in Dolores Park and it feels right, for the first time since I arrived in San Francisco, to hold another woman's hand in mine. For the first time, the presence of other couples around us isn't a brutal reminder of how lonely my life has become since I moved here.

"Which one?" We both know it's a lame joke. I've only ever talked about Jodie.

She leans her weight onto me. "Come on."

Karen has turned out to be quite the foul-mouthed little spitfire in the bedroom, always asking for more, making demands, because she knows what the consequences will be.

"She wanted another child, I didn't." It's how I usually sum it up. It has proven very effective to shut down conversations I don't want to have.

The first time Jodie left me alone with Troy, I was a nervous wreck.

"Can you pick him up from school and watch him for a few

hours, please?" she'd asked over the phone. "I really would like to escort this kid to his new foster parents. I'll be back as soon as I can."

"Sure," I'd said, like it was a logical sequence of events. I guess it was. Jodie and I had been dating for a few months. I'd gone to pick up Troy with her from school and Gerald's house a few times. I knew the drill, so to speak. That didn't mean I had confidence in my own abilities to babysit a seven-year-old. Was I supposed to hold his hand when we walked down the street? Pour him a glass of milk when we arrived at Jodie's? I didn't even have a key.

But Troy, perhaps because he was a child of divorced parents, displayed a great deal of independence—he didn't need me to walk him home from school at all, or so it seemed. Nevertheless, we walked side-by-side, and I queried him about what he'd learned that day. I could just about manage second-grade math with my numbers-challenged brain so I tested him with some sums as we headed to Jodie's place. He solved all of them in no time.

When we reached Jodie's building he produced a key and let us in. Once upstairs, he poured his own milk and started playing with an early-model cell phone Gerald had given him.

"I'm texting my dad," he said. "I would text Mom as well, but she doesn't have a cell phone."

I didn't even have a cell phone back then, but I quickly added it to my list of objects to acquire as soon as I quit my ADA job and found a law firm to join. If Gerald had one, I wanted one too.

"Can you show me?" I asked, and took a few steps in his direction.

"Sure. Look." The screen was tiny and so were the buttons he pushed, but it seemed easy with his agile child's fingers. "I'm texting Jake. He's had one for ages."

I'd heard Jake's name mentioned in conversations between Troy and Jodie. The pupils at the private school Gerald paid for all had cell phones.

I watched Troy's little fingers push the keys in quick tempo until he stopped to show me what he'd typed, before pressing a button with a green telephone on it to send.

"It's so cool," Troy said.

The D.A.'s office had only acquired its first personal computer a few years earlier. It was only a matter of time before Gerald bought one for Troy—perhaps he'd already done so and Troy had one in his giant room at his father's house, despite Jodie's opposition. She'd only agreed to the cell phone because it made her feel safer to know that Troy could reach her and Gerald at all times. Jodie and I had only been dating a few months and I stayed well out of her and Gerald's parental disagreements. Troy already had two parents, and I doubted he needed a third.

After that first time, I started picking up Troy from school at least once a week—saving Jodie quite a bit in babysitter fees. Some days, I would have work to finish and I'd sit at Jodie's dining table while he continued building something elaborate in Lego. Other days, I'd join him on the floor, my long legs often an obstacle, and the hours until Jodie arrived home would pass as if they were minutes.

But, throughout the time we spent together, I was always aware that I was not an extra parent to Troy. He already had a mother and a father. As we grew closer, I saw myself as more of an aunt-like figure in his life. I didn't need to be anything else to him.

When Jodie started talking about having another child, it unsettled me because this boy or girl would be ours. There would be no Gerald living around the corner. No other name on the birth certificate. I would be a mother—a thought that scared me so much it cost me everything.

"I just don't have it in my DNA, Jodie," I said to her. "The maternal gene does not exist within me."

"That's so not true," she said. "What about Troy? You are so great with him."

"It's not the same." I never knew how to explain it adequately to Jodie without hurting her feelings.

"Why not?" she insisted. "What would be so different?"

"Everything." There wasn't a thing between us that wouldn't change if Jodie had another child—and that's how I always saw it: Jodie having another child as opposed to the two of us as a couple going through all the steps to conceive of one.

"Only in the most exhilarating way," Jodie said.

"I've just joined a top firm, Jodie. I can't just hop out of the office and pick someone up from daycare or school anymore." Did she really think that I'd paid my dues at the D.A.'s office, working for a pittance for years, to throw all that hard work away and dedicate my life to another human being for the next eighteen years?

"As I can tell you from experience, working a full-time job and being a mother are not mutually exclusive. I can call millions of additional witnesses to the stand if needed. Yes, life will change. Things will be crazy for a while, but there's no unwritten law of the universe that says you can't have both, Leigh."

How was I supposed to tell this woman I loved so deeply that I didn't want both? That before I met her, the thought of becoming a mother had barely crossed my mind? That her, me, and Troy was more than enough for me. That I was so selfish as to sometimes curse Gerald when he asked if we could take Troy for a night during his week. That Jodie co-parenting a son was about as much as I could take, no matter how much I cared for him?

I never did tell her these things. Not until it was too late.

"You don't want to talk about her?" Karen caresses my hand with her thumb.

"There's not much to say." I could probably fill a thousand pages detailing my sentiments regarding Jodie—how meeting her changed my life—but I'm not the sharing kind. And it feels as if my wounds have only just begun to heal.

"It's not good to keep it all inside."

"Why do you want to know?" If Karen is going to go all shrink-like on me, I need to go on the defense.

"Because... I feel as if I'm competing with a ghost from your past."

"It's not a competition." I unlace my fingers from hers and wrap an arm around her shoulders instead.

"It sure does feel like one at times," Karen says.

Karen and I have only been seeing each other a few weeks. What is she expecting? "Really?"

"You're so guarded, Leigh. I'm just trying to find a way in." She puts her head on my shoulder. "I like you, that's all."

"That's all, huh?" I stop walking and face her, cracking a smile. "I like you too." I pull her close for a kiss, and while I shut my eyes, inwardly I scream. *Look at me kissing another woman in the park. I can do this. I'm over Jodie Whitehouse.*

But when I kiss Karen it's not the same as when I kissed Jodie. Karen knows too much. She has too much knowledge on how to push my buttons and, even more so, she doesn't need me the way Jodie did.

Jodie and I used to take Troy for walks in Central Park. It was our go-to Sunday afternoon activity on the weekends he was with us. We'd just sit on a bench in silence and watch him play and it's that simple sort of happiness that has eluded me completely since we broke up. As if my life no longer has room for tiny pleasures like that.

On weekends when Troy was with his dad and the weather was nice, I'd take a case file to the park, and I'd read it but never attentively because I could never keep my eyes off Jodie when she was engrossed in a book and she'd suck her bottom lip into her mouth without knowing she was doing it, because she was lost in the story, and she was totally relaxed, and I could almost physically feel the happiness we shared.

She was my soul mate.

When I break from the kiss with Karen I want to answer her

question with those words, but that's just not something you say to a person you're courting. I may enjoy inflicting pain in the confines of the bedroom, but I'm not cruel in other aspects of my life.

"Let's sit," Karen says and tugs me toward a bench lining the path. She's so tiny she can pull her feet up onto the bench with her and still sit comfortably. "I guess I'm just trying to understand what made Jodie so special."

She hasn't finished quizzing me just yet. But how can I possibly describe to her that it was everything about Jodie that made her the perfect match for me? Her kindness. Her fighting spirit. Her big, big heart. Her green eyes, and how they could sparkle when I introduced her to a new, unexpected activity after dark. The kind of mother she was to Troy. The way she folded a tea towel just so. How an upturned corner of the living room rug could drive her nearly mad. The softness of her shoulder when she leaned into me after a long day at work, looking for the sort of comfort I was convinced only I could give her. Her long-standing crush on *L.A. Law*'s Amanda Donohue.

I sigh, hopefully indicating that I don't like where this conversation is going.

Karen turns to me, her arms folded around her tucked-in knees. "I don't mean to give you the third degree. I guess I just want to gauge if you're ready for this. I'm not interested in a casual sex partner. I want more, and I think you do, too."

"I do." I nod to emphasize my point.

"Sorry to be so lesbian about it."

"I like the fact that you're such a lez." I cover one of Karen's hands with mine.

"I like many other things about you." Karen slants her head to the right and bats her lashes.

"Come closer." I swat her knees away and she unfolds them so she can shuffle toward me. I grab her by the back of the head and kiss her, so as to stop the thought flitting through the back of my mind: Karen will never be Jodie.

Our lips meet again and again and I focus on the fact that she doesn't need to be Jodie. Nobody else can and will ever be Jodie to me ever again. This is Karen, whom I'm very fond of, and who turns me on, and that, frankly, is much more than anything I've felt since I left New York.

CHAPTER TEN

"What are you thinking?" Amy asks.

Her question jolts me. Have I told her about how Leigh used to ask me that? If I did, I don't remember, but I have been drinking more than I should of late, and sometimes I wake up not remembering exactly what I've said the night before.

"Nothing," I reply. Above us, boys' feet stomp the floor. In a room adjoining the living room, Rosie's sleeping in a bed Amy bought for her especially, so she could nap at her house. The plan is for me and my children to go home after she wakes up. It's what we always do on a Sunday evening. "Just daydreaming."

I wouldn't call this a quiet Sunday afternoon. Amy's had to go upstairs twice to break up a quarrel between her two boys. They seem on edge today, but they're teenagers, so that's nothing out of the ordinary. Troy's been up there with them for a few hours and I presume he's doing all right. Rosie refused to go down for the longest time for her afternoon nap, so Amy played with her until Rosie's stubbornness gave way to extreme fatigue and she as good as fell asleep while maneuvering her toy chicken around the floor.

"You seem troubled," Amy continues. "Is it work?"

I'm glad Amy is not the type of person to ask too many direct questions. She could have inquired about when I'm finally going to take steps to move in with her, but I think we can both do with the peace and quiet of avoiding that dangerously loaded topic right now.

"I could use a longer weekend." I glance at Amy, who's sitting by the window, the light catching in her hair.

"Couldn't we all?" She opens her arms wide. "Come here."

I scoot over to her and lie down, putting my head on her upper thigh. When she starts stroking my hair, running her fingers through it and lightly massaging my scalp, I'm brusquely reminded of how Leigh used to do the exact same thing to me.

Since Amy has asked me to move in with her, and I reluctantly agreed—more in spirit than in action, so far—tension has grown between us. Unspoken, because neither one of us is very keen to address it, but it's there. In unguarded sighs, in phone calls cut short, and in these precious moments of quiet that we have, which we don't want to ruin by discussing our living arrangements.

When Leigh raked her fingers through my hair, whether it happened after sex or not, I felt every caress shoot through me as though it was her love for me itself making physical contact with my skin. The biggest tragedy of Leigh and I breaking up was that, before we couldn't get past our clashing aspirations in life, we hardly ever fought. We had nothing to quarrel about. The ease and pure exhilaration of being with her is what kept me from starting the much-needed discussion about having more children much sooner and in a more serious manner.

When Leigh and I danced around a subject, it didn't feel like it does now with Amy. I happily avoided it because I had Leigh Sterling by my side. Leigh, who, when I took her to Gerald's house in The Hamptons for the first time, recited a self-written poem for me on the beach. Leigh, who drew our initials in the snow with a stick on the sidewalk outside of our building, and who, I knew, would do anything for me, except the one thing that I wanted so badly.

When I did bring it up in a serious conversation for the first time, I tried very hard to not bombard her with it.

"Troy adores you," I said after she'd put him to bed one night.

"Likewise." She fell onto the sofa right next to me—Leigh would never sit at the other end of a sofa if I was in it. I could listen to her for hours on end about how she believed Troy was so smart for his age, and so incredibly sweet.

"I've always wanted two." My heartbeat picked up speed.

"You've said." For once, Leigh came to lie with her head in *my* lap. She stretched out on her back and stared up at me.

"I'm not getting any younger."

"You *are* getting hotter, however." She smiled and I knew what she was trying to do so I ignored her remark.

"I'm serious, Leigh." I trailed my fingertips through her gel-slicked hair, getting stuck there as well.

"I know you are, sweetie."

I shook my head. "I don't think you do."

"I love Troy to bits."

"I'm not talking about Troy. I'm talking about Troy's potential sister or brother."

"Look, Jodes, if this is a real, burning desire inside of you, we need to address it. But not after nine on a Monday evening. I'm not dismissing you, but give me some time to think about it."

Troy was ten years old by then. I couldn't allow myself to wait any longer, whether Leigh agreed to it or not.

Now, with my head in Amy's lap, when I try to remember how our civil, quietly spoken conversations turned into full-blown arguments about who exactly was being the most selfish, I fail to pinpoint the exact time. It happened in stages. One discussion ended with a snide remark. The following one was halted abruptly by a few words said in an accusing tone. But, from the very beginning—from that time she lay with her head in my lap looking up at me—I'd been able to sense that we'd never see eye to eye on the subject.

"Are you thinking about *her*?" Amy asks. When feeling insecure,

75

it's easy to give in to paranoia, I conclude, so I don't reply to Amy's question in a harsh tone.

"No, babe. I'm not thinking about anything in particular." Keeping the peace is high on my agenda. I don't want any more fights. I just want to lie here with Amy and enjoy a few more minutes of quiet.

Then, even before I hear it, I see the baby monitor light up green. Rosie's awake. This is how most conversations between Amy and me end. Kudos to her for not making a big deal about that. I count my blessings and get up to fetch my daughter. She'll be hungry now. Amy will feed her—she claims it's important for bonding, and who am I to argue with that?

After Rosie's been changed and fed, I call for Troy. Getting two children and their belongings in a taxi requires my full attention—lest I forget the frog Rosie sleeps with—and my goodbye to Amy is quick and almost methodical.

Sitting in the backseat of a taxi driving away from Amy's house in Brooklyn doesn't sting me nearly as much as it should.

Not the way it stung me when, in the beginning of our relationship, before Leigh had moved in, she would leave my place on Sunday evening to go back to hers, do laundry, and get ready for the work week, and all I wanted the second the door closed behind her, was for her to come back. To break all protocol and just move in, because I already knew that she belonged with me, and nowhere else.

Shortly after Leigh joined Schmidt & Burke, I came down with a massive flu and was bed-ridden for days. Luckily, Troy was at his dad's and he managed to avoid our germ-filled apartment.

I spent the first two days in a fever-induced half-sleep, not very aware of my surroundings. The third day when I ventured out of the bedroom in the middle of the afternoon, I found Leigh hunched over a stack of papers at the dining table.

"What are you doing here?" I asked. It was the first time since falling ill that I'd seen the time and I knew it was only three o'clock in the afternoon.

"What are *you* doing up?" Leigh dropped her pen and scanned my face.

"My back is sore from lying down for the past forty-eight hours."

"Come here." Leigh pushed her chair back. "I'll massage it for you."

"Seriously, Leigh. Why aren't you at work?"

"I'm working from home until you're better." She gestured with her fingers for me to come to her. "Making you chicken soup and all that." Leigh was as far removed from a staying-home soup-making kind of person as I'd ever encountered in my life. "Are you feeling better?" She cocked her head. "I should let Troy know. He'll want to see you. We've both been worried." She reached for the cell phone she'd recently bought. She and Troy were constantly texting back and forth, leaving me entirely out of the loop.

"I think I might be hungry," I said, not expecting her to have actually made any soup. But perhaps she'd gone to the corner store and got a can.

Leigh rose and walked over to me. I was still standing in the same spot. She curved her arms around me, not caring that I'd spent the past two days in bed sweating out a fever. "I called your mother and got her chicken soup recipe. I made the stock from scratch and everything."

"Am I stuck in the most absurd fever dream?" I asked, my head resting on her shoulder. "Who are you and what have you done to Leigh Sterling?"

"I know I don't contribute much to this household in the way of cooking, Jodes, but I step up when I need to." She pulled me closer to her. "I'm so glad you're feeling better."

"I'll have to be sick more often," I joked, but just having my hot cheek pressed against her shoulder was making me feel better by the second.

"Why don't you sit." She started walking me to the couch. "I'll get you a bowl of soup and text Troy. I'm sure Gerald will bring him over after school if he asks."

"Next you'll be telling me you and my ex have become best friends while I was fighting off the flu."

"Very funny," Leigh shouted from the kitchen.

Later, after a few more bowls of chicken soup, which I suspected my mother had made and brought over all the way from Connecticut, Troy arrived and the three of us sat cozily on the sofa, Troy perched against me on my left, and Leigh on my right. Despite not feeling very healthy yet, the combination of starting to convalesce, Leigh's chicken soup, and the fact that she'd worked from home the past three days—her biggest love declaration to date—made a different sort of delirium course through me. The two biggest loves of my life sat by my side while I was ill, when I needed them most, and I wondered if I'd ever been happier, and what could possibly top my sentiments of that moment.

The next day, Leigh left for work, having already stretched her option to not go into the office too far. When she closed the door behind her and left me on my own, I counted every hour until she came home. Throughout the day I felt much worse than I had the evening before when she and Troy had been with me, and it was as though I could, as of that moment, physically assess what love felt like.

CHAPTER ELEVEN

"I never see you," Karen says. "We've been dating for six months but it feels more like six weeks based on the amount of time we've actually spent together."

I'd been so passionate about Karen in the beginning. She couldn't have been more perfect. We shared the same kinky proclivities in the bedroom, and she was free as a bird. No exes hanging around. Fully secure in her lesbian status. No children and no desire to have any. A dentist with a flourishing practice. On paper, it should work.

"We both work too much. I know."

"No, Leigh. I work normal hours. You work insane hours." We're in her apartment in Nob Hill. When I rang the bell half an hour earlier—having knocked off work much sooner than I normally would have on a Tuesday—my head had been filled with the things I was going to do to her. How her pert little mouth would pout, and how the skin of her bottom would color pink under my touch. But she pushed me away as soon as I arrived and sat me down in the sofa for 'a much-needed conversation'.

"I have no choice. You know that. The offer of a partnership could come at any time. I can't start slacking now."

"That's what you have to say?" The side of her mouth twitches a little when she gets angry. I never noticed before. "Well, here's what I have to say." She expels a dramatic sigh. "I don't want to be with someone who rings my bell late at night for a booty call, and is up and gone again before I even open my eyes in the morning. We have no life together, Leigh."

"We have Sundays," I try, because even on weekends I spend many Saturdays catching up on cases in my home office. But I'm the firm's top litigator in San Francisco. I spend a lot of my time in court and juniors and paralegals can't do all my prep work for me.

Karen shakes her head. "You think you're so important."

I'm starting to feel under attack. "This is only temporary. We met at a bad time for me work-wise, that's all."

"Here's the order of importance of things in your life according to me. Work comes first, of course. Then you. And only then do I come into play. You can deny it all you want with your silver tongue and... Bambi eyes. But it won't work. I know what I feel."

I'm a bit taken aback by her accusation that I put myself before her and already arguments start stirring in my brain, but if I turn this into a proper fight, I'm not sure we can bounce back from that. I could take the other route, the only one we've tried and tested successfully. I could back her into a corner—literally—and fuck our problems away. But I doubt that will work with the mood Karen's in.

"You're right," I hear myself say. "I've been a selfish workaholic." I've only become so consumed with work since I moved here. Things were different in New York. Jodie made a lot of accusations toward the end, but she never blamed me for working too much. If anything, she spent too much time after hours worrying about the people she had in her care. "How about we set aside one night a week as a steady date night?" As the words come out of my mouth, I realize I'm signing the death sentence of our very young affair.

"One night a week?" Karen wrings her hands together. "Do you even hear yourself?"

It would be such a pity to lose Karen. I haven't invested enough of myself—and my time—in 'us' to be too heart-broken if it were to end, but she has saved me from doing a lot of things I don't want to do any more. Like bar crawling and one-night stands, and waking up alone on Sunday morning. I decide to fight for her.

"I'm sorry." I slap myself on the chest in dramatic *mea culpa* fashion, only to realize I'm being ridiculous. I don't want to end up hurting her more in the long run. We're very fond of each other, and the fact that she's demanding more of my time can only mean she has strong feelings for me. I also don't want to make any promises I can't keep, because she was right about one thing: my work does come first. I haven't worked my butt off for the past three years to lose sight of the prize now. That would surely make us both miserable, and not be conducive to romantic dinners in Sausalito and picnics with a view of the bridge. "I'm not going to lie, Karen. My work is important. I'm about to make partner, you know that. I have no choice but to put in the hours."

"At what cost, though? Have you asked yourself that?"

I know it's costing me her. Not the biggest price I ever paid. It hurts nonetheless. "If we'd met a year later..." I start.

"Save it. I know your type. Narcissistic to the bone. Think the world stops spinning if you work a few hours less a week. Total disregard for any balance in your life... and for the people who care about you." She chews the inside of her lip for a second. "I'm done, Leigh. When I'm with someone, I want to come first."

This reminds me of one of the perpetually returning arguments Jodie and I engaged in. Her telling me that Troy would always come first. Me replying that I had no trouble with that, that I understood, but what would my place be in the order of importance if she had another child?

"I'm sorry that I can't give you more." I really am.

"Oh, screw it. If you were really sorry, you would do something about it instead of sitting there almost relieved that you'll have even more time to spend on the job now, without someone begging for attention in the wings."

She's right. Every word Karen says is true. I'm out-argued by her precise analysis of our situation. I have no room in my life for love. Not now. At least, I learned a valuable lesson. I won't make the same mistake twice. All my energy will go to the firm from now on. At least until my name is on that letterhead, and for a few years after, of course, to prove that I'm worth it.

"I'll leave." I doubt there'll be room during this adieu for break-up sex. I admonish myself for even thinking that. I rise and head over to Karen.

"You just don't get it, do you?" Karen stares up at me the way she does on morning we do wake up together. As though she just can't get enough. A quality that has drawn me to her again and again— even if I had to resist working overtime once in a while. "Despite you... being you, I'm falling in love with you. Otherwise I wouldn't have bothered having this conversation. I would have just ignored you, and your weekly call, until you forgot about me."

I crouch next to her. Her display of sorrow is really getting to me. If I don't get out of here in the next few minutes, it will be very hard to leave at all. I put my hands on her knees and I can't help it, I feel something spark in my flesh. We have a physical connection between us that's hard to deny. "I have strong feelings for you too, Karen. But as you said... I am who I am." I've hardly felt more pathetic in my life. What happened to the Leigh who would fight for this? Who would at least make a valiant effort and try to make some changes to accommodate a woman who's declaring her love? When did I grow so cold?

"You're making this very hard on me." Karen finds my hands with hers. The skin-on-skin contact blindsides me. I need every ounce of willpower to fight the urge to pull her against me. I'm so torn. I've been in this sort of situation before. Do I ignore who I am and go all out for love? Or stay true to myself and choose the lonely road? If I couldn't change myself for Jodie, how can I possibly expect to be able to do so for Karen? "I'm not asking for the world, Leigh." Her nails dig into the skin of my hands. "If you stop and think for a moment, you'll see that." I look into her eyes. They're shiny with the onset of tears. "I'm not your ex."

Did she really just say that? Instinctively, I want to pull my hands away, but she keeps them chained to her trousers—those leather ones that drive me so insane. "Don't bring Jodie into this. That situation was totally different."

What tethered me to Jodie most was the fact that before me, she was a different person. I changed her, forever. That's a hell of a thing to walk away from. And I wonder how she's doing now. I've heard chatter about a baby girl. Is Jodie happy now? Does she have the life she always wanted? The one I, ultimately, couldn't give her?

"I'm not asking you to co-mother a child with me, Leigh." Karen doesn't back down. "All I want is some more of your time and attention." Her fingers are curled around my wrists. She knows where to apply pressure to make it hurt a little. She knows because I taught her. "We could have a really good thing together. Something you don't just find with any chick who walks into Cherries."

The nights I spent at that bar are still vivid in my memory. Talk about time wasted. The hours I spent drinking away the loneliness, followed by, more often than not, a few hours of disappointment in my apartment—never anyone else's fault but my own. Karen has a point. But she sure is blowing hot and cold, which I understand. She's emotional. Her feelings are on display. I'm not someone who shies away from commitment, and I'm not half the player I believed myself to be when I first arrived in this city. All I want, really, is a steady relationship. Karen knows this.

"What do you want?" I shake my wrists free from her grip easily. "Tell me what you want me to do, and I'll do my very best."

Karen exhales. "I want you to want to leave your office at a decent time in the evening so you can see me. I want you to look forward to that, instead of your next battle in court. I want to mean something to you."

I was expecting more practical instructions, like 'I want you to free up a drawer in your closet for my things'. All I hear now is that she wants promises I can't keep. Then again, I don't want to end up like Steve, my immediate boss in New York, whose wife divorced him two years ago, and who only gets to see his children every other weekend. He may claim he lives for the job, but I've seen his eyes drift to that picture frame on his desk.

"Look, Leigh, I'm not stupid." Karen's voice changes. "I know why you bury yourself in work." During moments of weakness, I may have talked about details of my life I prefer to keep under wraps, such as nagging doubts about the validity of my decision to leave New York. Once I make partner, I could go back if I wanted to. "But, put simply, there's so much more to life than work. I look at people's teeth all day for a living, I should know." The first chuckle of the day. "I didn't mean for this conversation to get so out of hand, I just—just want to make you see. Wake you the fuck up."

"I'm wide awake." I'm still crouched by Karen's side and my thighs are starting to cramp. I push myself up and fall onto the sofa next to her. "You're right, Karen. I shouldn't take you for granted like that. You deserve better."

"Better than Leigh Sterling?" There's a sparkle in her voice. First, she elbows me in the biceps, then, next thing I know, she's straddling me. "I don't think so." Her eyes shine with some sort of newfound confidence. "A better version of you? Oh, yes." With that, she slants her neck and finds my cheek, presses a kiss onto it. "I want you, Leigh. And I know you want me." She's breathing into my ear now, and a plethora of possibilities pops up in my mind. I could fuck her on the couch right here, as a sign of goodwill, but that's not really how we're wired. It would be better to make her wait for it. Make her strip slowly first. And have her stand with her hands against the wall for at least ten minutes, while I watch her backside wiggle in anticipation. I'm not walking out on Karen, and she's not walking out on me.

"I know what you're thinking." Her voice in my ear. "Do it," she hums. And then I do.

CHAPTER TWELVE

In a cruel turn of events, I end up breaking up with Amy in Gerald's beach house. It took years before I was able to return there, and then, when I finally do, hearts are broken all over again. As if the place is cursed. I'm definitely never going back.

It happens three months after we decided to move in together, and I still haven't made any efforts to break my lease, or ordered any boxes to start packing. I made several attempts. I have the letter to my landlord ready on my computer, but somehow I can never bring myself to click the print button. Every time I'm about to, a cold fist clenches around my heart, and a little voice starts yammering inside my head: *Are you sure, Jodie? That's a stupid question, of course. If you were, you would have printed, signed and sent this letter weeks ago.*

My parents have driven down to New York on Thursday and I've introduced them to Amy. The plan is for them to stay throughout the weekend and spend time with their granddaughter while Amy and I take a few days for ourselves in The Hamptons.

It was Gerald who suggested it. "Maybe it will speed up your decision-making process, Jodie," he had said and dangled the keys in front of me.

And now here we are. Late spring. The smell of barbecued meat in the air and the laughter of children mixing with the voices of their parents. The ocean wild, but perfect for long walks along its shore. Amy looks gorgeous in the twilight dusk, as if her skin tone and hair color were created to shine in this kind of light. And all I can think of is ways to not have this conversation. But there's no way out. It has been brewing for months, its undertones already coming to the fore in the car ride over here, when I was still worrying about Rosie, and checking my cell phone every other minute for a message from my dad. I was certain we'd never make it all the way there or we'd have to turn back entirely before reaching the Southern State Parkway. But my dad never rang, and just before we joined the Sunrise Highway, Amy put a hand on my knee and said, "This will be good for us, sweetie. We need to talk."

———

"Do you want to go for a walk?" Amy asks after dinner on Saturday. We're sitting on the upstairs deck overlooking the ocean.

"Sure," I say, anticipating how gorgeous she'll look on the beach with her hair untied and her freckles catching the last of the sun. I've practiced some responses to questions she will surely ask, but most of all I just want to know: why can't everything just stay the same? Are we not satisfied the way we are now? Most weekdays I stay in my apartment because it's much closer to work and, honestly— although I would never tell Amy this—during weeks that I have Troy, a house with three teenagers is just too busy for me after a long, hard day at work.

It's different for Amy. She works as an interpreter for the UN, and I'm not saying her job is not stressful, but I'd happily challenge her to do my job for a week and see how she comes out on the other side. After work, she always seems to have boundless reserves of energy to spend on the boys, not that they need much at the age they're at. Scott is sixteen and Ryan fourteen. All they want is to sit in their room or basement and play video games. But it's just their lingering, stomping, boyish presence that gets to me sometimes.

"You're miles away." Amy has hooked her arm in mine. We've taken off our shoes and the water nips at our toes as the waves roll in.

"It's just... this place. I have a lot of memories here. Good and bad."

"Ah... the notorious Leigh Sterling." She pulls me a little closer. "I know you broke up here, but that was ages ago, right?"

And yes it was, even though sometimes, it feels like it was only yesterday that she stood at the front door with her bag in her hand. "Yeah, but I haven't been back since so..." A gust of wind takes us by surprise and sweeps up Amy's hair. I can hardly expect my current girlfriend to feel too much sympathy for my painful memories of ending a faltering relationship with my ex. Amy has had to show a lot of patience with me already, and I'm sure she has limits, too.

"This is the present, babe," she says. "We are here together now. Let's make some new memories."

"You're right. Let's." I lean into her a bit more, and it feels good to be able to do that. To have someone by my side.

"So." She bumps her hip into mine on purpose. "The elephant in the room."

"Is it a pink one?" I joke, stalling.

"It can be, although its color is of lesser importance."

We stop and overlook the ocean. For a city girl like me, it has never lost its power. Leigh used to say that returning to nature is something most people crave on an elemental level. "How can it not be in our DNA?" she used to ask, when we came here, and stood in a spot like this, arms intertwined. "When we are ourselves nature's finest creation?" She still had the ability to mock herself then, to grin at overbearing things she said. Before things turned sour.

"Is it a sea elephant?" I find myself clinging to Amy's arm, unable to let go.

"Just tell me." Amy's voice has darkened. "Do you ever plan to move in or not?"

I don't say anything for the longest time because I don't know how without hurting her. I can't lie, but she's not going to like the truth either. "I have trouble letting go of my place."

"Why?" She turns to me. "You've lived there for such a long time. Don't you want a change? Live in a more"—I can tell she's searching for the right word—"adult place?"

I could so easily take offense. Tell her that not everyone inherits a house before they turn thirty.

"Or don't you want to live with me?"

I can barely stand her eyes on me. In that very moment, she looks like she already knows the answer. As though coming here is just part of some wishful thinking she has been doing.

"I shouldn't have agreed to move in with you. I wasn't ready." My words sound so cowardly.

"I just find it hard to believe that the reason why you don't want to move in is, and I say this with all due respect to the memories you've made in that place, because of a shoebox apartment which, more often than not, has some problem that needs fixing. Last summer it was the air-conditioning. Last month you had water seeping through the kitchen ceiling. I understand you can be attached to a place, but... don't you want something better for yourself?"

"Tell me honestly, Amy. What's your assessment of our relationship regardless of moving in together or not? Would you categorize it as simply wonderful and great, or lacking in certain areas?"

"For God's sake. Just say what you have to say." Amy raises her voice, not caring about a couple of other beach dwellers walking past us. "Obviously you have an issue with us, so just come out with it."

"Why don't we go back to the house?" I think it better to take the heat off. We haven't wandered far, and I need the time to gather my thoughts.

"Fine." Amy shrugs my arm off her and starts in the direction we came from. She walks so quickly I can barely keep up with her. Already, something inevitable is churning in my gut. No matter the outcome, it's going to hurt.

Back at the house, she heads directly to the fridge and takes out the bottle of Sauvignon Blanc she started at dinner. She holds it up to me wordlessly. Making it seem like too much of an effort to ask me if I want some.

I shake my head. She knows all too well I don't drink white wine. A few minutes later we sit on the sofa, Amy cradling a large glass in her hands, me without any beverage that might lend me some much-needed courage.

"So?" Amy asks. Her tone is milder now.

"I love you," I begin, "and I cherish our life together." Why didn't I say this months ago? "But…" I remember now. Because it's so bloody hard. "We don't have sex, Amy. We might as well be best friends or even roommates in your big house in Brooklyn."

She puffs out some air. "You do know why we don't have sex, do you?" There can't be more accusation in her tone. "Please don't tell me you're so ignorant that you don't have a clue." She shakes her head. I'm not sure if she wants me to reply. Either way, my nerves have turned into a liquid ball of fire in my stomach. All my muscles tense. "From the very beginning…" Her voice is small again. "You made me feel nothing but inadequate. Like what we did was never enough for you. I tried, Jodie. I did my best. And for me, it was enough, but in the end I just preferred not to disappoint you again instead of giving it another go."

Talk about a slap in the face. What strikes me most, though, is that in a year and three months as a couple we've never properly addressed this. "You didn't disappoint me, Amy."

"Oh, please." She drinks from the wine as if it's water. "You want… things… I don't even know what you want. All I know is that I'm not the person to give them… do them to you."

"I'm so, so sorry." I swallow hard. "I certainly never meant to make you feel inadequate."

"Look… what we have now, how things are. That's enough for me. I can live with that. Don't you think we're good together? Good enough to try harder?"

"This isn't about trying harder, Amy. It's about making each other happy."

"Don't I make you happy? You look pretty damn happy to me. There's so much more to life than sex, Jodie. We have our children. Our work. Our friends. Trust me, we wouldn't be the only couple to never do it…"

"But… don't you want to?"

"Yes. Of course, I do. But maybe we're just not compatible that way, even though we make a damn good match in many other departments."

"So, what do you suggest? That we both tone down our desires? That I move in and sleep in a separate bedroom?" I want to run out of the house, toward the ocean, and scream into the roar of the waves. Because, suddenly what I've been missing hits me in the stomach with full force. "Don't you want passion?" I ask.

"This was never about what I want, Jodie. I set my own desires aside for you long ago. And, well, I take care of myself on the many nights that we're not together."

Another slap in the face.

"What do *you* want?" Amy's wine glass is empty and she peers at the bottom. I can't look at her either. There's a reason why we don't have conversations like these.

"I don't want a relationship without sex and passion." Yet, I can't help but think of the implications breaking up with Amy will have on Troy and Rosie's life.

"And that's the real reason why you don't want to move in." Amy's quite matter-of-fact about it now.

"Moving in just seems… like settling for less."

"If I'm 'the less' I can't help but wonder who's 'the more'."

I shake my head frantically. "No, Amy, you're not less. If anything, this is my fault. You did everything right. I just want..." What do I want?

"You want someone like your ex." Amy says it as though she's been thinking about this as well. "I'm not her, Jodie. I never will be."

Maybe I do, but as I sit here and try to imagine my life without Amy in it, it only feels like I want her. "I know," I say, but don't articulate my further thoughts. *You're beautiful, sweet Amy Bernard, with the red hair, and feet that are always cold, and freckles in places I've never seen them before. You are Amy who sat with Troy for hours until he understood the German verb cases. Who knew what to do when Rosie had colic, when the endless crying was starting to get to me.*

"Either you make the commitment and move in or you don't and... this is over." Amy shuffles nervously in her seat. Where are the tears? The despair? Shouldn't this feel more like a knife through my heart?

"I—I can't move in, Amy. I just can't." I glance at her, expecting to meet anger, but I guess the lack of passion we suffered throughout our relationship is now also manifesting itself during our termination of it—as a blessing in disguise.

"Well then." She looks away again, rubbing her palms on her jeans.

And that's how it ends. With two words of conclusion as nondescript as, perhaps, many characteristics of our life together.

CHAPTER THIRTEEN

"I've given you two months to get your act together, Leigh," Karen says. "Nothing has changed. It's all just words, words, words." She delves into her purse and produces the key I gave her a few weeks ago, as a token of my commitment. "I won't be needing this anymore."

I can't say I didn't see this coming. But the partnership offer came two days after Karen and I had that conversation, and what was I supposed to say? "I'll gladly accept your offer, Mister Schmidt, but I'll need to work less because my girlfriend of only six months needs more attention."

Ironically, because I'm not in my twenties anymore, I'm tired as hell on this particular Friday evening when Karen raises the issue again, because I've just worked a seventy-hour week—of which seventy-five percent are billable hours—and my brain needs emptiness, or alcohol, or something else to unwind. But there's no chance of any of that now.

"I'm sorry." I know I have to let her go this time. It would be too selfish of me to try to keep her. We never made it past the frantic sex stage. Entirely my fault, I know, because more time spent together is required for that. But, honestly, it's not as if I ever felt bone-deep that Karen could be another love of my life. We wouldn't be sitting here again if that were the case. "You're right."

"I knew you wouldn't fight," Karen says. "Last time, I had to encourage you, and yet I was smitten enough to give you another chance. This time, I'm having enough self-respect not to beg." She brushes a tear from her cheek. One that rouses instant regret from my soul. "But I don't want this to be a relief for you. I want you to know, to really know, that this is killing me." She reaches for a hand-kerchief in her purse. "I hope you feel as shitty as I do now when you wake up alone tomorrow."

I frantically search my vocabulary for words to make this better, to ease the pain, but I come up empty. "You do deserve better."

"Fuck yes, I do." She runs the tissue under her nose. "I'm going." She stands suddenly. I thought she would have more to say, but why would she give me the satisfaction of wasting any more of her time on me.

"Hey." I stand and rush toward her. I can't let her leave as if she were just a stranger stopping by. As soon as I open my arms she falls against my chest, her curled fingers resting above my breast.

"I'm so sorry," I repeat. "You are a wonderful person, Karen. You're kind and funny and... the right amount of kinky." *And I'm sorry I never got to meet any of your friends. And that I had to bail on that party you invited me to last week. And that most of the phone calls I made to you were to cancel our plans.* I don't say these things out loud because they are water under the bridge, and, as she said earlier, "just words, words, words" and when have words ever truly changed anything? "I hope you find someone who does deserve you." Tears sting behind my eyes. Situations like this make me feel like a complete failure. Like I don't have it anymore, the stuff that makes relationships work. Like self-sabotage is all I know.

Karen pushes herself away from me, looks up at me one more time, and heads for the door.

"You're a fucking heartbreaker, Leigh Sterling," she mumbles and leaves. It sounds like the right description of me. I've broken my own heart the most.

After she's gone I pour myself a large measure of vodka. I look around my characterless apartment and decide to give my realtor a call tomorrow. I'm ready for that house now. I've earned it. I need to have at least something to show for—and something to come home to after another twelve-hour day.

My eyes rest on my phone. Out of nowhere, the urge to call Jodie creeps up on me. I glance at the clock. It's 11 p.m. in New York. Would she still have the same number? Does she still live on York Avenue? I still have her mobile and home number stored in my phone. I grab it and scroll to her contact details. My heart beats in my throat. I feel more alive than I have in months, maybe years. Suddenly, the distinct certainty that I have to do this settles within me. That calling my ex at this very moment is what everything in my life after we broke up has led me to.

Because with Jodie there were never any doubts about us making a viable couple. I knew after the first date. I knew weeks before I grabbed her wrists forcefully for the very first time. I couldn't explain to myself why I knew because it was just a feeling, a dizzy spark riding in my veins, making my heart beat faster for her. The way she gesticulated with her hands when she tried to make a point. How she tilted her head when a bout of shyness overcame her. The way she spoke of her job, one of the hardest positions to have in a city like New York, with such zeal, despite the lousy pay and heartbreaking stories that filled her days. I've never seen that kind of fire burn in anyone's eyes as long as I've been alive. Jodie cares. She cares about people everyone else has given up on. And she fights for them. She would rather have gotten fired than have lost a child in the system. But even someone with Jodie's determination and skill to bend the rules couldn't always make that happen. And when rules and the law and the system beat her, she always got back up again. Straightened that spine of hers and moved on to the next case, without ever forgetting about the child that had to be placed in a group home or detention center. Jodie always followed up.

The only time she really cracked was when she'd heard that a boy named Jamal had died. He was barely thirteen years old and already his life had been so unbearable he'd hung himself in a room he shared with three other foster kids. Not even I could cheer Jodie up after that happened. Not for weeks. Yet, she never even for a minute considered changing careers. Jodie never gives up.

I suggested it once, a few months after Jamal's death, after she seemed to have gotten over it for the most part.

"Do you see yourself doing this job until you retire?" I asked. It was our three-year anniversary and we'd gone to The Boathouse to get a good look at the park in autumn colors.

"Don't ask me that." Back then, Jodie hadn't picked up the habit of being snippy with me when I questioned something about her, so I was instantly taken aback. "This job is my life. Who else do these abandoned, abused, uncared for children have in their corner but someone like me?"

I swallowed my follow-up questions—Don't you want to make more money? Have a chance to be promoted? Do something less troubling?—right there and then.

Once she started talking about having another child with the same fire burning in her eyes, I knew I would never be able to persuade her otherwise. If anything, her perfectly articulated reasons to have another made it very clear that I shouldn't even try to stand in the way.

It's 8.05 p.m. My heart is still hammering away. I don't even need to ask myself if she was the one I let get away. I know that she is. Fuck it. I've just been dumped. I'm doing it. I dial her number. It rings. Once. Twice. Then voicemail, but the message I hear is not recorded by her. It's the standard one from her operator.

When she'd first gotten a cell phone, she never switched it off at night. "You never know," she said. I guess that changed when she had another child and sleep became more precious.

I don't leave a message. What would I say? If she'd picked up we could have had a conversation and I could have gauged her reaction, but I don't want to burden her with a message from me on her phone after all these years.

Deflated, I pour myself another vodka. I add a few ice cubes to lessen the sting. I hope the alcohol has the same effect on the sting that comes with being alone all over again. I've made some friends in San Francisco, but they're mainly people from work and more acquaintances than anything else. I don't really have a person I can call when I screw up an affair and who will rush over to my place and get wasted with me. My life might as well be defined by my work. Leigh Sterling, Attorney at Law—nothing else. Full stop.

I raise my glass and mouth 'to dentists' because the world needs good dentists. Although Karen never tended to my teeth in a professional way, I'm sure she's a fine one. And I guess it's only logical that she couldn't talk about her occupation with the same fervor that Jodie did. It's only teeth. I take another sip to stop my mind going down that road.

I let my eyes wander to the cabinet in the corner. I brought some stationery from the office just to be able to look at it. It took a few weeks for the name change—because I was never going to be anything less than a name partner—to trickle through to the office supplies, but it finally did last week. *Schmidt, Burke & Sterling.* It has a much better ring to it than just Schmidt & Burke.

CHAPTER FOURTEEN

After Amy, I have two more affairs that develop into the beginning of a relationship, until I put a stop to them a few months in. Muriel eventually forgave me for breaking up with Amy *for all the wrong reasons* and signed me up to a dating website. Following a few chemistry-less encounters, I found myself in a coffee bar around the corner from my place with a woman named Sheryl. After saying goodbye to Sheryl, I actually had a certain giddiness in my heart and the proverbial spring in my step. She was a foul-mouthed police officer with the most beautiful eyes and something in her demeanor—a certain determination I hadn't come across in a while—that promised fireworks in the bedroom. But, after the initial spark—and subsequent bedroom frenzy—started to make way for more conversation and getting to know each other better, I started to notice that we always ended up at her place and she showed little or no interest in coming to mine or meeting my children.

A single mother with two children is a hard sell and after it became apparent that Sheryl had no real inclination to include my kids in her life, things had to end. I was not going down that road again. But at least I had tried.

After Sheryl, I had a brief fling with the new girl in the legal department at work. Eve was ten years younger than I was, and she reminded me of myself when I was in my twenties. After office hours, we'd just drone on about work some more until it was time to go to bed—because we had to go to work in the morning. Eve was a dainty girl who wore blouses with lace on the collar and shiny knee-length skirts that didn't really do that much for me. After a few months, we decided we'd be better off as friends. I had tried again. Something Muriel was always on my case about. As though she'd decided to promote my relationship status to her most important hobby.

"Life is hard enough already. No need to go it alone," was one of her favorite sayings. I agreed, but for a woman in her early forties, with a body marked by childbirth, and two children to show for it, datable women weren't exactly lining up.

I meet Suzy on the day Troy leaves for college. She appears in the bar where I decide to stop for a drink after having waved goodbye to Troy and Gerald, who is driving him to Berkeley. If it weren't for Rosie, I might have joined them on their road trip, just for old times' sake. As a final farewell to my boy's childhood. And what a fine boy my son has become. He wants to be a lawyer, just like… I'm just about to let my thoughts wander to Leigh when a woman spills half of her drink on my table.

"So sorry." She has as thick a New York accent as I've ever heard. "I'm always a clumsy one. Did I ruin any of your belongings?"

I look from her to the table, which is empty bar a small puddle of what looks like Guinness. I shake my head.

"I'll be right back to mop that up." She flashes me a smile. "Can I leave that here for a second before I cause more wreckage?"

"Sure." She has the kind of smile that lights up a place.

"Hey, Dave," she yells at the barkeep. "I've done it again. Can you throw me a rag?"

Dave rolls his eyes and pitches a cloth in her direction. "You won't catch it," he yells after it. And sure enough, as soon as the rag reaches the proximity of the woman's hands it somehow ends up on the floor instead of between her fingers. She just shrugs and goes to work.

"I'm Suzy," she says to me when my table looks pristine, "Dave's sister. I just moved in upstairs."

I hold out my hand while I introduce myself. "Do you work here?" I ask after our handshake ends.

"Hell no." She tilts her head toward the chair on the other end of my table. "Can I sit?"

"Of course." I'm glad for the company, what with Troy on his way to becoming a proper adult and Rosie spending the day with her grandparents, who've come down to say goodbye to Troy. Our dinner reservation is hours from now. I presumed I'd need some time to put myself together. "Pleasure to have you." Little do I know at that moment that Suzy will almost be enough—almost.

"I start in the bank around the corner next Monday. I just moved back here from New Jersey after the most boring year of my life. I thought I could live outside of this city, but turns out I can't." She drinks from her beer and some of the dark liquid sticks to her lips. Black lipstick would suit her well, I think. She's the type for it. "You can take the girl out of New York and all that…" She narrows her eyes a little. "What's your story? I mean, I do know better than to ask that question to a woman drinking alone in the middle of the after-noon, but if you care to indulge me?" She shoots me a wink. "It beats unpacking."

I tell her about just sending Troy off, and one drink turns into three, and before I know it I have to rush to meet Rosie and my parents at that tacky restaurant they love to go to on Times Square.

"Stop by anytime, Jodie," Suzy says as she leans back in her chair and gives me a very obvious once-over. "You will most likely find me here every night. Dave needs some help making this place more glamorous." She yells the last bit so her brother can hear.

———

I'm back for more of Suzy a few days later. Just for a quick drink after work. I find her holding court at the bar, regaling a motley crew of bar flies with a story that features a horse and a pig. Her personality is magnetic and I can't seem to get her out of my head. I want to know more. During our conversation a few days earlier she made no mention of having a partner and when she referred to her ex the one time, she didn't call him or her by name. Besides, I know what flirting looks like.

I take a seat at the bar a few stools from her and order a martini from Dave. He not-so-discreetly signals Suzy that I've arrived.

"Excuse me, ladies and gentlemen," Suzy exclaims. "There's a lady here who requires my attention." Her words make me go all fuzzy inside. She kisses me on each cheek and her perfume drifts up my nostrils. Immediately, I regret not having arranged a babysitter. I'll need to leave in forty minutes to pick up Rosie.

"Let's slide into a booth," Suzy says and leads the way. She's dressed in the tightest pair of black jeans I've seen on a woman above forty, a black vest and not much else. Maybe she's making the most of her freedom to dress before she begins work at the bank. When I sit down opposite her, I notice a tattoo of a music note on the inside of her wrist. She's a wild one, I can sense it.

"I was hoping you'd come back." There's that smile again. Her hair is short but still manages to point to all sides, as if she hasn't owned a comb in years.

"I'm glad I did."

"Any news from your boy?" The fact that she inquires about Troy warms me to my core, just as her mere presence did on the day.

"I only call him once every day," I joke.

When I chuckle, Suzy gives a belly laugh. "How about the little one?" If she wants to seduce me, she's doing an excellent job of it. Appearing genuinely interested in my children really is the best way to go. Maybe I should just ask her out.

"She's at a friend's. I have to pick her up in a bit." I look at my watch. "Sorry I can't stay longer, but, erm, I—"

"Yes." Suzy is nodding vigorously. "Let's go out sometime." She's probably one of the least inhibited people I've ever met. "I would like that very much."

And just like that I have a date with Suzy Henderson, who lives around the corner from my building, whose muscles don't tense when I mention my children, and whose rock-chick exterior and big mouth make my head spin a little.

———

Because of Suzy's extensive knowledge of the bar scene on the Upper East Side we end up going on a modest bar crawl, ending up at Henderson's for a night cap. By the time Dave brings us two whiskeys I'm so hammered I wouldn't hesitate to go upstairs with Suzy if she invited me, although I'd probably end up falling asleep the instant I took my clothes off.

Our first date is pleasant enough, and I get schooled in interesting facts about my neighborhood, but Suzy seems to like a drink, and I find it hard to keep up. Thank goodness it's Friday night and I'll have an entire weekend to recover from this bender.

"God, I'm so tempted to take advantage of you." By the time Suzy says this in her clear, booming voice, I'm not shocked anymore. She peppered our entire evening with forward phrases and come-ons like that. I adore the fact that she has zero qualms about showing interest in me. "But I think, for first dates' sake, it is required that I walk you home and kiss you chastely on the cheek outside your front door instead." She has finished her whiskey already while mine remains untouched.

I chuckle and gesture for her to have it. "I would prefer to remember our first kiss." I look into her blue-grey eyes. They're alive with amusement and joy.

"To our next date, then." She raises her glass and scans my face, her eyes halting at my mouth. "Has anyone ever told you that you have the sexiest lips this side of the Hudson?"

"Oh really?" I curl said lips into a pout. "Who lives on the other side of the Hudson?"

Later, when she walks me home, the heat of the alcohol warms my flesh, but it's also Suzy's presence next to me that heats me up. She's exciting and full of promise and entertaining and, as it turns out, a bit of a lady as well.

As promised, she kisses me gently on each cheek, throws in a stiff, lingering hug—and oh, her body pressed against mine already feels so good—and then leaves. By the time I make it upstairs, my muscles are still tingling and my skin is even more flushed.

I pass by the picture of Leigh and Troy and consider that I haven't felt like this after a first date since the one I went on with Leigh Sterling.

———

My first time with Suzy happens on our third date. Our second one got cut short because Rosie got sick and I received a call from the babysitter a few minutes after I'd sat down at the restaurant. Suzy was such a good sport about it that I was tempted to take her up on her offer to accompany me home and take care of Rosie together, but I guess we both understood that it was more out of politeness that she offered, because a second date was really a bit soon for introducing her to my daughter. Moreover, I wasn't in a hurry to introduce anyone to my children after Amy, because if things didn't work out again it would also be their heart I'd be breaking—and I'd done it to Troy twice already.

For our third date, Suzy invites me to her apartment above the bar for a takeaway and a bottle of wine. We both know what that's code for. By then, I'm so hot for her that in between replying to emails at work, I daydream about kissing the lines of that tattoo on her wrist—much to Muriel's delight.

"Good God, girl," she says, "you're making me miss that exquisite thrill of the first few dates. Have some consideration for a woman who's been faithful to her partner for two decades."

And it *is* thrilling. Knocking on Suzy's door is such a rush, I'm slightly dizzy by the time she opens it. She's wearing tight jeans again, and they make her legs look even longer. She's not a fancy dresser, but I like her casual, no-fuss style. Almost anyone can look good in layers of make-up and the right skirt, but not everyone can pull off jeans and a t-shirt and make it look sexy and inviting.

"Don't mind the mess," she says after she's shown me in. "Dave hasn't bothered to move most of his stuff out yet. Lazy bastard."

"I only have eyes for you," I say.

"Oooh." Suzy brings her hands to her sides. "She flirts." She cocks her head to the side and looks me over. "You're such a posh girl, Jodie." She doesn't say if she thinks that's a good or a bad thing.

The bottle of wine I brought empties quickly, but when Suzy offers to open another I decline. "I don't want to be drunk for what comes next," I say, as I lean back in my chair.

"You're such a lightweight." She says it with a devilish smirk on her lips that ignites something between my legs.

"We'll see about that." I push my chair back and wait for her to come for me.

And she makes me wait, which only intensifies the pulse between my thighs. After a few slow seconds, she walks over and straddles me with her long legs.

"First," she says as she looks down at me, lowering her face toward mine slowly, "we kiss." And then we do. And I've only known one other time in my life that from the very first instant my lips met another woman's, I knew it would be special. I recognize the feeling as it jolts my core and awakens all my senses. With Suzy, it's the real deal. I don't know how I know, or how my brain processes this wishful thinking into actual information, but I feel it course through every cell in my body nonetheless.

Soon, we're tearing off each other's clothes and stumbling toward the sofa in a frenzy of blind, first-time lust. Suzy fucks me while gazing into my eyes, as though she already knows that I like to be watched like that, and I can see her lips curl into a sly grin—another massive turn-on—just before I'm about to come.

And, of course, our first time is not kinky, nor does it push any boundaries. That's not what first times are for. But when we lie in each other's arms afterward, our lips stretching into smiles against each other's skin, I vow not to make the same mistake I made with Amy, and I resolve to openly tell Suzy about my desires sooner rather than later.

CHAPTER FIFTEEN

W hen I first get the email I blink twice because I think I need to have my glasses adjusted. But there it is: the letters spelling out 'Troy Dunn' the way they've always done, just not in my mailbox. My heart in my throat, I click it open.

Hi Leigh,

I hope you don't mind me emailing you out of the blue—and after all these years. I'm an undergrad at Berkeley now, and the idea is to go to Law School after. I was wondering if you'd like to meet up sometime? Professor Steiger (who teaches Criminal Justice) speaks so highly of you.

I understand if you don't feel up to it, but I'd really like to catch up and pick your brain.

Best,

Troy

P.S. This has nothing to do with Mom. She doesn't know I'm contacting you.

I keep staring at the last sentence. How old is he now? I count on my fingers. He should be in his second year. I don't hesitate and hit the reply button immediately. I may not have a lot of room in my schedule for romantic shenanigans, but for Jodie's son, I'll free up all the time in the world.

Troy was eleven years old the last time I saw him. Saying goodbye to him hit me much harder than I had anticipated, but I could hardly negotiate visiting rights with Jodie because of the reason for our break-up. Plus, I knew it would only make things harder in the long run. A clean break, I thought. From mother and son.

Troy and I met at Jodie's apartment and as a parting gift I'd brought him The Death Star Lego set. He had mostly grown out of playing with Lego by then, but I had bought it for old time's sake. Because it was our thing and I wanted him to have something cool to remember me by.

I saw a tiny spark of excitement flicker in his eyes before they went dim with held back tears. After having to say goodbye to that boy, I swore I would never date a mother with non-adult children ever again, because of the total unfairness of it all. At least that was one goal I set and reached without having to go through a lot of trouble. Since Karen and I broke up, I haven't dated anyone, let alone a mother.

And, of course, in those moments when I looked into Troy's sad face on that rainy Saturday in early May 2003, the question came to me again: *why can't I do this for her? And for him? Am I really that selfish? Am I really putting myself and the pursuit of my career before this boy's happiness?* After all, Jodie had put her desires aside for me.

She'd waited until she believed she couldn't anymore, perhaps hoping, in vain, that the passing of time might change my mind. But time passing wouldn't make a mother out of me. Nothing would. Not even six years in the presence of Troy, for whom I cared deeply, but who already had two parents—and I wasn't one of them. I loved him, perhaps as a mother would love her son—I had no way of comparing—but I always believed that if I did, there would never be enough of that to go around for two of Jodie's children. How could I, a person who had zero track record of being interested in mothering children, ever be enough? Or be unafraid enough to try?

"Why are you leaving?" he asked in a small voice I had rarely heard him use.

I exchanged a glance with Jodie and she took over—she let me off the hook again. "It has nothing to do with you, sweetie." She put her hand on his shoulder and squeezed. "I explained it earlier," she said to both of us.

I had prepared some replies to possible questions, the way I did in witness prep but with myself on the stand and an eleven-year-old asking them. There was nothing of the lawyer left in me that afternoon. I wasn't a lawyer, nor a witness. Just a breaker of hearts.

"Can I have one last hug?" I asked, and shuffled a little closer.

I hadn't expected him to throw himself into my arms the way he did, and that floored me most of all. That unspoiled, unfiltered affection.

When I looked at Jodie, her son in my arms, I saw from the look in her eyes that she may one day forgive me for leaving her, but never for doing this to her flesh and blood. I would not forgive myself for a long time either, because to chip away a little at the innocence and, even for a moment, the easy happiness of a child, is not something you recover from quickly.

. . .

And now Troy is asking to see me. I reply that I would love to and that he should send me a few possible dates to meet. He responds not long after and a few days later I'm on my way to Berkeley.

He looks more like Gerald than Jodie, but he has her eyes, and that way of hers when he swats away the hair from his forehead with a flick of his wrist. When I extend my hand for him to shake, he pulls me into a hug, and I notice he's taller than me—he must get that from Gerald as well. Overall, he just looks healthy with youth and intense energy. And I have to dig deep to not show all that I'm feeling, have to strengthen my core and straighten my spine and hope that it's enough.

"Look at you," I say, and can't help but shake my head a little.

He shoots me a grin. I'm not sure it contains reflections of Gerald's smile because I didn't encounter that very much. It's not Jodie's, though. Even though it's her son I'm sitting across from, I'm bombarded with memories and nostalgic emotions. But Troy is an entirely different person now. He's all grown up, and I can only imagine how it must have torn Jodie up inside to send him off to college. Did it sting more because he decided to enroll at Berkeley?

"You look great, Leigh," he says. The early spring sunshine produces enough heat for us to sit on the outside terrace of the bar. "I have to admit I was quite nervous about emailing you, but I couldn't not, you know?"

"Yeah." It's way too late for an apology. And Troy seems to have grown into a nice guy, despite me leaving. Even though I know he didn't invite me for a drink to discuss his mother, I have to ask. Before I can say anything else, I need to know. "How's Jodie doing?" Luckily, I can keep my voice from cracking when I say her name.

"Mom's doing fine." Does she ever visit? I want to ask. Has she been here, in my adopted city? The mere thought sends a shiver up my spine. "And I have a sister now. Rosie. She's six and not at all annoying." That smile again.

Mom's doing fine. What does that mean? Is she with anyone? I can't bring myself to ask.

"She's seeing someone again." Troy answers my question for me. "It seems quite serious. Her name's Suzy. She's good fun."

I nod, hiding my discomfort. "Good to hear everyone's doing well." Unexpected panic floods me. What was I expecting? That Troy contacted me to set me up with his mother again? To hear that things haven't worked for Jodie on the personal front over the years? In the hope she might have let slip that she misses me? *Suzy.* Maybe I can get him to spill her last name so I can google her later.

"How are *you*?" Troy asks. His voice is light and he seems oblivious to the turmoil raging inside of me.

"I get by." A college student who's also the son of my ex is not someone I'm going to confide in.

"Get by, my ass." He slaps the tabletop with his fingertips. "You're the hottest lawyer in the Bay Area." He holds up his hands. "I'm going to be honest with you, Leigh, when I let it drop that I knew you, my status in my Criminal Justice class went right up."

I can't help but chuckle. Meeting Troy isn't about sentimentality. Troy was just a boy when it happened and for him it's all been water under the bridge for years. He's after the clout that comes with being associated with me. I'll happily oblige. "If we need to be seen together somewhere, just let me know," I joke.

I clearly remember the concentration on his face when we made one of these huge puzzles together. He must have been seven or eight, then. His little tongue sticking out from between his lips as he pushed a piece in place, followed by a proud grin.

"I can only take so much advantage of you." He sips from his Coke. "But I could use your help with an assignment."

"Cutting straight to the chase is a good trait for a future lawyer."

"Oh no, not right now. Please don't think that." He blushes. Maybe he does have more of Jodie in him than I caught at first glimpse. "I'm not that slick and harsh just yet."

"We'll work on that too, then." I send him a wicked grin. A short silence falls.

"Look, Leigh..." I can tell he's struggling to say something he's been chewing on for a while. "When you first left, I was angry. Mom explained, but I still didn't understand, you know?" His shoulders relax again. "For the longest time, I was convinced I never wanted to see you again." His lips form a thin stripe in between sentences. "But I grew out of that as well. I understand now why things didn't work out with you and Mom. And I realize it must have been hard for you as well. I mean, you and I were pretty close. So..."

"Thank you for saying that." I swallow the lump in my throat. "Are you going to tell Jodie that we met?"

"I don't know." He shrugs, indicating he hasn't given that particular matter a lot of thought. "Do you think I should?"

"Depends." Just thinking about it awakens nerves I haven't experienced for years. "If we see each other again, you probably should. She'd want to know."

"I guess." His face breaks out into a smile again. "Are *you* seeing anyone?"

"No." I glare at his white t-shirt which strains around his shoulders. At that dark mop of hair that keeps falling into his eyes. There's currently only one heartbreaker sitting at this table. "Not at present."

"Oh," is all he says, because what else can he say? "It was never the same with Mom's other girlfriends, you know."

A flutter in my chest.

"Well, she was single for a very long time after you—"

"I don't know if we should talk about this, Troy." My voice quivers.

"Why? Does it make you uncomfortable?"

"No, but Jodie might not appreciate you telling me about her love life."

"Maybe not, but I can tell you about *my* life, can't I?" Troy Dunn will make an excellent lawyer.

"Of course." Despite what I've just said, curiosity burns inside of me. I want to know everything, even though I'll only end up mulling the information he gives me over and over in my head, trying to draw comparisons, and hoping I still, somehow, in some crazy, illogical parallel universe, come out on top.

"Rosie and I only ever met Amy, and now Suzy. Anyone else she dated never made it past our front door when I was there."

She must have been so careful to keep Troy from being hurt again.

"Amy was all right. She had two sons my age, Scott and Ryan. It was fun to have brothers for a little while, I guess. We almost moved in with them, but then, for some reason, it didn't happen. According to Scott, it was all Mom's fault, but he never really said why."

"That must have been hard." The engine in the back of my brain starts churning. Amy with two sons. "Having other kids around and then having to say goodbye."

"I guess." He shrugs again. "For a while."

"Does Suzy have any children?" I can't help myself. It's like a door has opened, and I need to walk through it.

"No. She has moved in, though." He grins. "She makes such a mess. And you know what Mom is like."

While it was strangely satisfying to hear that Amy and Jodie didn't move in together, it stings that Suzy has made it that far. "Does Jodie still live on York Avenue?"

"Yep. Same old place. I don't think she'll ever leave there. Rosie has my room now, so I usually end up on the sofa when I go home. Or at my dad's."

"That must be rough. To have your room taken over like that."

"If it were anyone else…" He reaches for his phone. "But look at this face. You couldn't stay mad at her for more than five seconds either." He shows me a picture of a curly-haired girl grinning widely. Her green eyes hit me hard. The child in this picture is, put very simply, the reason why Jodie and I broke up.

"She's adorable." I can't hide the agony shooting through me like a freshly sharpened arrow, slicing through my flesh, puncturing everything.

Troy puts his phone on the table and looks at me. "Are you okay?"

But I don't want to fall apart in front of Jodie's other child. The irony of it would be unbearable. "I'm fine."

"Mom eventually told me why you broke up... I mean, I know..." He shuffles in his seat.

My own phone saves me. I didn't bother taking it out of my purse and I have to dig deep for it now, as if I have to linger in this moment of despair as long as possible. "Sorry, it's my boss. I should take this."

Troy nods and starts fiddling with his own device.

I talk to Steve for a few minutes and seize the opportunity to fake an emergency. "I'm very sorry to cut this short, Troy, but something has come up at work. I have to go, but I'd love to see you again." I fish a card out of the side pocket of my purse and hand it to him. "Call me anytime."

"I will." He stands. Does he want to hug again? He just puts his hands on my shoulders and squeezes. "You can be sure of that."

On my way back to the city, I do wonder if I'll ever see him again. Did he see me freak out? I wouldn't blame him for not wanting to deal with that. Rosie's picture flashes before my eyes. Not because I suddenly regret not becoming a mother, but because there were times when I tried to stop Jodie from becoming the mother of that smiling girl.

CHAPTER SIXTEEN

W hen we drive into San Francisco proper in a hire car we picked up at the airport, a bout of nerves hits me. But then Rosie yells something from the back seat and I'm pulled into the present again, away from the memories that have crept up on me on this journey.

We've come to spend a few days with Troy in the city. Leigh's city. I thought about getting in touch, because it's been years now, and surely we can be civil to each other, but I have Suzy and Rosie with me, and we're here as a family, and meeting up with exes doesn't really fit into our plans. Also, after all these years, I'm still not sure how I would react to seeing her again.

No, this trip is about family. The one Leigh never wanted. I've never been to San Francisco, but I presume it's a big enough city to not have to worry about inadvertently running into relocated exes. And we don't need a guide because we have Troy.

It's late when we arrive at the hotel. After we've freshened up, had a quick bite and put Rosie to sleep, Suzy and I are huddled on the bed together. I flick through the channels absent-mindedly, until an old episode of *L.A. Law* comes on.

"I love that show," I whisper to Suzy. I don't tell her Leigh and I used to watch re-runs religiously together.

"Oh," Suzy hums."Hey, was that an episode of *Sons of Anarchy* you just flipped past?"

"I don't know. You want me to go back?" Our arms touch.

"Not if you want to watch this." Suzy moves her arm away from mine. She's trying to say yes by saying no again. It drives me crazy when she does this. She re-adjusts her position so there's a gap between our arms.

"It's fine." I hand her the remote.

"No, you choose." She hands it back.

Ostentatiously, I change the channel.

"You didn't have to do that, babe." She leans into me again and focuses on the men on the screen riding their motorcycles, in which I have zero interest.

I don't know if these minor irritations are normal in relation-ships. Suzy moved in a few months ago, and I've caught myself suffering from rising levels of aggravation over nothing in particular ever since. They're not fights or arguments that we have, just tiny displays of not seeing entirely eye-to-eye on everything. Not that we have to, but sometimes it gets on my nerves that Suzy can so easily manipulate me into getting her way.

I wouldn't have asked her to move in if I hadn't considered our affair full of potential. I've had to give and take—mostly give when I really wanted to take—but it works well most of the time. When she got fed up with living above her brother's bar, and the noise and nuisance that comes with that, and said she was going apartment hunting, I decided not to make the same mistake twice. And I wouldn't have to leave my apartment if I asked her to move in.

Suzy has been good for me. And her timing was impeccable, what with Troy having just moved out when we met. Rosie adores her and vice versa. Our sex life is not as adventurous as I would like it to be, but at least we have one. She's easy-going, often messy to an extent that I have to keep myself from dangling a nonchalantly cast-off item of clothing in front of her and ask, "Are you really going to leave this here?" But I know she will just shrug it off, tell me what I want to hear, and do it again the very next day. Some people just don't have neatness programmed into their genes. That, too, I've learned to live with.

We had *the conversation* after we'd had sex a few times. I had tucked my head in Suzy's armpit post-orgasm and lay staring up at her breast, trailing a finger around her nipple.

"You're making me hot again," she whispered, her voice still husky from before.

"That's the idea," I said, decreasing the circumference of the circles my finger drew.

"Oh really?" I felt her shift against me. "What are you going to do to me?"

I pressed a kiss against her side. "I was wondering more what you would do to me." I took her nipple between my fingers and pinched —gently.

"Plenty of naughty things if you keep that up."

I squeezed harder.

"Ouch," she yelped, but there was humor in her voice.

I continued to squeeze.

She pushed herself up and looked down at me. "You're asking for it," she said.

"Yes." Something unclenched between my legs.

"Okay then." The tenderness she kissed me with frustrated me.

"Kiss me harder," I demanded.

She did, but it still wasn't nearly hard enough. I grabbed her by the back of the head and pulled her roughly to me.

When we broke from the kiss, which had been more biting than kissing, she looked at me earnestly. "Why so rough?"

"You think that's rough?" I drew one eyebrow into an arc.

"I don't know if you're aware, but you're always doing this when we make love."

Of course, I was aware. I was doing it for a reason. But I knew I couldn't bombard her with my wishes. I'd learned my lesson from being with Amy. "Yes, I think I'm aware."

"Why don't you tell me what it is you want me to do, so I can stop guessing." There was no annoyance in Suzy's tone, which was a good sign.

"Okay." I sat up a bit. "I like to be dominated. Tied up. Taken." The words came easier than I'd expected they would, perhaps because I'd had many years to practice them in my head.

"You want me to tie you up?" Suzy scrunched her lips together.

"Only if you would be open to that. I don't want to force you."

"I don't know. I guess I would need to think about that. Maybe read up on it." I hadn't anticipated that sort of careful reply from someone I'd come to know as free-spirited and daring.

"Okay." I was starting to feel self-conscious. This was not an easy ask. "I would appreciate that."

No more sex was had that night.

Suzy canceled our next date. She claimed her brother needed help in the bar because one of his staff had bailed on him. "Come by," she said. "But we won't have a lot of private time."

I was paranoid enough to check up on her. If it hadn't been for our conversation a few days earlier, I wouldn't have. Perhaps I thought I'd find her in a corner of the bar, curled up with some 'literature' instead of bartending a rowdy crowd. But she was indeed pouring drinks and working the customers the way she so easily could.

We were at my place on our next date—a home with many memories.

"Did you have a good read?" I asked, injecting some cheekiness into my voice. I didn't want our upcoming talk to be too heavy in tone. After all, what we were discussing was one of our main sources of fun.

"I did." She regarded me with those glittering eyes of hers. I'd fallen hard and fast for Suzy and I sat there fervently hoping I hadn't put our blossoming relationship on the line because of my question. "Very informative," she teased, and I felt it in my belly.

I sucked my bottom lip into my mouth and waited for her to say something else. Perhaps because I had brought up the subject, I had to be the one to carry the conversation forward, but the nature of it, the coming out as explicitly submissive, prevented me from doing so. I wanted her to know what to say and do instinctively. If that was a mistake on my part, I didn't perceive it as one at the time.

"I can do certain things, but, Jodie, I'm not sure what you think of me, or what kind of person you think I am, but this sort of stuff doesn't come entirely natural to me."

"I understand that." And I also already knew. If it had come natural to her, she would have shoved me against a wall already while delving her fingers under the waistband of my panties, and had me, on her own terms. "I'm just asking if you're willing to try."

"I am." She inched a little closer. "I can tell this is important to you."

I wasn't looking for a second Leigh, nor a second Amy. Just someone with a few qualities of both.

Suzy tried. Sometimes, lying with my hands tied up and her smoldering gaze on me, she managed to bring me out of myself. And maybe it wasn't exactly how I wanted it to be, but she made the effort—and I could hardly expect her to be Leigh, who'd had the great advantage of unearthing this side of me, and making everything she did to me a shocking surprise. The effort she put in was enough for me for a long time because all other aspects of our relationship pleased me, and at least she wasn't afraid to talk about it. Perhaps that was the open-mindedness I'd recognized in her at Henderson's that day Troy left.

· · ·

But now, in this hotel room in San Francisco, Suzy already half snoozing next to me, I can almost feel Leigh's presence. Or the promise of her presence. The way I did on nights when Troy was with his dad and I couldn't get to our apartment fast enough because I knew she'd be waiting for me—waiting to do her worst to me. And she always, always did. Like that day not long after my thirty-second birthday when she was waiting for me by the door.

"Give me your stuff, I'll put it away." She knew I wouldn't be able to relax if she just had me drop my coat to the floor. "Go into the bedroom, take off all your clothes. Don't lie down."

I hurriedly did what I was told and waited for her to join me, idly standing around, but not even touching the bed with my knee for support. I heard her shuffle around and then she walked in with her hands behind her back.

"I got you something, but you can't see, only feel." She had a wicked grin on her face. Back then, I hadn't told anyone yet what she did to me in the privacy of our bedroom. Not even Muriel. I just couldn't. I was afraid that some of the magic would go if I shared it. I was also still heavily processing the discovery of my own well-hidden needs. "On the bed. On all fours," she commanded. "Face away from me."

No kisses or other displays of affection had been exchanged yet. They would follow later. Softly and extensively. This always came first.

I crawled onto the bed and waited some more. I could hear Leigh put something on the chair next to the bed and remove some of her clothing.

By the time I felt her lean her weight against the bed, my clit was engorged, and I was ready. At least I thought I was.

She waited a few more seconds. I heard something rustle, felt her weight shift, and then nothing but excruciating, exquisite pain. Leigh had always spanked me with her hands, a belt, or a flogger up until now, not with... I didn't really know what it was. Only that its impact was wide and heavy and stung my cheeks like they would never recover.

I braced my body for the next blow, but to no avail. The pain crashed through me even harder, my flesh stung, and tears sprang from my eyes.

"Maybe you should count," she said, her voice emotionless.

Bam. She hit me again with what I was starting to believe was a paddle. "Three," I said.

"Oh no, no, no." I heard her huff out a disdainful breath. "Start from one."

I didn't know how many more of these I could take.

"One to ten. It's very simple," she said.

Ten more? Surely she couldn't be serious? Surely my ass was striped bright red already and well on the way to pleasing her.

She slapped me again, hitting only my left cheek. The pain vibrated through me, connecting with my clit. Wetness oozed from me. Before Leigh, I had absolutely no idea pain could feel this good. That, if someone pushed me the right way, I could take just about anything. Leigh had always known.

She alternated between my cheeks for number two and three and paused for a few seconds before launching into number four, five, and six in quick succession.

By the time I had to say "Seven" my voice came out too muffled.

"Again, Jodie," she said. "And count properly so I can hear you."

Leigh was never one to show mercy. That's what I liked about her the most under these circumstances. The way I could always count on her to make me dig a little deeper, to look for an even greater rush of pleasure than the one I was growing accustomed to.

I counted out the last three blows, agony converting into excruciating bursts of pleasure in my flesh. Then, nothing again for a few long minutes. I didn't hear Leigh move and she didn't say anything. I knew she was admiring her work, something I reveled in even more. Her glance on my ass. I knew what would come next. Meanwhile, a thick, slow pulse had taken over my pussy lips, converging in my clit.

Where I had expected to feel her fingertips run over the tortured skin of my behind, I was startled by the sensation of something that was not made of flesh. Instinctively, I turned my head.

"Look ahead," was all Leigh said. "Or else." *Or else.* So much of what she triggered in me was based on the words 'or else'. And I was always ambivalent about them. Eager to please, but also curious as to what new heights they would take me. Sometimes, when I didn't obey, when I pushed boundaries, she saw through me and said, "I know what you're trying to do and that doesn't work on me." But, sometimes, she gave in and indulged me with another round of spanking, or an extra finger where I wasn't expecting it.

That day, I had no desire to determine what lay behind her 'or else' and I stared in front of me, at the curtains, of which the pattern was just a collection of smudges through my tears.

It only took me a minute to figure she was trailing the tip of a dildo over the curve of my behind. The only thing I didn't know was if it was one from our collection or a new toy. And if new, how wide and big it was.

I could hear her breathing become labored—just the tiniest display of losing composure. I never let on that I could tell from the speed of her breath when she was going to start fucking me. I kept it as a secret that served me well. As a tiny means of clinging on to a sense of control.

Soon after, the tip of the dildo reached my pussy lips. It slipped through easily.

"Spread wider," Leigh said and tapped my bottom with a few fingers. A gesture that normally wouldn't hurt, but brought tears to my eyes after the paddle strokes she had delivered earlier. I slid my knees as far apart as they would go.

Without further ado, she slid the toy inside of me. Gently at first, so I could get used to it, but it didn't take long for her thrusts to become bolder, demanding more of me. I felt the dildo's girth splay me open, but for Leigh, I always took it easily.

The skin of my behind burned, and the strokes she delivered

with the toy touched me and filled me and satisfied me and I didn't need my clit to be touched. Leigh's mantra, almost from the very beginning, had always been, "Your clit is for quickies. I want to earn your climax." She never failed to do that.

Then, while fucking me savagely, she flicked her fingers against my ass again. Not hard, but with enough gentle force to have the pain re-ignite. It spread through me like wildfire. It started as pain but then changed into a stinging warmth, a blanket of delicious hurt covering me. She kept hitting the same spot with her fingers and with the dildo inside of me until all my thought processes crumbled and I was just a body being taken.

Everything around me turned to liquid heat and painful pleasure and the highest highs of abandon.

When I came, my muscles spasmed, clenching the dildo deep inside of me, and the pain radiating from my ass washed over me like a wave that cleansed me of everything that had accumulated in my brain since we last fucked.

After, Leigh hurried to my side, looked into my eyes briefly, before kissing the tears from my cheeks. We lay like that for a long time, until most of the pain had subsided, and all my tears had dried up. Afterward, she let me fuck her, but in a much more subdued way, because neither one of us needed it to be any other way.

Suzy's completely asleep now, and on the TV something is being set on fire. I change the channel, hoping to catch the last of the *L.A. Law* episode, but it's gone to a commercial break, and I'm not sure I should be watching it right now, what with the trip down memory lane I've already taken.

CHAPTER SEVENTEEN

"Will you please tell Jodie about us…"—I don't immediately know how to quantify my relationship with Troy—"… meeting up." By the time he's preparing for his final exams, more than two years after he first contacted me, we've been seeing each other almost every month. As it turned out, I *did* have spare time to bestow on another human being. Of course, these hours I spend with Troy can't be compared with courting a lover. Yet, I find myself anticipating our meetings, often in student bars in Berkeley where I stick out like a sore thumb. Because of what he represents in my life. A small part of Jodie. The more we see of each other, the more of Jodie I recognize in him. His sense of social justice, I gather, is much more evolved than his peers'.

"I don't know how she will react." Troy came into the city to meet me. I considered inviting him to my house, but something stopped me.

"I understand that." More than I let on. "But it doesn't mean she shouldn't know."

"What difference does it really make, Leigh?" He rips tiny pieces off a paper napkin and fidgets with them endlessly. "Mom's in New York. You're here."

I don't know how to explain this to Jodie's son. I can't even properly explain it to myself. "It just feels wrong to do this behind her back."

He waves me off, as he's done so many times already. I try not to inquire about Jodie too much, but sometimes it happens without me thinking about it, or he blurts something out about her, and the conversation automatically meanders in that direction. More often than not, we just chit-chat, and on occasion, I find myself thinking we chat like, perhaps, a mother would with her son. Although that really is taking it too far, especially given what has happened between Troy's actual mother and me. But when you've sat up with a boy when he was seven and had the stomach flu, and when you've taken him to soccer practice, and spent hours with him assembling puzzles and Lego constructions, part of that lingers in your soul.

What would he have called me if I had stayed? There was one time when I had picked him up from school. We walked home together, Troy gesturing with his hands and telling me about his day in excited tones. I gave him my keys to open the front door because he'd forgotten his own set and it just came out. "Thanks, Mom," he said. I tried to ignore it as best I could, and Troy just went about the rest of his day, but later, after dark, when Troy was in bed, I told Jodie.

"Troy called me Mom today."

Jodie sat with her head thrown back against the armrest of the sofa. She'd had an emotionally exhausting day. Her head shot up. "I guess that was to be expected at some point."

"It doesn't bother you?"

"Of course not. Why would it?"

"Because I'm not his mother." It came out all wrong. It was not what I meant. Not really. Although it was the truth.

"So it bothers *you*?" Jodie pushed herself up.

"No, I just think it's confusing when he calls us both Mom."

"Fine. I'll talk to him."

That was the end of the conversation. Troy never called me Mom again. I never knew what Jodie said to him, but I always regretted not having the balls to talk to him myself. To inquire why he had called me that. If in his child's brain it had just been a logical consequence of me living with him, or more of a conscious decision. Or even a way to coax a reaction out of me.

"Is Jodie coming to your graduation?" When, at the end of his second year, Troy told me Jodie was traveling to San Francisco with Suzy and Rosie, my heart had skipped several beats. They would stay in the city for a few days. Did I wish for him to arrange something? I told him I needed to think about it. It would have been different if Jodie had come alone, or with only Rosie as a companion. The mention of Suzy, whose name only occasionally popped up in our conversations, made me decide against it. Unsure if I could bear sitting through polite conversation with Jodie and her new girlfriend, I didn't take Troy up on his offer.

"Not sure." Troy shrugs. "You know what Mom is like." Do I? Still? I know he's referring to money, though. It makes me think of the house I've just bought, all large and shiny and empty, with no one waiting for me in any of its many rooms. Jodie still lives in the barely-two-bedroom apartment we once shared, because it's rent-controlled and she probably can't afford to live anywhere else, has this boy as her son and Rosie as her daughter, and how is that for acquiring wealth?

———

Troy has finished his exams when he tells me Jodie and Suzy have broken up.

"Oh," is all I say at first. This time, I *have* invited him to my home and have even attempted to cook us a meal.

"You know what I think sometimes, Leigh?" Troy asks. He has changed so much since that first time we saw each other again almost three years ago. Gerald's easy self-assuredness shines through his actions much more. "I think she may still love you."

As a rule, I don't drink when I'm with Troy, but I open a bottle of red wine there and then. "Why would you think that?" I don't look at him while I drive a corkscrew into the cork of the bottle.

"It never works out with anyone else."

"That doesn't mean anything." I glance at him. At this boy who I have invited to my house and who is about to eat my interpretation of chicken parmigiana. "Do you mind if I have a glass of red tonight? Rough day and all that."

"Sure." He doesn't ask if he can have some, but sips from the Sprite I've poured him instead. He's twenty-two. We could share a drink, but I guess it doesn't feel right for either of us. "Why are you single, anyway?" he asks. We usually don't venture into this conversational territory. Troy has told me about a few girls he's dating, but his affairs never seem to last longer than a few weeks, and he never pours his heart out to me. He isn't the type.

I chuckle nervously. "I work too hard."

He shakes his head. "Mom works hard and she finds the time. Even Dad is with Elisa now, and he must work eighty hours a week."

"Yes, well, I work even harder."

"Don't you want to be with someone?"

"I do." God yes, I do. "But it's not that easy."

"Why? Because you're a lesbian?"

That question takes me aback more than any other. I take a few gulps of wine. "Is this a cross-examination, Counselor Dunn?"

"No, of course not." He fidgets with his fingers. He can never sit still for more than a second. "We're friends, right? I'm just curious."

"It's not because I'm a lesbian." I start preaching. "I just haven't really met anyone I've wanted to get serious about for a long time."

He seems to accept that as a valid answer. "Will you come to my graduation ceremony?"

My eyes widen. "If you want me to." Perhaps no one else will see it like that, but I do feel I should be there. Even though I don't really know how to define our relationship, we are, indeed, friends.

"I do. I really do." The intense sparkle in his eyes almost makes me well up.

"Promise me one thing, though." I consider another glass of wine. "If Jodie decides to come, which I suspect she will, you have to tell her about me before the ceremony. She needs to know, Troy." There's no way Jodie will miss her son's graduation.

"Fine. I promise." He glares at me from under his lashes, the same way Jodie used to. "Don't you want to know what happened with Suzy?"

"I'm not sure it's my place to ask." The question's been on the tip of my tongue since he told me.

"Mom dumped her. The same way she did with Amy. So, you know, now she's single once again."

What does he expect me to do with this information? "I'm sorry for her."

"Yeah, me too, I guess."

"How about some food?" Jodie is single again and there's a good chance I'll run into her in a few weeks' time. The prospect fills me with dread and hope at the same time.

"I'm starving," Troy says in the way only men his age can.

CHAPTER EIGHTEEN

The day before I fly first class with Gerald to San Francisco for my son's graduation ceremony, Suzy calls. Again.

"I don't have time for this," I say, rather harshly. "Rosie's ill." I regret my tone of voice instantly. None of this is Suzy's fault.

"Do you want me to stay with her while you go to Berkeley?" Suzy asks. We were together for almost four years and breaking the pattern of our familiarity has been difficult. Being a single mom again has been even more difficult.

"No, I'll ask Muriel."

"I'll happily do it," Suzy insists.

"It's better if you don't."

"Can I at least come and see her while you're gone?"

"I don't know." Admittedly, I don't know what is best for everyone involved in this situation. I do know Rosie would love to see Suzy. They've lived together for more than two years. From Suzy's incessant phone calls since we broke up, it's impossible for me not to know how much she misses Rosie—and me. I'd never pegged her for the über-clingy type. Another thought I instantly regret. It's just that by the time I had worked up the nerve to end our relationship, I was rather fed up with Suzy.

"I'll call you later, okay?" I need a break from this conversation. I need to think. And I need to pack and console Rosie, who has been looking forward to this trip for a very long time, but is now too sick to go.

"Please do," Suzy says, as if she expects me not to. She hangs up and I sigh with relief.

Staying with Suzy would definitely have been the easier option. Things were never bad between us. No blazing rows kept us awake at night. Ours was a silent, treacherous down-fall. One that kept me awake at night nonetheless.

I go into Rosie's room to find her fast asleep. I put the back of my hand on her forehead. She still feels too warm. I've considered canceling my trip, but I have two children, and I haven't seen Troy in such a long time. Although he will be back in New York soon enough, I still think that, as his mother, I should be there for the ceremony. Perhaps I *should* allow Suzy to stay with Rosie. It would comfort her. But I have to think about the long-term consequences. If I let Suzy come over too much, Rosie will never get used to her moving out.

Hurting Rosie was, ultimately, what hurt me the most during this break-up. She had that same look on her face as Troy did when Leigh left. When will my mistakes stop repeating themselves, I wonder? I probably shouldn't date again until Rosie's old enough to understand that, sometimes, between grown-ups, things just don't work out.

I pass by the hallway mirror and ask myself, "What does that mean, though? Do you even understand?"

I glance back at my tired reflection. Good old Muriel will stay with Rosie. She and Francine love her to pieces. I won't even have to ask. All I will have to say is that Rosie won't be able to go with me to Berkeley, and she will offer to take care of her.

"That doesn't answer my question," I say to myself, like a woman who's about to lose her mind.

I had to break up with Suzy. It seemed that every day another personality trait of hers, one I had easily put up with for years, started grating on my nerves. Until it added up to me actively trying to avoid her.

The day before I asked her to leave I sat crying on Muriel's sofa. "It's really hard to explain, but it's like I've fallen completely out of love with her for no reason."

"There doesn't need to be a reason, Jodie. Sometimes two people only have a limited time together. Not everything is forever. That's just a fairy tale. And a conspiracy by the wedding industry."

"What about you and Francine?" I asked in between sniffles.

"We've just found a successful way of putting up with each other's shit. That's all. There's no magic."

"Then why can't I do that?"

"Because, sweetie, everyone is different."

"I don't understand," Suzy said. "What's wrong? We have a great life together. We're a family."

"I can't be with you anymore," I insisted. "It's not your fault." Try telling someone you've shared your life with for several years that you don't love them anymore without breaking their heart. "It's all me. You're not to blame."

"There must be something I can do." Suzy was a fighter. "Do you need some space? Some distance? I can go stay with Dave for a while, but don't do this, Jodie. Don't pull the plug on us like this." She was being very practical about it. I presumed the actual shock would come later.

"I've thought about this for a very long time." Months on end, I had mulled the inevitable decision over in my mind, on my way to work, on walks to court, en route to Rosie's school. Could I not be a bit more lenient? Perhaps with time some of the old sparks would return? "And I'm sorry to say it's over." By the time I told her I was able to be quite matter-of-fact about it. I'd done my crying already. I'd already grieved for what we once had.

I had tried to explain it as calmly as possible. I'd arranged for Rosie to have a sleepover at her friend Gracie's house, and had knocked off work early so I was home before Suzy arrived. I wondered if saying the actual words might make me change my mind, but looking at Suzy's devastated face as I broke the news only reinforced the feeling that I should have done this months ago. But I was always waiting for a change, for a tidal wave of magic to make things better. To make me a better person. Someone who loved their partner for eternity.

"That's all you have to say?" Suzy asked. "After four years? After I've taken care of your child like she was my own." I thought it a low blow to involve Rosie in this situation, but I understood.

"I'm sorry."

"But… what have I done wrong?"

"Absolutely nothing." There was no relief to be found in this moment. I knew both of our lives would get worse for a while until they got better. "You can stay for as long as you need to. We will tell Rosie together."

Suzy shook her head in disbelief. "I'm not staying in a house where I'm not wanted." Then she started to cry. Not hysterically. She had too much self-respect for that. "Is it sex?" she asked, sort of out of the blue. "I've tried to comply with your wishes as best I could, and I know that's why it didn't work out with you and Amy."

"No, Suze, no." Of course, sex had something to do with it, but that most certainly wasn't Suzy's fault. And I had learned my lesson after Amy—and altered my expectations accordingly. *It's just, when I try to imagine myself a few years from now, there's no scenario in which I can picture you by my side.* I didn't say that out loud because I considered it too cruel.

Perhaps she had come into my life at a time when I needed someone most. There was so much comfort to be found in falling in love with Suzy Henderson. I was in love with her, but then it faded, and everyday life mundanity took over until I felt I had nothing left to hold on to.

"Couples go through phases," she said next. "It can't always be good."

"It's not a phase." That sentence reminded me of what I'd told Gerald when I finally figured out that it was a woman I wanted to be with.

And now here I stand. My spirits low because of the break-up and how badly Suzy is taking it. Because my little girl can't see her brother graduate. But also with an undefined flutter in my stomach, because I'm flying to San Francisco. To Leigh's city.

CHAPTER NINETEEN

I can feel Jodie's eyes on the back of my head, like a rifle's laser sights. I told Troy over and over again that, if he didn't tell his mother about us seeing each other, it would be a bad idea for me to attend his graduation, but he was adamant. He wanted me there. He even said that, if it hadn't been for me, he might not even be graduating, but I saw through that one easily. He was just being dramatic.

He only told me yesterday that he hadn't been able to work up the nerve to tell Jodie about our friendship.

"I should have told her years ago," he said, "now it feels like I've been doing something bad."

I'm afraid to move. I stand here as though my neck is stuck in a medical brace and I can only look straight ahead. I know Jodie's a few rows behind me with Gerald. No sign of Rosie. It's as if I can feel them talking about me. I can imagine what's going on inside Jodie's head right now. She must be furious because what right do I have to be here on this day? If only Troy had told her.

It's Troy's turn on the podium, and even though it's probably inappropriate, a ripple of pride runs through me when he waves from the stage. His wave is not aimed at me, of course, it's for his parents, but then he does glance in my direction, and I can't help myself, I turn around and locate Jodie in the crowd instantly, as though my vision is a radar trained to only ever find her. I smile. She doesn't smile back. Then she shakes her head.

My heart is in my throat. Perhaps I should just leave. Pretend this moment never happened. But I can't just walk away from Jodie. Not again. Not now that I've actually seen her.

I patiently wait for the rest of the students to be called to the stage and have their moment. Every time one passes, my heart starts beating faster.

After the official part of the ceremony has ended, I watch Troy as he heads in Jodie and Gerald's direction. Should I just walk up to them? After having seen Jodie shake her head at me like that? As if that gesture could erase my being here.

I take a few steps toward them. I'm not just going to stand here as if I don't belong. Troy and I have a relationship now, and I'm here for him. Although I've been on edge since the day he asked me to attend. The prospect of seeing Jodie, which would be inevitable, caused a few more sleepless nights than I had expected.

"Mom, I hope you don't mind I invited Leigh," I hear Troy say. His voice is that of a man who knows he's guilty. "I didn't really know how to tell you, but we've been seeing quite a bit of each other." *Good one, Troy,* I think. *Lay it on her here and now.* Inwardly, I roll my eyes. But if you can't do stupid things when you're young, when can you? He beckons for me to join them. I paint a confident smile on my face.

"Jodie." I don't really know what else to say. "It's been too long." I don't know what to do either. Standing face-to-face with her has me reduced to a brainless creature. I extend my hand. Troy has to nudge her in the elbow before she shakes it.

The meeting of our palms is quick and awkward. I decide to direct my attention to her ex-husband.

"Gerald. How have you been?"

"Truth be told, I hadn't expected to see you here today." He ignores my question, but focusing my attention on him allows me to regain some of my wits.

"Troy wants to go to law school. Who's he gonna call, right?"

"I've learned so much from Leigh already, Mom," Troy says. Oh, christ. That boy sure knows how to push Jodie's buttons. "Can she come to dinner with us?" he asks.

I have to step in. I also don't particularly feel like having dinner with Gerald. "That's quite all right, Troy," I interject. "I'll take you out some other time." I shoot Jodie a quick, apologetic glance.

"For old times' sake, I guess," Jodie says. A shudder of something —Satisfaction? Nerves? Guilt?—rushes through me. Gerald doesn't look too pleased about his ex-wife's impromptu decision.

"Awesome," Troy says, holding up his hand for a high-five. I don't care how silly it looks, and I slap my palm against his with a big burst of inexplicable joy coursing through me.

"See you at eight at Rudy's," Troy says to me. "I'll call ahead to let them know there'll be four of us instead of three." He pulls me into a hug. Afterward, I can't help but glance at Jodie again. The years have changed her, of course, but she's still Jodie. I think of that night after Karen broke up with me, and I tried to call her. What would have happened if she had picked up? And what is seeing me so unexpectedly doing to her? Despite Gerald's presence, I'm glad I'll get to spend some time with her.

"I believe you've earned yourself a beer, buddy," Gerald says to Troy.

I wasn't expecting that move from Gerald either. He's giving me an opening here. I have to take it. "I know a great coffee place a few blocks from here," I say to Jodie. "Catch up?" My heart is almost bursting out of my chest. Seeing her makes my insides churn with nerves but, at the same time, joy sparks within me, and it seems to multiply by the second.

"Why not?" Jodie replies, but she looks at Troy, as though she's doing *him* a favor. He hugs her in response.

"Thanks, Mom." He lets go of Jodie and addresses Gerald. "Come on, Dad. I know just the place."

Jodie and I stand in silence for a while.

"How about something stronger than coffee?" she asks, finally meeting my gaze.

"Oh yes." I can actually feel my confidence coming back, like a coat I had misplaced, but found again and it still fits me like a glove. "Come on, we'll take my car."

I drive us to the same place where I first met Troy again. We manage to find a table on the back patio and we both order martinis —dirty with two olives—the way we used to.

"You're at a considerable advantage here, Leigh. You knew you would see me today. You had time to prepare. Whereas I, frankly, am still recovering from the shock," Jodie says as soon as the waiter goes back inside.

"It's just a conversation, Jodes. There are no advantages or disadvantages to be had." I didn't mean to call her by her nickname. It just came out.

"Christ, always the lawyer," she says awkwardly.

"But you're right. I've known for a while that I'd be seeing you —and I've been nervous about it ever since." I can't wait for that drink to arrive, although I must not overindulge. I'm driving Jodie, after all. How long has that been? Since we drove to The Hamptons for the very last time. The drive back to the city from The Hamptons has managed to stay lodged in my memory despite its blurry, dreamlike quality. Two hours of my brain playing ping-pong.

"I know you hated me for a long time after, Jodes. That weighed heavy on me. I wish we could have had a cleaner break—" Oh no, I said it again.

"There are no clean breaks when so much love is at stake." Jodie's tone is harsh.

"I know, but at the time, it was the only way for me. I hope you can see that now."

"No need to revisit. You made your reasons very clear. Sometimes, it just doesn't work out."

I can't help but shake my head. "Don't give me that. The end of our relationship was not a matter of 'it not working out.'" Finally the waiter returns. "It was a matter of wanting totally different things from life."

"I don't see the difference, but if you say so," Jodie says.

"We were right for each other on so many levels." I take a few quick sips. I need them.

"And yet here we are. Sipping martinis like virtual strangers."

"I wish it didn't have to be like that." I take a bigger gulp now. "I wish you didn't feel the need to be so defensive."

"That's a good one coming from the woman who, in all of my life, broke through my walls the most." Jodie hesitates for a second. "I had no choice but to build them back up again after we broke up. Doubly fortified."

"I couldn't stay, Jodie. It would have made us both miserable."

She nods. We both know. "Are you, huh,"—she pauses again— "seeing someone?"

"Not at the moment." Not for a long time, I think. "If I were, she wouldn't be too happy I'm meeting up with you."

"How do you mean?" Jodie's green gaze rests on me.

"Because no one else ever lived up to you. To what we had together." In a way, it's a relief to finally be able to say this. Not to anyone else, but straight to Jodie's face. "Obviously, I didn't realize that at the time."

"Regrets?" Jodie asks. Her spine is straight, but her voice wavers a bit.

"It's hardly fair to sit here now and claim that I regret my decision, after all this time. Let's just say that, on a personal level, my life didn't exactly work out as I had planned."

"As opposed to it doing so brilliantly on a professional level?"

"I'm good at my job. Always have been. But it came at a cost."

"We all have a price to pay."

"You have Troy and Rosie. No price is big enough for that."

"That might be true." She looks away from me. "Doesn't mean I didn't miss you terribly."

"Comes with the territory of breaking up." My glass is almost empty.

The ringing of Jodie's phone interrupts our conversation. She grabs for it hastily in her bag.

"Tonight?" I hear her say without hiding the disappointment in her voice.

"It's okay, honey." *Honey?* Who is she talking to? Rosie? "You'll be in New York most of the summer. We can celebrate for weeks on end." It must be Troy. Is he canceling their—and my—dinner plans? Hope flares in my chest. More of Jodie just for me.

"Yes. Just catching up…" Jodie says before hanging up and staring at her phone indecisively.

"Stuck with me?" I ask, unable to mask the twinge of hope in my tone.

"Looks like it." Jodie looks at me and I can tell—I still can—she's not too unhappy about this situation.

"I'm not going to lie, Jodie. I love Troy to pieces, but that ex-husband of yours, well… I'm glad I got out of that particular dinner. Imagine the riveting conversation. I'd much rather spend the evening with you." I don't hold back when I stare at her. "That is, if you want to, of course."

"If I had known my son would ditch me, I would have booked the red-eye back to New York. Rosie has the flu. Poor thing." She's lost in thought for an instant. "I hated that I had to leave her behind this weekend, but I couldn't do that to Troy. And she's in good hands with Muriel."

"Troy has shown me pictures of her. What a cute little thing. And quite the mouth, I hear?"

"It's a rewarding thing, you know, motherhood. Hard to put into words. But we're all different, I guess." Jodie's tone has gone hard again.

"Do you really want to go there again?" I slant my body over the small table. "Or do you want to enjoy the few hours we have together tonight? I, for one, am very happy to see you. And I've never blamed you for the choices you made, despite the fact that all they came down to was that there was no longer room for me in your life." I lean in a little closer. "And don't, not even for a split second, think it didn't hurt me every bit as much as it did you."

She holds up her hands, displaying her palms.

"How about another drink?" I smile at her, hoping to convey that she should say yes.

"Sure."

I hold up my hand to signal the waiter. "Tell me about Suzy," I ask, although I have no right to.

"What did my son have to say about her?"

"We never gossip about you in that way, Jodie. I promise. We both respect you too much for that. Anyway, Troy claimed he never really got to know her."

"You ruined me for a lot of women." A grin breaks on Jodie's lips.

"Oh sure, blame me." I grin back. "Any other woman would thank me, by the way."

"As I'm sure many have."

"Ha." I feign indignation. "I'll admit that for a while after we broke up and I moved West, I played the field. But, as you well know, I've never really been one for one-night stands and affairs going nowhere. I need more than that. Much more."

"Only total surrender."

"Oh, Jodie." I can't stop looking at her. All these years of not being with her, not experiencing what only she has ever given me. "Tell me what you're thinking right now." I can't be a hundred percent sure of the quickly changing vibe between us, but I take a chance, anyway.

"I'm too old for your games now, Leigh," she says, but I can tell she's at least a little bit interested. I can tell by how she flutters her lashes and fiddles with the cuff of her blouse.

"It was worth a try."

"Was it?" She looks at my hands. Perhaps she remembers what they can do.

"Where are you staying?" I need to make my move now. "I'm only asking because I'd much rather do something else with you than sit here and get drunk."

"You remember well." Jodie cocks her head.

"'Fondly' would be a better word for it." I empty my drink. "Back in the day you were much quicker to say yes."

"What can I say? I was thirty years old and still so easily impressed."

"Hm. I disagree." I eye her glass, hoping it will make her empty it quicker. "I think, that particular day, what you needed more than anything, was for someone to sweep you off your feet."

"Cut to Leigh Sterling, who did a sterling job."

"We were such different people then."

"What kind of person are you now, though, I wonder?" Jodie asks.

"Evidently not the kind who can persuade you to invite me to your hotel with one well-aimed, smoothly delivered sentence. Not anymore."

"You're so much more than that. Always were."

"I'm not playing games right now, Jodie." I can hear the urgency in my voice. "What would you like to do? I feel like we have this chance here, time for something unexpected… to get reacquainted, perhaps. I don't know." I shake my head. "As far as relationships go in my life, ours still counts as the most significant one I've ever had."

"Is Troy setting me up in some way? Obviously, he wanted me to see you again. And that whole basketball game excuse he just called me about… is he playing lawyer tricks on me?"

"I don't know, but does it really matter?" The joy I experienced earlier is soon making way for a slew of painful memories.

"Did you ask him to arrange this?"

"I would never use your son like that." This time I don't have to feign indignation. "We may well be sitting here together with a whole evening stretched out in front of us because he wanted it, but if that's the case, it's his doing alone. Not mine." I swallow hard. "You're also free to go whenever you want."

She holds up her palms again. "This is emotional for me, too."

"I know. I shouldn't have said that, it's just..." I tilt my head and find her eyes. "I hadn't expected you to have this effect on me, still."

"Let's go to my hotel," Jodie says suddenly.

I don't say anything, just call for the waiter. Jodie leaves some money on the table, and before I fully realize what is happening, I'm driving us to the hotel where Jodie is staying.

CHAPTER TWENTY

When we step into the elevator, I half-expect Leigh to start kissing me, but this is eleven years later, and all the boundaries we once carefully set have vanished, and when I look at myself in the shiny metal of the door, I see a different woman—outside and in. Yet, I want her to. I want someone to do that to me again. To take away all the things that always simmer somewhere in the back of my brain, to take away that longing that's been building in my gut for years. And I only want Leigh to do it. She's no means to an end. She's my ex-partner. The only one who ever knew me well enough to take me to the place I needed to go. Because the things I want, you don't just ask of someone. Or, at least, I guess you could, but it would take away half the pleasure.

The elevator cabin is silent, apart from a buzzing hum, and the sound of our breath, coming as regularly as always. Yet, beneath my skin, my blood is sizzling. I start making up a list of all the things this is not, but I realize quickly that I don't need to. I don't need to overthink this, or think about it at all. That's the whole point of inviting her to my room.

The best part of this entire elevator ride, which is about to come to an end, is that I get to experience both sides of the thrill. I know Leigh and the familiarity between us reassures me, yet I haven't seen her in years and there's the excitement of newness crashing through my flesh as well. Do I still love her? I ask myself as we exit the elevator and I guide her to my room in the furthest corner of the hallway. Do I? If I do, it's in a totally different way than before. The love that remains after the hurt has been dealt with. A more sedated, stable kind of affection based on memories and shared experiences and the life we once lived together. But, no matter what we do or how hard we try, we can never, ever get that life back.

As soon as we walk into my room—the one Gerald has generously paid for—which is swanky and large and boasts full-length windows on one side, Leigh starts scanning her surroundings. The curtains will have to remain open, of that I'm sure already, but she's also looking for props. I wonder if I would be offended if she unearthed some sort of toy from her bag, a flogger perhaps, or handcuffs. If I would be able to forgive such presumptuousness. But not even Leigh Sterling can rise to that level of audacity, and I remember what she used to say to me. "You have no idea what you give me when you take the pain." But I did, and I still do.

"Drink?" I ask.

"Just some water, please." To my surprise, Leigh dodges my glance when I look at her.

"Are you okay?" I try to make my question sound casual as I snatch a bottle of water from the minibar and pour its contents into a wine glass.

"I don't know." Is she having second thoughts? What was I expecting anyway? A re-run of our first date? "I think I know what you want from me, but I can't read you like that anymore. Too much time has passed." She takes the glass I hand her and deposits it on the desk she's leaning against. "I'm also not sure we are people who can just do this once and walk away, especially with the history we share. I'm only speaking for myself, of course. But this, for me, can never be casual. Not with you."

"What are you trying to say?" My heart is thumping away beneath my ribs. I grab the tiny bottle of Scotch I took from the minibar earlier and start to unscrew the top. Are we not on the same page, after all?

"I *do* have regrets. What if you *were* the one I let go? After you, my life did not become what I wanted it to be, and you know why? Because, yes, I'm good in court, and I was made partner well before I turned forty-five, and I made much more money than I could ever spend, because what would I possibly spend it on? Myself? I'm always working, anyway, because when I come home at night, to my gorgeous house, no one's there."

The person standing in front of me is so far removed from the Leigh I expected to encounter in my hotel room, I need to blink. "Why don't we sit for a bit?" I gesture at two club chairs flanking the window.

"I'm sorry, Jodie. I know this is not what you signed up for." Leigh sighs when she crashes into the chair, and there's nothing regal about her posture anymore. It reminds me of the day we broke up. She looked like her spine had shrunk several inches, and her voice had lost all of its liveliness. Leigh never had to tell me she was hurting, I always knew well before she had the nerve to fess up.

"I didn't sign up for anything." I sit down opposite her, trying to find her eyes, but she keeps looking away. "You're a bit young for a midlife crisis." I try a joke.

"It's you." The words come out as a whisper. "I usually don't feel like this. Perhaps because I don't allow myself to. Or because I don't have time for self-pity, but mainly because I'm not the type to dwell and look back like this on the choices I've made. But seeing you... actually, if I'm being truly honest, it started when Troy contacted me for the first time. That kid." She shakes her head. "I could have been there for all of it—his first girlfriend, his first year in high school, his first everything—but I walked away."

"Please stand up," I ask, leading by example. I extend my hand

and wait for her to take it. She does, letting her fingers brush over mine before truly grasping them, and pulling herself up.

"If I were you, I'd kick me out as well." A hint of a smile breaks through the sadness on her face.

"I'm not kicking you out." *I always wanted you to stay*, I think, but don't say out loud. "Who knows why we make the choices we make, Leigh? All we know is that they make us into the person we're meant to become. You're a hot-shot lawyer now, which is, by the way, quite a sexy thing to be. You know, in an Amanda Donohoe eighties kind of way." At last, the first hint of her trademark grin. "You're only forty-five. And as you just said, you're not someone who looks back often, so look to the future. One of the big advantages of the life you've lived so far is that you have no strings attached. You can be or do whatever you want."

Leigh's grip around my fingers grows firmer, yet I'm the one who leans forward and instigates the first kiss. "For example, you can do this." I tip my head and inhale her scent before pressing my lips to hers. I wish I could say her scent roused a million memories from my soul, but I've given birth to another child since she left, I've lived a whole new life, and the smell of my ex-lover is as new to me as all the rest of this.

"I need to know how *you* feel," Leigh says, as we pull back from what I can hardly describe as the passionate lip-lock I had hoped for.

"How I feel?" Despair clings to my voice. "Confused, horny, ready..." I ramble. "I want you, Leigh. That's how I feel."

"You want me for the person I once was to you." Leigh brings her face closer again. "You want me to tie you to that bedpost over there" —her eyes dart away from me for a moment—"and push five fingers inside of you."

It's exactly what I want, but I'm not sure I should just give myself away like that. It doesn't really work that way—never has.

"Most of all," Leigh continues, "you want me to stop talking." Her eyes bore into mine, and I can tell she's getting there, that she's getting herself ready. "And take charge."

Almost imperceptibly, I nod, and I feel everything falling away. The years we haven't seen each other, the pain we caused each other that has colored our memories, and, perhaps in both of our cases, altered our view on life as well. Because isn't our life made up of the people that we love? The people that have the power to fundamentally change something about us? Apart from my children, no one has ever had as profound an effect on me as Leigh Sterling. She knows it too. I see it in the way her facial expression is changing. Eyes that seem to look straight into my soul. That knowing, lopsided smile. Even in the way she tilts her head, exposing the length of her neck, as ever, a question in the slant of it: are you ready?

In a flash, her hands are on the back of my neck, pulling me in. The kiss that follows is much more invasive. There's nothing exploratory or cautious about it. It's a declaration of intent. The way Leigh claims me with her tongue now is how she'll claim me with her fingers later.

When we break from the kiss, I already feel out of breath and my knees are giving way. Not even the best sex I had with Suzy comes close to this thirty-second kiss from my ex. Apples and oranges. There's no use comparing the two.

CHAPTER TWENTY-ONE

"You'd better undress and bend over," I tell Jodie. She obeys instantly, just as she used to.

I keep my glance on her while she unbuttons her blouse and lets it drop to the carpet. Eleven years ago, Jodie would never have just discarded a piece of clothing like that.

When only her underwear remains, she pauses. I arch up my eyebrows, just as a matter of encouragement. The years have changed her body—how could they not? I hope she can tell that I think she's as beautiful as ever from the way I'm looking at her.

She unclasps her bra, hesitates for a moment before dropping it, then quickly takes off her panties as well.

"You know the pose." I move out of her way, wondering if she still does.

She bends over and presents her ass to me.

I'm momentarily floored by how easy she's making it on me, and by how she still seems to trust me after all these years. Maybe, when you love the way we did, it never really goes away. Maybe something lingers, the way people can survive with a piece of shrapnel in their body after an accident. It hurts. And it's an almost constant reminder. But survive they do.

I look at Jodie's behind in silence a few seconds longer. I know what that does to her. I also know what it does to me.

I quickly remove my blouse and then trace a finger up the curve of her ass. I feel her flinch underneath my touch. I can't lift my finger from her skin. I run it up and down her cheeks, reacquainting my fingertip with this body that has given me so much pleasure.

When I'm finally able to drag my finger away from her flesh I suck it into my mouth, as though it's the quickest way to savor her. I also know where my finger is going next, and some moistness wouldn't go amiss.

The fragility I displayed earlier leaves me, and I bring my finger to her behind again. Let her feel it's good and wet so she can draw her own conclusions about where this is going. And I fully realize this is going very fast, but there's no other way for Jodie and me to do this. Falling into bed smiling, caressing each other until the next morning, that was never how we did things—except perhaps for the first few times we made love, when I hadn't fully gauged her yet.

My finger inches closer to her crack. Oh, to be able to see her face right now. That face I've missed so much, that I've conjured up from memory many a night over the past eleven years. Those green eyes. Those long lips with their color of bruised plums—still her favorite lipstick. I was always sure a deeper meaning lay behind it, but if it did, she never admitted to it.

Has anyone else done this to her? Has Suzy ventured here? I can't help but wonder these things, but, as far as I know, she's not stayed with anyone longer than with me.

I only apply gentle pressure, just so she knows what to expect. And this image in front of me, Jodie offering herself to me like this, it's so *us* it brings a tear to my eye.

"Get up," I say, making sure no sentimentality shows in my voice.

Jodie pushes herself up and a smile flits along her lips when she sees I've taken off my blouse. Her eyes stop at my abs. I have a fully fitted gym in my house. It's not as if I needed the room for my offspring, I want to say, but it would be a joke in extremely bad taste.

"Face the window," I instruct.

While she does, I unbuckle my belt.

"Hands on the glass, ass out." Jodie was always coy about doing it in front of the window, but when I let a finger drift along her pussy lips I could always tell how much it aroused her.

She's gasping for air already and it's as if I can tell by the tautness of her muscles and the eagerness of her breath that no one has demanded this of her in years.

Our eyes meet in the reflection of the window.

"Let's give them a show," I say, and move behind her. With a fingertip, I mark the spot where I will slap her. I easily remember where it always used to hurt her the most.

I let the leather of my belt crash down on the spot I traced. Jodie's body jerks.

"Fuck," she hisses, and her hands slide down the window a few inches.

I know what she needs to get over the bite of the first slap. Another. The sound of the leather cracking on her skin injects jolt after jolt of fireworks into my blood. It's not as if I haven't done this with other women. Karen comes to mind, but it was never the same. I was Jodie's first. We made this happen together and created something between us that can, quite possibly, withstand eleven long years of absence.

"Mmm," I groan, just to give her a little something to hold on to. A tiny sign of approval.

Whack. I treat Jodie's other butt cheek to the same, but instead of just two strokes, I let them come down hard and fast. Asking her to count now would be beyond cruel.

One last crack of my belt and the reflection of her face in the window gives me a lump in my throat. I haven't been faced with such surrender in a long time. So much of what we had between us is still there. It rose to the surface the instant my belt connected with her flesh.

And I want to grab her, kiss her, tell her all the things I've saved up over the years, but I need to end this ritual properly. I let my finger trace the marks my belt has left, rubbing the pain into her flesh even more. Nobody has ever hurt for me the way Jodie has.

Then I can't stop myself from taking her into my arms any longer. I glue my body to her backside and the contact of our skins nearly makes me cry. Nearly.

"Is that what you wanted, Jodie?" I ask. I feel her body give a little in my embrace. "Answer me." I find her gaze in the window's reflection.

"Yes," she says, her voice hoarse.

"On the bed," I command, but I find myself unable to step away from her—I've done enough of that in my life. Instead of making room for her to move, I press my nose into her hair and inhale her scent.

At last, I give her the space she needs to turn around, but still I can't fully find the persona I usually so easily adopt in the bedroom. I grab her by the back of the neck and kiss her deeply. I recover quickly, as if a little bit of her is enough for now, and end our kiss abruptly.

"Go on," I say, not allowing for any more hesitation. "You know the drill."

By the time I've stripped off the rest of my clothes, Jodie is in position on the bed. She lies on her back, her fingers curled around the railing.

I loop the belt I used on her earlier and fasten it around her wrists nice and tight.

"Spread your legs." I crawl to the back of the bed and take in the sight. Her pussy lips glisten with moisture, and I can't let her know how seeing her like this affects me. "Wider," I say in a stern voice. She lets her knees fall farther to either side.

"You really want this, don't you?" I can't look away from Jodie's pussy. I can hardly stand the thought that other women have touched it, but I know it's a highly hypocritical, useless thought. "You want to be fucked so badly, don't you, Jodie?" I tear my gaze away from between her legs and look her in the eyes.

"Yes." Her tone is more defiant than I had expected. Time to take her down a peg.

"How many fingers, Jodie?" I ask. "Three?" I chuckle. "Nah, three is nothing for you. I know that much. Four perhaps?" I let my gaze drop down to between her legs again. "Or do you want everything, Jodie? Hm?"

"All of it," she rumbles, her breath ragged.

"Are you sure?"

"Yes," she says, like the first time she asked me to do this to her. I haven't reached the exact headspace I need for this yet. Maybe this was the way it was destined to go between us this afternoon, but it doesn't mean it's easy. This is as far removed from just sex—from just two bodies meeting—as I've ever been. All the memories, the regrets, the mistakes that lie between us, and yet, look at us now. I'm about to fuck her, give her everything, and I feel nerves rage in my belly.

"Yes," she says, her eyes on me. "And you know it."

I put a hand on Jodie's lower belly and I can hear her breath catch in her throat. I marvel at how her skin breaks out in goosebumps at the slightest touch of my hand. I look up and see impatience glitter in her eyes. Perhaps she has waited for this moment as long as I have. My waiting was never entirely conscious, except in those rare moments when I got completely hammered on martinis and, as they say, the truth just lay there, all bare and obvious for me to see at the bottom of my glass. I could hardly describe those as conscious moments, though. Only fleeting instances of longing that passed when the next day came and the new morning light erased them.

I guide my fingers to her cunt. No hesitation. I need to be inside of her now. Three slip in easily. Jodie gasps for air but doesn't close her eyes, and that's when I truly see her. A state of abandon is not that hard to reach when you know how to push someone's buttons, but this is not just abandon on Jodie's face. I halt the motion of my fingers, just let them be inside of her, all of Jodie clasping around them while I look into those green, green eyes. And I already know there will be no walking away from this. Those eyes, that glare, even the new lines that have gathered around her mouth, they're my home. Three seconds inside of Jodie is all I need to know that, eleven years ago, I made a big mistake.

I start fucking her and she groans in response.

"Oh fuck," she says. "Oh, Leigh."

Hearing Jodie say my name unravels something inside of me, but I need to stay focused. I fuck her quicker, before pulling out and giving her everything she asked for. Slowly, slowly, I cover my hand in her wetness, and I fuck her with everything I have. Not just my hand, but my entire being. I should have known when I walked away from her after our last fuck, on the floor of her apartment. I broke down in Sonja's spare bedroom as soon as I deposited the suitcases Jodie had packed. I howled from sheer physical pain, but I thought that was normal. I was so utterly convinced I'd made the right decision, and it *was* the right decision at the time, but only for a brief while. I should have gone to see her when Muriel cornered me. I should have reversed our fate when I had the chance.

Jodie's eyes are glazing over. "Relax," I say because I have something else in store for her. What I hinted at earlier. I slip my free hand from her belly to beneath the hand I'm fucking her with. Jodie's eyes widen. She knows. Her eyes close.

I push my hand deeper into her pussy, while I circle her sphincter with the index finger of my other hand. I have to look away from her face. I need to see what my hands are doing.

I also can't look at her when I start to cry.

I let my finger slip past the rim and I can't help but sneak a glance. Tears run down Jodie's cheeks as well. Her eyes flicker open and shut, but I don't think she sees anything. She's lost in the moment and, perhaps, this is the sight I missed the most. The sight of total surrender. Her wrists bound. Her body completely open to me, a display of trust, a vision of what years apart can't erase.

I can feel her pussy starting to contract around my fist. Her body stiffens, then relaxes. Time for my hand to retreat, to leave Jodie Whitehouse—this time, it won't be forever.

Our eyes meet and Jodie seems taken aback by my tears. But all I see are my desires reflected back at me. We both knew well before entering this room that this would not be an ending again. I untie her wrists, massaging and kissing them where my belt dented the skin.

"Good grief, Jodie," I whisper in her ear as I push her down and stretch next to her.

Jodie wraps her arms around me and faces me. Our cheeks are sodden with tears of relief and nostalgia and—I know this—love. I hold her tight, hoping it comes across that I intend to never let her go again.

"Maybe you should come to New York sometime," Jodie says. My heart flutters. I don't know how to reply with words. I need to let a burst of happiness wash over me before I can find them.

"Maybe I will," I say, gravely understating my true emotions, but Jodie knows. I know she does.

CHAPTER TWENTY-TWO

The next morning when I wake up early because we never did take the time to draw the curtains, Leigh is still fast asleep beside me. I take in her relaxed face; her lips are slightly parted, her eyes a bit baggy from the crying.

I check the alarm clock and my first thought, as always, is Rosie. It's only 6 a.m. Gerald and I will meet Troy for breakfast at 9 so we can catch the midday flight to New York.

Would it make Troy happy to see me appear at breakfast with Leigh by my side? It's a thought I'm not ready to entertain just yet.

Last night, Leigh and I got caught up in long hours of reminiscing, lying in each other's arms while avoiding drawing conclusions. Until we fell asleep, naked, our arms lightly touching, just as they always used to. What should my first words be to her when she wakes up? I can't stop looking at her. Her hair is pointing in all directions and one cheek is a bit wrinkly from lying on her side. It reminds me of lazy Sunday mornings when it was Gerald's week with Troy, and an entire day stretched out in front of us. The immense feeling of comfort to be spending the day with someone you love, doing the things you love, unencumbered, free in the union we then, still, chose.

My wrists are stiff, despite Leigh's incessant stroking of them last night, after the fact. When I stretch, my butt cheeks sting in the most satisfying way, and my pussy feels tender. I think of the time we have left, the few hours between now and my leaving for the airport. Would she really consider visiting me in New York? If all the things she said last night are true, she just might.

As much as I love watching her sleep, time ticking away from us gets the best of me. Leigh's lying on her back, the duvet half thrown off, and I remember what it was like to wake up beside her every morning. A small but significant blessing, because what better way to start the day than laying eyes on the woman I love? The woman who taught me more about myself than I ever deemed possible. After she left me, waking up was always the hardest—especially on days when Troy was at his dad's. But I've dealt with the emptiness of those mornings. Time has, for once, softened the memories that needed it most. And look at me now? Mother of two children, *and* in bed with Leigh Sterling. The most crucial of our differences dissolved as the years have gone by.

I trail a finger along her collarbones, only hesitating for a split second before dragging it down across her torso, to her left nipple. It's still limp with sleep, but not for long. I encircle it with the tip of my finger, but I need more. I move so I can take it in my mouth. As I wrap my lips around it, Leigh expels a light groan, followed by, "Good morning to you too."

Her voice instantly undoes me a little—although sparingly used, it was always an important instrument in our love-making—and I let her nipple slip from my lips to look at her.

"Morning." Leigh's face breaks into a smile that makes my heart sing. A grin so unselfconscious and free, it makes me realize I could fall in love with her all over again. "You should probably do it, you know," I hear myself say.

"What?" Leigh pulls me close to her, until my ear reaches her lips.

"Book a ticket to New York, you mean?" Her voice is a horny whisper, full of promise of things to come—if she does book that ticket.

I nod, my cheek now against her lips. I turn my face toward her fully, to look into her eyes. No more words are needed now. I lean in to kiss her, and this kiss, this morning, with early sunlight illuminating us, and the memory of last night in our hearts, is one that travels all the way through me, its divine sensation settling in the pit of my stomach. I won't fall in love with Leigh again because I already am. Perhaps it started when she loosened her belt from her trousers—although that would mean reducing the moment to one of pure physicality. To the mere promise of sexual satisfaction, and it was so much more than that. If I know one thing, back in the day and now, it was never promises keeping us together. And it was never just the scorching scenes in our bedroom Leigh managed to create. It was—is—much more than that. Then and now. Because how do you forget a love like that? The life we shared, the companionship, the deep friendship and understanding that connected us much more than Leigh tying me up ever could, they were the hardest to lose.

How Leigh was there for me after rough days—and in my profession, a lot of days are heartbreaking—not just with legal advice and a shoulder to lean on, but how she knew the right, lighter words to say to cheer me up. How she could disarm me by arching up her eyebrows and pulling her lips into a silly grin. How, when I came home, I'd find her building an intricate Lego construction with Troy, his whole being so in awe of her—and how I felt that too, then.

"How about next weekend?" Leigh asks when we break from our kiss.

My bruised pussy lips are pulsing again and, despite knowing I need some time to recover, I already want her again. I feel it in every bone of my body. Leigh is inventive, she'll find a way to give me what I need. She always did.

"Can't wait," I say, as I feel tears stinging behind my eyes. Because this love of ours is greater than time. It's greater than the sacrifices we felt we needed to make. The sum of it is more than our separate desires. Maybe we didn't see it then, but I clearly see it now.

"I'll stay at the Library Hotel. I love that place," Leigh says.

"Nuh-uh." I shake my head. "You're staying with me."

"If you insist," she says.

"I do." I lean in for another kiss, and I can already see it. Leigh waking up in the bed we used to share. The four of us going for breakfast because Troy will be home from college. Rosie will have a million questions to ask. Leigh will rest her hand on my knee and I will look the three of them over. The three people I love most in the world.

"My other nipple feels neglected," Leigh says when we come up for air. "And this too." She takes my hand and guides it between her legs. I know what to do.

———

Our goodbye a few hours later is fraught with emotion. Leigh keeps glaring at me, giving the impression she can't quite believe the night we just had. I have trouble processing it myself, but I need to drag myself out of my current mindset, ignore the sting of my ass cheeks and focus on packing.

"Here." Leigh hands me her belt. "Something to remember me by." Before she releases it, she lets the leather slide through her fingers suggestively. Having it presented to me now makes me think back to yesterday's tears—mine, but especially hers. What is going on behind those eyes of hers?

"I won't forget you that easily." It was hard enough the first time.

Leigh's only half-dressed, but the clock is ticking and I need to see my son at breakfast. I no longer feel the need to admonish him, though it feels odd to have him involved in this. She comes for me and grabs me by the neck again.

"I've never forgotten you," she breathes into my ear, and I know it's true. Perhaps some people can have several true loves throughout their lives, but for me, there's only been one. It's her. I can't be sure what the future will bring, but I do know that, if we do get back together, it won't be a repeat of our previous relationship. There's no tuning back into old habits in the cards for us. I have an eight-year-old at home. And I'm a decade older, and hopefully wiser.

I check the clock again. "I have to go, Leigh." Instead of pulling away, I let her kiss me, and the touch of our lips swoops through me the way it has always done.

"Say hi to Troy for me." She chuckles and grabs the rest of her clothes. "And call me when you're back in New York." Her gaze lingers, waiting for a confirmation.

"I will."

One last quick kiss and I'm out the door. Part of me hopes she'll wait until I return to fetch my luggage after breakfast.

———

When he sees me approach his and Gerald's table Troy rises and opens his arms wide. I can't wait for him to be back in New York. To spend some proper time with him.

"I'm so sorry about last night, Mom." He pulls me into a tight, forceful hug. When did my little boy get so tall and strong?

"Sure you are." I sit across from him and examine his grinning face before saying hello to Gerald. "How was the game?"

"Do you really care?" Troy asks, still with a smirk on his face.

"Just checking if ditching your mother was worth it, Troy-toy." I send him a knowing smile back.

"How was your evening?" Gerald asks.

The chair feels extra hard against my bruised butt cheeks. "Interesting," I say. I don't want to quiz Troy in front of Gerald.

"I'm sorry about that, too, Mom." Troy is just a barrel of apologies this morning, though he doesn't come across as very repentant. "I know I should have told you much sooner that Leigh and I were friends. I just... never found the right time to tell you."

Friends? "I agree." I'm not letting him off the hook for keeping that a secret from me. "You should have said something." A waitress comes by and pours me a cup of coffee. "Especially because you've become quite... close."

"I know." He nods solemnly and I can so easily see he's not telling me everything.

"So how is Miss Sterling these days?" Gerald asks.

I wonder if she's still in my hotel room—the one my ex-husband so generously paid for. "Doing quite well for herself."

"How wonderful." He can't hide the sarcasm in his voice, not that I expect him to. Gerald has always been courteous with Leigh and any animosity between them always seemed to come more from her side. As though she couldn't stand the fact that I'd once been Mrs. Dunn. As though that had left a permanent stain on me—one even she couldn't erase.

"Let's order some food, shall we?" I say, diplomatically. Although I'm not hungry. My stomach is too aflutter with memories of Leigh. And exciting possibilities for our future.

CHAPTER TWENTY-THREE

I take Friday afternoon off in order to arrive in New York at a decent time. I don't want to knock on Jodie's door after midnight. Over the phone, I expressed my doubts about staying with her. What would she tell Rosie? Would I sleep on the couch? But Jodie told me not to worry about Rosie just yet. She'd sleep over at Muriel's and we could all meet for brunch on Saturday. Brunch with Muriel, I thought. What a delightful prospect. But only for a fleeting second because my mind was too hung up on Jodie and having the apartment to ourselves on Friday evening.

When I finally ring her bell an hour later than expected courtesy of 'mechanical issues' with the airplane, I'm so amped up, so ready to have her melt in my arms, I'm unprepared for the shock of just standing there. Of waiting for her to open the door for me in the building where I used to live—where, undoubtedly, throughout my life, I have been the happiest.

"Hey stranger," she says when she does open the door. Everything is treacherously familiar, but it's also not. The walls are a different color, and the sofa is in a different corner. Toys spill out of a box next to the kitchen door, and a large half-finished puzzle is spread out on the floor next to it. "Come in."

I drop my bag and take Jodie in my arms. I'm grateful to be able to close my eyes for a few seconds, and while I do so, I consider that arriving here, after all these years, feels much more like coming home than stumbling into my own house in San Francisco after a long day at work.

As I head out of the hallway I spot a picture of me and Troy in front of a huge Lego construction. I feel strangely honored that a minor souvenir of me has remained in Jodie's home.

"God, it's odd to be back here." I unbutton my blazer and glance around. She has a new sofa and a new dining table. I scan the walls for pictures of a person who might be Suzy, but can't immediately identify one.

"Drink?" Jodie has a silly grin plastered on her face.

"Oh yes." I sit down. The carpet is still the same one we had that bout of break-up sex on. I hope she had that cleaned.

"Do you still like a good red?" Jodie stands next to the drinks cabinet a few feet away from me. On the plane, I had visions of entering the apartment and slamming her against the door, the way I used to do, but the power of nostalgia seems to have me in its grip and I'm much more emotional than aroused right now.

I nod and look at Jodie. She has slipped into a pair of jeans—definitely after-work attire. Muriel and a good number of Jodie's colleagues used to wear jeans to work all the time but Jodie is not the type. She's wearing a baby blue blouse and whereas ten years ago it would have been tucked in tightly, she wears it loose now. But we've seen each other naked. I've let my eyes wander over the most-hidden parts of her body, and I know the score.

Jodie pours the wine. "A gift from Dan Mazlowski if you can believe it. Remember your old colleague?" She hands me the bottle, as though I need to read the label before I can drink it. "He's made quite a career for himself."

"I'm sure he has." Uninterested in the origin of the wine, I put the bottle down and raise my glass. "I guess we should drink to Troy," I say, my voice a bit hesitant, "for bringing us back together."

Jodie shakes her head. "He's sticking to his story that it was not a set-up."

"That boy will make a great lawyer very soon." I clink the rim of my glass against Jodie's and look her in the eyes. In all our time apart, I've never encountered irises as green as hers.

We fall silent and sip. The thought flits through my mind that the feelings we had for each other in Berkeley might have just been intensified melancholia. That the feeling might be unreproducible now that we're sitting here, in the same room where the disagreements started. That the magic might be gone. And we can't just fuck again. I want to ask about Jodie's exes—I've never been good at dealing with those—but right now is not opportune timing. Of all the things I had imagined I'd be doing right now, searching for words was not one of them.

"I told Muriel about, erm, our night in Berkeley." Jodie eyes me over the rim of her glass.

"Good old Muriel." Did she ever tell Jodie I ran into her not long after we broke up? And that she advised me to make contact? "What did she have to say?" Nerves tumble down my stomach. It still feels like most subjects should be carefully danced around.

"She gave me an eye-roll or two." Jodie chuckles. "You know what she's like."

"Look…" I feel agitated like a teenager on her first date. Insecure. "I've been thinking about moving back to New York for a while." I just blurt out the words. I haven't particularly spent more time considering coming back of late than at any other time over the years I went West. I also realize this is the wrong thing to say at this time. I just hope Jodie can see that I'm ill at ease. And that I'm sorry.

"Oh." She drinks, shifting uneasily in her seat. An image pops into my head of how she would look with her back against the wall and the button of her jeans flipped open. I'm all over the place. I have no idea what to say to Jodie Whitehouse. Being here is undoing me.

"I shouldn't have said that." I try a smile.

"I'm glad Troy did what he did," Jodie says, her gaze on me. "I'm glad I saw you again, Leigh. And I felt it too. That pull. All those memories. It was a crazy night, but a few hours in bed together can hardly erase all that has happened." She sighs. "Granted, it would be easy to just fall into bed"—an image of Jodie with her wrists tied to the headboard drifts through my mind—"but, I don't know if that's such a good idea. Eleven years is a long time."

I nod but still don't know what to say, until it comes to me. The truth that has been building in my subconscious for over a decade. The truth I was always too afraid to face. "I should have stayed." I put my glass down. "In the back of my mind, you were always there, Jodie. Even when I was with another woman, I was always silently comparing. I mean, I had to leave the city to get over you... and still I didn't see. I should have stayed. I should have been there when you had Rosie. I should have been there for everything because now, I sit here, and I want you so much it's nearly paralyzing me, but there's this huge gap between us. Not just caused by the years we've spent apart, but by the completely different lives we've led. I should have done it for you, Jodie. Gotten over myself and the pursuit of my precious career." I can't hold back a tear from sliding down my cheek. It's just the one though, like a dramatic metaphor for all the years I've spent alone.

"I disagree."

A jolt of hurt makes my head spin. She might as well have punched me in the stomach.

"You've changed," Jodie continues. "I can easily see that. What happened between us has changed you. And it's easy to sit here and think it could have worked if you'd stayed, but we were so miserable by the end. I would never have wanted a child to grow up in that atmosphere." Jodie deposits her wine glass on the table as well. "But how many people get a second chance? I, for one, had never expected you to sit in my apartment ever again. Our split hurt me so much, but I realize it was necessary. We wouldn't be who we are now if we hadn't broken up."

"Clearly you've been happier than I've been." Self-pity doesn't really suit me, so I straighten my spine and attempt a grin.

"I had a child, Leigh." She shuffles closer. "Here's my proposition." Her thigh is nearly touching mine. "Let's look to the future instead of at the past. What happened did so for a reason."

"Yeah." In response, I inch closer to Jodie. I'm not sure how serious she was about not falling into bed. My entire week has been consumed with images of her under my control. Of her bottom striped pink by my hand.

"I'm glad you came all this way." Jodie leans her head against my shoulder. "It feels like I missed you more during this week than I did the past eleven years combined."

Warmth spreads in my belly, and not just because of her touch. I brush her hair away from her ear so she can clearly hear what I'm about to say. "I want to fuck you." Because, before we can calm down and really assess this situation, I will need to possess her many more times. I will need to see her face scrunch up with ecstasy and hear her voice grow hoarse with pleasure.

"Okay," Jodie says, as if she, too, feels that we need to fuck this tension between us out of our system. As if it's the only way. It probably is. But it feels wrong to order her to go into the bedroom because it's not my bedroom anymore. She's slept with other people in that bed. Or perhaps, those ghosts need to be exorcized as well. It doesn't take me as long to find my bearings as it did in Berkeley when I was still too stunned by the shock of seeing her. First fully clothed, then naked, then with her hands tied to the bed.

I tune back into the fantasy that has dominated my nights—and days—since last weekend. "I brought something." Jodie slips off me when I get up. I head toward my bag and grab it. "Wait for me in the bedroom. Get naked. I need to use the bathroom."

Then I see it, what I've been waiting for since I arrived. That spark in her eyes. That upturned corner of her mouth. She's so beautiful, and so Jodie—every inch the woman from my memories. I can't wait to look into those eyes when I fuck her.

Silently, Jodie goes into the bedroom and leaves the door open. I enter the bathroom and peer at my reflection for a second. I'm back, I think, and for an instant, it feels as if I never left. Then I quickly disrobe and strap on. I paid a visit to my favorite shop in the Castro last Wednesday and picked this one out especially for our New York reunion. Just the feel of the dildo, as I maneuver it through the ring with my hands, leaves me weak at the knees.

Jodie's eyes widen when I walk into the bedroom. Then her lips stretch into a grin. "On your knees," I say. "Here." I point to the spot right in front of where I'm standing. "Now."

Jodie hurries off the bed and kneels before me. "You'd better make it nice and wet because I didn't bring any lube." I did, of course, but she doesn't have to know that. In my fantasy, I added, "And I'll be damned if I'm going to use any of the stuff Suzy used on you," but I decide against that particular line. It's not necessary. Jodie's open mouth is hovering over the tip of my silicone cock already. "Eyes on me."

I didn't pick the smallest model, and that's an understatement. Jodie has to strain to wrap her lips around it and keep looking at me at the same time. I give her some time to find a rhythm and to get used to the action, but not too much, before grabbing a fistful of her hair and giving it a good tug. I yank at it until she stops. "You can do better." Her eyes are coated in tears already. She must be severely out of practice. When she sucks the dildo between her lips next, I give a little thrust, just to let her know I mean business. "Deeper," I growl. And she lets it slide further into her mouth until her eyes are bulging, and the sight unhinges something inside of me. No one has done this for me in such a long time. Her eyelids flicker open and shut as she works on my cock, until I say, "Enough." She lets it slip from her lips. Her mascara is smudged, a look I've always loved on Jodie. I give her a second to catch her breath.

"On the bed on all fours." I need to spend some time with her ass first. This was not part of my fantasy scenario either, but I can't help myself.

I wait until she's in position and then crawl behind her and let the dildo dangle between her legs. It's shiny with her spit and I need to stop myself from shoving it into her there and then, but that would just be giving her what she wants, and I do have some restraint left. I slither it against her pussy lips, let the tip graze against her clit, before pointing it at her ass cheeks and smearing them with saliva and her own wetness. My finger follows the dildo, meeting her flesh, and my own clit swells against the fabric of the harness. I could quite possibly come while fucking her. I spread her cheeks, just because I can, and because the sight never fails to arouse me, just to give the impression I'll be fucking her ass. I want to, but I want to look into her eyes more. I knead her ass cheeks, my fingertips leaving marks, and then let my fingers wander down to her cunt. I spread her lips and gather moisture. I just brought the lube as a precaution—because after so many years you just never know—but Jodie is sufficiently wet. I transport some of her juices to the dildo and rub it in my hand, lubricating it for entrance.

"Turn around," I hiss. I move to the side so Jodie can flip onto her back. "Legs wide."

Her teeth sink into her bottom lip. Whatever anyone else has done to Jodie in this bed and in this room, I'm ready to make it disappear. I'm ready to fuck the Suzy out of her—although I hardly think that's still necessary. It's more for me than for her. And even more than earlier, I feel as though I'm coming home.

I maneuver in between her legs and guide the cock to her glistening pussy lips. It has always astounded me how wet Jodie can get for me. My clit thumps against the panel of the harness. I need to fuck her as much for myself as for her.

"I'm going to fuck you so hard," I say, and Jodie drives her teeth further into her lips. She'll draw blood if she keeps this up.

By instinct, I guess, she brings her hands behind her head and holds on to the railing, but this is no time for restraints. This is us fucking in our old bed. I need her hands on me for that.

I push the tip in, eager to thrust, but, although I know full well how much Jodie can take, I give her some time to adjust first. I don't know how long it has been since someone fucked her with a strap-on. I do know it's been years since I felt the straps of a harness slice into my flesh, and that all that I have missed is bubbling to the surface in rapid, hot bursts.

I look at her pussy as I splay it open with my cock, then cast my eyes to her face. Jodie's mouth is open, her eyes narrowed. With one swift thrust, I'm deep inside of her and she gasps for air.

I lower my torso over her and plant my palms either side of her head. This is what I dreamed of. Me fucking Jodie while looking into her eyes. It's everything I hoped it would be. Plus, with every stroke inside of her, with every forward movement of my pelvis, my clit grazes against the inner panel of the harness. At first, I'm not entirely sure I want to lose control like that—and I wouldn't allow myself to with anyone else but her. But this is Jodie and I can tell she's getting aroused by the groans coming from my mouth. She releases the bed post and brings her hands to my shoulders, her nails digging in.

"Oh yes," she says. "Oh yes, Leigh." I fuck her harder, and by now my wetness must be overflowing from the harness, must be mingling with hers when I thrust, and the thought of our bodies meeting like that, and the realization that this is actually happening —that I'm fucking Jodie in her bed in her apartment in New York— spurs me on. I give her long, deep strokes and when she lets her head fall back I demand she look at me, and she does, and when her eyelids flutter open, and the green of her eyes shines through a film of tears, I let go. I come while inside her, and I can barely keep my own eyes open for it. I force them open, however, because I want to see.

"Come for me," I ask, although, admittedly, it sounds more like begging in that moment. An aftershock runs through me, throws me off-rhythm, but this is Jodie beneath me, and I know she hasn't changed that much that she can't come for me anymore when I ask. I see the orgasm ripple through her, her muscles shuddering, her mouth widening, her nails leaving marks.

"Oh fuck," she moans. And I look into her eyes, green slits in her face.

I stay inside of her a few more seconds before slowly retreating.

The harness and dildo are a nuisance now and I want to get them off me, but not as much as I want to kiss Jodie. So the silicone is sandwiched between us as I press my body to hers and kiss her for the first time today.

CHAPTER TWENTY-FOUR

It's a useless ride really—except for romantic purposes—but Rosie said she didn't mind the trip to the airport, so we see Leigh off together on Sunday evening. Rosie ended up staying at Muriel and Francine's for two nights in a row.

"Does that make me a bad mother?" I asked Leigh, who really was not the right person to ask.

"Nothing will ever make you a bad mother." She said the right thing but spanked me harder afterward nonetheless.

The three of us sit squeezed in the back of a taxi, Rosie half on my lap, Leigh's shoulder pressed into mine. I can't explain what she does to me, but maybe I needed a break from that intense longing in order to have another child. In hindsight, there were many justifications for our break-up. As many as there are now reasons to try again. Because, en route to JFK, it hits me again that the failure of my affairs with Amy and Suzy was all down to me. It wasn't so much that they couldn't give me what I craved in the bedroom, but what Leigh did give me. What she's given me now. And after a weekend of almost nothing but fucking, she still leaves me wanting more.

"When can I go on a plane again, Mommy?" Rosie asks.

Leigh nudges her in the arm and takes on a conspiratorial tone. "I'll work something out with your Mom, Rosie. I think both of you should come and see me soon."

I have to stop myself from suggesting next weekend. I would even let her pay for it. But we are not hormonal teenagers. We are women in our forties with responsibilities and full lives—and my parents are coming to New York next weekend.

"Do you want to take this slow?" Leigh asked me in bed this morning.

"You're the one who suggested moving back to New York as soon as you set foot in my apartment on Friday." I smiled at her, indicating it was a joke, but it felt like a lesbian cliché nevertheless.

"Touché," she said while searching for my nipple with her fingers. "Forgive a smitten girl for being nervous."

"'Smitten' I can live with." I caught her fingers with mine and brought them to my mouth. "'Girl' is stretching it a bit far." I sucked her fingers deep into my mouth and conversation was stopped again.

Now I'm about to say goodbye to Leigh, to watch her plane fly off, with nothing but a Skype date to head home with, and no clear idea of when we'll see each other again. Although until last weekend, I hadn't seen her for eleven years, this separation now seems cruel and harder to deal with. Once more, in a moment of despair, I find myself holding on to my daughter. The awkwardness of kissing Leigh goodbye in front of Rosie doesn't stack up against the pure need coursing through me to feel her body press against mine one last time before she goes.

"I love you," Leigh unexpectedly whispers in my ear, after we break from the kiss, but still have our arms wrapped around each other. "Always have."

Her words connect with something deep inside of me, maybe my soul, maybe the nostalgia of all the memories that have come flooding back, or maybe the part of me that's been missing since we broke up. "I love you too," I hear myself say, becoming more of a cliché as the seconds tick by. But it comes from the bottom of my heart.

Leigh folds her long body and crouches by Rosie's side. I had intended for them to spend more time together. I really wanted her to get to know Rosie—to, perhaps, show Leigh that the pain we suffered through was for the best reason imaginable.

"It was very nice to meet you, Rosie," she says, and seeing them together like that is almost too much. Tears well in my throat, but when you become a mother you learn to swallow your own tears in favor of your child's, and I try to apply that technique, but it doesn't seem to work when Leigh is standing next to me. "I will see you again very soon."

Rosie folds her little arms around Leigh's neck as far as they will go, and Leigh's face peeks through Rosie's curls, and I see her eyes are moist, too.

"She's a very affectionate child," Leigh says after she's stood back up.

"She's a hugger, all right. She'd hug the taxi driver if I let her." I smile down at my little girl. What would have happened if she hadn't had the flu last week? Would everything have been different? Would we all be standing here saying goodbye?

"I'd better go." Leigh blows Rosie and me one last kiss. I watch her make her way to security, and this seems to take too long for Rosie because she's already tugging at my sleeve.

"Don't be sad, Mommy," she says. "Leigh said she'd see us both soon." To her, all words are still the truth. But, when it comes down to these words, I do know that they are.

———

"So you're getting back together with her?" Muriel asks. I'm not feeling like work this Monday morning, and we've ditched it for half an hour to get a coffee at the Starbucks around the corner from our office.

Yes, I want to scream, but I don't want to offend Muriel's natural
—and logical—skepticism too much.

"Just like that?"

"Not 'just like that'..."

"How then?" Muriel enjoys playing devil's advocate.

"For starters, it will have to be long distance for a while..."

She doesn't let up. "For a while? Have you booked the U-Haul
already?"

I shake my head at her obvious comment. "Why are you giving
me such a hard time about this? It's hard enough as it is already."

"Just making sure your head's still screwed on the right way, girl."

I gaze into my coffee dreamily. "I know this sounds foolish, but
it's as if I know for a fact that she will never hurt me again..." I can't
help but chuckle. "Well, not emotionally, anyway."

It's Muriel's turn to shake her head. She throws in an eye-roll as
well. "You're my best friend, Jodie Whitehouse, and I consider myself
an open-minded woman, but that part I never really understood."

"There's no need for you to understand." I go all warm inside at
the memory of Leigh entering my bedroom fully strapped on. Not of
the first time, but on Saturday night, when she fucked my ass with it.

Muriel gives me a judgmental 'uh-huh', but I know she's not
judging, just playing. Apart from Leigh, she probably knows me the
best.

"Well, I have some news as well." She taps her fingers on the
table. "This weekend I plan to ask Francine to finally make an honest
woman out of me. Got her a fancy-ass ring and everything."

"Oh." I've always admired Muriel and Francine's relationship, but
in any other circumstances I wouldn't go all mushy about this. I do
today. "That's just..." I choke up.

"I was going to ask you to be my maid of honor but if you're
going to cry about it, I may need to revise my choice." Muriel shoots
me a big smirk.

"I'm just really happy for you." And for myself, I think. The
sniveling doesn't seem to stop. I barely shed a tear after I broke up

with Amy and Suzy, but the rivers I cried after Leigh must still be fresh on Muriel's mind as well.

"You have a strange way of showing it." Muriel shuffles her chair a little closer. "The way you're bawling now, it makes me wonder if you've been secretly infatuated with Francine for years."

I chuckle through my tears. "Not with Francine," I say.

"I know." Muriel throws an arm around me. "Now stop ruining my blissful moment of announcement with your emotional fragility." She squeezes my shoulder.

"I mean it," I say. "I'm so happy for you." And for me, I think, even though it feels like such easily breakable, flimsy happiness.

"Don't be happy for me yet. She still has to say yes." Muriel is patting my biceps now.

"True." I manage to pull myself together a bit. "Do keep me posted on that." I can finally smile at my friend. It's not my habit to fall apart like this.

"Can you spank someone via Skype?" Muriel asks. "'Cause if you can, just have her do that. I'm sure it will make you feel better."

I spend the rest of the day as an overly emotional but ridiculously happy wreck.

CHAPTER TWENTY-FIVE

"You seem so much more relaxed these days." I've taken an entire week off to spend with Jodie in New York. Steve could hardly argue because since I moved West in 2003 I must have accumulated a few months' worth of vacation days.

"I'm much older now," Jodie says. We're sitting on the exact same bench we used to sit on when we took Troy to the park. "And everything is different."

"That pile of dishes in the sink is probably what threw me the most."

"I'm sorry. I really wanted the place to be spotless for you." For a second, Jodie looks genuinely concerned. "But my night scrubbing days are over."

"Who would have thought?" I nudge her with my knee.

"Who would have thought you and I would be sitting on this bench again one day?" Jodie looks happy. Because of the physical distance between us, and because Skype sex is not my idea of a good time, she and I have had to talk much more than we would have done if we'd been in the same city. During our last call, I touched on the subject of moving back to New York—a subject I'm keen to pick back up today.

"I tried to call you one night from San Francisco," I blurt out in response. "Karen had just broken up with me because I was being a shitty girlfriend and I thought, fuck it, I'm calling Jodie. It went straight to voicemail, though, but I sometimes wonder what would have happened if you'd picked up. If we'd been ready."

"We'll never know." Jodie has her eyes trained on Rosie, who's playing with some other kids on the swings. "But I'm fairly certain you and I could never have just been friends. We were never meant to be friends. Amy and Suzy are exes I could be friends with, but you... never."

"Gee, thanks," I joke.

"Not that I'll ever be friends with Amy. I don't blame her for holding a grudge. I was a pretty shitty girlfriend myself."

"Speaking of being girlfriends..." Even though I know the answer to my question because it can't be more obvious, nerves rattle me. "Are we... girlfriends again?"

Jodie chuckles. "We are women in our forties, Leigh. I hardly think the term 'girlfriends' applies." She averts her gaze from the playground and looks at me. "How many times have we fucked since Berkeley?" She pretends to count in her head, then nods. "Yes, I think we can call that going steady." She breaks out into a crooked, purple-lipped Jodie-smile.

"Can we just pick things up again, though, Jodes?"

"Just pick things up?" She shakes her head. "Eleven years have passed. So, no, of course, we can't. But... I think that... I can only be truly happy with you."

"It's funny, but Troy actually said something of the sorts to me about you a while back."

"I guess he knows his mother well." The smile fades from Jodie's lips. "And he was always extremely fond of you."

"I've made many mistakes in my life, Jodie."

"You've changed a lot," Jodie says. "Are you the same person who always claimed that motherhood was not in her blood?"

"I am and I'm not," I say. "But, yes, I guess people do change."

"But so fundamentally?" Jodie urges. "To change your mind on such a big issue?"

"I didn't change my mind, Jodes." I shift position, straightening my spine. "Life did." I gaze into Jodie's green eyes. "Life without you." I pause. These words are of the utmost importance. "And how hard it hit me when Troy emailed me." I look away briefly. "I suffered after our break-up but I buried myself in work and found other means to forget. But it wasn't until I met up with Troy that first time that I realized how much pain I had caused everyone—myself included. I'd always so firmly believed I was saving us and, regardless of us needing to spend time apart, and everything happening for a reason, when I saw him again, something clicked. Something I hadn't allowed to compute in my brain for a long time." I steady my gaze on Jodie again. "I nearly broke down in front of him. After he showed me a picture of Rosie and I realized that what I had been so afraid of, what I had been so convinced of not wanting, was a smiling little girl." I shake my head. "Perhaps things would have been different if I'd met someone else, but only now can I see that I was never even open to the option. Your memory was always lurking in the background. It has always been you, Jodie." Tears have been brimming since I began this impromptu speech and they are now close to breaking.

Jodie shuffles a little closer.

"There are many rational reasons for the years we spent apart. I guess the most convincing one is that I wasn't ready. That I couldn't see past my own goals to meet yours until after I'd gone eleven years without you. And it's true that I've always believed that I wasn't a mother, that I just didn't have it in me. Not the desire, nor the necessary skills—or time for that matter. But then I look back at what Troy and I had, and my persistence in not wanting to be called Mom or even feeling like his mother, but, actually, I was doing everything a mother did. I did have his best interests at heart. I attended his soccer games. I attempted to make him an edible dinner once in a while." I try a shy smile. "I sat up with him when he was ill. I worried about him after dark. I wondered about his future."

"Okay," Jodie says and gives me one of those smiles that drive me wild. "It was very obvious you weren't ready for the things I wanted. Even though 'ready' is probably not even the right word."

Rosie comes running toward us. Her eyes twinkle and her curls bounce around her head. She has the same eyes as Jodie and Troy.

"Thirsty?" Jodie asks.

Rosie nods and Jodie produces a juice carton from her bag. Rosie tips her head back and drinks it with both hands clasped around the carton. Once it's empty, Rosie wants to give it back to Jodie, who refuses to take it.

"You know what to do with that."

Rosie gives her a quick pout, struts to the garbage can on the edge of the playground, and then rejoins her friends.

"She's so adorable." It's more thinking out loud than engaging in conversation.

"You used to say that about Troy when we came here with him." Jodie's tone isn't resentful.

"I know. He *was*."

"Do you want to come live with Rosie and me?" Jodie turns toward me.

"I'm certainly moving back to New York. I've worked my butt off for that firm the past decade. I don't think anyone can refuse me the request." I stretch my arm along the back of the bench, finding Jodie's neck with my fingers. "Do you really want me to move in straight away?"

"Why not?" Jodie's eyebrows twitch. "I *know*, Leigh. I know here." She taps her chest dramatically. "I know that we belong together. Why waste any more time?" She shuffles backward, leaning into the grasp of my fingers. "It's so obvious to me now. When Amy asked me to move in with her, all I had were doubts. With Suzy…" She pauses.

Suzy, whom I'm bound to meet once I move back, whom Rosie calls 'Auntie Suzy'. "Even with Suzy it wasn't the same. Not by a long shot. I've never known the way I do when I'm with you."

"You've grown more sentimental with age as well." I squeeze Jodie's neck between my fingers.

"So what? There's something to be said for becoming a sentimental fool."

"Back to York Avenue…" Some serious down-sizing will be in order, but I don't want to break the magic of the moment. Has anything been done to the place at all since I left?

"I know it's cramped, but we'll figure something out." Jodie puts a hand on my thigh. Her touch makes me melt.

"I'll start packing as soon as I get back." And put my house on the market, I think.

"I predict we'll be sitting on this very bench twenty years from now. Troy might have children by then. We can take our grandkids to the park."

It's the 'our' that almost makes me well up.

CHAPTER TWENTY-SIX

Leigh is flying back to San Francisco tomorrow and I can't sleep. It's still the same alarm clock that sheds its faint red light into my room—these objects, if treated right, are indestructible. It makes me think of the sleepless nights I spent here on my own over the years. The weeks of agony before breaking up with Amy, during those nights that she believed I should have spent with her in Brooklyn. The long, frantic dawns worrying about what to do about Suzy, whose presence in my apartment—and my life—seemed to be getting bigger and bigger. Too big for my comfort.

But, mostly, I reminisce about the nights I tossed and turned while missing Leigh. She's a wide sleeper, who likes to stretch her arms and legs, claiming her territory—funny how she's even like that when sleeping. From what she's told me, for the past eleven years, she has mostly slept alone, not having encountered many reasons to improve her sleep etiquette. I'll need to get used to having her in my bed again. In *our* bed.

Even though I can't sleep, it feels right. Leigh and I spent many a sleepless night in this bed together as well. She stayed up with me when Troy was sick and his fever worried me. She sat by my side until the morning light broke when a boy whose case I was responsible for committed suicide and I nearly went to pieces with grief and frustration.

One night, when we'd been together for about a year, we remained awake all night, giddy with excitement, dreaming up our future. Leigh would say silly things like, "I'll become D.A. and you can be my trophy wife" or "we'll move into a penthouse on Park Avenue." I would tickle her until she took the trophy wife remark back. I ignored the Park Avenue comment.

Sometimes, just before falling asleep, she would say something along the lines of, "Are you sure you locked the door, Jodes?" Just to tease me, because she knew all too well I would need to get up and check. Afterward, she'd make sure I was exhausted enough to go to sleep right away once she was done with me.

Now, she seems to breathe heavier than she used to. A light purr comes from her side of the bed—which is also half my side. Just after we broke up, I was convinced that as soon as Leigh moved to the other coast, some lucky woman without any desire for children would snap her up and never let her go. How could that not happen? Turns out Leigh didn't allow herself to be snapped up. The other day she said that, for her, the years we spent apart could be easily summed up in one word: lonely.

She turns on her back and shoves her hand into my shoulder in the process. Maybe in a few years a gesture like that will irritate the hell out of me, but now, on the cusp of our second life together, it only makes me smile. I take her hand in mine. I don't want to spend our last night together asleep. I start stroking her palm, realizing that we are too old to pull an all-nighter, but I don't care. I want to look into her big brown eyes. I want to make plans for our future again. Real plans.

"Can't sleep?" she says when she opens her eyes.

"It's not easy with someone like you in my bed." I give her a mock sigh.

"Because I'm too sexy?" Her lips curve into a crooked grin. Her cheeks are slack with the remnants of sleep. She looks so relaxed, so completely where she needs to be.

"Because you take up too much room."

"Would you like me to sleep on the sofa?" Her hand is stroking my belly, but she knows I don't want to do what she's thinking of because of Rosie sleeping in the other room. Not an issue I ever had with Suzy—because Suzy never made me scream the way Leigh does.

I curve my arm around her back to let her know she's not going anywhere until she has to leave for the airport tomorrow.

"Remember when you lay here with me one night and you proclaimed you'd become D.A. one day?"

"I said that? No way." Her hand keeps flitting along the sensitive skin of my belly and my C-section scar.

"That was before you got dollar signs in your eyes and joined Schmidt & Burke. When I still believed you were idealistic like me." I let a finger skate along her cheek.

"I was never idealistic like you. Never to the same degree, anyway."

"Perhaps we would never have met if you hadn't worked for the D.A.'s office. Or I would have been put off by your criminal defense lawyer ways if we'd met later."

"Too many 'ifs' for this hour of the night, Jodie."

"What happened to the Leigh who could stay up until morning and dream with me?" My finger has reached her hair. I've spotted some gray ones above her ears, but I haven't told her yet.

"She's tired." In the semi-darkness, I see Leigh's eyes sparkle nonetheless. "But I'll tell you this, just so you'll never forget." She inches a little closer. "You and I were destined to meet, I'm sure of it. And, no, I don't care if that sounds too sentimental for the sane people we consider ourselves to be. Only a few days ago, I believe, I heard someone talk about sentimentality and such." She chuckles. "A wise woman, I seem to remember, considering her age and so on."

I dig my fingertips into Leigh's scalp. "I guess it would be equally foolish to consider whether we're going too fast?"

Leigh pushes herself up a bit, her hand falling away from my belly in the process. She looks fully awake now. "It's not foolish at all, but, like you, I just… know. I know that I want to be here with you. Being anywhere else right now would make me more miserable than I've been in the past eleven years combined."

"I'm not having any seconds thoughts, either." I scoot closer and wait for her to kiss me.

"We should get some sleep though, Jodes," Leigh says after.

"Fine." I crash down and turn on my side, my back to her. "Spoon me, please. And don't fall asleep before I do."

Leigh folds her tall body around mine and whispers, "You know what happens when you're too bossy for your own good." She's asleep within minutes.

I still can't sleep, not even with Leigh's arm resting on me, with her breath in my ear. Or, perhaps because of it. The short conversation we just had about her becoming D.A. reminds me of the day she got hired at Schmidt & Burke.

"I solemnly swear to you, Jodie Whitehouse, that it will become Schmidt, Burke & Sterling within the next ten years," she'd proclaimed. By then, I had seen Leigh in various states of ecstasy, but never when her job was involved. Pure happiness seemed to radiate from her skin, and I absorbed it gladly. I wanted nothing more than for Leigh to be happy, for her to get everything she wanted in life. She'd had to go for several interviews before they finally offered her a contract, and I had supported her every step of the way.

I'd even considered it a privilege to see Leigh with her confidence frayed at the edges—she was never one to totally crack—and to see her fidget with her fingers uncontrollably, her eyes going all dark and serious.

"I hadn't pegged you for the nervously pacing type," I said, the night before her last interview. "It's in the bag already, surely. I'm certain all you'll need to do at this point is manage to hold a pen in your restless fingers long enough to sign on the dotted line."

"This is no joke, Jodes," she said in her formal court voice. "I've wanted this for a long time."

I guess I could see it then, on full display, how blind desire can make a person behave. How having eyes on the prize can chip away at their common sense.

Although Leigh had made it clear from the very beginning that she wouldn't be a career ADA, she had consulted me extensively before finding the law firm she wanted to join and getting to work on accomplishing that goal.

"You're an inextricable part of my life now, Jodie," she had said, "I need to know how you feel about this."

By then I had worked for the ACS for more than five years and I had seen many an excellent ADA join law firms. It always made me a little sad because it meant that the private sector would, once again, gain what the state was losing in experience. I didn't object, of course. If that was all it took to fulfill Leigh's deepest wishes, she could become the slickest lawyer she needed to be, put in the required hours to make her name partner ambitions clear, and attend after work drinks to suck up to people who were silly enough to need it. Leigh always had my support. Between the two of us, Gerald, a string of regular babysitters, and Muriel and Francine, we had Troy's wellbeing more than covered.

Most of that blind ambition has gone now. She got what she wanted—and life has changed her.

Carefully, I extract myself from her grasp and watch how she rolls onto her back. I'm ready to start again with this new, mature, wiser version of Leigh Sterling.

CHAPTER TWENTY-SEVEN

"Your house is so big, but you hardly have any stuff," Jodie says.

"I've gotten rid of a lot of things already." It strikes me that I brought zero lovers to this place. I invited one woman back once, but I had to ask her to leave before we could actually become lovers because I'd totally misread her and she tried to shove *me* against the wall.

"All the sex toys you used with other women, you mean?" Jodie stands by the window, looking out. The things I want to do to her in this house.

"I told you. I had one semi-serious relationship and I screwed that one up as well."

"Was she"—Jodie turns around, curling her fingers around the edge of the window sill—"kinky like me?"

Jodie seems to be suffering from the same affliction as me: irrational jealousy of ex-partners. "Oh yes," I tease because Karen might have been the right amount of kinky for me, but it was never the same as with Jodie.

"Did you… do things with her that you didn't do with me?" She sinks her teeth into her bottom lip and that's how I know this is foreplay. So much for both being the jealous type.

I discard the box I'm filling and walk over to her. She's already positioned perfectly in front of the window. I stop a few feet away from her and look her in the eyes. "I did." It's not true, but it doesn't matter.

"Do it to me."

Blood rushes to my clit. Since our reunion, I've let Jodie fuck me a lot more times than when we were first together—as though I've been in a constant, unquenchable state of arousal. As though merely dominating Jodie isn't enough anymore.

"I let her tie me up and fuck me any way she wanted to," I say.

Jodie narrows her eyes. She doesn't believe me. That too doesn't matter. If I tell her to fuck me, she will.

"Any way she wanted to?" Her voice quivers.

I fold my arms over my chest. "Yes."

"With your hands tied up?"

I nod.

"Do… you want me to do that you?" Jodie understands that this would not be a matter of reversing roles, and that, throughout, I would be in full control.

"Yes." I keep my voice steady, but lust rages in my blood.

"Now?" Her fingers hold on to the ledge a bit tighter.

I nod again.

Jodie sucks her lip into her mouth. It turns me on more. I don't crave to have my hands immobilized, but I do want to see what tying me up would do to her. I want to see the look in her eyes when she loops a belt around my wrists.

"Come here," she says, and I bridge the gap between us.

Her hands go straight for my belt and when she unbuckles it, liquid lust pools between my legs. She tugs the belt from the loops of my jeans and inspects it. She might not have laid her eyes on it many times, but she sure has felt it crack against her ass on numerous occasions already. Last night, for instance, when she arrived at my house. She'd said she wanted to see it before I left for good and promptly booked a ticket to San Francisco. That particular belt and Jodie's behind became intimately acquainted all of last night. She barely got a chance to see the house.

She unbuttons my jeans next. "You do the rest," she instructs, in a voice more sure of itself than I had anticipated.

Methodically, I take off my clothes, and just to grate on her nerves a little, let them fall to the floor.

"Sit on the window sill with your arms stretched above your head." Jodie moves away from the window. It looks out over a bunch of backyard bushes and I know that, disappointingly, nobody will be able to see.

Once I've found my position, Jodie looks me over for a second, and I can see the excitement glitter in her glance. It matches the thrills chasing up my own spine. I hike my knees up and spread wide for her without her having to ask—my own little triumph at this moment.

She proceeds to fasten my wrists to the handle of the window. They're not tied very securely, but it's the thought that matters most. Jodie has never seen me like this. I've never been in this position. The newness of the situation sets something off in my blood, and I need to swallow the words 'fuck me now' because they have no place in this scenario.

Jodie hoists her t-shirt over her head and stands before me in her bra and jeans. My clit stands to attention more. My nipples are so hard they almost hurt.

"Let's see how many fingers Leigh Sterling can take," Jodie says, and the way she pronounces the words, without a trace of doubt in their tone, makes my head spin. She doesn't bring her fingers to my pussy lips, though, but instead circles one around my clit—something I hardly ever do to her. "You'd better not come," she groans, and I can tell that, now that she's touching me, she has trouble controlling herself. How wet she must be. The prospect of touching her cunt later brings me another few seconds closer to climax.

"Because I haven't fucked you yet." She keeps trailing her finger around my clit, and I make a mental note to commend her on her torture technique later, but right now, I need to wriggle my ass and hold on to something inside myself in order not to come at Jodie's finger.

"How many do you think, Leigh?" she asks. "Three? Four?" Her finger halts its motion. "All five?"

Admittedly, I have to swallow hard at these questions. It could be that I overplayed my hand. Speaking of hand... Jodie's hand is now lowering itself between my legs. Her fingers lightly skate over my drenched lips. I look down at her hand and my pussy, but I don't have a lot of room to maneuver so I can't make out how many fingers she's actually planning on fucking me with.

I don't reply to her question because I realize that the biggest thrill lies in leaving it up to her. How far will she go? Can she even do this? Jodie has fucked me before, of course, but never like this. And never with more than three fingers.

"Let's start with two and work our way up, shall we?" Jodie looks astoundingly gorgeous in the moment that she says it. The light illuminates her face and brings out the green in her eyes. And those lips that always go a bit crooked when she speaks. I wouldn't mind those on my clit later... Two fingers inside of me stop my thought process. Jodie is gentle, but with her other hand, she finds my breast and pinches my nipple.

I'm so aroused I could probably come after a few more strokes, but I know the rules of this game better than anyone.

Jodie increases the rhythm of her fingers and I wrap mine around the belt tightly. She doesn't say she's adding a third finger, but I certainly feel how she spreads me wider. She doesn't give me a lot of time to adjust, either, and amps up the speed with which she's fucking me again. I'm starting to unravel. It begins somewhere beneath my ribs and soon seizes my muscles.

"Jodie, I—" I can't take it anymore, I want to say, but the words die in my throat and the grin Jodie shoots me saturates my flesh with another bout of lust and the thrill of coming for her like this, hands tied, surprises me with its strength.

Jodie's fingers retreat and she holds two of them up to me. They're wet with my juices. "I lied," she says. "I only used two."

I burst out in giggles while she unties the belt. Once my arms are free I pull her toward me. "I'll have you for this."

"I was hoping you would." Jodie pushes herself back and glares at me.

"Very well." I hop off the window sill and tell her to take off her jeans and take my place.

I don't bother with tying her up. I only have eyes for what lies between her legs. Her pussy is soaked, her lips puffy and a deep red, her clit so swollen she'll probably come with just one flick of my tongue against it. And I can't help myself. I need to taste her. When I kneel in front of her, I think that not everything has to stay the same. We're not the same people anymore in so many more ways than I had first believed.

Jodie's hands are in my hair as I let my tongue touch down on her lips first, trailing between them, and then I feast on her clit. I suck it between my lips and flick my tongue against it while my nose inhales everything of her.

"Oh, Jesus." Jodie's fingers tug at my hair. Her heels dig into my shoulders.

I lick Jodie in a way that I hardly ever do: gentle, deliberate, not withholding anything. Soon her thighs are clasped against my ears and she expels a high-pitched roar.

When I push myself free from the grip of her thighs and look at her, she's snickering with her back pressed against the window.

"What?" I ask.

"That was certainly different." She hoists me toward her.

"Wouldn't want you to get bored." I'm still a little ambivalent about what just happened.

"Bored?" She presses a kiss onto my forehead. "Did you really let your ex fuck you like that?" There's insecurity in her voice.

"Of course not." My mouth is pushed against her shoulder.

"I knew that." She grabs me by the shoulders so she can look at my face. "I did."

I nod. We'll continue this conversation later—probably in a similar situation and without words. "If you want me all settled in before Muriel's engagement party, we'd better get a move on. I thought you came here to help me pack."

"Oh, I can pack as well if you want me to," Jodie says, a wide grin on her face.

"Don't push it." I fall back into her arms and kiss her.

As soon as I came back from that first weekend in New York with Jodie I started dropping hints at the office about moving back East.

"We could use your expertise to expand the Boston office," Steve said at first.

"No," I replied. "I'm needed in New York."

CHAPTER TWENTY-EIGHT

Rosie's a flower girl at Muriel and Francine's wedding. She walks down the aisle with the biggest look of concentration on her face.

Don't cry, don't cry, don't cry, I tell myself. She has experienced a growth spurt of late and I can't help but wonder if in a few years' time both my children will tower over me. Leigh sits on my right and Troy on my left. He's almost finished with his first year of Law in Boston, which is only a four-hour drive away so I get to see more of him.

With the money from the sale of her house in San Francisco Leigh bought a townhouse on the same street as Gerald.

"Imagine that," I said. "Next you'll be having dinner parties together."

"He's not too bad, I guess," Leigh said when we celebrated after we'd signed the deeds. I'd protested at first, of course. My financial independence, however difficult it has proved over the years, has always been a point of pride for me.

"Don't be so Irish, Jodie," Leigh said. "Your name needs to be on this title. It's the only sane thing to do." I knew she was right. If I was finally going to give up my apartment on York Avenue, I did want my name on the papers. "This is our house."

"What's with all the sniffling, babe," she whispers in my ear now. "Are you going through *the change?*" I know she's only saying that to make me laugh—and make me snap out of this emotional haze—but I've actually wondered the same thing lately.

"Shut up. I need to focus." But I well up again as I see first Muriel and then Francine strut toward the front. Muriel is beaming, a bright smile plastered on her face, and she winks at me when she passes and turns to take her spot for the ceremony.

Leigh doesn't know what I have planned for after this wedding, which I should give my full attention. My best friend doesn't get married every day, after all.

"We're going to *Muriel's wedding*," Leigh has repeatedly said to Rosie over the past few days, but the joke was always completely lost on the girl. She has no interest in Australian movies from the early nineties. Leigh, on the other hand, convinced me to watch the film with her. We have a TV set in our bedroom now. What we watch most on it, when we have the house to ourselves, is a video Leigh made of me while I penetrate myself with a dildo for her. She says nothing has ever made her come as hard as fucking while that video is on.

I didn't realize until a few weeks ago that being a maid of honor is really only an honorary title. At least when it comes to this wedding.

"I don't want no attention on you," Muriel said when I asked her about my duties. "It's bad enough I have to share the bridal spotlight with Francine. Just organize me a bachelorette party and that'll be that."

I want nothing more than for everyone's gaze to be trained on the happy couple. Rosie's job is done and she rushes to my side. I put a hand on her shoulder. So does Leigh.

The wedding officiant says a few words about both of them and then proceeds to proclaim their union.

"Seriously?" I had asked Muriel when I went wedding gown shopping with her. "White?"

"What else am I going to wear? Red?"

"Cream or beige or that lilac one over there doesn't look half bad."

"Sometimes I wonder if you know me at all." She scrunched her lips into a defiant pout. "I'm having a white wedding." Muriel could never stay serious for very long. "Well, dress-wise at least."

Now, her dark skin contrasts heavily with the white of her dress. Francine looks dapper in a white suit with soft violet accents. If she wanted to wear any other color, I'm certain her wife-to-be set her straight—so to speak—soon enough.

"You have to cry at your own wedding," I said to her last night. "I mean, you won't be able to stop yourself."

"I'm sure you'll do all the crying for me," Muriel said in her typical Muriel way. "I'm from Harlem. We don't cry in Harlem."

"I'm from Connecticut, which is not exactly the state best known for its tear-shedding inhabitants either."

"Do you, Muriel Ilene Williams take Francine Watts to be your lawfully wedded wife?" the officiant asks.

"I do," Muriel says in a loud, booming voice, lest there's someone at the back whose hearing aid is not working. And I see it glitter in the corner of her eye. Or perhaps it's the way the light slants through the window to her right.

Francine says "I do" next, after which they exchange rings, carried by Francine's nephew, James, and the ceremony ends.

"Stay behind for a bit," I say to Leigh after she gets up. My children are in on this and I want them here for this moment. Having them present is important to me.

Rosie stands grinning beside Leigh. Troy, a real man now, with a beard he refused to shave off even for this occasion, shifts his weight from one foot to the other nervously.

"What's going on?" Leigh asks. The place is emptying rapidly.

I feel for the box in my pocket and go down on one knee. Rosie's already squealing with delight.

"Leigh Sterling." I look up at her. "Will you marry me?"

Leigh glares at me, then shifts her gaze to Rosie and then to Troy. Her face breaks into a smile. "I can hardly say no in front of your children, can I?"

I feel the tears coming already. I won't be able to stop them now.

"Yes," she finally says. "A million times yes."

Rosie's jumping up and down. Troy is wringing his hands together. I wonder if he's holding back tears as well, or perhaps he's just embarrassed by his old Mom's antics. But, as far as I'm concerned, almost a year after his graduation from Berkeley, I wouldn't have just proposed to Leigh if it weren't for him.

Leigh pulls me up. "That's why you wanted to wear trousers?" She doesn't wait for a reply and throws her arms around me. Rosie hugs me from the side and from behind Leigh's back, Troy gives me a thumbs-up.

———

"I can't believe you still managed to steal my fucking thunder." Muriel does not look like a blushing bride. "You had the audacity to propose on my wedding day!"

"It... just seemed fitting," I stammer, gauging if she's actually mad —she certainly looks it—or if she's toying with me.

"You could have told me." Her hands are at her sides. "But fuck it, Jodie. Let's just make this party one big love fest." She pulls me into a hug that lasts much longer than our usual ones. "I'm glad you found each other again." When we let go, she peers at me. "I see now that no one else could ever be more perfect for you."

"Will you be my maid of honor, then?"

"Damn right I will be." She pulls her lips into a smirk. "And, no offense, but the bachelorette party I will throw you will not be as tame as that cocktail shaking class you set up." She nods as though very sure of something. "I'm taking you to Atlantic City."

The DJ changes the pace of the music to a slow song and I recognize the intro to "Show Me Heaven".

"For you," Muriel says. "So you can have a mushy dance with your fiancée."

I shoot Muriel a smile and, as I wander over to Leigh, I know that, if this had not happened, if Leigh and I had never seen each other again, my life would still have turned out sort of all right because I have a best friend like Muriel.

"May I have this dance?" I ask, bowing solemnly.

"You may." Out of habit, Leigh puts her hand on the small of my back as she guides me to the dance floor. I drape my arms around her neck and gaze up at her.

"Opening dance at our wedding, I presume?" Leigh quirks up her eyebrows.

"Everything is open to debate."

"Not everything." She slants herself toward me and kisses me lightly on the lips.

Troy wolf whistles at us. He's being a good sport and dancing with Rosie, who really should be in bed by now, but Muriel and Francine are her favorite aunts and her Mom just got engaged.

"How long have you known you were going to ask me today?"

I huff out an embarrassed chuckle. "I guess the idea first dawned on me when Muriel told me she was planning to propose to Francine."

"When was that?" Leigh cocks her head to the side.

"The Monday after you came back to New York for the first time." I push myself a bit closer toward her. "But it didn't... crystallize until a few months later," I say in my defense. "And hey, it beats blurting out that you want to move back to New York after just one night together."

"Fair enough." She leans her forehead against mine. "The real question, however, is how you managed to keep Rosie from telling me?" We both look at her dancing with Troy and she waves at us.

"Oh, I only told her three days ago. I knew from the start that would be a lost cause." We both wave back at Rosie. "I told Troy a few weeks ago when I went to see him in Boston. He finally admitted to arranging that basketball game excuse with his friend. There was a game, but he would never have gone if he had seen there was hostility between us. Then we would have ended up having dinner with him and Gerald."

Leigh shakes her head. "That boy."

Indeed, I think, that boy.

I sneak another peek at my children dancing together while Leigh pulls me closer to her, and the biggest rush of happiness moves through me.

CHAPTER TWENTY-NINE

I t's hard to believe this is actually happening. It's an even further stretch that I agreed to have the wedding here, at Gerald's house in The Hamptons. But, perhaps, we had to come back and do it here —to right a wrong.

I'm rather notorious for my closing arguments in court, often speeches I slave over for hours, writing draft upon draft until they're perfect, but I haven't spent nearly as much time on any of them as I did on getting my vows right for this day.

It's a small group that has gathered here. Our parents. My brother Lex, forty and single. Perhaps he hasn't met his Jodie yet. I should tell him later that he shouldn't despair. Not that I think he does. Sonja. Steve and his third wife. Muriel and Francine. Ginny and Susan and their twins. Gerald and Elisa, whom I really think brings out a different, better side of Jodie's ex-husband. Rosie, of course, who's taking her role as only bridesmaid extremely seriously. And Troy, who, for the very first time, has brought a girl home. Her name is India, even though she's all American. She's studying computer sciences and looks like she spends too much time indoors, but she's sweet and Troy is very affectionate with her.

Jodie's reciting her vows first. She's gearing up for them now. I love her to bits, but I already know she won't make it through them without bursting into tears. She wasn't always like this. She claims to have changed in that department since she had Rosie. I also know that I'll need to read her vows on paper later to fully grasp them.

"Leigh," she starts. She's dressed quite informally for her own wedding. The Jodie I once knew would have been horrified at the idea of getting married in a linen pants suit. But here she stands. Her hair in the wind, eyes blazing. Those purple-painted lips—still the same lipstick—ready to pronounce the words.

After she asked me to marry her, it stung just the tiniest of bits because I had wanted to be the one who asked *her*. But I got over that by the time we left Muriel and Francine's wedding party.

"I decided to ask you to be my wife because, despite the years we spent apart, I've loved you all along. You once said to me that your passion for me eclipsed everything else, and I've always remembered that."

There we go. Her voice is ascending into a higher register already. I teased her about it last night, but she wouldn't have any of it.

"You'd better let me read them now because we both know you won't be able to say them tomorrow, babe," I said.

"I may surprise you," Jodie tried.

"Fine, but just a word of advice: keep it short. It's easier to cry through two or three sentences than through four pages of love declaration. I know how you feel about me already, anyway."

She didn't say anything, but I did notice later that she was huddled over a piece of paper and I might have heard some strike-through noises made by the tip of a pen.

It's not that Jodie's words don't matter to me. They do. But what we have between us is hard to put into words. We can try, but we both know we can't pour our feelings into a string of vows. We've been apart, and we know that's the last thing we want ever again.

Nothing better to tie a couple together than an eleven-year separation.

"My passion for you..." The rest of Jodie's sentence gets swallowed by a sob. I can just make out 'equally' and then she goes silent. Our guests, who are standing around us in a casual set-up, shuffle around nervously a bit, but they're all familiar with Jodie so they know the deal.

"Oh, screw it," she stutters. "I love you, Leigh Sterling. I bloody well love you."

I squeeze her hand and look into her eyes. What does she see through her tears? The woman who left her or the woman who came back? I'm both, of course.

"Leigh," the officiant addresses me, "would you like to recite your vows?"

I most certainly do, I think, and clear my throat.

"Jodie." We decided long ago to not use traditional wedding vows, but to say something straight from the heart, and in our own words, instead. "This love, our love, is one that only comes along once in a lifetime." I curl my fingers around hers a little tighter. "When we met, everything changed. Because how could it not? Never in my life have I met someone more responsible, caring, sensual and with a heart so big it has room for all the foster kids in New York City." Damn, I'm starting to well up a bit too. But someone chuckled when I said 'sensual'—I bet it was Muriel—and it keeps my tears at bay.

"During the time we spent apart, no one even came close to you. No one." I grip her hand a bit tighter still. "Perhaps it's sad that I needed to be away from you, to be removed completely from your life, to see that there's only one woman on this planet for me. It would be ludicrous for me to stand here and to vow that I'll be forever faithful to you because there is not a person in this world who thrills me more than you do. And you know that when I say I only have eyes for you that I mean it." Regardless of my restraining efforts, the first tear slips out of my eye. "I don't believe it's possible to love another human being more than I love you. To fit together better with someone than how we fit together. To reach a level of happiness higher than what we've reached now. I love you, all of you. I love your family. Your children, Troy and Rosie. And I love all of us together."

Jodie is in tears. Perhaps it was a bit much. We still have to get through the 'I do's'. My own cheeks are hardly dry either. I want to give the officiant a hurry-up glare, but I can't keep my eyes off Jodie. The words I just spoke don't convey half of what I feel, but it was never words that tethered us to each other the most. It was only when we started using more words, and the arguments got heavier with them, that we started drifting apart.

The officiant finally proceeds. He must be used to this. All these emotions so blatantly on display. All this joy. I wonder what it does to a person. I hope he's not single.

During my years of loneliness in San Francisco, I never even considered marriage. Not just because it wasn't a legal option then, but because I was as far removed from the prospect as I could be. Now, though, not even a year after seeing Jodie again, I stand here and I say 'I do' with such pride in my voice, I believe it may just erase all the mistakes I made.

When our lips meet for the formal you-may-kiss-the-bride moment, I don't want to let go. Muriel never hesitates to inform us that her wedding night—as are most newlyweds' first nights together—was a big dud. She and Francine both crashed into bed exhausted from the day's events. I vowed to myself that this would not be the case for Jodie and me. It wouldn't suit us. Additionally, we have the hormonal advantage of our reacquaintance, with the accordingly high levels of arousal in our bloodstream.

When we finally break from the kiss, Jodie looks at the small group of people around us, and I follow her gaze. Rosie's smiling and crying at the same time. Troy and India are headed in our direction. So are our parents. It feels strange to be congratulated for my love for Jodie. She crouches down and picks up Rosie, who really is too big to be carried in her mother's arms, and a new rush of warm, all-encompassing love washes over me. I love that girl and there's nothing I wouldn't do for her. She knows it too and is already starting to take advantage of it.

"Come here." I hold out my hands to take Rosie from Jodie. She folds her arms around my neck and puts her head on my shoulder. No words are required. It reminds me of when she and Jodie waved me off at the airport that first time and she threw her little arms around me. What that impromptu hug told me was that everything would be different the second time around. And it has been. Jodie is my wife now. She put a ring on my finger. I know what the next step will be, but I haven't told her yet. First, we must celebrate.

The congratulatory part of the afternoon passes quickly. Jodie's not like Muriel in the sense that she didn't want to invite every distant acquaintance to our wedding.

"I don't want a big fanfare. I just want to be married to you," she said. "But it would be impolite to not at least invite our nearest and dearest."

When Gerald, an excellent neighbor and a surprisingly good cook for someone who works all the time, suggested his beach house as a venue, I guess it resonated with both Jodie and me. As though the only way to come full circle was to hold the ceremony here.

"Are you sure?" Jodie asked, after we'd already agreed.

"I do have one concern," I said. "You've taken your exes there. It might be awkward, what with the memory of them."

"Don't worry about that. I've forgotten all about them." It was just a manner of speaking, of course, because Jodie stayed friendly with Suzy for Rosie's sake. Apparently, Suzy was able to do that—I suppose I admire her a tiny bit for that. I've met her and I guess I can see what drew Jodie to her. But, to my utmost relief, she hasn't become that close a friend that Jodie invited her to our wedding.

Champagne flows freely well into the night. Most of the guests have booked accommodation in the area. This includes Gerald, who gallantly claimed that his house was ours for as long as we needed it.

I also presume he didn't want to stay here on his ex-wife's wedding night.

"How strange," Jodie said, when we arrived here this morning, "that Gerald and I have grown closer since you arrived back into the picture. Who would have thought?"

"Life is strange," I replied enigmatically. And it is.

Jodie's just freed herself from a conversation with her parents. I always got along fine with Don and Eileen Whitehouse, but I guess—just like anyone would—they had their suspicions when I suddenly re-appeared in Jodie's life. She leans with her hip against the sofa and I beckon her over.

She struts over and her gait is not entirely straight. It doesn't matter. I want to tell her now.

"Let's go out back for a minute," I say.

She cocks her head as if to ask 'Really? You want to fuck me now?'

"I need to ask you something important."

"How sneaky to wait until after I've said 'I do'."

She puts her hand in mine and I guide us to the back patio. She leans into me immediately, her lips on my neck.

"I'm serious, Jodes." I let my fingers run through her hair briefly anyway.

"Okay. I'm all ears." She backs away from me a little, but I can still smell her perfume.

"I've been thinking about this for a while..." I gaze into Jodie's green eyes. "I was wondering if you would be willing to consider me adopting Rosie. So she can have two parents."

Jodie's eyes widen. "For real?"

I nod. "I would hardly joke about that." I recall the time Troy called me Mom and my stunted reaction to that. It's certainly not that I suddenly believe that motherhood is my true calling and any life without it is incomplete. "I love Rosie, and I think it would be advantageous to cover all legal bases."

"I'm not saying no, Leigh, but you are springing this on me... and, truth be told, I'm rather tipsy."

"I felt it was important to ask you today."

"All legal bases, huh..."

Perhaps I could have phrased that better. "I don't want you to be the only one she yells at when she reaches the rebellious stages of puberty."

Jodie chuckles. "How about we continue this conversation tomorrow."

"Agreed." I tug her toward me again. "Mrs. Sterling."

She looks up at me. I'm just joking. We're both keeping our names just the way they are. "I honestly have no idea what ever possessed me to take Gerald's name. Back then, it was just the obvious thing to do, I guess, but in hindsight it seems so ludicrous."

I nod my agreement. "Now," I whisper, "I believe I see a wall with your name on it."

"Just kiss me," she says, and I do.

I STILL REMEMBER

Her hair is styled differently now, but her eyes are still the same dark-chocolate brown. They stare at me with the same amazement that buzzes through my unsuspecting bones. Amy Waters. Twenty years ago I loved her with an intensity I didn't understand. I never told her, but looking at her now, at the way the edges of her mouth quirk up, suppressing that distinct pout I dreamed of for months on end, I realise she must have known.

"I have the name Jane Smith here in my appointment book." Amy's eyes quiz me. Or maybe they mock me for the dreariness of my chosen alias. I never was really good at reading her. Too much emotion in the way.

"People tend to freak out when I book under my real name."

"And they don't when you show up?" She bites her lip. There are many reasons why this situation could unsettle her. None can be as nerve-racking as unexpectedly standing eye-to-eye with the girl—a woman now—I silently adored in high school.

"Sure, but then at least I'm present to manage the fuss." I look different in real life than I do on TV. Some call it dressing down, but I'm never more comfortable than in jeans and t-shirt. On the air, my face is covered in layers of make-up and the top half of my body— the only part visible—is styled down to a tee by Jake and Andrew, *The Morning News with Elise Frost*'s wardrobe managers. Sans make-up and in leisure wear, I hardly ever get recognised. This time it's different though. Amy and I, we have history. And I had no way of knowing she owned The Body Spa.

"How long are you in town for?" Is that a tinge of accusation in her tone? Of course, it's my fault we lost touch. We had laid out our plans. That's what best friends do in high school. They think it will be the two of them forever, think that ten years down the line they'll be bridesmaids at each other's wedding. Only, I always knew my future didn't hold the kind of wedding Amy started planning for herself as soon as she turned twelve.

"For the weekend. It's dad's sixtieth." I shuffle my weight around as I try to identify the tumbling feeling in my stomach. So much has changed since we last saw each other a few days after our high school graduation. I barely even thought of Amy the past few years. We're grown-ups now, and as good as strangers. Still, all that was left unsaid between us seems to rush through my mind now.

"How is Ralph?" Amy's voice is still a well of calmness. It always was, even when she leafed through bridal magazines at the age of sixteen and dreamed out loud about marrying Brett. I wonder what happened to her dreams. Does she have the two suburb-required children? Good heavens, did she marry Brett?

I shrug off Amy's question because I don't want to discuss my father. This small talk seems so inappropriate, so lukewarm, so out of sync with my memories of her. "How are you, Amy?" I ask, painting on a smile.

She wears a black spaghetti strap tank top, showing off spectacular collarbones. Her dark curls are pinned up into a bun, but she always had a mane that couldn't be tamed and a few stray ones frame her face. She looks tanned and healthy.

"Twice married, twice divorced." She wiggles her fingers as if she's proud of the fact they hold no rings. "You?"

I can't help but think of Celia and how we left things back in New York. She moved out more than three months ago but the bed still feels empty without her. And didn't I just ask Amy how *she* was doing? I didn't even hint at inquiring about her marital status, but here she is, offering up the information freely, as if it sums up her entire life since we lost touch.

"My love life's a bit of a disaster, but I can't complain about the rest." I smile apologetically. I don't know why I always do that when I refer to my career and how it has skyrocketed over the last few years.

"I watch the news every morning. It was so strange at first, you know. That you were this girl I played hooky with..." She pauses for a moment. "Shared my first cigarette with." The gentle lines on her face crinkle into a melancholic expression before she sends me a wide smile. The Amy smile. The one that always got me. "And gosh, you come across so well on the screen, Eli—" She hesitates again. "Do you still go by Eli?"

No one has called me Eli since Amy. Eli expired the day I left town—and Amy. I shake my head and grin, because I can't help myself.

"Ahum." A girl in white slacks who I hadn't even noticed before clears her throat. I suspect she's my designated massage therapist.

"If you don't mind, Sarita," Amy addresses her. "I'll be taking care of Ms Smith myself."

"Sure." Sarita turns on her heels and leaves the reception area.

"I hope that's all right," Amy is quick to say.

My pulse quickens at the thought of Amy's hands on my body. "Of course." I give her my camera smile—the one that hides everything.

"Please, follow me." She moves from behind the reception counter and leads me to a door on the right. As teenagers, we were always about the same height, but she seems so much taller now. She wears a pair of black linen trousers that flow around her long legs. We walk into a waiting area with low couches and soothing music. "Would you like some tea first?"

"Sure." I nod eagerly. One part of me can't wait to get on Amy's massage table, but at the same time my heart hammers frantically in my chest. I watch her as she pours two cups of tea from a pot next to the kettle. Her movements are graceful and easy, just like I remember.

We'd been swimming in a small pond behind Amy's house. It was cordoned off from their garden by a bunch of pine trees and, as the afternoon progressed, the sun dipped away behind the trees, leaving us with early evening shadows. We were wet from the water and the sky was the colour of summer: blue streaked with soft yellows and dashes of pink I never understood. The colours that would forever remind me of Amy.

It was the height of my crush on her, a few weeks before we'd leave high school forever. All my energy went into trying to keep my eyes off her as she adjusted her bathing suit while we let the last of the heat dry our skin. I tried so hard not to look at her that all I did was stare in the distance.

"What's wrong, Eli?" Amy playfully pinched me in the side, catching me by surprise. I swathed her hand away as if it were a vile mosquito, quickly regretting my impulsive reaction. To mask the turmoil ripping me apart inside, I shot her a quick grin before rolling on top of her and pinning her arms above her head.

I stared down at her, every cell in my body tingling. Her dark eyes smiled up at me and a surge of something I couldn't control swelled inside my gut. I closed my eyes for a second and saw what was going to happen next. I was going to lean down and kiss her. I saw myself do it on the back of my eyelids. I could almost taste her lips and smell beyond the heady mixture of sun and lotion on her skin.

When I opened my eyes, it seemed as if hours had passed, but it was still the same Amy squirming below me on the grass. It was the same pond giving away its summery sparkle to the falling darkness. Amy's eyes were still the same mocha brown and her hair the same shock of wild curls, but I had changed. I'd never come so close and suddenly I realised it was the closest I would ever get.

"Eli?" Amy's voice never really suited her until now. It was always the voice of a grown woman with endless legs, strong hands, and pronounced collarbones.

"Sorry. Miles away." I take the cup of tea she hands me and, awkward as I feel, sip from it immediately. The tea is scalding hot and I burn the tip of my tongue but I don't say anything.

Amy looks at me over the rim of her cup while she, wisely, blows on it to cool the liquid. Her eyes radiate a softness I don't recognise. But we are different people now, even though I feel myself slipping into my teenage skin again—and adoring Amy silently. Me, of the endless chatter on TV, the never-ending banter I've made a career of. A few minutes with Amy and I'm sixteen again.

"Why don't we get on with it." She places her cup on a small table next to the chair she sits in, one leg folded over the other. She looks at me, her eyes almost watery now, and in that one glance I see it. In that instant, I realise she always knew. "I give a mean massage, even if I do say so myself." She erases the moment with a quip and a smile and I don't know what to think.

The words *massage* and *Amy* seem to flash in my mind in big red letters. My brain can't process the two of them together, as if it has neatly shelved any physicality away from the memory of Amy.

This morning when I drove past The Body Spa in my rental car, it just looked like a good place to book a massage. Now, it seems to have become a feverish dream location from puberty. A throwback to a time in my life I remember fondly, but don't revisit very often.

"Sure." I get up and we stand shoulder to shoulder, just like years ago in gym class.

"This way." Was that a tremble in Amy's voice?

Our arms brush together and, despite being fully dressed, it still has an instant impact on the flow of blood in my veins.

"It's only a massage," I tell myself. I treat myself to one every weekend. Usually, I nod off about halfway through to wake up invigorated after. Usually, the person administering the massage is Raj, a man with golden hands whom I'm not attracted to in the slightest.

The situation is quite different today, because, no matter how I twist or turn it—no matter how many years have passed—Amy is still that dark-haired girl who walked to school with me every single day of our senior year. She's a woman now, but twenty years ago, my heart beat in my throat every time she waited for me at the corner of the street. Emotions I deemed erased by life a long time ago, seep back inside my brain as we walk to the therapy room.

And I know what comes next. I'm a massage aficionado and,

usually, I don't even think twice about it. It's second nature to me and massages are simply not a clothed activity.

"You can undress over there." Amy points to a door. "You'll find a towel. Please take everything off."

She might as well have planted a kiss on my lips, that's how flushed I suddenly feel.

Amy's tone is professional though, as is her demeanour. She adjusts the volume of the music in the room. "Do you mind if I put on something a bit unconventional for a place like this?"

I shake my head as she locks her iPhone in the dock without waiting for my reply. I already know what she has in mind.

Legs shaking, I head for the locker room. I close the door and lean my head against it for a brief moment. From the other side of the wood I hear the first notes of 'Round Here'. Amy and I listened to it endlessly the year we turned sixteen. No song could ever be more ours.

Nostalgia washes over me as I slowly undress. I scan myself in the mirror on the wall. A TV job has made me vain enough to hire a personal trainer. For all its shallowness, I take great pleasure in spotting a hint of tricep when I watch myself back on screen. I run a finger over my arm, but can't begin to imagine what it will feel like when it will be Amy's finger. I know that I somehow need to steel myself for what's to come. But it's just me and a towel in a dressing room. And a slew of ragged memories.

I wrap myself in the plush cotton of the towel. It's wide enough to cover me from the top of my breasts to under my knees and long enough to fit snugly around my body. I take a deep breath before stepping back into the therapy room.

Amy waits for me with a big smile, Adam Duritz's voice humming in the background. I may have dreamed of a situation like this twenty years ago—Adam's warm voice and me about to get naked for an eager Amy—but if I did, I forced myself to forget long ago. My brain is busy taking it all in. I'm also nervous and, truth be told, quite turned-on by the sentimental strangeness of it all.

"Please, get comfortable on the table while I wash my hands." Amy turns away from me to give me the privacy I need to settle on the table. I climb on and lie down on my belly while covering my backside with the towel. My face finds the hole at the head of the table and I try to at least pretend I'm relaxed.

My field of vision is limited to a basket of flowers on the floor below me. I can only rely on sound now.

"I prefer not to talk during a session as I feel it hinders relaxation." Amy's words float above my head. I'm fully aware of the nakedness of my skin and I wonder how she sees it. I wonder how this makes her feel. Her footsteps approach. She has taken off her shoes and she's barefoot. She adjusts the towel briefly and the air that flows underneath is enough to instigate a mad pitter-patter in my chest.

Her hands are so close, almost as close as I dreamed they would be when we were teenagers.

All my memories of Amy seem to be bathed in the warm colours of summer. We'd ridden our bikes to a record store a few miles away, a CD-sized plastic bag dangling from both of our handlebars. When we arrived at our spot by the pond in her backyard, she tore the wrapper off the case. The album cover was orange, on it the title *August & Everything After* seemingly scribbled in handwriting. We'd only heard 'Mr. Jones' and 'Round Here' on the radio and had no idea this record would become the soundtrack to our friendship, the notes rousing nostalgia from my soul forever after.

Amy pried the in-lay from the case and unearthed a pen from her bag. Without explanation, she wrote something on the back of the booklet and handed it to me.

It read: 'Amy + Eli Forever'.

She grabbed my copy from my hands and repeated the process, marking both our CDs with what looked like a couple's inscription.

Maybe I should have said something then.

. . .

Amy starts the massage by lightly running her fingertips over my entire body. The motion is quick and over in a flash, but my skin breaks out in goosebumps nonetheless. I need to use all my energy to hold back a sigh. The next thing I feel is the drizzle of warm oil on my back and shoulders. She rubs it on my skin before applying any pressure. I melt into the table the way the lotion does on my skin.

Gradually, her fingers dig deeper into my flesh. Her thumbs press into the muscles surrounding my neck and I think I must be in heaven.

I love a good massage and I treat myself to one as much as I can, but this is something entirely different. I can feel my nipples poke into the soft towel covering the table already and my breath does not come with the relaxed huff-and-puff that I know from massages administered by Raj.

When we were teens, Amy and I spent the majority of our time together, but our relationship wasn't a tactile one. Neither one of us were big on hugs and impulsive displays of affection. We expressed our friendship by always being there and nodding our heads to the drum beat of the Counting Crows. God knows what would have happened if Amy were a hugger.

Amy's fingers wander along my spine and seem to dent my skin permanently. The difference between being touched intimately by someone you care for as opposed to someone whose hands you've simply come to admire is striking. Every touch of her hands on my skin—and I seem to count a hundred per second, but my brain lost processing power a while ago—releases a current of energy in my flesh. I know it's sexual and the pureness of my first bouts of teenage lust bubbles to the surface. Nothing happened between Amy and me then, and I have no reason to assume it will now, but I am Eli again. Beneath Amy's hands, there's no sign of the national TV news anchor. There is only the memory of those very first seeds of long-ing, innocent but oh so present. Then and now.

She stretches her body over mine to reach the small of my back, an area dubbed by Raj as 'my problem zone'. I sit in a chair most of the day. That's how glamorous my life is.

It's as if Amy can sense it—years of experience must have done that to her fingers—and she pushes deeper to undo the knots in my muscles. And I simply can't help but wonder what those fingers must feel like inside. What it would do to me if they slipped. I shut down the thought as quickly as I can, because I can't go there. Although it seems like the perfect place for it, this is no time for thoughts like that. The towel beneath me feels fairly absorbent, but I fear I may slide off in a puddle of my own wetness if I go down that route.

Her fingers knead the flesh of my back and shoulders. Up and down they roam for minutes on end and—despite myself and the feverish thoughts crashing through my brain—I'm about to reach that state of zen-like calm, of shutting off the world and just returning to myself. But then it happens. Her finger brushes against the side of my breast, which protrudes a bit as I lay on my belly.

Amy doesn't apologise, she simply continues, but it feels as if my life has just changed considerably. As if the world has shifted and new possibilities have been born. This happens all the time during massage therapy, of course. The number of times Raj has accidentally brushed his fingers along my breast equals the number of times I haven't cared an iota about it. But the furtive skating of Amy's finger along my skin there feels more like a promise. An opening. Maybe a declaration.

Both of her pinkies glide along on either side now, and I never before realised how sensitive my skin is there. Maybe this is just the way she does her job. Or maybe she has a few buried emotions rising to the surface as well.

Every time her fingers dip a little too low, a flash of heat tumbles through my bones, all the way from my spine to my toes. Goosebumps have made way for hot flashes and then—oh no—an involuntary moan escapes me. I snap my mouth shut as soon as it happens, but it's too late. I've given myself away. I lay there dying a little bit, my face pressed into a hole, my eyes fixed on Amy's toes. Her nails are painted a deep red and—I may be losing my mind by now—it's the most beautiful colour I've ever seen.

But Amy is a true professional and she pretends nothing happened. She must have heard though, her ears are not that far removed from my over-enthusiastic mouth and the volume of the music is high enough to make a point, but low enough to easily fade into the background when not given any attention.

She moves her field of action more to the middle of my back again, with long kneading motions of her hands. She covers a lot of ground and drags the heel of her hand all the way down to the curve of my ass, her fingers slipping briefly underneath the edge of the towel. This expansive movement also causes her belly to sweep against the top of my head every time she stretches forward, which does not help with the hot flashes I seem to be experiencing at regular intervals now. So much so, in fact, that I can't distinguish the flashes anymore from the fire that has started simmering beneath my skin. How long can I hold off the inevitable explosion?

I never officially told Amy I'm a lesbian. She probably read about it in a gossip magazine when it went public a few years ago. Maybe this is her revenge. But we were sixteen back then, and while the knowledge of something being different was always very present within me, I hardly had a clue myself. Twenty years ago the word *lesbian* was not one you heard often. I knew I had a mad crush on Amy and sometimes I simply believed that it was completely normal but just not outspoken, while other times the sheer strength of my feelings for her obliterated any notion of it being different. All I knew was that I loved her and that, in the end, she could never love me the same way.

After a last soft caress of my back, Amy pads to the middle of the table. Without saying a word, she removes the towel. At first, I think she's just adjusting it—that touching me underneath it has made it slip—but she doesn't put it back. That's something Raj never does.

The conditioned air of the room breezes across the skin of my buttocks and a new onslaught of lust rips through me. If this is revenge, or a test, I don't stand a chance. But I don't move and let Amy carry on wordlessly. Adam Duritz launches into 'Anna Begins' and I still know the lyrics by heart so I try to focus on those instead. They're complicated and quick so that works for about thirty seconds, until Amy drizzles oil on the back of my thighs and then, all the way up the burning cheeks of my bum.

Whatever happened to a simple neck massage, I wonder, when her fingers hit my skin. They're soft and warm and I melt again. But this time, after the brushing of her fingers against my breasts and the exposing of my butt, I melt differently, as if the wetness of my centre has spread throughout my body and has liquified every bone beneath my skin.

When her fingers dip a little too low the first time, I have no doubt she knows exactly what she's doing. She still applies pressure to the muscles in my thighs, but it's as if I can sense her focus shifting. She doesn't pay nearly as much attention to the outside of my legs as to the inside, but every time she's on the verge of touching me really inappropriately, she pulls back.

I can hear her inhale and exhale quickly over the music and I try to determine if this is the breath of a woman performing a massage or foreplay.

Then, just when I think I'm about to dissolve in a puddle of my own wetness, her hands move to my calves. Every single one of the cells between my belly button and my knees throbs wildly. A sensation I could probably cope with if this was a stranger venturing into the territory of a massage with a happy ending, but this is Amy Waters, the girl I wrote bad poetry for in high school. The girl who once told me that the two lone freckles on the left of my nose were the cutest thing she ever saw, after which I spent at least two sleepless nights thinking up ways to grow more.

Amy's nails trail along my ankles, but they don't stay there very long. Up they come again, and the closer they get to the massive erogenous zone every inch of skin within an arm's length distance of my bum has become, the more moisture I can feel trickle out of me. Can she see? The room is dimly lit and my face—with cheeks as flushed as a blazing fire—is safely hidden in the hole of the table, but is my excitement visible to her at all?

The answer comes in the shape of her finger tracking the line where my butt becomes thigh. I know enough about massages to realise this is not standard procedure in respected establishments. When her bold finger meets the wetness spreading from between my legs, it doesn't waver. Instead, it dives lower and lingers there, barely moving. Instinctively, I find myself spreading wider. I didn't mean to, but if I try to close my legs now it could be perceived as disapproval and I don't want this to stop.

Amy takes advantage of the better access I offer her and now traces the tip of her finger along my pussy lips. Up and down it goes, skimming my lips, which are swollen and soaked and ready to be parted. Has she ever even touched a woman like this?

Her fingertips continue to play with my pussy non-intrusively, almost tickling, but it's enough to send wave after wave of smouldering heat through my blood. I'm afraid to make a noise that will break the spell she's under. I'm afraid to face the consequences of having her stop now she's gone this far.

Her fingers start probing deeper, sliding between my folds and I inadvertently press myself against them, meeting her lazy strokes. It feels as if my entire body has transformed into a slithering mass of want. I'm close to abandon, close to asking her to please fuck me, when her fingers retreat.

My heart thunders so furiously beneath my rib cage I fear my torso might pulse upwards with every beat.

"Turn around, please," she says as if this is the normal midway point of any massage therapy session. But there's a strain in her voice, a slight tremor informing me she might just be as turned on as I am.

And I want nothing more than to flip over, but then I have to face her. How can I meet her gaze after she has touched me like that? But I'm not the one who started it. I only came here for a massage.

I free my head from the hole and push myself up slowly. Before looking up, I try to swallow away the nerves bunching up in my throat. There are a lot of things I want to say, but I don't want to ruin the moment by speaking.

Amy is fumbling with something at the sink when I finally turn around. She has her back to me and, silently, I lie down and wait for her.

"Close your eyes," she whispers as she approaches.

I do as I'm told.

The process of sprinkling oil on my skin is repeated. A drop crashes down on my erect nipple and I can sense Amy's hesitation before her fingers descend on my flesh and spread the lotion. She stands at the head of the table, her belly close to my scalp again, and I can hear her sharp intake of breath as her fingertip brushes my nipple.

It's different lying on my back, all exposed like that. I try to keep still as Amy's fingers knead my breasts, but it's impossible. She's watching me now. She's seeing the emotions running across my face and the way my skin crinkles into goosebumps as she touches me. I only came to town to celebrate my dad's birthday and I had no way of preparing for this level of intimacy. I decide there and then I have two choices. Shut off my brain and enjoy the physical bliss Amy's hands provide—no matter the emotional fall-out later. Or do as I did years ago. Work myself into a frenzy over how she makes me feel, decide I can't deal with it anymore, and leave.

But this is now, and Amy's hands have already ventured much further than I ever dreamed they would. She's the one who slipped her fingers between my legs and whose nails are now tracing circles around my nipples.

"Oh god," I groan as she pinches my nipple and leaves me with no choice at all.

"Don't move," she says, her voice hoarse and throaty above my head.

And I stay still but I have to open my eyes. I have to see her. Just as our gazes lock, her hands squeeze my breasts.

I could cry for the teenager I was once was. A young body filled to the brim with an inexplicable burgeoning lust for Amy. If time is supposed to heal all wounds, what is it doing now? Coming home is always a fleeting exercise in dredging up the past, no matter who you see or don't see. But then you leave and forget about it all over again, a bit more with every departure. How will I ever leave this behind?

Amy's eyes seem to tell me everything I need to know—in this moment, anyway. Because what really happened to us are the things that didn't happen. The conversation we never had. The feelings I never shared. If this is her way of saying we're okay, then I'm fine with that.

She gives my breasts one last gentle squeeze before abandoning them. Her left hand trails downward along my chest as she walks to the side of the table. She leans her hip against it and I follow her with my eyes. Her face is tanned, but I can easily spot the blush below her cheekbones.

She searches for my eyes again, and arches up her eyebrows a fraction, as if asking for permission. It's a little late for that, I think to myself, but I know what she means. The time for foreplay has ended.

I want what's going to happen next so much, my body breaks out into a shiver. She puts her hand on my belly to calm me down, but it hardly has the required effect. Her fingers already point south, to that moist mess of a pussy of mine.

Shouldn't it have been the other way around, I wonder? Should I not have been the one seducing her? But this role reversal—if you will—turns me on more than the prospect of Amy's fingers inside of me.

It reminds me of hot summer nights alone in my bed. I left the curtains open to see the last of the light fade away, while I dreamed of Amy's face before she kissed me and told me it was all real.

It can't be more real now. Amy's one hand travels lower, while her other one stays on my belly, driving her nails into my skin. I spread wider, because it's all I ever wanted to do for Amy.

Her eyes are on mine when the first fingertip enters me. Something shimmers in the chocolate brown of them. As her finger slips all the way in, I realise it's lust. The same lust shaking my bones.

It's more shock than anything else rattling through me as Amy starts to fuck me slowly, almost leisurely. A hint of a smile plays on her lips, as if this was the only possible outcome of us running into each other the way we have.

All the years of friendship we shared flash through my mind in that moment. The time I almost kissed her. The day we took dozens of pictures at a photo booth, my face drawn into a serious frown in all of them because Amy was sitting on my lap.

But Amy has her finger inside of me and, as she slides it back, I feel the tip of another one getting ready to slip in. And yes, this is sex —unmistakably so—but it's also much more than that. My pelvis bucks upward to meet Amy's thrusts. Her gaze doesn't waver and I feel moisture build behind my eyes. Because this is too much. The essence of what is happening right now has been with me as a fantasy for more than twenty years.

In the silence between two Counting Crows songs, I can make out the sucking noise Amy's fingers produce between my legs. It stokes the fire in my belly even more, and when her other hand starts to travel south as well, her fingers tickling the trimmed hair down there, I'm about to spontaneously combust.

I know she's going for my clit and I know that when she reaches it, I'll be lost. The moment will pass forever. Confusion, nostalgia and years of pent-up lust descend from my mind into my blood.

Amy thrusts deep with the two fingers of her left hand as her right index finger brushes the side of my clit. My muscles contract at the touch of her finger against my swollen bud. I want to pull her close and kiss her, but Amy is calling the shots, and I don't want to break the spell she's under.

She finds a rhythm with her hands. A deep stroke with one hand, while the fingers of the other circle my clit. It's more than enough to send me on my way to the deliverance I've been waiting for what feels like forever.

Amy in her mum's high heels. Amy in boxer shorts and a tank top at her cousin's sleep over. Amy by the pond, careless and with the promise of everything shimmering in the darkness of her eyes. Amy right here, right now. Eyes blazing and fingers on fire inside of me. Her muscles working underneath her skin as she takes me.

I throw my head back because her glance is too much for me to take in that moment when my body surrenders. It all crashes through me, lightning quick fireballs reaching the end of my fingers and my toes at the same time. The walls of my pussy clamping tightly around her fingers. The pleasure that shoots up inside of me through her hands, which are, in the end, mere extensions of her eyes and what I've seen pool in them. I had to wait twenty years and maybe that's why it feels so good, life-changing even, but definitely shattering the world as I know it for a brief instant.

Amy doesn't slide her fingers out of me immediately. She leaves them inside to linger for a few seconds as I find her eyes again. I know that mine are filled with tears of release and a slew of other emotions I don't have the presence of mind to identify.

"Jesus," I say, because, at times like this, it always seems like the only appropriate thing to say.

Amy looks at me in disbelief, her eyes wide and her lips slightly parted. As if she's just slipped back into her skin after an out-of-body experience. Gently, her fingers leave me and I have as much a clue of what to say as she has.

Mute, she stares at her hands and I know, despite being the one naked on a massage table, I have to step in.

My muscles are weak and soft from the massage and the climax, but I pull myself together. "Hey," I say, while I push myself up. I shoot her a reassuring smile. "You really do give a mean massage."

She seems to snap out of her trance and starts looking around the room. I hope for the towel she took off me at the beginning of our session. I'm not sure if it's possible to feel more naked than I am, but I do.

Thankfully, Amy locates the towel on a chair behind her and, instead of simply handing it to me, she steps toward me and wraps it around my bare skin.

"I wish I knew what to say," she whispers in my ear as her arms fold around me.

For all the intimacy we just shared, this unexpected hug touches me more than Amy's fingers inside of me.

In response, I curl my arms around her waist and hold her. I realise this is the first time I've intently touched her this way.

"Whatever it was you wanted to say, you've said it loud and clear." My cheek is pressed against Amy's chest and I can hear her heart hammer away at a ridiculous pace.

I can't help myself, because the next thing I know, my fingers snake down her back, finding the hem of her tank top, wanting desperately to feel the skin underneath.

She gives me one last squeeze before freeing herself from our hug. She doesn't pull completely away though, and in the motion, my fingers wander to her sides. I look up at her and I can't shake the feeling there's something more going on here than two old friends reconnecting in an unexpectedly physical way.

"Eli, I..." she starts. Her fingers play with the white towel that's slung around my body. "I really don't know what came over me."

"I'm not complaining." I slip off the table so I can stand tall and face her properly. The towel starts sliding down, but Amy catches it and fastens it with a tight fold above my breasts.

Again, it's an intimate gesture. There's only one way I know how to acknowledge it. My hands are back on her waist and I pull her close. The short, ragged puffs of her breath travel across my cheeks.

Slowly, I slant my head to the side and lean in for that kiss I should have gone for years ago.

Amy doesn't display any signs of hesitation as our lips meet. I figure it's a little late for doubts after her fingers brought me to orgasm mere minutes ago.

My fingers travel the length of her arms, all the way to her face, where I cup her chin. The towel slips off me anyway—and Amy lets it—but I'm past caring. I'm ready to be naked with Amy again.

Amy's nails trail along the skin of my back as our tongues dance with one another. The kiss seems to freeze time and I have no idea how long we've been at it when we finally break apart.

"We should talk," Amy says, but her breath comes out in chopped puffs and her body language doesn't exactly signal a talking mood.

But I probably need this conversation more than Amy, and I'm dying to hear what she has to say, so I nod before ducking down to grab the towel again.

"That thing obviously does not want to stay on your body," she jokes. "I can see why."

For an instant, I'm flabbergasted, and a flush rises to my cheeks. While I'm still grappling to come up with a response, Amy moves in again and pecks me on my burning cheek. "There's a shower through there." She points to a door behind me. "Take your time. I'll wait for you at reception."

I grab my belongings from the dressing room and head for the shower, all the while wondering if I'm not trapped in a dream. I don't want to wash away the oil Amy rubbed into my skin, but as I do and my hands caress the spots she just did, my mind already wanders to the next step. I'm not leaving town until I've touched Amy the way she has touched me.

After I've put myself together as best as I can, smelling of lavender and satisfaction, I find my way to the reception area. My legs are still a bit shaky and my cheek still tingles where Amy kissed it last. I half-expect reception to not be there and wake up in my old bedroom in my parents' house, sweaty from a passionate dream. But there's Amy, leaning against the reception desk, one ankle crossed over the other. She looks so different from when I first walked in. A lot has changed since then.

"I presume you have a party to go to tonight." Amy's voice is playful, almost seductive.

I remember the reason why I'm in town and all the prying questions on my relationship status I have to look forward to. "Yes. Oh, joy." I check my watch. "But it only starts at seven."

Amy draws her lips into a pensive pout. "Let me check with the boss if I can take the rest of the day off." She tucks her chin in and looks at her own chest. "Great. She agrees." She sends me a wide smile and I'm sixteen again.

We exit The Body Spa together and I wait for her initiative as we stand around on the parking lot in front.

"Did you know I live in my parents' old house now?"

Due to the fact I appear on TV five times a week, Amy probably has a lot more superficial knowledge of me than I of her. I realise I know nothing about her life. "Really?" But, oh gosh, the memories that place holds.

"Yep. Do you still know the way?"

I nod. I could never forget. "See you there in ten minutes."

I step into my rental and notice my hand is shaking when I put the key in the ignition. I'm going to Amy Waters's house. It's the only thought occupying my mind as I drive the route I could take blindfolded—still, after all these years.

I used to ride my bike to Amy's house. An old beat-up BMX I inherited from my older brother. I'd attach cards from a deck to the spokes with clothespins and pretend it was the scooter my parents would never allow me to have.

The Waters house is still in the same spot in the same street, but that's about all that still resembles the memory I have of it. The bricks are no longer red and the roof is flat instead of slated.

I sit staring at the sleek, whitewashed walls of the rectangular shape in front of me, when a knock on my car window wakes me from my daze.

"Coming?" Amy's arched-up eyebrows ask—just like they've always done.

I get out of the car and, apparently, I can't hide the look of bewilderment on my face.

"If this surprises you, wait until you see the inside," Amy teases. But I'm not really interested in the inside of her house—not for now, anyway. I want to go round the back and see if the pond is still there. That pond where we passed hours of our youth just lying around and dreaming out loud of the kind of life I knew I would never lead.

Amy catches my glance and it's as if she can read my mind. "Come on." She curls her fingers around my wrist and drags me to the path circling around the house. "You can admire my flair for interior design later."

My pace quickens as we approach the backyard. To my surprise, not a lot has changed. The pine trees are still there, and so is the pond. I can see its surface flicker through the spaces between the trees.

A rush of tears pricks behind my eyes. I have to breathe in deeply to stop them from crashing through.

"I've spent a fortune redoing the house, but this is still my favourite spot." Amy stands behind me and her voice sounds exactly the same as then, except, everything is different now. I turn around to face her.

"Did you know?" I ask, the words coming out a bit shaken.

Her face mellows into a soft expression foreign to me. Is this how she looked at her husbands when they proposed? How did she regard them when the divorces came through? But I'm no different, not having had a romantic relationship last longer than a few years. I broke my record with Celia, who, in the end, I also successfully managed to chase away. I blame the job. Presenting the morning news doesn't make for a lot of date nights. Or maybe the right woman simply hasn't come along yet.

"How could I not?" Her fingers intertwine with mine. "You were my best friend, Eli. Of course I knew."

My heart beats in my throat. Why did I never say anything? What if our years of friendship turned out to be one big missed opportunity? What if it could have been so much more than me sneaking glances and pining for her secretly?

In my teenage mind, Amy was the cruel one for, supposedly, never being able to return my affections. But in the end, I was the one who left without looking back.

This baggage hangs heavy in the air between us, thick like the remnants of summer clouding the late afternoon.

"I'm sorry for leaving like that." The words tumble out of me like a confession, like something that should have been said ages ago.

"Hey," she yanks my arms up by the wrists and places my hands on her hips, "I always told myself you simply loved me too much to stay." Amy was always the brave, hopeful one. But when she puts it like that, my defences against the tears burning behind my eyes crumble.

"Gosh." Tears stream down my cheeks and I can't wipe them away because Amy is holding my wrists.

"You're here now." Amy leans in and presses her lips against my cheek.

It's the simple truth. I'm here, by Amy's pond and she just kissed me again. I'm no longer Eli the lovesick teenager. I'm Elise Frost, the morning news anchor who caused a riot on a lesbian website when she dared to exchange her signature glasses for a new model.

"I am." Amy's been running this show long enough. Unafraid of whatever happens next, I loosen my wrists from her grip. I bring my hands to her cheeks and draw her near. When our lips meet, the past falls away and I easily shake off whatever's left of my teenage self. We're two grown women and this couldn't be more perfect.

While our lips meet again and again, I trace my fingertips over the skin of her arms until they find the hem of her tank top. I don't just want to get underneath, I want it off of her. I hoist it over her chest and break the kiss to pull the top over her head. I've ogled those collarbones long enough. As gorgeous as they are, I need more.

Heat travels through me at high speed and I do hope there will be time for slow caresses and endless gazing into each other's eyes later, because I can't stop myself now. My actions border on the edge of frantic when I pull the straps of her bra down and scoop a soft breast out of its cup. Feeling its weight in my hand brings me pause, though, and I stop to worship it. My lips are drawn to the dark brown of Amy's nipple and when I taste it, I taste her. I taste afternoons riding our bikes along the high street, looking for excitement. I taste the sun that slanted across the tops of the pine trees when we sunbathed in this very spot. I taste our history.

Amy's hands are in my hair, her fingertips zapping electricity through my scalp. I fall onto my knees and drag her with me onto the grass. It's an unexpected struggle to get her bra off amidst the tangle of limbs we have become, but I want her naked beneath me more than I've wanted anything in my life.

I think about the times I laid down next to her on this indestructible patch of grass, dreaming up the courage to do something about the heat that throbbed under my skin.

Between the mad frenzy of tugging off our clothes and getting our hands on each other's flesh, I see all of my dreams come to life. I see it in Amy's eyes. The same desire I once suffered from, now sizzling between us, years too late but, simultaneously, right on time.

I marvel at the strong muscles gleaming beneath the skin of Amy's thighs as I strip off her trousers. Her legs are tanned, and why wouldn't they be with a backyard like this. Before I rid her of the last piece of clothing—her panties—I make sure I'm as half-dressed as she is and take everything off except my knickers.

Stretching my arms alongside her head, I look down at her, at the desire chasing away any doubt from her face and the ripple of her biceps as she brings her hands to my hair again. I'm beyond words, so I let my mouth crash down on hers and I kiss her.

Amy's elbows lock around my neck and the way she holds me

close to her couldn't express my own emotions better. It's as if I found something I didn't even know was missing, but can never let go of again.

"Do it," she hisses into my ear when our lips break apart for a split second. "Fuck me, Eli."

And maybe it's in the way she pronounces my childhood nickname, or maybe it's the heat coming off her skin mixed with the nostalgic power of our surroundings, but the tears start stinging again. I'm quick to swallow them away and peck a moist path down her shoulder, over her exquisite collarbones, stopping at her breasts. I bend my elbows so my own nipples skate along her stomach. They're hard and stiffen further as they meet the soft skin of her belly. I suck one of her nipples into my mouth and rub my teeth against it.

"Ooh," she moans, and it's enough to set my pussy on fire. My entire body seems to vibrate as I nibble on Amy's nipples. And then the scent of the grass hits my nose and a light breeze rushes over us, making my skin break out in goosebumps, and the picture is complete.

I travel lower, kissing my way along Amy's belly button until my lips reach the hem of her panties. My tongue slips under briefly and already her muscles contract. I take the hour of foreplay she experienced when she fucked me on her massage table into consideration, and proceed. I place a trail of light kisses on the panel of her panties, before pulling it aside and exposing her pussy to the air. Then a whole new perfume hits my nose, pure arousal blending with the promise of a beautiful late summer night.

I look at her puffy, shiny lips. At how pink and perfect they are, and how wet they are for me, but before I threaten to get overemotional again, I press my mouth to her pussy and inhale.

"Oh god, yes." Amy breathes heavily, twining her fingers through my hair.

I push myself up and, while removing her panties from her legs, find her gaze. I remember how she hardly blinked earlier that afternoon as her fingers meandered towards my pussy. We have a lot to talk about. Later.

After positioning myself comfortably between her legs, my arms cradling her hips for support, I lick Amy Waters's pussy for the first time. I believe it must affect me much more than her, despite the fact that, the instant my tongue connects, her pelvis shoots up and her nails may leave permanent scratch marks on my scalp.

I trail my tongue all the way along her lips and let it circle around her clit. Every time I repeat the action, my tongue burrows a bit deeper between her folds and I taste her musky, heady perfume.

"Eli," I hear her murmur, and I'm so lost in the trance licking her puts me in, she has to grab me by the hair to get my attention.

"What?" I scan her face for signs of pain or discomfort, but a big grin awaits.

"Straddle me, please. I need to taste you."

I begin to think I know exactly what went wrong in Amy's two marriages, providing they involved the opposite sex. The way she fucked me so assuredly earlier and now this question are hardly signs of someone new to the lesbian lifestyle. I'm also beginning to wonder how much of my life I wasted by leaving Amy behind twenty years ago.

Happily, I oblige. I slip out of my soaked underwear and crawl up to her.

"Are you sure?" I ask, more to tease than to know, because I recognise certainty when I see it and it's staring right back at me.

In response, she pulls me on top of her and there I sit, my legs wide above Amy's mouth, hers spread in front of me. Never in my wildest dreams, I think, before lowering myself, my knees sinking into the grass of our youth.

When her tongue grazes against my lips the first time, I nearly crash through my elbows. My nipples press into Amy's belly as I position my mouth over her pussy. When she sucks my clit into her mouth, white heat crackles through my skull and I all but lose it again.

I have Amy's pussy to attend to, though, and this is not an opportunity I want to waste. I'm in no position to add fingers to the mix, so I put all my effort into licking her. Every time Amy sucks my lips or clit into her mouth, I do the same, until my brain reaches the point at which it can't compute anymore. Amy's tongue flicks my clit, while my own face is buried between her legs, breathing her in, lapping at her essence. And then it's too much again.

I come. My knees shuddering against her shoulders, and I could scold myself for my lack of self-control, because I certainly haven't given as good as I have gotten yet, but really, who could blame me for that?

I regroup quickly, because it's also a little bit a matter of pride, me being the out and proud lesbian in this alfresco sixty-nine position. I launch a fresh onslaught of licks on her clit, because she can't be that far off. I trill my tongue against her swollen bud and I feel her fingertips scrape my buttocks.

"Yes," she says and it spurs me on. Her body trembles underneath mine, her nipples hard pebbles against my stomach. "Oh god." And I sense the climax making its way through her body, pulsing through her muscles, but I only stop licking when she gives me a light pat on the backside.

I topple off her onto the grass and I can feel a fit of giggles build inside of me. This is what it came down to? A quick rumble by the pond?

"Come here," she says, and opens her arms as wide as her legs earlier.

I nestle in the crook of her elbow, and we both lie in silence for a while, waiting for our breath to steady and for our brain to find the words. Amy speaks first.

"I do hope for your sake none of my neighbours have zoom lenses on their cameras."

In any other circumstance, a blind panic would have rushed through me at the mention of nosy neighbours, but not when I'm in Amy's arms.

"No one recognises me without my glasses and fancy tops on, anyway."

"I did." Amy draws me closer, and a million questions race through my mind, but, perhaps because of the early-evening sun dipping lower behind the trees, I'm all of a sudden very aware of the reason for my visit and how I might not make it to my father's big birthday party on time and in a presentable way.

"I don't suppose you want to be my date tonight?" Reluctantly, I wrestle myself free from Amy's embrace.

She pulls me back in. "Don't we have some lesbian processing to do first?" Her hands shoot up my back and, instantly, set my skin on fire again.

"Not the kind you have in mind right now." I smile against her neck. "I have to go."

"Will you come back after?" I revel in the obvious tension in Amy's biceps, a big indicator she doesn't want me to go.

"I don't have to tell you what the Frosts are like, do I? It might be a late one."

"As long as you don't leave town without a word of warning." Amy's voice is a whisper, barely able to be heard above the rustle of the wind.

That's exactly what I did years ago. One day, I simply couldn't take it anymore. I couldn't be witness to Amy and Brett's blossoming romance one minute longer. So I left. It was as much self-preservation as it was cowardice, because I failed to say goodbye.

"I promise." This conversation should not take place while we're both naked in Amy's backyard. "I really have to go now."

As I scramble for my clothes, sadness overtakes me. What if twenty years is not enough to forget the hurt I've caused her? What is this, anyway? Because, I may want to bring Amy breakfast in bed tomorrow morning, but as far as I know she's still a twice-divorced heterosexual woman—and nothing has changed at all, except for the few grey hairs sprouting from my scalp and the deepening laughter lines Joe, my make-up guy, always makes fun of.

Amy watches me leave. She's still naked, not making any effort to cover herself up. I bend down to kiss her on the forehead—and to commit the scent of this afternoon to memory.

It was the beginning of summer after our high school graduation. Amy and I both knew we'd be going our separate ways at the end of it, each to colleges miles away from one another. But we had one last summer of lounging by the pond, talking about boys—in Amy's case —and trying to muster up the courage to tell her how much I loved her—on my part. We had big plans to visit each other during breaks, and the Christmas reunions we'd stage would be epic.

Because I couldn't bring myself to tell her, I felt more like a fraud every day. One afternoon, something inside me broke. I was sitting by the edge of the water, eyeing Amy as she ducked above and below the surface. When she pulled herself out, a million water drops clinging to her skin and reflecting the summer sun, the vision I had of her was too much.

No one knew how I felt, and I couldn't tell my best friend. Insecurity, teenage hormones and the overwhelming sense of not having a clue as to who or what I was, knotted into a ball in the pit of my stomach. It sat there growing every time I looked at Amy. And I looked at Amy a lot those days.

"Brett's bringing his friend Paul tonight. You know, the handsome one from basketball." Amy plunged herself down next to me, spraying my skin with water drops. "Surely, he must be good-looking enough for you, Eli."

I resented the fact that she just didn't see. That she felt the need to set me up with boys I wasn't even remotely interested in. That she assumed I was just like her. At the same time, I knew it was wrong to feel that way. And I wanted her so much. I wanted to kiss her and tell her to forget about Brett and Paul. We spent all of our time together and we got along so well. Why was that not enough?

But I knew it didn't work that way.

"I have to go." I started getting up, for once almost more repulsed by Amy's half-naked body than turned-on.

"Now? Why?" Amy arched up her eyebrows. "You are coming tonight, aren't you?"

"I'll see." Suddenly, I couldn't get out of there fast enough. "I'll let you know," I said more to myself than to her, as I made my way out of Amy's yard.

When I arrived home I told my parents I had changed my mind and did want to enrol in the summer school programme my college offered. They'd been keen for me to attend, and shipped me off a week later. Six weeks before I was supposed to. I saw Amy one more time before I left.

Throughout my dad's birthday party, my mind is on Amy. On how her fingers dipped so eagerly between my legs during the massage, and how, despite the undeniable intimacy we shared, everything else has been left unspoken.

I have to skip town early enough the next day to make it to the newsroom on Monday. I feel as if time is slipping away from me again, just like it did that last summer. The same kind of pressure builds in my gut, and by the time the party ends, I'm torn. It would be so easy to sneak off the next day, and pretend it never happened. To not have to face any consequences and just move on.

But I saw the fire in Amy's eyes—a fire I might have been too young to see when we were teenagers, if it was there at all. I've felt her fingers inside of me and her tongue between my legs. And how can I possibly run away from that, no matter what she has to say?

Instead of going to bed after the last guests have left, I borrow my mother's bike, because I'm too tipsy to drive a car, and cycle to Amy's house.

It's late and the air has cooled off, but an alcohol blush burns on my face and I have the memory of my afternoon with Amy to keep me warm.

When I arrive at Amy's house, everything is quiet and dark. For an instant, I wonder if it's appropriate to disturb her night rest, but I tell myself she'd want me to. I park my bike against a bunch of low shrubbery and, not wanting to ring a loud and intrusive doorbell, go round the back.

As I approach I hear a crackling noise I quickly identify as fire. To my surprise, Amy lounges in a deck chair, wrapped in a quilt, by an iron fire pit I hadn't noticed before—understandably, as earlier I was suffering from a severe case of tunnel vision.

"I was hoping you'd show up," she says as if she's been expecting me. "This time." There's no malice in her voice, only a playfulness and maybe a hint of hope. She looks up at me, a small smile tugging at the corners of her mouth. "I couldn't sleep."

A bit wobbly with too much wine in my blood, I crouch beside her. "I know an excellent remedy for that."

Amy's eyes sparkle in the light of the flames. She circles her fingers around my wrist again, and I'm glad for the extra support.

"This is all terribly romantic, isn't it?" I quip, because I have a lot of things I want to say but I don't really know where to begin.

"Let's go inside, anyway." Her fingertips already scorch my skin and I'd follow her anywhere. This time, I would.

The day I said goodbye to Amy without her knowing was an ordinary Wednesday. I was leaving for summer school the next Monday, but Amy was joining her family on a road trip to the coast the day after and wouldn't be back before I left.

We sat in the kitchen at my house, eating scones my auntie Ella had brought over. Amy loved scones, mostly because no one in her family knew how to make them properly. A big dollop of cream stuck to her nose, but I didn't tell her because it looked so adorable. I believed that if I remembered her face like that, more goofy than sexy, I'd get over her quicker.

For Amy, the summer still seemed to stretch itself out endlessly.

A few weeks of no responsibilities and expectations had that effect. I sat there, looking at her and the cream on her nose, and the thought of leaving her behind made all the words die in my throat.

I let her rattle on about another party she was planning next week when she got back. I'd have to bring scones—preferably the ones my mother made—and everyone had to wear a white t-shirt, but I shouldn't forget to bring my bathing suit. And could I possibly get my hands on some beer?

I just nodded and watched her being Amy, cringing every time she mentioned Brett, and even more so when Paul's name came up.

At a bit past four—I remember because we had an old cuckoo clock in the kitchen that had just chimed four times—she got up because she had to take her little brother candy shopping for the road trip.

We didn't hug, because we weren't that type of people. Just a quick wave, and she was gone, out of the kitchen, our house, and my life.

I stayed glued to my chair until my mother came home from work an hour later, debating if I should go over that night to say something. But I knew I couldn't do that because I couldn't possibly face the accompanying questions.

I should have, but I couldn't.

"I should have told you," I say as I stand in Amy's kitchen. It's a dimly lit, stark white, handleless cupboards affair with lots of stainless steel and a host of Smeg appliances lining the countertops.

"I can't disagree." Amy leans against the fridge, out of which she has taken two beers. She hands me one—as if I need more booze. "But I understand why you didn't."

"Look, um, Amy…" I start to stutter. "I can't help but wonder if you, um, you know…"

"You couldn't ask me then, and you still can't ask me now." Amy's fingers hug the neck of her beer bottle. I stare at her hands because I can't look her in the eyes. She steps closer, puts her bottle on the counter, and lifts my chin up with one finger. "Ask me, Eli."

It reminds me of how she begged me to fuck her earlier today. I didn't hesitate then.

"Are you…" I begin. Her eyes are on me, just like they were when she slipped her fingers inside of me, and I suddenly realise I'm about to ask the most redundant question ever. So, I kiss her instead. I trail my lips from her mouth to her ear. "If you're not into women, I'm not either," I say.

"My sexuality is very fluid," she whispers back. "Always has been."

I snicker at the cliché. "You could have said." My lips descend to the hollow of her neck.

"I had no idea back then, Eli. Don't you think I would have told you otherwise?"

"To sum things up." My eyes have caught sight of the swell of her breasts. "I knew but I didn't say and you didn't know, but you would have said."

"Whatever you say, Eli." Amy's hands tug at my jacket. "All I know is that when you came into my spa, my heart started beating like mad and I wanted to tear your clothes off."

She's doing a good job of that now. Her fingers start unbuttoning my blouse, while my own hoist up her sweater.

"Good thing you're in the right profession for that then." After I pull her top over her head, our eyes meet. I see something shimmer in them, and I don't know if it's regret or promise, infatuation or pure lust, but it doesn't matter. We're Amy and Eli and we spent endless summers in this house. We ate dinner in this kitchen, which doesn't remind me at all of the kitchen of our youth, and I push Amy against her fancy Smeg refrigerator and flip open her jeans. And nothing could feel more right, more full-circle than this.

My hand moves quickly under the waistband of her panties and she's so wet it astounds me, but I don't let that deter me, because I realise I haven't done what she's asked me yet. I haven't fucked her yet.

"Stay," she mumbles in my ear, when I slip a trembling finger in between her hot, moist folds. "Not for the night, but for a week, or a month. Don't go, Eli. Please."

And as her words transform into throaty groans, I know I won't be going anywhere soon. As I fuck Amy, at last, there's nothing else I want to do but stay with her. The walls of her pussy clutch around my fingers and I dig deep, as deep as I can, as if the deeper I go, the more it will make up for lost time.

When I look at her, her eyes are already starting to glaze over. Maybe she's waited for this as long as I have.

"Yes," I say. "I'll stay." In the back of my mind, all the arrangements I have to make start rearing their head, but I ignore them easily, because, at my fingertips, a miracle is about to happen. I can sense Amy is about to come already, that her body has been on the brink all day from fondling me—and seeing me again. And I feel heat rise through my own flesh before it pools between my legs. I'm with Amy—I feel what she feels—when her knees buckle and an incredulous look takes over her face. And I can hardly believe it either, but it's happening right in front of me—to me, to us.

"Oh fuck," she says, and I swear I can feel my own pussy unclench as she lets loose on me. As she bangs the back of her head against the door of her refrigerator and the climax roars through her muscles.

I stare at the delicate skin of her neck while Amy catches her breath—my fingers still inside and her head still tilted back—and a knot I had long ago deemed not there anymore fizzles away to nothing in the pit of my stomach. When I exhale, it's not only used-up air that gets expelled from my body, but years of repressed feelings and, from the corner of my eyes, a few tears of relief and pure happiness.

Gently, I slide my fingers out of Amy and I press myself against her, finding her neck with my lips. After I've kissed a path to her ear, I whisper, "What will we do when I stay?"

I feel her body contract against me when she giggles. "I'll teach you how to give the perfect massage." Amy's voice is low and husky, and I might be bone-tired and drunk—my head swimming from too much booze and finally sinking my fingers into Amy—but this night is not over yet.

* * *

After calling my producer at the network to lie about a family emergency and claiming I need a week off, I head back to the bedroom where Amy still lounges.

She arches up her eyebrows when I walk through the door, her face lit up by the sun because there was no time to close the curtains last night.

"We have seven days to figure this out." I have no idea what I mean when I say it, but the prospect of spending a week with Amy makes me want to burst out of my skin.

Amy's quizzical expression transforms into a wide smile. She extends her arm and I grip her wrist so she can pull me back into bed with her.

"Who knew," she says as she draws me on top of her, "that it could be so easy to make you stay?"

I realise I'd best get used to wisecracks about me leaving town so stealthily twenty years ago. "Let's go outside." I kiss Amy on the tip of her nose. "I want to swim in the pond like old times."

"Old times, huh?" Amy paints a wicked grin on her face. "You mean lusting after me silently while I pretend I don't notice how you stare when I wear a bikini?"

"Absolutely not." I sink my teeth into the soft flesh of her earlobe. "No bathing suits allowed." I push myself up from the bed and the robe I borrowed from Amy splits open.

Amy eyes me. "I can hardly say no to that." She jumps from under the covers and snatches the fabric off me. Stark naked, we run down the stairs, through the kitchen and into the playground of our youth.

I'm sixteen again when I dip my toes into the water to test the temperature.

. . .

I first felt it when I sat in my familiar spot by the edge of the pond, timing Amy as she tried to swim as fast as she could from one side to the other. My job was to focus on my waterproof watch—something I'd always done with great determination before—but this time around, I couldn't keep my eyes off Amy as her body cut through the water towards me. It was an afternoon of just us, before Brett appeared on the scene and stole precious moments of our time together.

I didn't know what a lesbian was and I had no idea it was even possible for a woman to fall in love with another woman. But when Amy pulled herself out of the water, drops raining down her skin and lingering in her hair, I knew I was in love. I knew because not only did the sun catching the hazelnut in her eyes look like the most beautiful sight in the world, but later that afternoon, when I had to go home for supper, it suddenly hurt that I couldn't spend every waking moment with her.

"You weren't timing me," Amy said, her hands on her hips and, to punish me, she swung her head from left to right so the cool drops of water splattered from her hair onto my hot skin.

"Stop it." I looked up at her, at the grin on her face, which all of a sudden seemed unbearable as well as totally addictive. Because I had no idea how to handle myself, I pushed her back into the water, jumping in right after her, because I didn't want her to swim away from me.

She ducked under and yanked me down by the ankles and, just like that, an innocent game we'd played all of our lives, caused my body to pulse in places I'd never paid much attention to before.

This time, it's Amy who pushes *me* into the water. It's freezing cold, but not for long, as she dives in and wraps her body around me. I feel her pubes rub against my skin and her nails scrape along my back.

"I love this pond so much," Amy says before she kisses me and the world seems to disappear for a moment. "We have so many memories here," she whispers when her lips reach my ear.

She embraces me under water and it hits me, exactly like it did on that afternoon twenty years ago, that I'm in love with her. Maybe I still am or maybe it's just nostalgia mixing with confused memories. Maybe she was the one all along or perhaps she'll always have the same effect on me, either way, I rake my nails over her skin and bury them in the lush flesh of her behind, my body all fired up again. Because Amy in this pond might be the closest I'll come to everything I've ever wanted in my life.

With one hand, I cup her buttocks, while the other travels to her belly. Her legs are spread out in front of me, her body enveloping me, her breath on my neck as her lips nip at my skin. Despite being surrounded by water, I feel how wet she is for me again. There's not a hint of hesitation as my fingers find her opening and I slip and curl them inside. Her body tenses around me, her nails burrowing deeper into my flesh.

"Ooh," she exhales, her mouth so near.

My body takes over because my brain has shut off. This is as close to primal as I've ever been. I fasten my pace, exploring her under water, her mouth now on mine, her moans disappearing down my throat. Her nipples are hard, wet peaks against mine, moving up and down with the rise and fall of her body as she rides my fingers. I press my thumb against her clit, circling it slowly every time I thrust deep. The sensation of having her in my arms, her body so close she almost melts into me, while my fingers are buried inside of her, is enough to make my muscles tremble and my knees go weak.

Amy holds onto me for dear life as I try to stay standing in the water, bucking under the force of her approaching climax. The sound of splashing water mixes with her groans in my ear, until she goes silent and her body clamps down on mine, nearly squeezing the breath out of me, and her pussy clenches around my fingers.

"Jesus Christ, Eli," she says, "I think I might fall in love with you."

The sun colours the water around us pale yellow as I slip my fingers out of her. Amy's legs are still wrapped around my waist, as if she can't let go, and I trace my fingertips along her sides and hold her close.

I commit the moment to memory, the soft slapping and the magical tint of the water, the pressure of Amy's body against mine, the words she just spoke, and decide that from now on, this will be my benchmark for happiness.

NO GREATER LOVE
THAN MINE

1

ANGELA

"You have no choice," Harriet says. "I wish I could get you out of it, but you have to go see Roger."

I tap the toe of my shoe against my boss's desk. I don't care if it annoys her—in fact, I'm pretty sure it does, and am glad of it.

"Maybe you can work something out with him," she says. "But administratively, my hands are tied."

'Administratively' is one of Harriet's favorite words. Especially in combination with explaining how tied her hands are exactly.

"That'll be the day," I scoff, "when Roger lets a woman off the hook." I hang my head in desperation. "How is this guy still working for the department?"

Harriet leans over her desk. "You didn't get this from me, but I hear he's on his way out."

"About ten years too late, but still, some good news today."

"There can be much more good news soon. Five mandatory sessions is all it takes." Harriet fixes her gaze on me. "I need you back on the squad, Angela. As soon as possible."

I shuffle in my seat and, inadvertently, wince.

"If you're physically ready, of course."

"Just a bullet to the shoulder," I say sarcastically. "Comes with the territory."

"I hope you know I don't question your mental readiness to return to work." Harriet sends me one of her attempts at a smile. She used to be my partner. I know smiling isn't her forte.

"But someone in HR does," I say.

"We have to cover our bases. That's all it is." Harriet tilts her head. "Five hours of your life spread out over two weeks. You'll have the rest of your time to recover from whatever Roger Bradley's therapeutic skills unearth from the depths of your soul."

I snicker. "It's not funny. I just want to work. I'll even have you chain me to a desk for the coming two weeks."

Harriet arches up her eyebrows. "If you only had an ounce of desk jockey blood in you, you'd be sitting on my side of this very desk right now."

"But action is what gets you killed." Even though it was a through and through, sometimes it's as though I can still feel the bullet lodged in the flesh of my right shoulder.

"Don't even say that." Harriet and I worked side by side for seven years, until she got promoted.

"Fine then. I'll go waste my time in Roger's office." I make to get up. It's not because I don't have all the time in the world to talk, but I know that the captain of our squad has a million things to do.

"Call me after," Harriet says. "Screw confidentiality."

"Yes, boss." I give her a faux-salute and leave her to tend to her many administrative tasks.

———

I've been lucky enough to never have to avail of Roger Bradley's services during all my years as a police officer with the LAPD, but I've heard all the stories.

I hope Harriet's right about him being on his way out, although it doesn't help me much now, as I sit in a nondescript waiting room, wishing it was evening already, and my hour with Roger over.

It's not just his reputation that gets my hackles up. I'm not a believer in talk therapy and the prospect of having my soul shrunk sets my teeth on edge. It's just a formality, I repeat in my head, as I see how the seconds tick by on my wristwatch. Maybe I can try something with Roger, get him to sign the necessary paperwork without me having to sit through five actual sessions with him.

The door to Roger's office opens and a colleague I know vaguely —I think he works in Vice—walks out. We nod our recognition, or perhaps our commiseration, and he walks off. The door remains open, but I'm not being called in. Maybe Roger needs to make some notes on the mental wellbeing of his previous client first.

A few more minutes pass and I just sit there waiting in front of an open door. I check my watch and it's not 4 PM yet, that's true, but only about fifty seconds off.

When the seconds counter on my watch turns to '00' a woman appears in the doorway. A woman who is decidedly not Roger Bradley.

"Detective Hill," she says. "I will see you now."

For a second, I'm chained to my chair. At the sight of her, I simply can't move. My legs have lost all their power.

I mumble something, but nothing sane comes out of my mouth. What happened to Roger Bradley? It would be a delight to have a therapy session with him now that I'm faced with the alternative. Because this will be a trip down memory lane I swore I would never take.

2

JACKIE

I've had time to prepare for this. Still, seeing her knocks me for six. It's been twenty years, yet I could pick Detective Angela Hill out of a crowd of millions. She has aged, of course. Twenty years in this job will do that to you, yet her essence has remained the same. Those pale blue eyes—the undeniable sparkle in them. She's not in uniform anymore, but she still tucks her blouse tightly into the waistband of her trousers, revealing a fine figure.

"You're not Roger Bradley," Angela says, after I've closed the door behind her.

"Very perceptive." I point at two club chairs facing each other near the window. "Please, sit down."

"I'm not sure I should stay," Angela says. "It must be against some protocol." She fidgets with the wristband of her watch.

With any other client, I'd put a reassuring hand on their shoulder, but I can't do that with Angela.

I sit down, hoping she'll follow my lead. "I assure you, it's perfectly fine."

"Where's Roger?" She sits down and slings one leg over the other, her arms crossed over her chest.

"Mr. Bradley has been suspended. I'm covering for him until a suitable, more permanent replacement is found." I find myself distracted by a freckle next to Angela's nose. Has that always been there?

"Okay." Angela eyes me through narrowed lids. "So, am I to assume that you'd rather be somewhere else instead?"

I give her a hint of smile. "Whatever gave you that idea?"

"You've read my file. You know what happened. It's LAPD procedure for every officer who's the victim of a shooting to see a shrink. But I'm fine. We can just skip this whole thing."

I relax my hands on the armrests of the chair, hoping to inspire some calm in my reluctant client. "Is that what you were going to say to Roger?"

Angela presses her lips together and nods. "I probably would have gone about it differently, but I figure you owe me, so I might as well be direct."

Ouch. The knives are out already.

"Interesting."

"Please don't do that typical shrink thing and bring your hand to your chin, nod thoughtfully, and only say 'interesting'. None of that shit's going to work on me. I just want to get out of this. If you cared for me at all." She stalls. Something twists deep in my gut. "Then you'll at least do this for me."

"Angela, please," I implore. "We have an hour. Maybe we can talk."

How can it be that I still remember her lips on mine so vividly? How those blue eyes stared into mine as she pushed a finger high inside me. A drop of sweat trickles down my spine. Maybe I should have protested more when I saw Angela's name in Roger's appointment book. But what could I have said? Detective Hill and I have a secret history together?

Angela shakes her head. "It would have been nice if someone had alerted me to this."

"I agree and I apologize. Believe me, these are not the circumstances under which I wanted us to meet again."

Angela scoffs. "As if you ever wanted that."

I deserve that. I deserve every last ounce of scorn she sends my way. "I got called in to take over from Roger a few days ago. I've been in over my head. I didn't ask for this either, but this is the situation as it is." I try a smile, although I know it won't work on her. Or no, I can only guess. It's been twenty years, and even back then we didn't know each other that well. "How about we just begin?"

Angela purses her lips. The way her eyes blaze with anger, I half expect her to make a locking up gesture with her fingers, followed by throwing away the imaginary key. She gives a stern nod.

"Would you like to begin by telling me what happened?" I'm glad there's a safe distance between us. About three feet separate us. More sweat pools in the small of my back. I'll need to change my blouse if I keep perspiring like this.

"You already know what happened." There's nothing but accusation in her tone. "Or did you not read my file?"

I read it last night and again this morning. I skimmed through it again during my lunch break, my glance always halting at her picture. Those eyes. They could cut through steel.

"I'd like to hear it in your own words."

Angela rolls her eyes. "I can't do this." She throws up her hands. "How can you possibly expect me to? I haven't seen you in two decades and then, boom, here you are. And you expect me to talk about something I have no desire to talk about, with you, of all people." She massages her temples.

"I know it's not fair."

"Not fair," Angela repeats under her breath. "You should know a thing or two about that."

I swallow hard. I try to hold her glance, but it's my own that skitters away. I can't look her in the eye—it's a privilege I squandered years ago.

"It's probably meaningless now, but I'm so sorry about what happened back then." My hands go all clammy. "My choices were very limited. I had Carl to consider." No matter the agony of the moment, my voice fills with joy when I say my son's name.

Angela holds up her hand. "Save it. Whatever you're going to say is twenty years too late."

"Everything's different now," I say, not sure what I mean.

"At least your ex-husband became commissioner." Angela's voice is all venom. "I hope it was worth the sacrifice."

"I didn't do it for him."

"Truly, it doesn't matter. I don't care. I'm just flummoxed because I was expecting that poor excuse of a human being Roger Bradley to receive me in this office for a therapy session, not the woman who broke my heart so ruthlessly, so..." She pauses, then waves a hand. "Well, you're the therapist. I hardly need to explain it to you."

"You don't. I understand. If it's any consolation, it's a shock for me as well. To see you again after all these years." I refrain from telling her that, despite all the hard feelings between us, I'm happy to be sitting across from her. To be able to look into the cool blue of her gaze whenever my eyes dare to wander there.

She huffs out some air. "I felt so much anger towards you." She shakes her head. "Once the anger subsided, I was sad. For a very long time."

"I'm sorry." I have to ask. It's none of my business, but there's an acute need inside me to obtain this information. "Did you, um, find someone... after me?"

Angela's eyes grow wide for an instant, then she just shrugs. She just sits there and it's as if I can still see some of the sadness inside her. As though, faced with me, she's trying to hide it so well, pulling up all her guards that, in her zeal, she's forgetting to conceal the most vulnerable parts of her.

"I shouldn't have asked. I'm sorry."

"This is turning out to be one big apology session for you. I hope it's cathartic." Her tone is all bite, but something has softened in the blue of her eyes.

"It's not." I wish I could at least say to her that if I could go back in time, I'd do everything differently, but I can't do that. My child came first. Although, perhaps his happiness was the perfect cover for my cowardice. "Here's what I propose." I have to meet her halfway, even if by doing so I'll be neglecting my professional duties. But I'm not the right therapist to help Angela with her possible PTSD. There's too big a conflict of interest. "I'll write you down as having taken today's session and I'll find someone else to take over from me for the next sessions. But—"

"Of course there's a but." She taps her fingertips on her knee.

"You're my last client for today. How about we go for a drink instead? I know I could use one."

The corner of her mouth quirks up briefly, only to plunge down again, pulling her lips back into their dismissive slant. She doesn't say no immediately. "If I don't go for a drink with you, will you make me sit out the session?"

"I'm not blackmailing you into having a drink with me, Angela. You're free to leave if you want to."

She rises and walks behind the chair. She plants her hands on the back of it. I don't spot any rings on her fingers. "I know a place not far from here. Classy enough to not be crawling with cops." A small shift in her lips again. "I'm not fit to drive yet, which is bullshit, but there you have it." She straightens her spine and, for a split second, grimaces. "I'll be taking a cab."

"Give me the address. I'll follow you." I suppose it's a step too far to propose we ride together.

3

ANGELA

I arrive first and don't wait for Jackie before ordering a Scotch on the rocks. I take a seat at the bar and then I do wait. I wait for Jacqueline Cooper, or I guess it's Smith again now. I take a sip, then another. I need it. The booze slides down me with a deliciously relaxing burn. This is far better than any mandatory therapy session. Although I may actually need therapy after seeing Jackie again.

I've downed half my drink by the time she arrives. I didn't tell her about the parking situation on this side of Sunset. She has worked for the police force all her life. She should know these things.

She pulls up a bar stool and sits next to me. She glances at my drink and motions for the barkeep.

"Two more, please." She points at my glass, which only has one finger of amber liquid left. She slides around on her stool, turning more toward me, but not fully. "This is a better setting, don't you think?" She casts her gaze around the place. It's nothing much—and the comment about it being classy was a definite lie. I don't even know why I said that. But I've been coming here for years and I've never spotted one cop I know.

I give her the satisfaction of nodding. Perhaps I shouldn't be here —I should be protecting my heart more. Staying out of trouble. But I was never going to say no to Jackie Smith inviting me for a drink, especially if it got me off the hook from therapy.

Jimmy, the barkeep, puts two tumblers of Scotch in front of us. "Enjoy, ladies," he says. He doesn't wink, but still gives us this look. Like Jackie and I shouldn't be sitting at his bar together. Wasn't that always part of the attraction between us? I push the notion aside. Jackie and attraction don't fit into the same thought anymore. That's what happens when someone rips out your heart and then tramples all over it.

"To times gone by," Jackie says.

"Really?" I give her a look. "That's what we're drinking to?"

She looks less nonplussed now than earlier, when we were in Roger's office. More at ease with a tumbler of Scotch in her hands, in the low light of the bar.

"To your speedy recovery," Jackie starts again. She holds up her glass.

I quickly clink mine against it, then take another sip. If I keep up this tempo, the impossible might happen, and I might become happy to see her again.

"Seriously, though," Jackie says, "How are you feeling? Right shoulder was it?"

She rests her dark gaze on me. An intricate pattern of crow's feet creases around her eyes. It catches in the light of the candle on the bar. It makes her look as though I'm seeing her in a dream.

I pull a face that's supposed to confirm what she just said. I take another sip and make a deal with myself. I shouldn't have agreed to this drink if I'm not going to say anything.

"Yep, hit me just next to my vest. The shooter had aim, I'll give him that."

"Did they get him?" Her brow furrows, giving her a concerned look. There was a time when I'd have given anything to have her look at me like that.

I nod. I don't want to talk about the shooting. If I'd wanted to do that, I would have stayed in therapy. "What you asked me earlier," I say. "Whether I found someone after you." I stare into the dark-honey liquid in my glass, then look up at her. She still has the same expression on her face, but perhaps it's now laced with a hint of trepidation. "Have *you*? After your divorce?"

"Not really." She swings toward me a bit more. "I mean, I tried, but, you know."

"When you tried, do you mean you dated men? Or women?"

She chuckles. "Wow. Still as direct as ever."

Something in me wants to mirror the smile on her face. "I assure you that I was trying to be circumspect."

"I dated both," Jackie says. "Rather unsuccessfully."

"Really?" It's hard to believe. Jackie may have broken my heart, but she's still a striking woman. I never really stood a chance against her advances.

"Is that so surprising?" She raises an eyebrow.

"I thought suitors would be lining up for the likes of you."

She sends me another smile, a dazzling one. "After Michael and I divorced, I just wanted to be on my own."

"When did you divorce?"

She thinks for a second. "Thirteen years ago."

"That's a long time to be alone." I drink again because I need time to process this information. Jackie has been single for thirteen years. I don't know why the number of years shocks me so. Or is that a pang of regret rushing through me?

"Maybe I'm like you. Married to the job."

I shoot her a quizzical look. "Was that in my file as well?"

"I can read between the lines."

"What else did you read between the lines?" I'm not a fan of therapists—for which Jackie is one of the biggest reasons—but I'm curious nonetheless.

"You refused a promotion seven years ago. I guess that means you're still not sick of flirting with danger."

"I hardly refused." My reply comes too quickly.

"I don't much care for reading between the lines, anyway. I'd rather hear all about it from you," she says.

"All about what?" I trace a finger over the rim of my glass.

"You." Her voice is husky. It must be the booze.

I burst out into a chuckle and shake my head. "Let's not pretend," I say. "We won't see each other again after tonight."

"If that's what you want." Her glass is still half full, so it can't be the Scotch making her sound so audacious. Or maybe it's too strong for her—maybe she's one of those women who have drastically curbed their alcohol intake after fifty. But she looks too damn good in a bar setting for that. That tumbler of Scotch sits too naturally in her hand. My gaze stops at her hand. An image of her fingers approaching my mouth flashes before me. Those fingers skating along my lips. I couldn't get enough of them, yet I was only granted one night with them.

"Do you want something else?" I have to ask. She's practically forcing me.

"I wouldn't mind seeing you again."

"Why?"

She flicks her tongue over her upper lip. "Because… it almost feels like serendipity. Like too good a chance to pass up."

"A chance at what?" I try to conceal the indignation that rises in my chest, try not to let it reach my voice. I fail.

"I don't know, Angela, but…" She does that flick of her tongue again. "I know I hurt you, probably beyond repair, yet I'd like to try."

I shake my head. "A chance to make yourself feel better about how you treated me back then?"

"No, God no." She inclines her body forward a bit. "A chance to explain. A chance to tell you that… it was hard for me too." A crack in her voice. "So incredibly hard."

"I don't need an explanation. What good will that do me now?" I finish my drink. I slip off my bar stool. "And you don't deserve the relief of giving me one." I turn away from her. "Jimmy, can you put these on my tab. I'll pay next time."

"You're leaving?" Jackie asks.

"Yes." I cast one last glance at her. "So you know what that feels like." With that, I'm out of there.

4

JACKIE

"Mom, please," Carl says. "I know you don't believe in the institution of marriage anymore, but I've yet to make all my mistakes. Pay attention."

Two days ago, I was much more excited about my son's upcoming nuptials. Then I saw Angela again. She's been on my mind ever since. I can still see her walking out of that dingy bar, leaving me there on my own, feeling totally out of place. Despite her injury, she walked out straight-backed, without so much as a glance behind her.

"I'm really not the person to ask for advice on this."

"That's why I'm here," Jeffrey, Carl's best friend—and soon to be best man—says. "You just have to do the Mom thing and nod at appropriate times. You don't even have to pay that much attention, Jackie. Just enough to make Carl feel loved and sufficiently noticed."

I want to make a bridezilla comment, but I fear it would hurt Carl in his current state. Ever since he started planning this wedding, about three years ago it seems, he's been gradually losing his usually outrageous sense of humor.

"This one or this one." First he puts an off-white pocket square in his blazer pocket, then a pale pink one.

"The white one," I say.

"The pink one," Jeffrey says at the same time.

Carl rolls his eyes and sighs dramatically.

"This is not helping."

"Honey, I know the right color for the tiniest piece of fabric seems hugely important to you right now, but let me tell you, in the grand scheme of things, it means nothing."

Jeffrey makes a loud buzzing sound. "Wrong thing to say, *Mom*."

"Fine," I say on a sigh. "Go with the pink one."

"Jeff, darling, can you give us a minute," Carl says.

"Sure." He plucks his phone out of his pocket. "I'll use it wisely to find my future husband on Grindr." He sashays out of the room.

"What's going on with you?" Carl asks.

"Nothing, honey. I'm sorry."

"You can't fool me." He puts the pocket squares on the table and sits down next to me. "I know I've been going nuts over this wedding, but I can still tell when my momma's upset." He tilts his head the same way I do. A subtle incline meant to convey empathy. He's too much like me, my son. "Is it the wedding?"

"No, honey." I'll need to give him something, even though he has no idea of Angela's existence. "It's just some work stuff. I'm subbing for someone and some of the cases are… not as straightforward as I'd like them to be."

"Like what?" He rubs his chin—one of his father's moves.

"You know I can't talk about that."

"I'm not buying it. You have work stuff going on all the time, but it never makes you so absent-minded. Your favorite son's getting married." He grins, baring a row of perfectly white teeth. "Unless…" He leans his shoulder into me. "It's something else." He makes a spectacle of examining my face. "You've got that look about you."

"What look?" I'll be the first to admit that seeing Angela again has thrown me, but surely not to the extent that my son can read it off my face.

"You've met someone." He quirks up his eyebrows. "A gay son is a perceptive son. Never forget."

I chuckle, hoping I can laugh his comment away. "It's nothing. Now back to you. What were we on? Pocket squares, was it?"

"You're a fool to think I'm letting you off the hook so easily." He gets up and pivots toward the table. "This conversation's not over, but, for now, we can get back to me."

"Let's get Jeff back in. He's better at making sartorial decisions," I say.

Carl nods, but before he calls for Jeffrey, he whispers, "Is it Sondra? I know you really liked her."

If only, I think. I shake my head. The irony is that if I'd left my husband for Angela twenty years ago—which seemed like a gigantic impossibility at the time—I would probably not be so close to my child. And he wouldn't even have noticed how seeing her again has affected me.

I stare at Angela's phone number. It's right there in front of me, in her file. Her personnel file picture, taken a few years ago, staring back at me—again. Yesterday, before leaving Roger's office where I've been spending half days, I almost took the picture out of her file and slipped it into my purse. Until I realized we live in a digital age and I snapped a picture of it, so I'd have it in my phone. When I got home I was afraid to look at it though, because I feared what it might do to me.

It's not just her eyes that undo me. It's the complete absence of a smile. Police officers are not supposed to smile when they get their picture taken, but in Angela's, there's not even the slightest hint of joy. Her eyes, though piercing, are dull. The corners of her mouth drawn tightly, deeply down. There's such acute sorrow about her and I can't help but wonder: did I do this to her?

It's a ridiculous thought. No one stays sad for twenty years over what was basically a one-night stand. Yet this is the thought that persists in my brain, that's been swirling, messing with me, since I saw her again.

It's why I want to call her.

So I do.

She picks up after the second ring. "Detective Hill." Her voice is emotionless and direct, like her.

"Hi, Angela. It's Jackie." My heart pounds in my ears.

"Yes." She says it like a statement.

Maybe this was a big mistake. I'm not sure how to get the words past my lips. Even though we only spent a short amount of time together, I can so easily imagine the scorn on her face.

"Did you have something to say?" she asks.

"Yes, um, I wanted to say that, um…" I've turned into a stuttering teenager. "You're off the hook for therapy. I'll sign the papers and give you a positive evaluation." What am I doing? Committing fraud to please her? Is my guilt really still that big?

"That's nice of you." A hint of something else in her voice.

"But I also wanted to ask if…" I take a deep breath. "If you'd go to dinner with me." I spit out the words as fast as I can, lest they retreat, robbing me of any chance to see her again, forever.

"Is one a condition of the other?" Angela asks.

"Sorry?"

"Are you blackmailing me into having dinner with you by not requiring me to follow through with the therapy?"

"What? No, Angela, I'm not blackmailing you. I won't force you to have dinner with me. I'll draw up the necessary paperwork and send it to the HR department at the end of next week, after you should have had your last session, regardless of us seeing each other again. You have my word." I brace myself for a snide remark about how worthless my word is.

"Okay," she says. "When?"

My heart leaps all the way into my throat. I debate inviting her to my house, but it's too much. We need neutral ground. "Tomorrow night? I know an exquisite Greek restaurant in Silver Lake. I'll text you the address."

"Okay," she says again, like this is a business transaction.

"Eight?" I can't believe she said yes.

"I'll be there." A short silence follows. "But, Jackie," she says, "don't go getting any ideas in your head." The dry thud, with which she ends the call, rings in my ears for minutes after.

5

ANGELA

"You never told me how things went with Roger," Harriet says. We're eating sloppy tacos and drinking beer at a bar around the corner from the Hollywood police station, a monthly tradition we started when we were partnered up, and have kept going since.

"Roger Bradley has been suspended."

"Already?" Harriet sips from her bottle of Dos Equis.

"Guess who's taking his place?"

Harriet shrugs. "Clearly, I'm out of the loop."

"Jacqueline Cooper."

Harriet puts her taco down. "No shit."

"Oh, yes." Once, probably on one of our taco nights, I got so hammered, I told Harriet all about Jackie and how she so cruelly broke my heart.

"What happened?"

"You know. We came face to face after all these years. Some of the old anger resurfaced. She tried to apologize. It was all very messy and awkward."

"But she's still your therapist?"

"On paper." Even though she's my boss, I don't bother lying to Harriet. There's no point.

"What does that mean?" She takes another long drag of beer.

"It means I'm having dinner with her tomorrow night."

Harriet brings her bottle down onto the table with a loud bang. "You're having dinner with Jackie Cooper?"

It sounds crazy to me too. I give Harriet a slow nod. "It's Jackie Smith now."

Harriet chuckles. "Well, well."

"Not like that." I can't help a tiny smile from spreading on my lips.

"Like *what*?" A smug grin appears on Harriet's face.

"It's not a date, it's just…" I have no idea what it is. "She asked me and I said yes."

"Good for you."

"We'll have to see about that." I'm not even sure why I agreed. Maybe twenty years is long enough to put what happened between us behind me.

Harriet nods. "I know she did a number on you."

I shrug. "Water under the bridge now."

"And we all get lonely sometimes, even die-hard single ladies like yourself." She twirls her bottle of beer between her fingers.

"Oh please, not the loneliness speech again." I reach over and stop the spinning of her beer bottle mid circle. "You're only on your second beverage of the evening and we're going there already?"

Harriet emits something between a chuckle and a scoff. "Just because we're no longer partners doesn't mean that I no longer look out for you."

I give her an offended eyebrow raise. "Last I checked, I was plenty old enough to look out for myself."

"You know what I mean." She cocks her head.

I shake mine. "I appreciate your concern, but I'm fine."

"I know that, but maybe I want better than just plain old fine for my bestie."

I dramatically puff some air out of my cheeks. "How about you give me some department gossip instead of wishing all kind of things for me." I narrow my eyes. "Although I'm not sure you're the right source for that, seeing as you had no idea Roger Bradley has been suspended."

Harriet taps a finger against her temple. "There's only so much space in here."

We both burst out into a chuckle. Mine is mainly born from relief because we've changed the subject from my non-existent love life.

———

When I get home, after drinking quite a few more beers than my doctor recommended while still on painkillers, I don't go through my usual routine of gulping down a glass of water, brushing my teeth, discarding my clothes on the nearest chair, and falling into bed pleasantly tipsy.

I head into the spare bedroom which doubles as a study and unlock the bottom drawer of the desk. When I stick the key, which I keep in a separate spot, into the lock, it doesn't immediately want to turn. It's been that long since I used it last. I twist the key back and forth until the lock snaps. I open the drawer. It only holds one item. A group photo.

I look at the twenty-year-younger version of myself first and conclude I could have aged worse. Not taking a promotion that chained me to a desk has a lot to do with that, although opinions on that vary. And a gunshot wound to the shoulder hasn't exactly helped with my youthful complexion of late. Still, it could have been worse. No middle-age spread and the wrinkles on my forehead have been kept to a minimum.

Yet, I do see something in that picture of myself that I no longer see when I look in the mirror. Wonder. Hope. The very expectation of a life filled with love.

My gaze wanders to the person all the way on the right. The instructor who was tasked with teaching a group of reluctant police officers all about the psychology of domestic abusers. She stands tall, her gaze focused, her shoulders back. Her hair was long then, slung over her left shoulder. Jacqueline Cooper, now Smith.

The picture was taken at the end of the week-long seminar, when I had already fallen head over heels in love with her. Maybe that's what I see in my glance. And maybe that's why I've failed to find it there ever since.

Because she gave me all the hope in the world, only to take it away again after giving me the most delicious taste.

I run my fingertip over the picture, as though it will allow me to feel her skin again, the way it felt against mine, so promising and intoxicating.

It still stings that she's been divorced for thirteen years. During those years, did she think about contacting me? Does she keep pictures like this one as relics of a past that never turned into a future?

With a sigh, I put the picture away. That's enough reminiscing for one night. And I must get my beauty sleep. After all, I'm meeting Jackie for dinner tomorrow evening. The words don't sound right in my head. Like a great impossibility—the greatest of all. Because how do you sit across from someone to enjoy a meal together, when you've had to cut that very person out of your heart in order to survive?

But I said yes. For some reason I may never understand, I said yes. I said yes to her once before and look where that got me. I can always cancel. But I'll sleep on it first.

6

JACKIE

"The squid's really good," I say, because it's true and I have no idea what else to say. It's not that Angela has dressed up for this dinner. She's wearing a similar style pantsuit to the one she turned up in for our therapy session, her blouse tucked in tightly. Yet, there's something different about her. Something about her has mellowed.

"The squid it will be then." Angela puts her menu on the table.

"Thank you for coming."

"A small price to pay for being able to get back to active duty in two weeks' time."

"If you look at it like that." On my way to the restaurant, I've decided to give Angela the first fifteen minutes of our time together to get all the snide remarks out of her system without calling her out on them. I figure fifteen minutes is the very least I can give her. But I will not indulge her too long at my expense. I may have made the wrong choice in her eyes, but for me it was the right one. A difficult one, but the correct one nonetheless.

"Tell me about your son," she says, surprising me. "How did Carl turn out?"

"He's the most wonderful man." An involuntary smile spreads over my face. "He's getting married in six weeks. He's been going crazy over it for what seems like the past six years, even though they've only been engaged for six months."

"Cold feet?" Angela asks.

"Quite the opposite." I chuckle. "Very hot feet." Is that a hint of smile I detect on Angela's face? "I'm surprised he hasn't scared Beau off yet with his nuptial hysterics."

"Beau?" Angela quirks up an eyebrow.

"His fiancé."

"Your son's gay?"

"He is."

"Carl is marrying a man." Angela says it as though she needs to hear the words out loud to process them.

"He sure is."

Angela shakes her head and makes a weird giggling sound.

"What's so funny about that?"

"It's not funny, just strangely ironic."

"I don't follow."

Angela gives a full belly laugh. "You didn't want to be with another woman because of your son, who turned out to be gay himself."

"One doesn't have anything to do with the other."

"I'm not saying it does, but you do have to see the irony of it."

I scratch my nose. I still don't get what's so funny about the whole thing.

"Have you told him about us?" Angela asks.

"No. His father and I were still together when, um, we happened." I swallow hard. "But he does know I also date women now."

Even though I've already admitted this to Angela before, this seems to amuse her again. She paints on a grin I can't decipher, then says, "Tell me about the last woman you dated."

I'm saved by a waitress stopping by to take our order. We both order the squid and I ask for a bottle of the house white wine.

After the waitress has walked off, I hope Angela is keen on a change of subject, but she plants her chin on an upturned palm and looks at me. "I'm listening," she says.

I hope the sigh I expel tells her I'm not comfortable discussing this. Not because I'm about to tell her about a woman I dated, but because it's Angela I'm telling about this woman. "Her name's Sondra. It didn't work out."

A different waitress comes by to open the bottle of wine and pour us each a glass.

"That's brief, even for you," Angela says before taking a sip of wine. "Good choice. The wine. Not the woman. At least I gather from the oceans of information you're drowning me in." She chuckles heartily.

"She was younger and still had children living at home. You know how complicated that can be."

"Actually, I don't know that much about it." Angela's on the warpath tonight. Perhaps she's been on sick leave for too long.

"A child will always be a woman's first priority."

"So I'm told." Angela leans back and does the silent thing, probably hoping I will fill the void in conversation.

"Look, we may as well address the elephant in the room." I don't know if it's the few sips of wine I've had or just the effect of sitting across from Angela Hill again—across from this woman who once made my heart skip many beats—but I need to say this. "I should never have let things go as far as they did between us. That's on me. It created expectations that were impossible for me to meet."

"Do you regret our night together?" She trains her steely detective gaze on me.

How can I possibly say I regret it? I wouldn't admit to that even if I knew it was what she wanted to hear. "No." Even though it's been twenty years, I still get rushes of remembrance. Flashes of how her touch set me alight, of how it undid something in me that had thus far remained tightly locked up. "My only regret is that I had to hurt you."

"I don't regret it either. After all, I was single and available."

"You knew my situation."

Angela purses her lips and nods. "I think we can ignore the elephant from now on."

"Tell me about the last woman *you* dated," I quickly say, before she starts interrogating me again.

She chuckles. "I solemnly swear it's not a cop-out when I say there's really nothing to tell."

"How come?"

"I'm not relationship material," she says matter-of-factly. "Simple as that."

"I don't buy that."

"Well, it's not your call to make, so…"

"Fair enough." I try a smile. "Let's change the subject to something a bit more comfortable."

"Yes, let's have some small talk." The intensity of her gaze on me says she'd rather leave the restaurant than engage in chitchat—she was never the kind.

We are rescued once again by the arrival of our dishes.

As I stare at my plate, I ponder the possibility that twenty years has been too long. Maybe too much has happened and we have nothing left to say to each other—and the things we do find to say are too contentious. Maybe for us, there's no such thing as water under the bridge, and the night we shared—those few hours of surrendering to what we both wanted more than anything at the time—should be forever relegated to the confines of our memory.

I glance up at her. She sends me a goofier grin than I was expecting.

"You were never good with silences," she says. "Which always struck me as odd for someone in your profession."

"I usually am," I say. "Good with them." I don't say that it is, and always has been, her very presence that unnerves me. "Maybe not as good as you though."

"Well, in my job, I dare say, the stakes are even higher. Some well-timed silence can work wonders in an interrogation room."

This sparks another kind of memory. "Remember at the seminar, when I asked you to role-play an interrogation? I kept asking you to show more empathy for the perpetrator, but you couldn't do it."

"I was a rookie," Angela is quick to say. There's a flash of something in her eyes. I only meant it as a joke, but it looks like I may have offended her professional pride.

I don't say that at the age of thirty-five, she was hardly a rookie. But a lot has changed in policing the past two decades and when Angela was at the academy, empathy was probably a word not often mentioned.

"How's your squid?" I ask instead.

"Tender as can be. Good recommendation." She holds my gaze for an instant. Her eyes are icy blue, but I remember the warmth in them. I was never able to forget that. The change in her when I had my hands all over her. Out of nowhere, a stab of desire slices through me, and I know, in that moment, as I remember how the look in her eyes can be transformed, that I want her all over me again.

7

ANGELA

W*hat do you want from me, Jackie?* I want to ask. *Absolution?* But she doesn't strike me as a woman who is after absolution. She strikes me as someone who has made peace with the mistakes of the past a good number of years ago. There's an air of calmness about her that I admire. A dignity she didn't possess all those years ago.

"Did you leave Michael or did he leave you?" I ask. Instead of dessert, we've both chosen something stronger with our coffee. Jackie holds a glass of brandy in her hand, while I'm nursing a tumbler of whiskey.

"I left him, although, by the time I made the decision, there wasn't much actual leaving to do."

"What does that mean?" Sometimes, when I scan the delicate features of her face, the almond shape of her eyes and the way the left side of her mouth is always slightly curled upward, I wish we weren't in this Greek restaurant. I wish we were back at that bar off Sunset where the light is more forgiving and I don't look like a police officer who took a bullet three months ago. It bothers me that I didn't look my best when I saw her again.

"It means that we had grown so much apart, the divorce was a mere formality."

"Did you have more affairs?"

Jackie scoffs. "I would hardly call what we had an affair, Angela."

"My opinion differs." My pulse ticks up. Did she not fall in love with me the same way I did with her?

"We slept together once."

"But we dreamed of doing it many more times." I clear my throat. "Well, I did, at least."

"If you're asking if I fell in love again while I was still married, I didn't." Jackie runs her finger over a perfectly sculpted eyebrow.

"Were you in love with me?" I seem to have gone into full-on detective mode—the non-silent kind. After all, this is a serious matter of the heart I'm investigating. And I never before got a chance to ask.

"You know I was." There's a vulnerable edge to her voice. "I was crazy about you."

Me too, something inside me screams. But I choose silence now.

"But after your divorce, you left it up to chance whether we should ever meet again."

"Of course I did." Jackie takes a slow sip from her brandy. "I thought about you a lot, but I could hardly give you a call and say, 'Hey Angela, guess what, I'm divorced now.'"

I merely shrug to indicate my disagreement. I don't think I should say it out loud.

She inclines her head. "Seven years is a long time and I knew I'd hurt you."

"It's fine." What else can it be? I can't really see it as a missed opportunity—that one had come and gone seven years earlier already.

"How about we drink to Roger Bradley," Jackie says. "Or is that in bad taste?"

"He used his position to assault vulnerable clients." I shake my head.

"Point taken." Jackie casts her eyes downward. "How about we drink to destiny putting us back on each other's path instead?"

"I'll happily drink to that." I prove my point by bringing my glass to my lips. "But please don't tell me you believe in any of that stuff. Destiny and what-have-you."

"Would that lower your opinion of me even further?" For the first time, Jackie unleashes her Jackie-cackle. A low-bellied bluster of a laugh that's so infectious, the corners of my mouth quirk up instantaneously at the sound of it.

"I won't deny you hurt me." I drink again, to gather bravado this time. "Because you did. But, as I just said, I'm not relationship material so I honestly don't think you and I would have amounted to very much, given the chance."

Jackie arches up both her eyebrows—I remember her fingertip skating over one of them earlier. I long for her finger to repeat its motion. Jackie regroups and gives me what I think of as her practiced shrink look. "Would you say you believe in relationships at all?"

"I do, for some people. Just not for me."

"That's an unusual opinion. May I ask why?"

"Because what are the odds that every single person on the planet is the same and wants the same thing? I've never needed all the fluff that comes with being in a relationship. I'm perfectly fine on my own."

"A little defensive, but I'll take your word for it." She bares her teeth in a wide smile. "But, for the record, I strongly disagree. I think that you and I, we could have and would have made it just fine."

It's my turn to scoff. "Easy enough to say." I look away.

"It's not, actually. It's very hard to say. In fact, it hurts me quite a bit to say this to you."

I drag my gaze up from her hands to her face. "Are you serious?"

She nods, her eyes narrowed. "We had what it takes."

"And what might that have been?"

"Chemistry, for starters." Her smile isn't nearly as wide anymore. "And a one-in-a-million connection."

"But also vastly different lives. And chemistry only takes you so far."

She huffs out some air and waves her hand about. "We can speculate all we want. The fact remains that I'm sad we never had a chance."

A short silence falls. This time, I'm the one who feels the need to fill it.

"Why did you ask me to dinner?" I ask.

Jackie looks into her glass of brandy, from which the liquid is rapidly disappearing. Then she casts her eyes back up and holds my gaze. A shiver runs down my spine. "Because I had to see you again. I let you go once. I wasn't about to make the same mistake all over again."

Her eyes are dark and brooding and not a fiber of my being doubts her words. When someone looks at you with such intensity and says something like that, it can only be the absolute truth. "Things are very different now." My attempt at sounding confident in my reply fails spectacularly. Why is my voice so shaky?

"We can't change the past, no matter how many times we rehash it." She runs a finger over the rim of her glass this time. I'm mesmerized by it. Her fingers seem to evoke something inside of me. "And we may both be in our fifties, but according to Carl sixty is the new forty, so I say we have a whole lot of future still ahead of us."

The scar on my shoulder itches, reminding me of how fragile life can be.

"What are you saying, Jackie?" I take a sip of whiskey, its heat scorching my throat.

"I guess what I'm saying is that I'd very much like to see you again." Jackie's all confidence now, her dark eyes ablaze with the passion I once knew. "That's me putting my cards on the table."

I swallow down hard. The evening has definitely taken a turn. Despite my hard feelings toward her, I can't wait to see where it will end. I nod, giving her something but not too much. I drink again because I don't know how to play this. On the one hand, I don't want her to think that her breaking my heart can be erased by buying me dinner but, on the other hand, I do appreciate her gesture—and her company most of all.

"What do you say, Angela?" She does the head tilt that did me in all those years ago. "If I ask you to have dinner with me again, will you say yes?"

"I will." It's how it always was. This unstoppable force inside of me has taken over the driver's seat. Just like twenty years ago I knew full well that she was married and had a teenager in the house, I walked into it with my eyes wide open. Even though I knew I shouldn't, that nothing good could ever come of it, I followed where she led. Tonight, it's like a case of history repeating itself all over again—except that she's single now, and her son is about to get married.

Jackie has shown her hand, and it's a winning one.

"That makes me very happy." Jackie stretches her arm and reaches for my hand on the table. She covers it with hers and gives it a light squeeze. "Are you free this weekend?"

The touch of her skin on mine winds back the clock two decades. I'm in my thirties again and desperate for more of her touch. She's pushing it. I withdraw my hand, leaving hers lonely on the tabletop. "I'm on sick leave, so."

She gives me a smile that says she understands why I'm blowing hot and cold—because I am. I'm flustered and confused; flattered and afraid. Sitting across from her at the end of this meal is making me feel more than I've allowed myself to feel in a very long time. Years—no decades. I don't do relationships and, hence, I'm not very good at expressing my emotions. Jackie is a counselor, she must be able to read it off my face.

She signals for the waiter and asks him to bring her the check. While we wait, she slants over the table and says, "Come to mine Saturday evening. I'll cook for you."

8

JACKIE

A week ago, Angela Hill was but a distant memory. Tonight she's coming to my house for dinner. I've had a hard time focusing on any of my clients' tales, because her face keeps popping up at the most inopportune moments. Those sharp cheekbones, that steely gaze. Her wavy hair, shorter than it was before, which I long to run my fingers through. That slice of desire that coursed through me during dinner hasn't left. It has taken up permanent lodgings inside of me, flaring up when I'm trying to fall asleep at night, and when I open my eyes first thing in the morning.

And I remember that it was the same twenty years ago. I should have stopped it. I should have been the wiser one and taken my responsibilities more seriously, but when it came to Angela Hill, I had no control.

I stare at my reflection in the mirror. Is it nostalgia pushing me to rekindle this, I ask myself. But what do I know? It's probably a bit of everything. Because I do clearly remember that, for that brief moment when I allowed myself to lose control, I didn't feel like Jackie Cooper, mother to Carl and wife of the deputy commissioner, any more. When I took Angela to bed, I was Jackie Smith, a woman with options. A woman in bed with another woman, feeling all the things Jackie Cooper never could. Even though it was all too brief. We only had one night, because real life can't be so easily erased.

I have to remember my own words. The past is the past. Too much has happened to let it stand in the way. But that's easy enough for me to say. I had a life to return to, a son who needed me. What did Angela have? Who waited for her to return home after our night of passion?

I shake off the thought, smile at myself in the mirror, and head into the kitchen. I'm not stretching my culinary skills to the limit tonight. I'd much rather spend my time chatting with Angela than slaving away in the kitchen.

My phone starts ringing and for a split second I fear it's Angela calling to say she can't make it. I look at the screen. Carl.

"Hey, Momma," he says, in that way of his. "Nervous for your big date?"

I regret telling him, but he's just like his mother—an expert at reading someone's mood. He's far better at prying information out of someone than I am, however. He's the kind of son a mother can bare her soul to.

"I'm not nervous."

"Of course you are, but that's okay. It's only normal."

I didn't tell him that I knew Angela when he was still a boy. That's a conversation for another time. All he knows is I'm having someone over for dinner—someone I like, a lot.

I listen patiently. Carl thinks, because he's getting married and I'm single, he knows much more about dating and relationships than I do. He probably does.

"Just be your glorious self. No woman can resist that. And if things don't go according to plan, excuse yourself and text me. I'll call you and pretend I have an emergency. You know the drill."

"I'm fifty-eight, Carl. I'm not going to have my son fake call me when I'm on a date."

"Suit yourself, but know the option is there. What are you cooking?"

"Roast chicken."

"Damn, Momma. You're going all out." I can hear the irony in his voice.

"Hardly."

"I envy you your night. Beau is dragging me to a Log Cabin event." He sighs dramatically and I can easily imagine the accompanying eye-roll. "Can you please remind me why I'm marrying a white republican?"

"Because he'll make the perfect son-in-law." We've had a version of this conversation since Carl first had the hots for Beau.

"As long as we never talk about politics at the dinner table."

"Correct." Angela has only ever seen a picture of Carl, and he was still so young then. I'm getting about a million miles ahead of myself, but for a short moment I allow myself the indulgence of imagining their introduction. Carl would be his usual charming self. How would Angela react? It's too hard to predict—I don't know her well enough yet.

"I have to go, Momma," Carl says. "Call me tomorrow, okay?"

"You'll have me on the phone before eight," I joke.

"Make it a decent time. Love ya." He makes a smacking sound into the phone and hangs up. A pep talk from my son is always welcome. But from now on, I'm on my own.

———

Angela is dressed a bit more casually when she appears on my doorstep, beige linen pants with a pale-blue blouse on top. She offers me a bottle of Sonoma Pinot Noir and I'm pleasantly surprised by her choice.

When I've escorted her from the hallway into the living room, she says, "Divorcing the commissioner must be lucrative." She casts her gaze about the room. It lands on an artwork of a near-naked woman sprawling over the city of Los Angeles. "I've seen this before." She walks toward the wall.

It surprises me that the artwork sparks a memory in her, although perhaps it shouldn't. I resist the temptation to jog her memory further. At some point, I'd like her to come to her own conclusion about it.

She stares at the artwork intently while tapping a finger against her lips. "Why is this so familiar?" She turns to me.

"It'll come to you." I give her nothing else but a crooked grin. "Drink?"

"Whatever you're offering."

"Shall we sit outside? It's a lovely, smoggy Los Angeles evening."

She quirks up her eyebrows and follows me to the patio outside.

"Remind me to never invite you to my place," she says. "I couldn't bear the disappointment on your face."

I pour us each a glass of white wine from an ice bucket next to the teak table. "Lest you think I bled the esteemed police commissioner of this city dry, rest assured I made my own money over the years."

Angela sits down and, as soon as she does, kicks off her sandals. "By unearthing the depths of people's souls?"

I snicker and shake my head. "By making the most of my proximity to Hollywood."

She tilts her head. "You sold your soul to the devil?"

"Kind of." I hold up my glass. "You might have heard of a little TV show called *Criminal Intent*."

She nods. "The one where every single week a woman gets brutally murdered, if she's lucky. If she's not, she gets raped as well," she deadpans.

"If you put it like that." I can't help but chuckle.

"I never really watched it," she says. "What's your involvement?"

"Together with a friend, I came up with it. My friend's still an executive producer, while I sold my stake in the whole business a few years ago."

"Selling your soul's a lucrative business, indeed."

"Let's just say I wasn't very happy with the direction the network wanted to take the show."

"So, in the end, you did the right thing." She peers at the glittering water of the pool, then back at me. "If you've made all this money, what are you doing replacing the likes of Roger Bradley?"

"Helping out where I can."

"Atonement," she says, "for inflicting that awful show on humankind."

"Ouch." It doesn't really hurt my feelings. I know the show's reputation and nobody remembers the first two seasons, when the storylines were far less grim, and I still had a say.

"I'm sorry. I shouldn't judge like that. I've really never watched it. If I'd known, though." She sips from her wine.

"Would you have watched?"

"With great interest." Her gaze wanders again.

"How's your shoulder?"

She looks at it as though its condition can only be assessed by doing so. "To be completely honest, but don't tell anyone at work, it's still quite painful." She sighs. "I went to the shooting range this morning, and it was not good."

"Sorry to hear that."

"You can't rush a healing wound." She purses her lips. "Much as I would like to." She inhales a lung-full of air and lets her head drop to her shoulders, looking up at the sky. "Christ, this place is unbelievable. It's so peaceful. It's like I'm not in the city anymore."

"It's quite a change from Downtown."

"Even with a place like this, you haven't been able to scoop up a significant other?" There's glee in her tone. Is she flirting? "That I'm alone in my shabby two-bedroom in Culver City, that's no wonder, but you." She throws her arms wide. "With this."

I shrug. "I had to learn the hard way that a mansion on the hill isn't a babe magnet."

"Maybe you've been trying to attract the wrong kind of babes."

"I'm also not very interested in anyone who could fall into the babe category." I look into her eyes. "Give me a hard-as-nails police-woman over a babe any day of the week."

Angela lets out a loud cackle. "I remember now, Subtlety was never really your strong suit. Not when it came to... certain things." She doesn't look away. In that moment, it feels like we're on the same page exactly.

"What can I say? I'm getting on. I have no time for subtlety any longer."

"Valiant effort at an excuse." The corners of her mouth curl into a smile. "But as a seasoned detective, I see right through it."

"Obviously." I wish she was sitting closer to me. I'd put a hand on her arm, but from where I'm sitting, I'd need to lean over uncomfortably.

I haven't seen Angela in two decades, yet sitting here with her feels totally natural. Like something we should have been doing all our lives.

9

ANGELA

When Jackie takes me inside for dinner, I'm still trying to get over the view from what she described as her patio, which I'd call more of an outside living room.

She leads me to the dining table and I sit facing the artwork I stopped at earlier. I recognized it instantly, but didn't want to say. I didn't want to start our evening that way.

A replica of it hung on the wall of the hotel room we spent the night in. We both thought it a great piece and saw it as luck shining down upon us, what with having found the only hotel room in the world without tacky wall decoration.

I can't believe she went out and bought the exact same thing—and gave it such a prominent place in her spectacular home.

"I have made for you"—She shows up next to me with a plate in her hands—"Roast chicken with assorted roasted vegetables."

"That looks delicious."

"Thank you." There's a hint of smugness in her smile, but it doesn't bother me in the least. "Enjoy."

She sits down across from me and I lose all interest in the view behind her, no matter how breathtaking it is. Jackie's wearing a beige sleeveless top and it takes most of my willpower to drag my glance away from her arms as she picks up her cutlery. Maybe it's the piece of art hanging so close to me that shifts something inside of me. My sentiments about tonight seem to be evolving in her favor with every minute that passes. My reluctance seems to evaporate.

"Not hungry?" she asks, a lopsided grin on her face.

I give her my version of a bashful smile, which I've been told has nothing bashful about it, and cut off a piece of the chicken she has served. I chew with gusto and end with an exaggerated 'hmmmm'. I really need to pull it together.

Jackie puts her fork down, leans back, and studies me.

"It has come to me," I say. I point at the wall. "I remember." I spear another piece of chicken onto my fork. Jackie may have produced the moistest roast chicken ever, yet the taste of it is lost on me tonight. My senses are otherwise occupied. It's as though I'm discovering her all over again. Jacqueline Cooper version 2.0. I may not have been very impressed with *Criminal Intent* the few times I watched it, but I am impressed with how she has leveraged it into securing her financial future—and this dream of a house. The way she's looking at me, as though she can somehow sense my emotions have made a leap, isn't helping.

"I'm glad you do. It always stuck with me." Her gaze softens. "It was the first piece of art I bought for this place." A small smile appears on her face. "At first, Carl, who thinks himself an interior designer just because he watches all those home decoration shows on TV, mocked me relentlessly. He said it was too on the nose, too kitsch. But even he has come to appreciate it."

"Did you ever tell him about… us?" I ask.

Jackie shakes her head. "I couldn't at the time and by the time he was old enough… what we had was so long ago."

I pause to reflect. I put my fork, with the piece of chicken still pronged onto it, down. "Back then, I was too hurt to accept it. But I do understand why you did what you did. For Carl."

Jackie narrows her eyes. "I hope one day you can forgive me."

"That day may be today." Something twists inside me. The guard I've been desperate to keep up since I came face-to-face with Jackie again shatters as I sit here glancing at her. At her high, patrician cheekbones. That dark, intense glint in her eyes. The way the color of her skin makes the beige of her top seem bright as the sky outside. I don't step back in time twenty years—that's not possible because of the life we've lived since—but how I felt about her then rushes back, floods my senses, causes a riot in my stomach that makes it impossible to touch another bite of the food she has prepared.

In that moment, I realize I want her. I've always wanted her—and only her. There's never been anyone else and it's, at the same time, a harrowing and exhilarating feeling. Because I'm sitting across from Jackie in her house, with the same piece of art hanging above us that once graced the wall of the hotel we made love in twenty years ago.

I see something strain in her muscles. She's holding something back. It's not words. It was never words that we had between us. It was something much more far-reaching than that. Passion. Wordless and deep. Unmistakable. It's quickly coming back now, all the feelings I've kept bottled up for years. They're overtaking me and Jackie looks me in the eye and I know the next step needs to come from me. It's the only way. I was the slighted party. I need to make the next move—the one that backs up the words I've just spoken.

I push my chair back. I stand and look at her for an instant. It's been twenty years so it's statistically impossible not to have met another woman who could rival her in beauty and grace, yet that's how it feels. I remember what I said at the Greek restaurant about the unlikeliness of every single person on the planet wanting the same thing: a relationship. I still stand by my words, but I feel they no longer apply to me. Not when I'm looking at Jackie like this.

I slowly walk over to her. She looks up at me. When she rises from the chair to her full length, she's a few inches taller than me, and I remember how that used to make me feel. Not when we were lying in bed—because that only happened once—but when I looked at her during the week-long seminar. Back then, I didn't much care for the subject of psychology of domestic abuse or whatever it was, but I very much cared for the instructor. That eloquent, elegant woman with shoulders so broad they didn't quite match her delicate demeanor.

Her shoulders are still as impressive, and her arms, my God, I can't wait for her to hold me in those arms, and erase the last twenty years from my life.

I've stood up and walked over to her, but that's as far as my move will go. I'm too undone to take more initiative. Past hurt turned into apprehension wars too much with the sudden desire inside me.

"Kiss me," I whisper. "Please."

Jackie doesn't say anything. She tilts her head, takes a step closer, and folds her hands over mine. The touch of her skin stokes the flames of lust inside me. Maybe I never came here for a meal, maybe it was about this all along. Jackie's touch. This moment of pure joy just before she kisses me. Because I know she won't deny my request. I know she feels the same way. Otherwise, why would she have taken the time to break down my barriers? This woman sees something in me I haven't seen in myself for decades. She sees the desire that's still alive inside of me, while, all this time, I was convinced it had died years ago.

10

JACKIE

My heart beats furiously in my throat. To see Angela like this again, ready to surrender to me, after all these years, is taking my breath away. But I must keep my wits about me. She's the one who walked over to me. She's the one who has just asked me to kiss her. So what am I waiting for? It's what I've wanted to do since she stepped into Roger Bradley's office. Or no, since I spotted her file among my new clients. And here we stand, hand in hand. A dream come true. I'd best not screw this up as well.

I tilt my head and look into her eyes. There's not a hint of that icy steel in them. They're all warmth and sparkle and desire. Angela Hill wants me. The realization hits me like a blazing ball of fire. I touch my lips to hers and the floodgates of my memory open. My night with Angela was my first time with a woman. How did I ever walk away from that?

This is no time to think of my son, and rehash all the reasons why—I've done that enough over the past twenty years. This is no time to think at all. This is a time to feel. To revel in the sensation of her lips against mine. It's only the softest, briefest of pecks, yet the heat that spreads through me is the greatest I've felt in my life.

Because everything's different now and this means something. It's the start of something. Of a second chance. I know this in my bones.

Angela withdraws her hands from mine and runs her fingers up my arms. My skin instantly breaks out into goosebumps. Our lips meet again and as they do, she presses her palms against my biceps. I part my lips and try to find her tongue with mine. I come up empty.

I pull back and open my eyes. Angela keeps her hands on my arms, but the rest of her seems to have retreated. I don't say anything, just arch up an eyebrow.

She needs a moment. A few seconds to process what's happening. This isn't just any kiss. This is a kiss between Angela Hill and Jackie Smith. It makes all the difference in the world. Perhaps I should have known that very first time when we kissed, that I was never meant to kiss anyone else like that again.

Angela brings her hands from my arms to my chin, cupping my cheeks, and draws me to her. It's this very motion, this small act of her pulling me near, that I've craved so much, that it opens the floodgates of my memory even wider.

We were so much younger then, had so much more life to live, and we had no idea that it would be such a furtive thing between us. What's one night in a lifetime? Yet it has remained with me like a strong force ever since. Not always on a conscious level, that would have been unbearable, but the feeling of Angela's hands all over me has stayed with me through the years. To have her hands on me again now is a sensation so powerful, I can no longer hold back. I want to kiss her, yes I do, but I want to do so much more. I want to make up for all the kisses we were unable to exchange. For all the nights I missed her lying in bed beside me.

This time, Angela kisses me, and her tongue slips in from the get-go, inviting mine to dance with hers. And dance we do. I curl my arms tightly around her waist, hoping to convey that I have no intention of ever letting her go again, and kiss her like there's no tomorrow. As far as I'm concerned, tomorrow doesn't need to show up any longer. I'll always have this moment. The moment Angela came back to me.

And this kiss might be fraught with a million emotions, memories of missed opportunities and, perhaps, broken hearts, but it's also so much more. It easily transcends what we once were, and what we've come to mean to one another—vastly different things for each one of us. It brings us together, unites, gives us if not a blank slate, then at least a canvas we can paint over. On which we can create a brand new picture, although the one beneath it will always be there. Except no longer visible to the naked eye.

She kisses me again and again and I sweep my hands from her back, to her sides, to just next to her breasts. I need to find out how she has changed, or if I can even spot the changes. As our lips keep meeting, Angela becomes the same woman again who seduced me years ago—although she always said I was the one who seduced her. None of it matters.

I give her blouse a tug, making my intentions known, and this time, Angela doesn't need a moment anymore. She kisses my cheek, then the sensitive skin of my neck, until she traces a path back up to my ear.

"Take me to bed," she says, and they're the most beautiful words ever spoken.

I don't say anything, just look at her. I'm not one to be stumped for words, but I'm certain I can't get any past the lump in my throat. When something happens you've been dreaming of for twenty years, even though you knew you weren't even entitled to the dream version of it anymore, it's a lot to take in.

Silently, I take her hand and lead her down the hallway and up the stairs. My bedroom is the masterpiece of the house. One wall is a floor to ceiling window overlooking the always-twinkling lights of this impressive city below. Like me, Angela is a born-and-bred Los Angeles girl, and our love for our city was something we bonded over when we first met.

"Jesus," she says, and stands still in front of the window. "No artwork required on the walls in here."

I smile and pull her close again. "Especially not now you're here," I manage to say, and I don't care how incredibly cheesy it sounds. I already know she's going to make fun of me for saying this in the morning—but the morning is too far in the future. This is now, and I have Angela in my bedroom. Dinner is getting cold downstairs and, as far as I'm concerned, it's the best thing that could be happening to it.

"I want you," she whispers in my ear. Her words make me melt. Her touch sets my skin on fire. I resume my work on her blouse, hoisting it all the way out of her pants, and letting my hands travel underneath.

"I want you too," I say against the skin of her neck, and I feel her hands slip underneath my top.

11

ANGELA

Jackie has me exactly where I want to be: flat on my back, with her on top of me. A position I'd never dreamed I'd find myself in ever again.

We're only dressed in our underwear and I'm still glowing from the pure joy of peeling that sleeveless top off her, and slowly revealing more of her skin. The front of her body is pressed warmly to my side, her leg is slung over mine. I feel so much of her on me, I can hardly believe it—can hardly believe this is real.

Her lips are all over mine, our tongues entwined. When we break from our kiss, she looks down at me, her gaze intense and brooding. "Twenty years of foreplay," she says, her lips drawing into a smile. Her gaze flits to the right, to the scar on my shoulder. "But I'll be gentle with you regardless." She bends over and presses the lightest of kisses on my shoulder. "I won't hurt you ever again, Angela." My name is barely a whisper on her tongue.

"I got shot so I figure the worst has been done to me already."

"If you hadn't been shot, we might never have met again."

"Who knew getting shot could be such a good thing? Let's not tell the NRA, shall we?" I smile up at her. My shoulder wound doesn't hurt any longer, my brain is being flooded with too many feel-good hormones, my blood saturated with lust.

"It'll be our secret." She leans in to kiss me again and it's the kind of kiss that tells me, loud and clear, that the time for talking has ended. When our lips break apart next, and she skates a finger from my cheek, over my collarbone, to the swell of my breast, I follow its path with my eyes. The sight of her finger caressing my skin works in tandem with the sensations it's producing. I've only ever been this lit up for her. I never turned into a complete celibate—I had basic human urges to meet—but when other women touched me, it never felt like this. Life-changing. Like the mere touch of a fingertip has the power to reach all the way into my soul.

Her fingertip dives underneath the cup of my bra and my nipple presses against the fabric, screaming to be released. As though she heard the cry from my flesh, Jackie pushes the cup down and peers at my erect nipple. She leans in, waits a beat, then takes it between her soft, soft lips.

I close my eyes and revel in the pleasure that bursts inside me already. If this is how it feels when she's licking my nipple, I can only imagine how my body will react when she does the same elsewhere. She repeats the process with my other nipple, freeing it, regarding it with such heated intention, then sucking it into her warm mouth.

"Jesus," I say on a moan. This makes her look up, so I instantly regret not keeping my mouth shut. "Don't stop," I add, twirling my fingers through her short, jet-black hair.

She sends me a sly smile, then wraps her lips around my tortured nipple again. Before she sucks it all the way into her mouth, she grazes her teeth against it, and I'm about to lose my mind.

She kisses her way back up to my lips, and lets her tongue dart into my mouth. I hungrily press my fingertips into her flesh. I want her so much, so acutely, I don't think I can wait any longer. It's not just desire, it's a need so great, it lodges like a stone in my gut—a stone that can only be obliterated when I touch her the way she's touching me.

I bring my hands to her back and unhook her bra. Her hand is trapped between our bodies, and her thumb sweeps over my nipple. Desire flares and I clumsily fumble with her bra. I ignore the pang of pain in my shoulder as I try to find my balance.

Jackie pushes herself away from me and guides her bra off her body. She flings it into the room somewhere. It's still early in the evening and as I follow the trajectory of her discarded bra, I see the setting sun bathing our city in the most beautiful golden light.

Jackie helps me to get my own bra off and as soon as I lie back down, she goes for my panties. She peels them off me slowly and, as I lie naked in front of her, yearning is all I feel.

Jackie's glance skates over me. It sweeps up from my legs, over my breasts, to meet my gaze. The smallest of smiles plays on her lips. I'm so overtaken by desire that I have no room left in my brain to worry about how she may think I look. Our bodies are not what they once were. I, for one, have a prominent battle scar on my shoulder. But none of that matters, all doubts are erased by the energy crackling in the air between us. Besides, from the look in her eyes, I can only conclude that Jackie very much likes what she sees.

My most urgent longing is to get her panties off her. I want to see her the way she sees me; I want her to bare herself to me. Complete surrender is the only way for us to go and it surprises me how easily we're getting there. This is something we need to do, just like it was twenty years ago. No matter the consequences and how it may color our lives afterward, this was always inevitable. Which is why, if we couldn't be together, we could never see each other again.

All I have to do is stretch out my arm in the direction of her panties, and Jackie catches my drift. No doubt out of concern for my injury, she proceeds to take the last remaining bit of her clothing off, and reveals herself to me—it's even more intoxicating than that first time.

She sucks her bottom lip into her mouth. Maybe she's thinking about logistics—or wondering how she can go easy on me now that we're both naked and brimming with lust. I'm way ahead of her and pull her toward me. I maneuver onto my side, practically disabling my right arm so my shoulder is immobile and protected. I'm not a leftie but I think I can find the strength, and the dexterity, some-where. All I have to do is look into Jackie's demanding eyes. All the desire I feel running through me is reflected right back at me. All the years of not wanting to think about anything like this ever happening again, while the need for it roared inside me subcon-sciously. The release of simply lying here with her, our bodies hot with anticipation, is such a relief. As though something that's been off kilter for the longest time can finally slip into focus again. Easily. No effort required. This was how it was always supposed to be. Jackie and me.

Jackie cups my breast into her hand again and squeezes my hard nipple between her fingers. It's as though she has found the switch to ratchet my desire up another gear. I run a finger over the slope of her hip, over her thigh, then turn inward. I push her one knee away from the other, and, gently, let my finger roam toward her hot center.

I spread my own legs and shuffle as close to her as I can. Her hand starts moving south and as I run a finger over her soft, warm pussy lips, her hand reaches my own, pulsing lips. We stroke each other gently while we stare into each other's eyes. Her finger circles my clit and I expel an involuntary moan. This spurs her on and her finger slides down, into my wetness.

My own finger mirrors hers. The touch of her soft, wet lips revs up my excitement another notch. I push a finger high inside her and the combination of feeling her hot pussy clamp itself around me, while her own finger touches something deep inside me, is almost enough to push me over that invisible edge. I've had to wait twenty years for this and, it seems, my body has waited patiently along with me. But now that we're here, it can't contain itself any longer.

All the while, I look into Jackie's eyes. They've narrowed but I can still see the obvious spark in them, the revelation, the utter satis-faction of finally getting to do this again. She withdraws her finger and adds another. She fucks me harder, as though she's totally attuned to the rhythm of my core, my heart, my throbbing desire.

I mirror her action because this is what we are. Mirror images. Not because we look alike, or not even because our hands are doing the same thing, but in her, I see myself reflected back so perfectly. The parts of me I've kept hidden, that I've kept pushing down, ignoring and denying them throughout the years. That's why the look in her eye, despite the pleasurable action of her fingers inside my pussy, is what's getting me off the most. I see the person I'm meant to be, the woman I could only ever be with her.

When Jackie starts brushing her thumb over my clit as well as fucking me with increasing intensity, it all bursts open. All the memories, pent-up desires and, most of all, the present lust, the electricity between us, flowing from my body to hers and back through where we're touching each other so intimately, so inevitably. I give myself up to her and come at her fingers while I have two of my own fingers buried deep inside of her. Her eyes on me, her fingers inside me, her warmth wrapped around me. It all erupts into a deafening crackle of white noise in my brain and a burst of stars in my core.

I ride her fingers through this blissful climax, the sort of orgasm that I must have saved up for this very occasion. I cry out her name as my limbs stiffen.

"Oh, Jackie," I moan, as decades worth of tension flow from me at finally being able to scream out her name.

12

JACKIE

When I open my eyes I can't believe it for the first few seconds. My consciousness isn't fully alert yet, and the memories of last night are still aligning themselves in my brain. I blink and rest my gaze on Angela. She's really here. As of now, no matter what happens, it will never have been a one-night stand. We have two nights between us now—two nights of utter and complete joy. Although, for me, this time around, the guilt-free nature of our lovemaking gave it an extra dimension. As I roll over and curl an arm over her sleeping body, I don't have to worry about the repercussions of what happened between us having an effect on my life. There are no more heartbreaking choices to be made. I'm free. What happens next will all depend on Angela.

In my eagerness to press myself against her warmth, I've slung my arm over her in a less than delicate manner. It must have roused her because she stirs in my embrace and the sound she makes in the back of her throat awakens the lust inside me. I want her all over again, even more than yesterday.

"Morning," I whisper into her ear.

She rolls onto her back and even though her lips are pulled into a smile, it's tight—more like a grimace. She glances at her shoulder. "I'm not sure my doctor would approve of what we did last night."

"Does it hurt?" I place a gentle hand on her injured shoulder.

"A little." What her smile lacks in brightness, her glance makes up for in spades. "I'm supposed to be out of action for a reason."

"Maybe I shouldn't clear you to go back to work just yet." I press a kiss to her cheek. "Remember, I hold all the power."

"I'm pretty sure you shouldn't be in bed with me if you plan to exercise any authority over my mental wellbeing." Her smile breaks out fully now.

"Good God," I exclaim. "I'm worse than Roger Bradley."

"I hope you get suspended so we can spend the rest of my sick leave in bed together."

I burst into a chuckle. "We really shouldn't joke about things like that." My heart sings at her words, though. Angela wants to spend more time with me.

"If we can't joke about the many dark sides of life, and the many flaws of human nature, what can we do about them?" she asks matter-of-factly.

"You're absolutely right." I press myself a little more against her. "Last night was spectacular, by the way."

"It was." She folds her arms behind my neck and pulls me in for a kiss.

"Thank goodness it's Sunday."

"What are your plans today?" she asks.

"Devouring you some more... if you'll let me." I try a smile but I can't put all my heart into it before I know if she agrees with my plans.

"If you could feed me first, then we can open negotiations as far as the devouring is concerned." She pushes herself up a little.

I think of the discarded dinner downstairs. "I'm not sure I *can* feed you. You seemed quick to leave the food I made for you last night uneaten."

"No offense to your cooking skills, but there was something far more delicious on offer." She turns her head and looks out of the window. "I still can't get over that view."

"How about you enjoy it some more while I rustle us up some breakfast in bed."

Angela shakes her head. "Breakfast in bed is the most unpractical, overrated thing ever invented." She cocks her head. "At my age, I want to eat sitting at a table in a comfortable chair, thank you very much."

"All these false notions of romance we've been spoon-fed over the years." I throw the covers off her. "None of that here. Come on."

"Hey," Angela protests. "You promised you'd go easy on me."

I cover her naked body with mine, careful not to put any pressure on her shoulder. I want to ask her what went through her mind when the bullet hit her, but that's a conversation for another time.

"Is that better?" My breasts press into hers and the touch of her warm body against mine stirs that deep lust that overtook me last night again.

"Much." She kisses my forehead. "But I still need to eat first."

———

"I saw you. Once," Angela says. We've taken our breakfast outside and are overlooking the city. "I avoided all big police functions where I suspected you might turn up alongside Michael. I always made sure I was on a shift. It was easy enough to swap." She sips from her coffee. "But then, completely out of the blue, I saw you at The Grove." She shakes her head. "I never go to The Grove. But I was in the neighborhood and I promised my mother I would bring her back some cherries that night and, for some reason I will never fully understand, I said to myself, I'm here now, I may as well get some overpriced but convenient cherries from The Grove, so I can go straight to my mother's house after. So I did and there you were." She puts her cup down. "I immediately did a U-turn and went back to my car. No cherries were bought that day. My mother was very upset." She gives a light chuckle. "It was a few years after…" Her voice trails off. "And seeing you still hit me so hard. I couldn't understand it."

"I'm sorry." I put a hand on her knee but keep staring ahead.

"I'm not sure what I would have said to you if you'd seen me." Angela sits up a little straighter. She doesn't put a hand over mine.

"We can't get mired in what-ifs," I say.

"I know." She's the one who turns to me. "So, what do we do next? Date?"

"If you want to." I can't help a smile from spreading on my lips. "Do you want to date me, Angela Hill?"

"It beats making appointments with you in Roger Bradley's office." She can smile again as well. We'll never be able to erase what happened between us completely, but we can't let it stop us from taking another chance at happiness together. "And we can only meet here, never at my place."

I slant my head. "I'm dying to see your place."

"Well then next time *you* take a bullet, because compared to this palace it's the very definition of a dump."

"But it's *your* dump." I squeeze her knee. "And I want to know everything about you."

"Hm, you might want to see a shrink about that. That sounds a little obsessive." She winks. "I know one, but I'm not sure if she's any good."

"I want to know what I've missed," I say.

Angela shakes her head. "We should look to the future instead of the past."

I nod. "Okay." Inside the house, my phone starts ringing. I roll my eyes. "I bet you a thousand bucks that's Carl."

Angela just quirks up her eyebrows.

"I'd better get it. He can be a bit relentless about these things." I go inside and locate my phone. Carl's name appears on the screen.

As I press the answer button, I let my glance wander outside, where it lands on the back of Angela's head. With the way I'm feeling, there's no way I can hide this from my son.

13

ANGELA

"He's my son," Jackie says. "There's really nothing to be nervous about."

"So you keep saying, yet look at my hands." I hold up a trembling hand.

"Well, then, let me try another approach." Jackie steps closer. "I'm sure Carl's just as nervous as you are."

"I find myself wishing you hadn't told him about our previous affair. I feel like it puts me at a disadvantage."

Jackie shakes her head. "Carl's a grown man." She cocks her head. "Most of the time, anyway. When he's not acting like bridezilla personified."

I hear a car in the driveway.

"They're here." Jackie pulls me into a quick hug. "It's going to be fine," she whispers in my ear. "I raised him." She chuckles and because we're standing so close, her laugh reverberates through my body. It relaxes me a little.

Jackie heads to the back door to greet her son and his fiancé, Beau. What I haven't told her is that, as much as I'm nervous about Carl's reaction to me, I'm equally worried about my reaction to him.

For the longest time, I considered Jackie's son the very reason why she couldn't be with me.

"Hello, Momma," I hear.

I can't stand around here any longer. I'd better follow Jackie into the kitchen.

Carl throws his arms wide the instant he clocks me. "Angela," he says in a solemn tone. "How exquisite to finally meet you."

The boy—well, man—gathers me in his arms and embraces me. His hug is not tight, but measured. I hug him back with the same level of trepidation. In my job, I have to be able to read people, often in an instant, but Jackie's son is a tough one.

"This is Beau." A man who looks like the quintessential perfect son-in-law, as advertised in many a television show along the years, holds out his hand. He's not a hugger then.

I shake Beau's hand and respond to his wide smile with my own. Because of my relationship non-history, I've always managed to avoid introductions to parents but I conclude meeting a lover's children must be similar. Wanting to make a good impression. The unreasonable, yet gnawing fear of not being instantly liked.

"Let's sit outside," Jackie says. "There's a bottle of something upmarket in the fridge."

"I'll do the honors, Mom," Carl says. "You ladies sit down."

Jackie puts an arm around my shoulder as we head out to the patio. "See," she says, after we've sat down. "The worst is over now."

I crane my neck to look inside. Beau is standing in the kitchen with a bottle of champagne in his hands while Carl takes glasses out of a cupboard. They're not huddled over in a gossipy, conspiratorial stance. I turn back around to face Jackie and inhale deeply. She's right. That first moment of dread has passed. It will be all right.

———

"Here's to Mom having a plus-one for my wedding." Carl holds up his glass.

320

Beau rolls his eyes. "Once you get to know him better, you'll find Carl has quite the knack for bringing everything back to himself." He holds up his glass as well. "It's very nice to meet you, Angela, regardless of Jackie coming to the wedding alone or not."

I bring my glass to his. Jackie has talked to me about the wedding, of course. It's only a few weeks away and it's the main topic of conversation between her and her son. But we haven't actually discussed me accompanying her. Perhaps it's implied because I've spent most of the remainder of my sick leave in her company, even staying in her house while she's at work. It has done wonders for my convalescence. Or maybe it's all the mind-blowing orgasms I've been having. A smile flits over my lips.

"Wonderful to meet you, too. I've heard so much about the two of you."

"You will come, won't you?" Jackie has turned to me, her intense gaze resting on me. "You're free on the tenth of July?"

"I may need to go shopping first, but yes, of course I will."

"Oh, don't worry, girl," Carl exclaims. "You have a fine figure and I have some ideas running through my head already. Mom's wearing this beautiful, eye-catching, very mother-of-the-bride purple dress and I was thinking—"

"Carl," Jackie says with glee in her voice. "Angela's a grown woman perfectly capable of dressing herself."

Carl purses his lips, then takes a sip of champagne. He puts his glass down and throws his hands in the air dramatically. "Suit yourself." He narrows his eyes. "Quite literally, actually." He breaks out into a wide smile—it's the kind of smile that would light up even the darkest room. "But put me on speed dial in case of any sartorial emergencies nonetheless."

"Good grief, will I be happy when this wedding is over." Beau winks at me. "We can finally get on with our lives."

"Speak for yourself, darling," Carl says, then regards me intently. "Now let's not be rude. Perhaps we should talk about something other than the wedding. Angela, you're a cop, just like my dad."

I'm not sure whether this is a jibe at his mother cheating on his father with me twenty years ago. I return Carl's gaze and don't spot any malice in it. I see a lot of Jackie in it as well. Glimmers of good-naturedness. And what did she say earlier? That *she* raised him. This is just me making silly assumptions in my head.

"I am and have been for many years." The past three months I may not have felt like much of a police officer, but I'm going back to work on Monday. I've been officially cleared—physically and mentally.

I glance at Carl and Beau, then at the view behind them, and consider that, if it weren't for me being a cop, I would never have met Jackie. And if that perp hadn't shot me, I wouldn't be enjoying this moment with Jackie's family. Sometimes, it takes a stroke of bad luck to have another go at happiness.

14

JACKIE

I hold the dress in front of me and peer at my reflection in the mirror.

"To be honest, I was quite surprised when Carl told me you'd be wearing a dress," Angela says, lying on the bed.

I pivot and, while still holding up the dress, I bat my lashes. "Why would you say such a thing, Officer Hill?"

"Officer?" Angela quirks up her eyebrows. "That's Detective Hill to you." She pushes herself up. She doesn't seem to be in any hurry to get ready for the event my son has been dreaming of most of his life.

Angela hops off the bed. She halts right in front of me and rubs the dress between her fingers. "Let me show off my detecting skills for you. What material is this?" She brings the dress to eye level. "Hm, my powers of deduction seem to be eluding me at the moment." She gently tugs the dress towards her. "Why don't you give me this so I can inspect it a little closer."

I hand her the dress and as soon as she has it in her hands, she drapes it over the bed.

"Hey," I protest. "I need to put that on asap."

Angela shakes her head. "My powers of deduction have concluded that you have, at the very least, five more minutes." She rakes her eyes over my body. I'm only wearing panties. My pulse picks up speed. Angela pushes me against the wardrobe, against the mirrored door I was inspecting myself in minutes ago. I let her. Any protest I'd put up, now that she's pressing herself against me, would sound incredibly insincere.

"You never look more gorgeous than when you're dressed like this," Angela whispers in my ear, then proceeds to kiss my neck. She kisses a path to my mouth and presses her lips to mine.

I run my fingers over her arms. We've been all over each other for weeks, almost inseparable since we spent that first night together. We're making up for lost time, and there's a lot of time to make up for.

Angela knows time is of the essence now and starts kissing my neck again. Her lips descend and she takes each of my nipples into her mouth until they're as hard as bullets. Inside of me, lust surges. Angela's lips on my skin are all I dream about, all I think about. She traces a path down and sinks to her knees in front of me.

She plants hot kisses above the waistband of my panties before kissing my nether lips over the fabric. She wraps her mouth over my clit and I press my palms against the wardrobe for support. Her hot mouth pulls back and my clit pulses with need against my panties. Angela hooks her fingers underneath and pulls my underwear all the way down. I step out of them and spread my legs. My body hums with anticipation, my clit throbs with desire as I stand there, ready for her.

Angela glances up at me. We don't say anything, just share this look, this moment of extreme intimacy between us, and then she leans in.

I delve my fingers into her hair as she flicks her tongue over my wanting clit.

My knees buckle a little at her touch. When she sucks my clit all the way into her mouth, I feel like my legs might give out entirely.

Angela Hill, I think. The woman I love. Because I do. I can't realistically claim I've loved her for twenty years, yet as I stand here, pressed against my closet—the one I refused to come out of for her when I, perhaps, should have—while she has her mouth all over my clit, it sure feels as though I've loved no one else the way I've loved her. Despite the fleetingness of our first encounter, its power has always remained with me.

"Oh, Angela," I moan, because I like to say her name when she goes down on me—because I like how it sounds in this particular situation and, simply, because I can. No one else's name will roll off my tongue during this particular act ever again.

Angela's tongue flicks with more intensity—and she knows what I like by now. We've made up for a lot of lost time already. My clit is so sensitive to the ministrations of her tongue. I delve my fingertips into her scalp, needing something to hold on to, something of her. She licks and flicks and it all blends into a burst of pure joy, of delicious heat streaming through me, coursing to my extremities and back.

"Oh, Angela," I moan again. "Angela. I love you."

LOVELY RITA

S weat trickled down my temples as I danced for the first time in months. I didn't care if Rita showed up. I boogied myself into a state of indifference I'd been craving for weeks. Pushing my arms above my head, I relished the predatory looks my exposed belly button received. Being declared too monogamous for Rita's standards didn't spoil me for this crowd. Just because I wasn't one for sharing loved ones, didn't mean I couldn't enjoy the thrill of a one-night stand.

A girl dressed in black leather pants and not much else swayed closer to me. I'd been working on my abs tirelessly since Rita had left me, and now they were working for me. She pressed her hips into my behind and left them there, finding the rhythm with me. I guess you could call it dancing.

"Want a beer?" she yelled into my ear over the thundering bass.

I spun around to get a good look at her face. Hair tied back in a loose ponytail, some curls springing free. Intense black eyes and no makeup on her face. Zero resemblance to Rita.

"Yes, please." I shot her a smile. I was out of practice and fairly certain the sexy grin I was aiming for looked more like an insecure smirk, but she nodded and headed for the bar. I exhaled and brushed a strand of hair away from my forehead.

That's when I saw her.

A bundle of platinum-blonde hair. Lips red and full. A smile to die for. That glare that sent my heart racing and clit throbbing.

I gasped for air and scanned for emergency exits. Rita was not alone and I didn't feel like being introduced to her new girlfriend, who, no doubt, would still be so charmed by her she wouldn't mind all the talk of open relationships and the enrichment polyamory can be to one's life. I'm not one to judge—I just wanted Rita all to myself.

"I'm Liz." Leather pants girl handed me a cold bottle of beer. I wanted to rub it against my cheeks to make my burning blush disappear.

"Ali." I clinked the neck of my bottle against hers. "Thanks."

Liz followed my gaze, because, try as I might, I couldn't stop looking at Rita. She was the most beautiful woman I'd ever seen, with her big brown eyes and racially ambiguous skin.

"Do you know Rita?" Liz asked. I noticed the sudden twinkle in her eye, and I knew the score. This was a small-town club and Rita had probably taken half of the girls home at some point.

"She's my ex." It still stung when I said it. "It didn't work out."

I did try, but my heart had never hurt as much as when Rita had picked out a voluptuous redhead for us to have a threesome with. As if I wasn't enough.

"How long were you together?" Liz couldn't let the subject go. I totally understood.

"Seven months. Broke up three months ago." My night of forgetting Rita was not going as planned. Not only was she here, but I was trapped in a conversation with a stranger about her. That was Rita. Ever present and always on the tip of everyone's tongue.

Liz whistled through her teeth. Any attraction I had felt toward her seeped out of me.

Through the crowd, Rita made her way to where I was standing, resulting in a crazy pitter-patter of my heart.

"I've been looking for you," she said, her voice breathy and low. "Where have you been hiding?" As if she didn't know.

The woman trailing behind her was so pretty it hurt. She had a relaxed hipster way about her. Maybe it allowed her to stand things I couldn't possibly accept, no matter how much I wanted to keep Rita.

"I take it you've met Liz," I mumbled, avoiding Rita's question.

"Oh yeah. Good times." She poked her girlfriend in the ribs and flashed her a knowing smile. "Remember, honey?"

The gorgeous hipster was the honey now.

It wasn't so much anger rushing through me. After all, I could only blame myself for not being more compatible with Rita's ways. It was a big surge of raw lust gripping me at the sight of Rita's neck and her skin the color of brown butter. I had always wanted Rita. From the first second I laid eyes on her until this moment in the club, downgraded to the word ex, huddled between her current girl-friend and a lover for one night.

It was madness, still my blood pulsed with desire. Hot pangs of want were speeding through my veins. Heat gathering between my legs already. One look was always all it took.

"Please, meet Anya." When Rita smiled at Anya it was as if someone had reached into my chest and squeezed a cold fist around my heart. I'd never get that smile again. I'd relinquished all rights to it the day I disagreed with Rita's rules.

"Hey." Anya waved a long-fingered hand at me. She was a skinny jeans and tank top kind of woman, with long ash-blonde hair falling to her shoulders and subtly painted lips.

"Let's dance." Rita grabbed Anya's hand and pulled her onto the dance floor. Then she had the audacity to wink at me. My breath hitched in my throat and all I wanted was to drag her away from Anya and take her home. Have her do that thing she did to me. That thing no one else ever did.

Liz and I followed. She seemed as entranced as I was, the twinkle in her eye still present. We slithered our bodies between sweaty arms and backs and I started moving with the rest of them. Whenever I glanced in Rita's direction, which was about 95 percent of the time, her eyes were fixed on me. I knew that look. She knew I did.

No one danced like Rita. The music flowed through her bones and her muscles flexed and relaxed to the beat of its drum. It inhabited her and she was all the more mesmerizing for it. Plus, she kept eyeing me.

I finished the beer Liz bought me in a few long drags and made for the bar to replenish, needing a break from Rita's stare. It was obvious what she was playing at.

Drops of sweat flickered on her bare shoulders when she joined me at the bar. I ordered four beers and thrust one in her hand.

"Thanks," she said, while letting her finger glide over the back of my hand. "I'm so thirsty." She tilted her head back, exposing the delicate skin of her neck, and swallowed for what seemed like an eternity. "Anya likes you."

In a perfect world, I would have been over Rita by then. I tried to look away and ignore her, but the muscles in my neck didn't allow me to—as if they were still as infatuated with her as the rest of me. Instead, I stared into the brown of her eyes, took in the enormity of her smile and surrendered. I'd never be done with her.

"Do you want to play?" She inched closer. So close I could feel her breath on my cheeks. "Liz is welcome to join as well, of course. She's fun."

It was her unwavering confidence that always got me. Not a lot of people said no to her, because she acted as if the word wasn't even a possibility.

She brought her lips to my ear. "I know what you like."

I could barely move. She'd whispered me straight into a frenzy of desire. I inhaled and exhaled slowly to regain composure.

"I'd better get these to the others." I pointed at the bottles of beer on the counter.

She slanted toward me again. "I'll take that as a yes."

She wasn't too far off.

I weighed my options as if I had any. As if Rita's proposal hadn't erased all other outcomes to my night.

I could go home alone. I could take Liz home. All four of us could go somewhere together. Or I could ditch Liz—one less contender for Rita's attention. None of the possibilities had me alone in a room with Rita, but beggars can't be choosers.

My hands trembled when I brought the bottle to my mouth. My body wasn't giving me a lot of options. Throughout the seven months of our affair it had been reduced to nothing more than a bundle of want. Attraction-wise, no one came close. If she was offering it on a silver platter, I wouldn't say no—even if it meant including Anya. Even if it meant I was the extra for the night.

I found Rita's eyes, bit my lip and nodded. The smile she shot me alone was enough to send me reeling. She arched her eyebrows and tilted her head in Liz's direction, silently questioning her inclusion. I shook my head. If I was sharing Rita, one other person would do.

Fifteen minutes later, Rita, Anya and I sat huddled together in the back seat of a cab. I felt my blood beat through my veins as Rita's thigh flanked mine. It was only fitting she resided in the middle, like a queen amidst her minions. I wondered if Anya was as much a sucker for Rita's touch as I was. The answer was obvious.

Rita's flat hadn't changed. It was all red mood lighting and shag carpet. A faux fireplace guarded by life-size leopard statues in black marble. In anyone else's home they would have looked tacky.

"Hey." Rita pounced on me like a wildcat while Anya watched. Was she more of an onlooker? I hoped she was.

Rita's blood-red lips came for me. Her heady perfume hit my nostrils hard, and I inhaled as if my life depended on it. Her nipples poked into my skin through the fabric of our tops, and the prominent display of her arousal flattered me.

"You're in for a treat." There was that unflinching confidence again. There was no doubt in my mind that she was right. Every second with Rita was a treat.

Her fingers dug into my scalp as she kissed me, and my legs turned to jelly. Her smile shifted from generously broad to mischievously narrow as she pulled her mouth away from mine and glanced at me. She all but licked her lips.

"Come on." She grabbed my hand and guided me to the bedroom. I had fond memories of Rita's king-size bed, which, from my point of view, was a total waste of space because I always slept glued to her caramel-skinned body. She probably bought it with more advanced sexual activities in mind. It could easily fit three.

Anya followed us and hoisted her top over her head as soon as we entered the bedroom. All my attention had been so focused on Rita, I hadn't even noticed she'd gone through the night braless. As if it was a practiced routine, Anya inched closer and Rita stepped back.

"Kiss for me." Rita sat down on the bed, sucking her bottom lip between her teeth.

Anya's nails scraped over the flesh of my arms. A crooked, full-lipped smile played around her lips. She looked so pale compared to Rita.

She pressed her naked chest into me, rigid nipples stabbing into my breasts, and traced the tip of her tongue along my neck, over my chin, to my mouth. The room was silent except for the agitated coming and going of our breath and the touching of our lips. Rita sat stock-still on the edge of the bed, her eyes on fire and her head tilted sideways.

Despite it not being Rita on the receiving end of my kisses, the fact that she sat watching us was enough of a turn-on. Anya tugged at my T-shirt and I lifted my arms to allow her to take it off. After she one-handedly unclipped my bra, she leaned into me and breathed heavily into my ear.

"We're going to make you come so hard," she said, and it made me shiver. That was Rita's line. That's how I knew she spoke the truth.

My nipples stiffened into hard peaks as they grazed Anya's porcelain skin. She slid a finger under the waistband of my jeans and flipped the button open. Before coaxing me toward the bed, she lowered the zipper with her other hand, and pushed me down.

I found her eyes and saw the madness, the same madness I'd seen flicker in Rita's gaze so many times. The yearning for this kind of activity. The desire to live with an abandon foreign to me.

From the bottom of the bed, Rita yanked at my jeans until they slid off. Anya removed her own pants faster than I could blink. She didn't appear to be wearing any panties either. It figured.

Anya lay down next to me and, while circling one finger around my belly button, allowed me to enjoy the show of Rita undressing. The spectacle wasn't in the way she did it, slowly and totally aware of the effect she had on me, but more in how she held my gaze throughout it. The intensity brimming in her eyes left me panting underneath Anya's tickles. Her glance skimming over my bare skin was plenty of incentive for my clit to swell beneath the flimsy fabric of my panties.

As soon as Rita was undressed she hopped on the bed and pressed her body against my side.

"Let me prove to you once and for all"—Rita looked me square in the face—"that three pairs of hands are so much better than two."

Anya's circling motions traveled up to my chest, while Rita started stroking my inner thighs. She might have had a point.

Their lips found each other over my head and, instead of jealousy, bursts of sweltering lust rushed through me.

Anya, on my left, pinched my nipple hard as Rita, on my right, trailed the top of her finger over the crotch of my panties. They broke their lip-lock to bestow all of their attention on me, and yes, it felt as if I were being fondled by a million hands at the same time. Fingers were everywhere. A frenzy of pecks, lingering tongues, and thrilling pinches descended on me.

Rita dragged my panties off me and my swollen pussy lips pulsed for her. Anya let a fingertip skate over my hard nipples while driving her tongue deep into my mouth. Instinctively, I spread my legs for Rita. I was so hot for her, so ready. The club, the cab ride, the little show—rehearsed lines and all—they had put on for me, it was all foreplay and I didn't need any more gentle coaxing. Juices oozed out of me as my clit throbbed to the quickening beat of my heart.

Anya moved the action of her mouth to my breasts and sucked a nipple between her lips. Rita trailed a finger through my wetness and I shivered in my skin. My muscles trembled and I pushed myself up to meet her, eager for her to enter me. Her lips parted slightly as she slipped a finger inside.

"Oh god," I moaned, because Rita's finger inside of me was all I ever wanted. She soon added a second one, while Anya nibbled on my nipples, her hands kneading and her teeth grazing.

With her free hand, Rita pulled the skin away from my clit, exposing it to the musky bedroom air. She didn't touch it; she just watched it as my juices gathered in the palm of her hand.

"Ready?" she asked, a surprisingly solemn expression on her face.

"Oh," I hissed in reply, no longer able to form words. I knew what she meant though, and my skin flared with anticipation. I was lost beneath their hands and tongues. A willing victim of their double act.

Rita curled her fingers inside of me and found the spot. The one, somehow, only she could reach. In response, I arched my back, my muscles stiffening. Anya's hand and lips kept arousing me, propelling me to new heights. Rita's fingers pushed inside, circling, curling, bringing me to the brink.

I found Rita's eyes and drank in her desire, because in that moment, she was mine. Or I was hers—again. All signs of irony had left her face. She pinned her gaze on me while her fingers touched me inside, the intent of them displayed in the twitch of her lips. Witnessing how Rita wanted me was all I ever needed. It wasn't a magical spot inside of me yearning to be stroked; it was the passion in her eyes and how it connected with every fiber of my being.

It started in my belly, a wildfire spreading through my flesh, seizing me. My pussy tingled and my nipples reached up. Flames tickled my skin. Desire burned through my bones.

I cried out as I came, fingers on my nipples and in my cunt. The climax echoed through me, bouncing through my body, again and again. I clenched the walls of my pussy around Rita's fingers, as though I never wanted to let her go again, before collapsing into the mattress, spent and voiceless.

Rita gently slid out her fingers, dragging them along my belly, coating my skin in my own wetness, and kissed me on the mouth.

"I told you," she said.

Anya kissed my left cheek and Rita pressed her lips against my right cheekbone.

I curved my arms around the pair of them before turning my face to Rita. "Lesson learned."

ACKNOWLEDGMENTS

Endless gratitude to my wife Caroline for supplying the idea for this novel, for always listening patiently to my crazy plans, and for being my partner in just about everything. To Maria for the unwavering enthusiasm when it comes to my stories and for the invaluable beta-reader essays. To Cheyenne Blue for being a stellar, honest editor and an equally excellent friend. To my readers, without whom all of this wouldn't be possible.

Thank you.

ABOUT THE AUTHOR

Harper Bliss is a best-selling lesbian romance author. Among her most-loved books are the highly dramatic French Kissing and the often thought-provoking Pink Bean series.

Harper lived in Hong Kong for 7 years, travelled the world for a bit, and has now settled in Brussels (Belgium) with her wife and photogenic cat, Dolly Purrton.

Together with her wife, she hosts a weekly podcast called Harper Bliss & Her Mrs.

Harper loves hearing from readers and you can reach her at the email address below.

www.harperbliss.com
harper@harperbliss.com